Windswept

The Mapweaver Chronicles Scroll I

by Kaitlin Bellamy

Windswept

First Edition: August 2018

For Mom
Your magic could never be written, or replaced

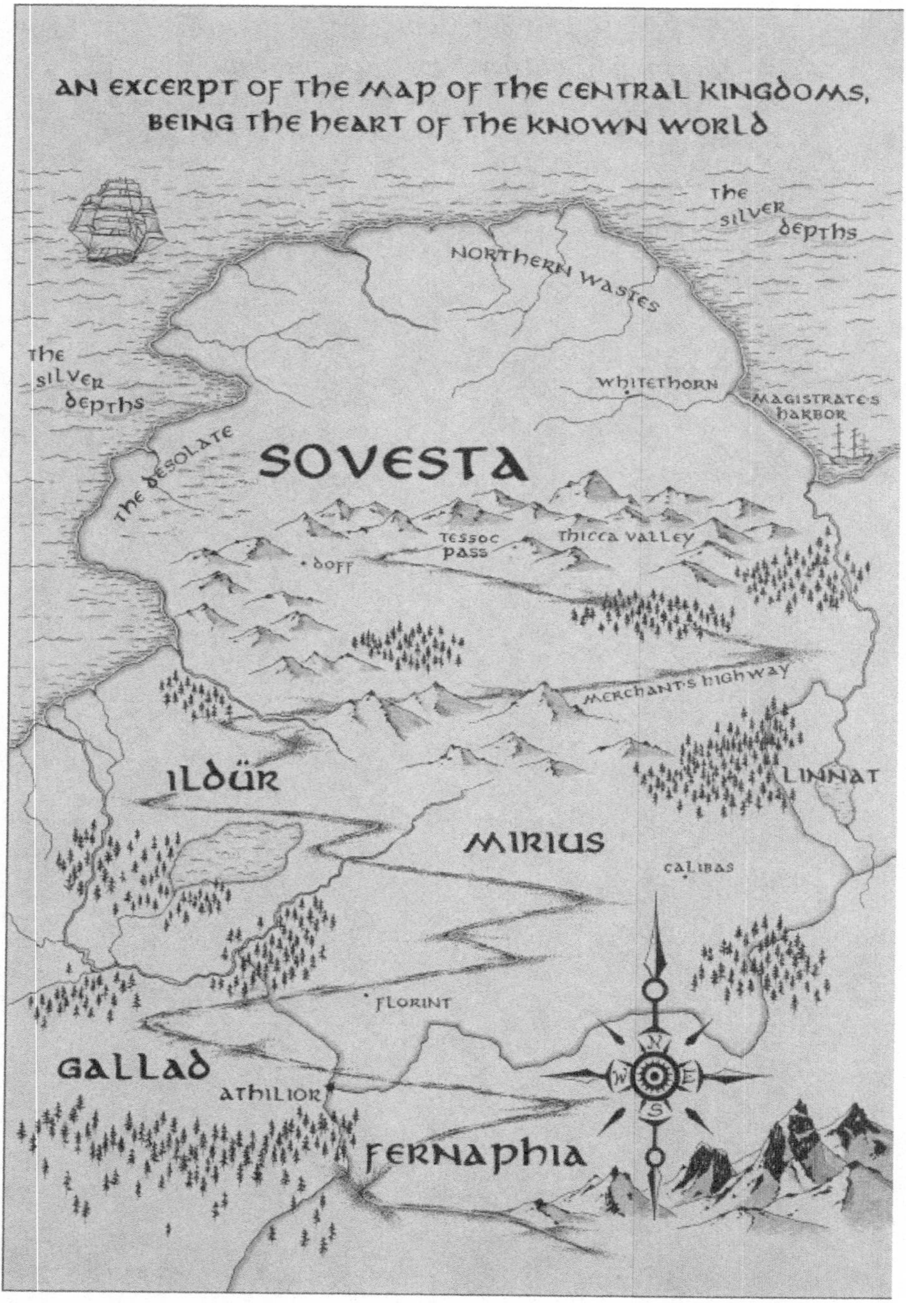
AN EXCERPT OF THE MAP OF THE CENTRAL KINGDOMS,
BEING THE HEART OF THE KNOWN WORLD
THE SILVER DEPTHS
NORTHERN WASTES
THE SILVER DEPTHS
WHITETHORN
MAGISTRATE'S HARBOR
THE DESOLATE
SOVESTA
TESSOC PASS
THICCA VALLEY
DOFF
MERCHANT'S HIGHWAY
ILDÜR
LINNAT
MIRIUS
CALIBAS
FLORINT
GALLAD
ATHILIOR
FERNAPHIA
N
W
E
S

Chapter One

Caravan

Fox sat cross-legged on the upstairs windowsill, nose pressed against the cold glass. His breath clung to the windowpanes, slightly obscuring his view with each steady exhale. Every so often he would raise a finger and sketch pictures in the foggy glass, briefly clearing a patch of window before his breath misted it over once more. Outside, a cold spring sunrise was only just beginning to brush the frost-covered grass, but Fox knew that the whole of Thicca Valley was awake. Awake, and waiting.

Even through the haze, Fox could see all the way to the outskirt farms. Every chimney was smoking, and every kitchen window was lit. Here and there he could see shadows moving in the weak morning light: children running to the valley pub, hoping for news, or mothers shaking out rugs and anxiously peering up at the mountain road. Downstairs, Fox knew his own mother was busy sweeping the stone kitchen floor. Again.

As if the house could possibly be any cleaner. But Father was coming home any day now, and Fox knew better than to argue when Mother started worry-cleaning. It was easier simply to take his chore assignments and do them without complaint. And so, Fox and Mother had both spent the last week washing windows and scrubbing doorframes, airing the bedding, and sweeping out all of the fireplaces.

It wasn't just Mother. Everyone got restless this time of year. Winter was releasing its tyrannical grasp on the valley, and spring was beginning to fight its way through the ice. And with that first hint of warmth, every Thiccan began looking west, watching for a sign of movement on the mountain road. The waresmen were coming home from their yearly trade caravan, bringing with them the provisions and coin required to make it through another year. They'd been gone all winter, and the moment the Tessoc Pass cleared, their wives and children started looking for their return. Fox's own father was among them, Thicca Valley's only trapper and fur-trader. Any day now, someone would spot that first wagon emerging from between the peaks. And until then, people watched, waited, and indulged their anxious little habits.

Something moved at the corner of Fox's vision, making him turn to look. A bird was winging its way toward the Five Sides, the valley pub. It was a small, grey bird, with a scrap of blue tied around its ankle. A short-range messenger bird, probably coming from one of the mines. As Fox watched, the bird disappeared behind the pub. He waited for several minutes, but no responding bird was sent out. A lunch order, then. Or a trivial piece of news. Nothing serious or urgent, and certainly nothing interesting enough that it might take his mind off waiting. So instead, Fox scrubbed the glass clean of its fine layer of mist and turned back to watching the cold and dark mountain road.

He'd heard once that the country of Sovesta used to be warm and prosperous. Now, looking out on the thick layer of frost that brushed the early spring grass, he found it hard to believe. The legend was that Sovesta had been favored by the gods. Then, it was a blessed nation, covered in rich, lush farmlands. Until a foolish king, hundreds of years ago, had offended the gods. Whether the king had stolen a god's daughter or wife, or enslaved the god itself, Fox didn't know. Every storyteller spun the legend a little differently. But the punishment was always told the same: a curse, throwing the country into turmoil. Sovesta became a ruined nation, dominated by snow and ice. The gods pulled the Highborn Mountains up from the earth to isolate Sovesta from the rest of the Central Kingdoms. It was even said that before the curse, magic ran thick in the bloodlines of many Sovestan families. But the gods stripped them of even their Blessings, leaving the country barren of any magical gift ever since.

Now, in Fox's lifetime, the brief summer months were crucial. Crops were planted early, sometimes even before the ground was fully thawed. The whole of Thicca Valley worked tirelessly throughout the waking hours to store food and supplies for winter. Children spent their days gathering firewood and fishing. Meats were smoked, the small farms were constantly tended and everyone prayed that the snows would wait to fall until after the harvest.

And then as summer ended, just before the Tessoc Pass closed, the valley's fire merchants, waresmen and traders would take to the Merchant's Highway, journeying south to sell their wares. Each year, Fox helped send his father off with the caravan, making sure his gear was in order and his goods were primed for selling. And, each year, Fox grew more and more restless as he was left behind. He knew that technically he was not *old* enough to be allowed to join the men, but he felt sure that he was *ready*. His fifteenth birthday was coming up this summer, and already he knew more about trapping than Father himself had at that age. But still, he was left behind. And so, he filled his time during the dark winter months in the only way that kept him sane: he practiced.

Fox glanced down at the foot of his parents' bed, where his welcome-home gift for Father lay, wrapped in thick brown paper. A rabbit-fur vest, and matching hat. All caught, skinned and treated by Fox himself, and carefully sewn together during the days of Deep Winter. Yes, *this* year, he was sure of it. This year, he'd be invited. This year, Father would let him officially begin his apprenticeship.

The sun had risen properly, with no sign of the traders, by the time Fox decided to finally abandon his windowsill perch. He slipped down to the floor and scurried across the hardwood planks to the ladder that led up to his room.

Houses were built to stay warm in Thicca Valley, nestled as it was in the Highborn Mountains. The cabins were tight and cozy, with rooms kept small to better hold the heat from the fires. Fox's "room" was more of an alcove set into the upper wall of his parents' bedroom. It was just tall enough that he couldn't quite stand upright in it anymore, but he needed little space. The walls had been carved into shelves and nooks for his personal things, and an old trunk sat at the foot of his sleeping pallet, just beside the ladder. A single row of firestones, set directly into the curve where the wall met the ceiling, kept his nook warm and softly lit.

Fox rather liked his little room. It reminded him of a den, or a burrow, and he'd always felt comfortable in tight spaces. It was one of the many reasons his nickname, Fox, was so appropriate. That, and his often uncanny animal instincts. He had a keen nose for weather and, somehow, managed never to get lost. He supposed this was why Father found him such an invaluable trapping companion. Of course, one of the other reasons his nickname was so apt was his size. While the people of Thicca Valley were often small and sturdy, Fox was simply small. He had none of the natural bulk that the miners were built with, and he could never spend his days hauling ore and felling trees like so many of the other youth his age. His talents were in his fast fingers, nimble feet and the ability to slip soundlessly to and from the forest path like so many of the beasts he and Father hunted.

Fox dressed quickly, pulling on his own rabbit-fur vest, and lacing his knives into place around his waist and thighs. He tied Father's old scarf around his neck as he slid back down his ladder, and finally made his way to the ground floor.

An overwhelming and mouth-watering bouquet of smells met him as he entered the kitchen. It seemed that Mother had moved on from sweeping, and had now thrown herself into cooking. A whole tub of freshly-peeled potatoes sat beside the large, circular firepit at the heart of the kitchen. A bundle of small, plucked chickens sat on the counter top, waiting to be roasted on the spit, but Mother herself was nowhere in sight.

The kitchen door was propped open. A cool breeze swept through it, airing out the cabin, and bringing with it two female voices. The lower one was unmistakably Mother. And the other? Fox smiled, scooped himself a cold cup of elk broth and a hunk of bread for breakfast, and went out to join them.

The raised porch curved most of the way around the cabin, built up several lengths from the ground to accommodate firewood storage underneath. Fox followed the voices around the corner, to the back stairs, where Mother sat with a young, dark-haired girl Fox had known all of his life. The two were up to their elbows in a basket of mussels, scrubbing grit and sand from their shells.

The girl looked up at his approach, a mocking smirk on her face. "Look who finally decided to wake up and join the living," she teased.

Fox hopped up on the porch railing, being sure to kick the girl gently in the shoulder as he did so. Laila Blackroot, the innkeeper's daughter, was Fox's closest friend in the world. His own parents treated her like family, and her father did the same for Fox. With Fox's father gone so often, and Lai's mother dead long ago, the Blackroot and Foxglove families had come to rely on each other quite comfortably. Lai pulled her weight as much as any of the boys, often keeping Fox company in his own chores. He returned the favor at the Five Sides when he could, and the two spent their warmer months running all over the valley. They hauled water, delivered food to the mines, cut firewood, and filled their nets with more fish than anyone else.

"Good that the mussels are back," said Fox through a mouthful of bread.

"Decent fishing won't be far behind," confirmed Lai. "And I'll be the first to find it. Been checking every day."

"There's a finely-knitted shawl and an iron bit in it for you if you give me first pick," said Mother, stopping to tuck a stray hair back into place behind her ear.

"As always, Mum Foxglove," said Lai.

Fox finished his breakfast while they worked, breathing in the cold morning air. It was fresh, filled with woodsmoke and the bite of frost. And, somewhere in the distance, *snow*. It would snow tonight, he could smell it. Around dusk, by his reckoning. And his reckoning was almost never wrong.

Soon, the mussels were cleaned and prepared for cooking, and Mother retreated to the kitchen once more. She made Fox and Lai promise to air out the stable before they left, and the two obediently set off across the small stretch of property.

The family's pony, Cobb, was out on the caravan, so Fox didn't spend much time in the stables during winter. But with the caravan on its way home, now was the time to ready it for habitation once more. As they worked, Lai chatted on about this and that. Her father's plans for the Homecoming Festival; the Bracken boys and their troublemaking; how much she loved the smell of fresh hay as she laid it down on the stall floor. And Fox was content to listen as the two worked their way through a steady stream of chores, preparing the stable for Cobb's return.

They had done this so many times, for so many years in a row, that it was a habit by now. Lai was a good hand's-breadth taller than Fox, and so it was she who pulled things from the high shelves and took to climbing up to dust the rafters. Fox himself kept to the floors and checking that the woodwork hadn't been compromised by the winter.

It was absorbing work, and easy enough to lose himself in. Even so, each time he passed the small window, or the open stable door, Fox found himself glancing out across the valley, trying to catch the slightest glimpse of movement on the mountain road.

"All that looking won't make him come home faster," said Lai finally, pulling bits of straw from her long black braids.

Fox rolled his eyes. "Easy for *you* to say. You've never had anyone go out! Your pa's got the inn, and all your cousins are miners, except Picck. No one in your family's a waresman." Fox kicked lightly at the doorframe, dislodging clumps of dirt and straw from his boot.

"But he's on his way home now, so it won't be too long to wait," said Lai, coming to stand beside Fox.

He smiled ruefully at her. "Always the cheerful one, aren't you?"

She placed her hands on either side of his face and grinned. "Have to be, don't I? Without me, you'd only smile maybe twice a year!" And she pushed, squishing Fox's face out of shape and making his lips pop out, startling a laugh out of him. "Ha!" Lai said triumphantly. They both knew perfectly well that she was the only person in the world who could get away with a move like that. Anyone else, and Fox would have punched them in the nose. But instead, she scurried away, laughing as Fox chased her all the way down to the river.

AN HOUR LATER, SOAKED from the knees down and armed with a fresh basket of mussels for the kitchen, Lai and Fox sloshed into the Five Sides Inn and Tavern. "Da, I'm home!" Lai called out. They heard a muffled reply from the basement. "C'mon," said Lai, "over here. He'll be up soon, I'm sure."

They heaved the soaking basket up onto a long table and collapsed onto either side of it, stripping off their wet shoes and stockings. This early in the day, the common room was completely empty. The long wooden tables were clean, the air free of the usual smells of pipe smoke and ale. A fresh pile of firewood was stacked neatly on the wide, stone hearth, and the dark wooden beams running from floor to ceiling were wiped clean of their nightly film of soot, bringing decades of carved initials dancing across their surfaces into sharp focus.

It was easy to imagine that The Five Sides had been around since the beginning of time, and certainly since the beginning of Thicca Valley. The tavern was the heart of the town, both in location and importance. It had been there all of Fox's life, and he spent more time in the tavern than his own home when Father was gone. But while it was a staple of Thiccan life now, Fox knew that it hadn't always been so. He loved to hear Lai tell the story.

"My grandpa was sixteen," she would say. "He was the youngest of six brothers, and he *hated* working the mines. So one day, he didn't show. Instead, he wandered around town, looking for another job."

But, of course, you didn't just *find* another job in the valley. You worked the life you were born into. Fathers taught their trades to sons, or the occasional nephew. Family businesses were passed down through bloodlines, or inherited through marriage. And every so often, if you happened to show a natural talent toward a certain profession, you might be taken on as an apprentice. But to leave your place in the community when you had nowhere else to go ... it was unthinkable. It was madness.

"Mad, that's right," Lai would say. "That's what they all called him when he knocked on the waresmen's doors, looking for work. They told him 'Go back to the mines, boy! You're no use to us here!'" And she would flap her hands, as if shooing away a flock of crows. "But he didn't go back. And when he refused to go back to the mines, his parents threw him out. So what do you do when you've got no place to stay?"

Once, when hearing Lai tell the Five Sides Tale to a group of younger children, Fox heard one little girl say excitedly, "No bedtimes!" Another time, a goat breeder's son piped up with, "You sleep in the barn loft, like my da does every time ma kicks him out!"

But the correct answer was, "You build a place of your own!"

Lai would continue. "He traded every favor he had to buy the empty scrap of land where the old bakery used to be, before it burned down. And he started to lay out a foundation and such, a wall here and a doorway there.

"And every night, men would come by on their way back from the mines. Or they would come into the town square from the farms, hoping to buy flour or trade with the fire merchants. And then, suddenly, the men were offering to help. They would help lay stones, or cut wood, just for a little while to take their minds off mining or the children or waiting for dinner."

It was Fox's favorite part of the story. He loved to picture it. He could just imagine all of the men in town, coming together for no good reason, but enjoying each other's company all the same. And then, as Lai would continue her tale, he would find himself wishing that he could have been a part of that accidental team so many years ago.

"It was summertime," Lai would say, "so the evenings were still light. Women started bringing dinners to the men out in the square, instead of making them come home to eat. And the whole valley watched and helped the building come together. And while grandpa didn't know what his new house was going to become in the beginning, he started to figure it out with those nightly parties. He hated mining, but he loved this. Being around all the people, and talking and laughing and eating together. So, the plan changed. The house kept growing and stretching, filling all the space he'd bought and even a bit more, but nobody minded. By the first snowfall of the season, he'd opened his doors."

It was all of this adjusting, and changing the design halfway through the building process, that gave The Five Sides its name. It was an unbalanced and sprawling building, and the far left wall was much longer than the right, but the valley loved it. And Fox, looking around at the polished oak bar, and the glowing embers in both the gigantic fireplace on the far wall and the circular fire pit at the heart of the room, loved it too.

"And, of course," Lai would say as she neared the end of her tale, "let's not forget the heroine of our story."

Everyone knew her name. It was carved ornately onto the mantlepiece for all to see, and it was always kept clean. Sometimes Lai's audience would answer excitedly, all at once. At other times, the name would trickle around the room in a series of whispers, like a breeze. "*Amaree.*"

"Grandad met the baker's daughter by accident one day. He was working on his own while everyone else was off in the mines. Almost all of the walls were up, and he was experimenting with different brews to give the men. Getting quite good at it, too. He was gathering blackroot at the edge of the forest when a shoe dropped out of the trees and hit him on the head."

This part of the story always made the girls in the audience giggle excitedly. And every so often, they would pipe in with the next few pieces of the tale.

"He looked up, and there she was!"

"And he said, 'What in Spirit's name are you doing up there?'"

"And she tried to jump down and run home, but he caught her around the waist and wouldn't let go until she told him why she was up in a tree, watching him!"

During one such outbreak, Fox distinctly heard one of the miners by the fireplace say to his companion, "Every girl in the valley hopes she can have a love story like this one. So steer clear of the woods in the springtime. Shoes dropping all over the place from eager hands."

"Amaree had seen Grandad trading in the valley square one evening," Lai would continue. "She heard him talking about spices and recipes with her father, and you might say she liked the look of him. The prospects for a baker's youngest daughter aren't the best, so Amaree took matters into her own hands. And when Grandad caught her that day, she offered her services." Here, Lai would smirk mischievously. "Offered, I say, but truthfully she wouldn't take no for an answer. When Grandad sent her home, saying he didn't need any help, did she listen?"

An emphatic "No!" from her listeners would echo through the common room.

"Every morning he would find her in the kitchen, pounding out dough and grinding cinnamon. And every morning he would kick her out. But she came back in the evening with the dinner customers. She'd sweep floors and clean up tables. Run drinks from the bar. She would stay until closing. For weeks this went on, until one day Grandad didn't turn her away. He handed her a key and said, 'Take the room at the far end. I never fill it anyway.' They were married at the midsummer festival, and the Five Sides remains, to this day, a tribute to the family they created here when they brought the valley together."

Fox had heard the story so many times, but it still made him feel warm and at home. He looked around the empty common room and smiled to himself, excited for nightfall when the place would fill up with music and miners and games.

A heavy tread on the back stairs announced the arrival of Lai's father, Borric Blackroot. Moments later he emerged, a fresh barrel of drink balanced easily on his shoulder. He was a massive bear of a man who made Fox's own father seem downright weak in comparison. "What's this?" he said, his booming voice echoing in the empty tavern. "Dripping all over my clean floor?" He set the barrel down and swept Lai up into his arms. "I ought to send you off to bed without supper. For a month! How would you like *that*, little missy?" he said. He sounded completely serious, and slightly terrifying, but Fox knew the man all too well. Sure enough, Lai laughed and planted a kiss on her father's cheek, and his false anger melted into a warm smile. "I suppose I'll let it slide, just this once." But Fox and Lai both knew that Borric would never punish her, nor would he ever need to. Lai did more than her fair share of work around the tavern, and the few times she actually *did* get into any real trouble, Borric would laugh it off and say "That's my girl!"

Fox found Lai and her father to be fascinating. They seemed to enthusiastically break the rules of Thicca Valley, where people were often smaller and stockier than they were in the south. But here was Borric, big enough to graze the sides of any door frame, and his daughter, slight and delicate and taller than all of the other girls. They were a mismatched pair if ever there was one, and they attracted oddballs and strays like moths to a candle. And Fox, quite proudly, was one of them.

Borric set Lai back on her feet. "Off to the kitchen then. Put those wet things up to dry, and take care of those mussels. You brought 'em, you clean 'em. Picck's got enough work to be getting on with, without you adding to it." As Lai scrambled into the kitchen, Fox scooped his boots and socks off the floor and nodded to Borric, who hoisted the ale barrel onto his shoulder again and said, "Your mother's doing well, I take it?"

"Very well, sir," said Fox. "She's cleaned the house so much this week, Father won't even know he's in the right place." And he followed Lai into the kitchen as Borric's hearty laughter filled the air.

The kitchen fireplace was already lit and crackling merrily, bathing the room in warmth. At the hearth, Lai was laying out her wet socks and tucking firestones into the toes of her boots to help them dry faster. As Fox joined her, there was a cheerful cry of welcome from across the kitchen. "Morning, Foxglove!"

Lai grinned at Fox, and he rolled his eyes. His full name, Forric Foxglove, was almost never spoken. He'd always preferred simply Fox. But Lai's cousin Picck, the kitchen boy, ignored this completely. Fox dropped his socks next to Lai's and turned to greet Picck with a resigned smile. "You owe me for that, Picck-ling," he said.

Picck smiled a wide, red-cheeked smile, and Fox felt his slight irritation simply fizzle away. Picck was so genial, and so delightfully odd-looking, that Fox could never stay mad at him for long. Lai's cousin looked absolutely nothing like her or her father. His hair was so curly and bushy Fox wondered how he ever ran a comb through it. His ears stuck out too far, and his nose was almost the only thing on his whole face that you noticed. Still, he had always been a good friend to Fox, despite his oddities. "Well, I'm working on something special just for you, you know," he said, giving Fox a quick punch on the arm. "Smell it out, and you'll get the first taste."

Obediently, Fox closed his eyes and breathed in deep. Rabbit; cinnamon sticky buns; fresh spring onions; rabbit stew with carrots and corn-silk mushrooms. And there, another scent. Fox felt a wide grin spread across his face as he opened his eyes. "My bread."

"Ha!" said Picck, clapping Fox on the back. "I tell you, that nose of yours could find a lost snowflake in a blizzard."

"The rosemary bread?" asked Lai. When Picck nodded, she squealed excitedly. "Oh, how long until it's done?"

"Another hour, but you get those mussels done and it'll make the time go by faster."

They set to work, sitting and scrubbing the mussels by the fire. As they did, Picck bustled around the kitchen singing.

Picck was nearly seventeen, but he'd been working at the Five Sides since he was nine. He belonged to Borric's younger sister, and while all her family were miners, Picck's lungs weren't right for mining work. But even from childhood, his family knew he was a very gifted cook. So, when it came time for him to start learning a trade, he moved into the kitchen, where he rolled out a sleeping pallet by the fire for himself every night. Borric had offered him a room, or even a space in the basement storage, but Picck refused time and time again. So finally, they just let him be.

The mussels were scrubbed clean and a whole bundle of onions chopped when finally Fox and Lai were excused with a hot loaf of rosemary bread each. They sat on the bar in the common room to eat it, munching away happily as they watched Borric wipe down the mantle. And then they sat playing cards, waiting for the tavern to fill.

The children were first in. As they finished their chores, they came looking for news. When Borric said he hadn't heard anything, some of them joined in the card game, and others went home to update their mothers. Then some of the shopkeepers wandered in and ordered drinks, and sat down to wait. Outside, a light snow began to fall as afternoon faded into evening, and Fox smiled to himself in satisfaction. His nose never lied.

The youth from the mines started trickling in, shaking snow from their hair and clothes. A handful joined in the game, but most sat, exhausted, by the now-roaring fire. By full dark, it seemed most of the valley was packed into the Five Sides. Farmers and their wives, and most of the miners. Almost all of the children had come back and were gathered on or around the bar with Fox and Lai. Many of the waresmen's wives were perched on stools by the fire, telling their neighbors over and over that no, they hadn't heard anything yet.

Hours dragged by, with heads turning every time the door opened and people pressing their faces to the windows whenever someone thought they heard something. But finally, when Dirrik Bracken fell asleep in his stew, the women of the valley seemed to decide that they'd had enough waiting for tonight. Fox watched as the tavern began to empty again, with mothers plucking their children out of the group and wives dragging their husbands away to bed. His own mother, who'd made a brief appearance for supper and then disappeared again, wasn't the kind to come and fetch him, but Fox knew on his own when it was time to go home. He said goodbye to Lai and fetched his warm, dry shoes from the kitchen, then journeyed out into the cold spring night.

It was still snowing, but Fox didn't mind. It would be over by tomorrow morning, he was sure. As he made his way home, his eyes kept wandering to the Highborns. He wondered if Father was as eager to get home as they were to have him. Well, he would ask him tomorrow.

Tomorrow. Fox stopped, frowning. He hadn't meant to think it, but now that he had he was sure. Tomorrow. The caravan would be home around midday tomorrow. He could feel it, just like the snow. He could smell it.

Fox rubbed his nose vigorously and then breathed in, focusing hard. There were the smells of the tavern behind him, and the Lillywhites' grain mill far off to his left. The familiar odors of the valley that he'd known all his life. And then, there was just the hint of something else. Something he couldn't place. But he knew it was the caravan.

He wondered for a moment if he should turn back, and announce to those few left at the tavern that the caravan was near. But, almost at once, he reconsidered. No one would believe him, of course. Why would they? Smelling the caravan ... it sounded like nonsense, even to him. Lai would believe him, perhaps, but she would be busy now helping her father clean up. If tomorrow came and went with no homecoming, then who had to know? And if they did show up ... well. That was another matter entirely.

FOX DIDN'T WASTE TIME waiting by the bedroom window the next morning. Instead he dressed at top speed, hurried through breakfast and then got right to his chores. By the time Lai came to see him, Fox had weeded the back garden, gathered wild goose eggs from the riverbank, and snared a beaver which he then traded for a packet of soap cakes. Lai found him on the front porch, scrubbing a pair of trousers in the washbucket. "Need a hand?" she asked, leaning on the railing.

"Nope," he said, "almost done."

"Good," said Lai. "Then you can come berry-picking with me. Dad says the timing is perfect, because the lingonberries are newly showing, and they're just tart enough for his pies!"

Fox looked up quickly from his washing. "Did he hear something? About the caravan? Because if he's starting to make his pies, it means he's preparing for the Homecoming and that means he knows —"

"No, nothing yet," said Lai. "He just wants to get things ready. He's waiting to make the crust, but he wants his berries now before the rabbits start getting at them."

Fox wrung out his pants and hung them over the porch railing to dry, thinking hard. Then, as casually as he could, he said, "Maybe he should start making all those crusts anyway. You know, just in case."

"In case?"

"In case the caravan comes home soon ... or today." Fox turned away from his laundry and went on quickly. "I mean, so many pie crusts must take a long time, right? And he should really be prepared, shouldn't he? Because there's always a chance that they could be home sometime today ... this morning, or afternoon, or ..."

"Fox?" said Lai carefully, "have you heard something?" When Fox didn't answer, she cocked her head to one side curiously. "What's going on?"

Lai would believe him. She had to. She was Fox's best friend in the entire world, and she had always been on his side. Fiddling with the hem of his sleeve, he said, "Last night ... I had a feeling. It was like I could smell them coming."

"Like with the snow?" said Lai.

"Exactly!" said Fox excitedly, glad she was catching on so quickly.

"So when are they due?"

"This afternoon. At least, I think this afternoon. This has never happened to me before, so I'm not exactly sure, and I don't —"

"You don't want to say anything, in case it turns out *not* to be true," Lai finished for him. She stood there for a moment, surveying him thoughtfully. Then, she seemed to come to a decision. She turned abruptly and started back down the road.

"Where are you —"

"I'll take care of it," she called over her shoulder. "Come by when you're done!"

Fox watched her go, a slight smile tugging at his lips. Not for the first time, he found himself amazed by Laila Blackroot.

AN HOUR BEFORE THE midday bell, Fox let himself into the tavern's kitchen entrance and stopped, staring around in amazement. A thin cloud of flour hung in the air, and he was almost overwhelmed by the smells of fresh berries and honey. Picck and Borric were rolling out and shaping pie crust so fast it made Fox dizzy just to watch. He found Lai in the far corner, peeling her way through a pile of small, pink frost apples.

"Lai?" he said. "What did you do?"

"Da, Fox is here!" called Lai, barely looking up from her work.

"Ah, excellent." said Borric, looking over his shoulder and spotting Fox. "C'mere, boy. I've got a job for you, too."

When Fox ambled over to the long counter, still amazed at the pie production surrounding him, Borric handed him a heavy bowl full of freshly-washed blackberries. "There's cinnamon in the cupboard over there. Just finished grinding it this morning. Go mix." And then he turned back to his crust and Fox hurried back to Lai's corner, fishing the cinnamon out of the spice cupboard on the way.

He sat cross-legged on the floor next to Lai's stool and began stirring cinnamon into the berry bowl, delighting for a moment in the mixture of smells. Then he said in a low voice, so as not to be overheard, "What's going on? What did you say to him?"

Lai glanced quickly over her shoulder to make sure her father was occupied. Then she said quietly, "I told him you got a messenger bird from your father, but that it wasn't set in stone and you didn't want to excite the whole town. Don't worry, your secret's safe with me."

His secret. Was it that? For a moment, Fox wondered what would be so wrong with telling Borric that he simply smelled the caravan coming. Like he could with the snow. His keen nose for weather was widely known, and Picck was fascinated by his ability to identify any scent. So why was this any different? Fox couldn't even explain it to himself. But for some reason he felt that if people knew, it would change the way everyone looked at him. For now, better to keep it to himself.

The midday bell rang from the heart of the town square, making Fox jump and drop his spoon into the thick berry paste. He looked up and met a pair of eyes that danced with excitement. "Well," Lai said, "go and look!"

Fox stood nervously and crept out into the common room, wiping his hands on his shirt front as he did so. He climbed up onto one of the high benches at a table by the window and wiped a spot of glass clear with his sleeve. His eyes found the mountain road, and for a moment he saw nothing but grey and snow. And then, a flash of color caught his eye, and he shifted his gaze. There, making its way down the last curve into the valley, was the caravan. Father was home.

Chapter Two
The Homecoming

Things started happening so quickly Fox could barely keep up. The bells in the square began to ring out again, and messenger birds filled the sky, heading to the mines and the outlying farms. Within minutes, the town square was filling with eager families, and Borric was stoking the common room fire. Then Fox was swept up in a flood of people taking refuge from the cold at the Five Sides. He scrambled out of the way and hid in the kitchen with Lai, who was pulling a hot pie out of the oven. "It's mad out there!" said Fox.

"As it should be!" said Picck, swooping in quickly to scoop the pie out of Lai's hands and set it on the cooling rack. "A little madness now and then is good for you, Foxglove. Embrace it!"

"Go," said Lai excitedly. "Go see your father!"

"Yes," said Picck sagely. "Go to him. Brave the madness!"

Fox grinned and hurried back to the kitchen doorway, peering out into the common room. He could hear cheering and whistles outside. He put one foot out the door and then stopped, hesitating. In a moment Lai was at his side. "Fox? What's wrong?"

Fox turned to her. "I was right," he said quietly. "I knew they were coming."

"Yes," said Lai, just as quietly.

"What does this mean?" he asked.

Lai bit her lip, for a moment looking just as lost as he felt. "I don't know," she said finally. She squeezed his shoulder, and Fox took a deep breath. Then, he plunged into the sea of bodies, threading his way through the crowd to the open door.

Wagons and carts of all sizes were parked outside the tavern. As Fox watched, a handful of women detached themselves from the crowd and ran to the caravan, throwing themselves into their husbands' arms. Children followed behind them, calling out and waving, and Fox craned his neck, looking around for his own father. But before he could look very far, he was scooped up into the air and squeezed in a strong hug. "Dad!" he said, throwing his arms around Father's neck and hugging just as tight.

After a moment, Father peeled him away and set him back down on the ground. "Let me look at you," he said, and Fox stood up straight. Father folded his arms across his broad chest. "You've gotten taller," he said sternly. "Taller is no good, you'll lose your nimble footing and then you'll be useless to me."

"Sorry, sir," said Fox, grinning. "I'll try to stop."

A broad smile broke through Father's thick, black beard, and he ruffled Fox's hair. "Well, it's the best I can expect, I suppose." Then, laughing, he put his hand on Fox's shoulder and said, "Let's go home."

They fought their way through the crowd to where Cobb was standing patiently with the other animals. Ponies, mules, and a handful of the tall, thick-haired goats that were sometimes used to pull the wagons. As Father carefully led their pony away from the herd, Fox caught a glimpse of Fire Merchant Terric's reunion with his wife. The two were wrapped in such a tight embrace that Fox was amazed either of them could breath, and Terric's wife was crying and laughing all at once.

"First winter alone for her," said Father quietly. "How'd she take it?"

Fox raised his eyebrows, taking in the woman's sobs. "About like that, without all the kissing and laughing."

They left the chaos of the square behind and hiked up to the house together, Cobb following placidly behind them. As they walked, Father told Fox stories of the trade caravan. "The *colors*!" he said reminiscently. "The rich autumn reds and golds. Ah, you don't see that kind of color here." He talked about the southern fashions and customs, and told Fox about the time he got to sell his furs to the ruling house of Mirius.

"What was their castle like?" asked Fox eagerly.

"Big," said Father. "Very, very big. I can't imagine what they *do* with all that space. They have rooms so big, they should never get warm. And of course, their castle was *nothing* compared to Athilior. The seat of the High King," said Father, answering Fox's question even before he asked it. "Each of the Central Kingdoms have their own monarchs or lords, but they all have to answer to the High King." He hummed in a dreamy sort of way and stared up at a lone piece of blue sky shining through the clouds. "Someday, I'll take you to Athilior. It's the most beautiful city of silver and white. There are universities and libraries, the famous temple district, and the biggest marketplace this side of the Westerling Sea."

Fox thought of that morning's breakfast of simple brown bread with a sigh, imagining what it might be like to have foreign spices and fruit. Every now and then Father brought back exotic treats, but they were gone all too soon.

The Sovestan lifestyle was simple, built around survival. The traders not only brought home money for their families, but many of the daily necessities that the people of Thicca Valley lacked. Father especially, his trade catering to the wealthy, kept the valley from disappearing. He bartered for needles and thread, cookware, knives, lanterns, buttons, fishing line. Tonight, when the three-day Homecoming Festival began, Father would set up shop at the Five Sides and start trading with the valley folk. And Fox, in his constant efforts to prove to Father that he was ready to be apprenticed, would be there for every moment of it.

Mother was waiting for them on the front porch, leaning against the railing with her arms crossed. Mother never ran down to the valley square with the other wives when the bells started to ring. She and Father had always preferred to have their reunions privately, it seemed. And so Fox, as he always did, turned left when they hit the front path and led Cobb to the stables, where he would remain until his parents called him in for dinner.

COBB WENT EAGERLY INTO his freshly cleaned stall and began tearing through his feeding bucket. Fox was completely ignored as he unloaded saddlebags and gear from the old pony's back. He hummed quietly as he worked, setting packages aside to be sorted later and picking bits of leaf and snow from Cobb's mane. He always took an extra long time brushing Cobb after the caravan's return, knowing that it was impractical to groom the animals thoroughly while on the road, as well as giving his parents as much time together as they might need. Slowly and deliberately, Fox worked over every inch of Cobb's thick, grey fur, singing softly.

Have you gone a-westerling
And seen the shining seas?
They say a buried treasure waits
Behind the salty breeze
Have you ridden Merchant's Way
And smelled the summer air?
The autumn gold and winter cold
Are barely moments there.
But if you go a-westerling
Or past the Southern Gates,
Remember me, wrapped in the hills
Where winter always waits.

Cobb had finished eating and was standing calmly, swishing his tail. As Fox began working a comb through the pony's mane, he said quietly, "I bet you never get tired of it, old boy. The lovely autumn weather and the long walks."

"He's the lucky one, isn't he?" said a voice from the stable door, and Fox jumped slightly. Father was standing there, leaning against the doorframe. "He gets the easy job."

"I didn't hear you come in," said Fox.

"Trapper's tread," said Father. "The gods' gift to we that hunt." He joined Fox in Cobb's stall and knelt down, cradling one of the pony's hooves in his lap. "New song?" he asked.

"It started making the rounds about a month ago," Fox said. Winter nights got very long in Thicca Valley. To pass the time, many of the valley folk would write new songs during evenings in the Five Sides. Favorites began to circulate, making their way into the mines and out to the farmlands, filling the air all year long. "I was there when Farradic finished off the last verse, and it sorta just stuck."

"It's beautiful," said Father. "It'll be one of the ones that lasts." They worked in silence for a bit. Then, as Father set down Cobb's last hoof, he stood and stretched. "Have you ever been up to the mines and heard them sing?" He leaned against the wall, gazing out the window toward the northern mines. "Early in the morning is best, just after the rest of the valley begins to wake up and the men have already been at it for a couple of hours. They pick a song, and it starts off quiet. But then, it swells and echoes. It fills the mountain, and it's like the earth itself is trying to speak to you." For a moment, he simply watched the evening snow begin to fall. Then he tossed his hoof pick into the grooming bucket. "For all of the colors and riches the southern lands have to offer, they don't have anything that sounds like that." He smiled at Fox. "Dinner will be ready by now. And then, you and I have a Homecoming to get to, don't we?"

"Yes sir," said Fox.

They left Cobb dozing in his stall and made their way back up to the house. As they walked, Fox thought about the miner's song. About how much Father seemed to love it. With the whole Merchant's Highway at his feet, and the stories he brought back every year, Father still preferred Thicca Valley. And Fox, who spent every winter honing his skills and trying to prove himself, couldn't wait to get out of it. As much as he himself loved his home, and all of the people in it, he was restless.

Fox spent his dinner watching Father across the fire pit. He watched as he and Mother exchanged quick kisses and held hands, and as Father took his time over every bite. He noticed for the first time how Father seemed to take in every stone as he looked around the kitchen. And then, all at once, he noticed how tired Father looked. This strong, laughing man was exhausted. He had hints of grey in his dark hair that had not been there last summer.

As the sun outside finally dipped out of sight, the bells began to ring out in the valley square again. The Homecoming Festival was beginning, with the Five Sides at its heart. Within minutes, Father and Fox were on their way, laden with trade goods to set out at the tavern, and Fox decided to put his worries out of mind for a while. The Homecoming was a chance to relax, to enjoy having the valley together after a long and lonely winter, and before the exhausting summer work began.

THICK, WET SNOWFLAKES began to fall as they entered the valley square, and Fox breathed in the smells of the Homecoming. Fresh hickory wood being added to the bonfire; roasting pigs; hot cider; Borric's pies and fresh honey cakes. Smoke filtered through the chilly air, wrapping around the rooftops and making the moonlight hazy.

"Stay for awhile," said Father. "Have a good time. I'll set up shop. And try to rescue me one of Borric's blackberry pies later."

As Father disappeared into the Five Sides, dancing broke out around the bonfire, sending long shadows darting across the shop fronts and the snow-powdered streets. Fox skittered off to the side to watch, enjoying the flashes of color from the Thiccan's holiday finery. For a time he simply stood there, taking in the dance. And then a hand darted out of the crowd and clamped around his wrist, pulling him into the swirling mass. Kimic Lillywhite, the grainmiller's daughter, was smiling across the circle at him. Fox suddenly found himself skipping around the square in a frantic Sovestan country dance, flecks of snow biting him on the cheeks and making his ears sting.

That first dance was followed by three more, until Fox's lungs were on fire and he had to collapse on the leather worker's shop windowsill. Kimic sat beside him, laughing and brushing snow from her hair. "Thanks for joining me," she said breathlessly.

"Didn't have much of a choice," Fox said lightly as he loosened his scarf.

Kimic smirked at him. "Oh come on, Fox. We both know you'd never get out there yourself."

Fox shrugged. "I like to watch. What's wrong with that?"

"It's just no fun, is all," said Kimic. She leaned her head back against the shop window. "It must be hard, being a boy," she said contemplatively. "You have to start working so much younger than us girls."

"Lai works just as hard as any of the boys."

Kimic rolled her eyes. "Yeah, but that's Lai, isn't it? She's different."

Fox felt a sudden rage surge up inside him, and he bit down hard on the inside of his cheek. He didn't know why, but something about the way Kimic said "different" made him want to hit something. Forcing himself to speak calmly, he said, "Well, what's so wrong with working hard?"

"Nothing exactly," said Kimic. "It's just a shame you boys can't have more fun sometimes." She sat up a little straighter and fluffed her skirt. "*I* can have fun until I get married." And then, to Fox's horror, she took one of his hands in hers and leaned in closer. "Don't you want to have fun, too? Come and dance with me again."

Fox stood so abruptly that Kimic lost her balance. "Sorry, gotta go help with the trading. Enjoy your dance." And he scurried away, quickly putting as many bodies between himself and Kimic Lillywhite as possible. As he made his way to the Five Sides he jammed his hands in his pockets, disgusted. Of course she was flirting with him. Every year, there were a handful of youth who thought they would get special deals and trades if they befriended Fox. Young men and women who usually didn't pay him any mind were suddenly acting like close personal friends. Kimic was a year older than him, and almost a head taller. She was always batting her eyes at the boys and spending her allowance on frivolous things. She would grow up to be one of those young women who would flirt with the married men, Fox was sure of it. And the way she talked about Lai, as though working hard made her less of a girl ... Fox was grateful for the chaos in the Five Sides, so he could put his mind to other things.

Father's table was in the back corner by a window, and he was already surrounded by an eager crowd, all shouting out offers and vying for his attention. Before braving the storm of traders, Fox ducked into the kitchen and begged a fresh blackberry pie from Picck. Then he wove a path through the crowd and slouched onto the bench opposite Father, sliding the pie across the table to him.

"Oh thank Spirit," Father said, and then he raised his voice to the clamoring valley folk. "Alright, alright I know everyone wants to have their say, but give a man some room, please!" The crowd backed away slightly, leaving Father to eat his pie in relative peace. "It's a madhouse this year," he said to Fox through a mouthful of blackberry.

Fox surveyed the trade goods piled on the table and the floor around it. "Looks like you made a good profit this trip," he said.

"Not only with these," said Father, gesturing around with his fork. "I've arranged a special surprise that I think everyone will be excited for."

Fox sat up on his knees and leaned in eagerly across the table.

"No sir," said Father quickly. "You will wait with the rest of the valley, and be surprised when they are." He finished his pie and shoved the empty plate across the wooden tabletop to Fox. "Take that back to the kitchen for me, and then I'll need you to find the lavender candlesticks in one of those packages on the floor. Farradic wants them for his wife, and he's made a solid offer." He caught Fox's eye, and laughed. "Don't give me that stubborn little face, you look just like your mother. It was only a day behind us, so be on the lookout tomorrow. But that's all the hint you get! Now off with you!"

IT. *It* was only a day behind, Father said. Fox and Lai sat in the Five Sides kitchen the next morning, trading guesses on what the special surprise might be.

"It has to be something big," said Lai. "Or else he would have just brought it with the caravan."

"Not necessarily," said Fox. "Sometimes there are items he trades for that have to get sent later. Like some of the more expensive fabrics."

"Hey," called Picck from across the room. "If you're gonna be in my kitchen, breathing my air, you'll keep working for it."

They turned back to the spring peas they were shelling and lowered their voices.

"What if it's silk from Vathidel?" said Lai.

"Or silver pallet shells from the Red Harbor?" said Fox.

"You're both wrong," said a voice from the doorway. Borric stood there, a knowing smirk on his face. "See for yourself. It's here."

Lai grinned excitedly at Fox as they set their work aside and hurried out into the common room. The Homecoming was still in full swing, with waresmen haggling prices all around them. Out in the square, children and adults alike were playing games, although at the moment many of them seemed to be watching something off in the distance.

"Come on!" said Lai, grabbing Fox's hand and pulling him outside. The morning chill was a shock after the warmth of the kitchen, but Fox tried to ignore it as he stood on tiptoes, trying to see what everyone was looking at.

"What is it?" he asked no one in particular.

The excitement in the square seemed to be swelling like a soap bubble, ready to pop at any moment. It seemed that people were not quite sure *what* was coming down the mountain road. And then a word began to be passed around the crowd. Fox heard it whispered from Grainmiller Lillywhite to Miner Farradic. "*Shavid*."

The Shavid. In Fox's lifetime, they had never visited the humble Thicca Valley. But he knew who they were. Everybody knew who they were. The legendary Shavid groups traveled from place to place, never setting down roots. It was said that they answered only to the wind, and they danced for the kings. Shavid players and magicians were always welcome in the highest places, and yet they were coming here.

Fox turned and caught Father's eye through the tavern window. Father winked at him, then turned back to his customers. Fox shook his head, amazed. Was there nothing Timic Foxglove could not do? And how could he, Fox, ever live up to the man's legend?

He could spend his whole life trying, that much he knew. But for now, the Homecoming was about to get a whole lot more interesting. Fox had no idea how Father persuaded a Shavid company to come to the valley, or how long they were planning on staying, but he was going to take advantage of every second.

Chapter Three
Shavid

The Shavid wagons were like nothing Fox had ever seen. Not the simple, sturdy carts that the caravan used, but tall, wide things painted bright colors and hung with everything from feathers and bells to cookware, making them clank and jangle as they paraded through the square. They were more like rolling houses than anything, with shuttered windows along the sides and brightly painted back doors. Even the horses that pulled them drew the eye, with ribbons woven through their manes and jeweled baubles dangling from their harnesses.

Fox had never seen so much color. Rich reds and oranges, and blues so bright they made the sky look drab. There were colors he couldn't even name, colors that he could only dream about from Father's stories. As he watched the Shavid come pouring out of their wagons, he rubbed his fingertips together, warming them slightly. These were colors so vibrant he wanted to reach out and touch every one of them, as though they might feel different than the colors in Thicca Valley.

And the *smells*. As each wagon passed, Fox caught a whiff of something new and beautiful and confusing. Something sharp and tangy from the wagon with the bright red door. Then a series of flowery scents from the wagon with the green door and yellow shutters. The last wagon smelled entirely of leather, but it was the richest leather smell Fox had ever experienced. There was something ... soft about the scent that he couldn't quite figure out.

The Shavid began setting up camp in an empty stretch at the western end of the square. Fox was amazed at how quickly and seamlessly they worked, almost like a dance. As he watched, three of the men began unfolding the side of one of the wagons, transforming it into a small stage at the heart of their campsite. Two more wagons were parked on either side, and they, too, were in the process of being transformed. Women were pulling out bright, patched awnings and long tables from the wagon sides, turning the wagons into selling booths before Fox's eyes.

"Hey!" shouted Lai in his ear, and Fox jumped. He'd been drifting toward the Shavid camp without realizing it. Now he stopped, tearing his eyes away from the whirlwind of color.

"Yeah?" he said sluggishly.

"I said come with me! I want to get some of my savings so I can buy something!" She grabbed Fox by the arm and pulled him away, back to the Five Sides. Reluctantly, Fox allowed himself to be dragged against the tide of Thiccans hurrying to get a closer look at the Shavid. Once inside the tavern, he followed Lai upstairs and to the end of the hallway, where she and Borric shared one of the rooms.

"I've been saving up all winter so I could get some new things during the Homecoming barter, but this is so much better!" said Lai. She dropped to her knees in front of the fireplace and pried one of the bricks loose. In the hollow space beneath it, she stashed her most precious things: money, her favorite doll from when she was younger, and a deep green hair ornament that she never wore. Fox saw the polished surface glint in the weak emberlight, and turned away. He'd seen Lai's treasure trove before, but that hair ornament was the only thing Lai had of her mother's. Looking in on it always made Fox feel as if he was intruding on something very personal.

Lai pocketed a handful of silver and replaced the brick. "Let's go!"

Downstairs again, they were briefly held up by a group of Lai's cousins, all sent to help with the extra tavern business. Fox waited impatiently as Lai issued them their tasks, then finally grabbed hold of her shoulders and pushed her from behind. He steered her all the way to the Shavid camp like this as she laughed.

A tall, broad-shouldered man was standing on the wagon stage, addressing the crowd. Fox dropped his grip on Lai and they squeezed up to the front of the gathering to listen.

"And so we thank you for welcoming us into your beautiful valley," the man was saying. His voice made Fox feel warm, as though he were sitting by the kitchen fire in the early morning. He was also dressed in the most remarkable clothes Fox had ever seen. His vest was bright red, and hung with rows of gold beads. Gold stitching winked from the cuffs of his deep blue shirt, and even his boots seemed to be patterned with golden leaves and feathers. Fox missed the next thing the man said, he was so fascinated by the colors. Suddenly, the man was bowing his way off stage, to be replaced by a handful of the other Shavid, all dressed in bright costumes and with masks tied to their faces.

The Shavid players put on a show like nothing Fox had ever seen. It was a comic piece about one of the gods falling in love with a milkmaid, and it had the audience applauding and cheering riotously. By the time the players took their final bow, Fox was holding a stitch in his side from laughing so much. Then the Shavid welcomed the valley folk into their camp, to trade and enjoy each other's company. Fox found himself shuffled forward by a mob trying to reach the seller's stalls, and he ducked quickly out of the way to avoid being trampled.

Lai had vanished, presumably joining the eager crowd. And so Fox began to wander on his own, taking in the colors and smells with quiet delight. He caught glimpses of jewelry at the selling stalls, and leather masks that mimicked the ones he'd seen on stage. A handful of boys were buying ornately carved wooden swords from one of the players, and Fox couldn't figure out why. Thiccans had no problem carving their own, what made these so special? For a moment he stopped to watch, frowning at two little boys as they squared off against each other in an empty patch of grass. And then as they began play-fencing, Fox stared in amazement. Multi-colored sparks flew each time the wooden surfaces met, and Fox could swear he heard the clank of steel-on-steel. As the children fought clumsily, having no real idea how to fence, it almost seemed as though they were no longer dressed in their festival clothes. As he watched, Fox could swear that they were suddenly clad in chain mail and armor. The vision flickered and shifted as the combatants moved, but it was there.

He turned away, staring around the rest of the camp excitedly. Tents as garishly bright as the wagons were being pitched all around him. They smelled of silk and fur and ink. Fox let his feet take over, wandering where they would with the rest of him simply along for the ride. He ducked behind the stage wagon, catching the briefest glimpse of flesh as some of the

Shavid began changing costumes for another play. He turned left, making his way deeper into the campsite.

His feet took him past an open tent, almost a pavilion. Inside, he saw a handful of Thiccan girls including Kimic, swaying their hips slowly in rhythm to a piper's tune. A tall, beautiful Shavid woman in a long flowing skirt was directing them, seemingly teaching the girls a foreign dance. As Fox scanned the scene, he caught sight of the piper, dressed entirely in multi-colored patches. Fox watched him, sure for a moment that he'd seen a shower of sparks pouring from the pipe's end, but he blinked and the vision was gone.

The next performer he came across caught and held his attention for several minutes. A juggler, dressed in a costume of cream and gold, was entertaining a small group. He was juggling what first appeared to be solid golden baubles, the size of spring apples. But as Fox watched, some of the globes began to shift sizes in midair, changing from egg-sized to large as grapefruit in the blink of an eye. The audience clapped for him, and the juggler bowed dramatically, sweeping one arm behind him and continuing to juggle with his free hand.

There. A deep-throated laugh, somewhere to Fox's left. And the strum of a lute. It was the man in the red vest, Fox was sure of it. He turned, looking for the source. There, seated on a low stool in front of a short, round tent was the broad-shouldered man who had made such an impression on Fox. He was surrounded by a handful of his company, all of whom were holding foreign instruments. The man himself was tuning a beautifully-carved lute, the only instrument in the whole collection Fox recognized. He looked up when Fox approached.

"Welcome, young master," said the man in that warm, rich voice. "How can we help you today?"

Fox looked over the small group. Two boys older than him, a man with a thick grey braid, and a woman whose dark red hair was cut so close Fox might have mistaken her for a man, if it wasn't for her form-fitting costume. They smelled of fresh soap and foreign spices and wood, and Fox felt a longing pulling at him that he could not explain.

"Look at the poor lad," said the woman sympathetically. "Speechless in sight of you, Radda."

The broad-shouldered man, Radda, laughed heartily. "Well there's no need for that," he said. "Come now, boy, what's your name?"

"Forric Foxglove. Fox."

"And what service might we offer you this fine afternoon, Master Fox?" He shifted his instrument into playing position, and Fox marveled that hands so large could even hold the thing without snapping it into kindling. "A song? A dance? A mythic tale of maidens and swords?"

"Or is there a love ballad you'd like us to sing to a lady friend?" asked one of the boys.

"We're best at the dancing tunes, though," said the other boy.

"And you really shouldn't ask for a tale," said the grey-haired man. "Our resident storyteller is up at the front of camp somewhere, and this one here," he jerked his head toward Radda, "has never been much with stories."

"Here now," said Radda in mock outrage. "I'm better than *you* ever were, Otter!"

"You embellish too much!" Otter spat back. "You turn what ought to be an end-of-night poem in to an epic that drags through 'till the morning embers!"

Fox smiled as his nervousness melted slightly. Feeling somewhat bolder, he cut in before Radda had a chance to reply. "Actually," he said, "I was hoping to learn a little bit more about ... you. All of you. The Shavid?" Now that he'd gotten started, he found he couldn't stop. It was as if he *had* to convey to them the longing, the need to know everything about them. "It's just, we don't get many Shavid here. Or any. Ever. You're the first troupe we've ever seen, that is to say *I've* ever seen, and I know you travel the Known World and you've seen so much more that there is to see than I can ever *dream* to and —"

Otter cut him off with a wave of his hand. "Alright, we get it boy." He looked at Radda. "For Spirit's sake, tell him something before he wets himself."

Radda chuckled and motioned for Fox to sit. He did so, waiting eagerly for Radda to set his instrument aside and begin speaking. "There is a legend of the creation of the Shavid." He looked pointedly at Otter. "I may not be a gifted storyteller, but there are some tales even *I* can spin to satisfaction."

He took a breath and looked Fox in the eye. "It begins, as all truly old stories do, with the start.

"In the beginning, Dream fell in love with Spirit. Over time, their union would produce the gods. But firstborn were the elements: Earth, called Shatza. Fire, called Zaru. Water, called Ralith. And Wind, called Rhin. Wind was the youngest of the four. She was blithe and vivacious, and told her father Spirit that she would never fall in love. When she finally did, as all women eventually do, her first kiss was legendary. It lasted one hundred years, and when it was over it broke into one hundred pieces. And that was the beginning of the Shavid."

Fox had heard stories before. There wasn't much else to do during the dead of winter. But this was nothing like the tales that were spun during the dark hours, when most of Thicca Valley would gather at the Five Sides and tell their favorite myths or make up new poems and songs. Those nights were warm and comfortable, as you nestled in with your friends and took turns telling your favorite parts of old legends. This, however, was something else entirely. From the very first words, Fox was whisked away to someplace new. He could feel warmth on his face with the word "fire," and feel his heart beat madly at the mention of love. And when Rhin shared her first kiss, Fox felt an ice cold pressure on his own lips.

"The Shavid are wanderers," Radda continued. "Following the wind, always moving from place to place. Never setting down roots. They make their unofficial home in a town called Wanderlust. It is a place that exists only once a year, and only for one purpose: to host the yearly gathering of the Shavid. A festival at summer's end, dedicated to the celebration of their patron goddess, and the birth of their people."

There were tents. Dozens of them, shimmering in Fox's vision. And the distant sound of a hundred wagons rolling through the woods toward the heart of Wanderlust. And brief, teasing scents flittering through the air, but disappearing before Fox could place any of them.

"The rest of the year, the Shavid travel in smaller groups, or on their own. Their magical Blessings are a reflection of Rhin's own passions. Music, dance, theatre. But their true Blessing is in their connection with the wind. It is Rhin's voice to them, whispering in each ear and heart. The children of Rhin answer to no master but the wind."

When Radda bowed his head, the story at a close, Fox realized he hadn't been breathing. He took a deep breath of ice cold air, pulling himself from whatever spell the story had wrapped around him as Otter clapped Radda on the shoulder.

"Well done. See? You *can* practice brevity when you really want to."

The musicians and Fox laughed, and the redheaded woman tugged playfully at the ear of one of the boys. "Come on, we'd best start getting ready for the show." The group began to gather themselves up, straightening their costumes and checking that their instruments were in order. But Radda stayed put. He caught Fox's eye and held his gaze.

"You're still hungry for more, aren't you boy?" Fox nodded, and Radda seemed to scrutinize him closely for a moment, as if there was something about Fox that he couldn't quite put his finger on. Then, he clapped his hands together and said, "Well, Radda Southwick is nothing if not a people-pleaser!" He dramatically swept up his instrument again. "Come now, ask me anything, and I will be honored to oblige."

"What did it mean, the magic Blessings?"

"Powers. Gifts. You know, the magic some people are born with."

Fox blushed slightly. Of course. Blessings. That's why he didn't recognize the term: magic in Sovesta was extremely rare since the curse. Fox had never even heard of anyone in Thicca Valley being born with magic in over four generations. "Oh, of course," he said to cover his embarrassment. "Blessings."

"Well, the Shavid Blessings are not like other magic. We don't usually appear from thin air, or read minds or walk in dreams. Our blessings live through our talents. Dancing, music, even sewing."

"Magic? In the music?"

The tall bard laughed. "Well of course, young master. For instance, I could make you see ... flowers." He plucked at a few strings, and a shimmering blanket of golden blossoms sprang to life at Fox's feet. "A bright spring morning in a land where the snow falls only in December." He began to play a lighthearted tune, and it suddenly seemed to Fox that the ice beneath his feet had turned into lush, green grass dotted with wildflowers. A sweet chirping chorus seemed to fill the air and, just for a moment, the sun was warm on Fox's face. But as Fox reached out to touch an iridescent butterfly that was winging past, it all dissolved in a flurry of snow, and cold settled over him once more.

Fox stared at the spot in front of him where the butterfly had been, barely registering the playful argument that had broken out between the musicians. It was only when Otter shouted "— whole forest of great white oaks, changing seasons! Now *that* was a performance!" that Fox came back to his senses.

"Maybe back then, but you couldn't pull that off these days, old man," said one of the boys, and Otter smacked him on the back of the head.

"You alright, Fox?" asked Radda quietly as Otter and the boys continued to snipe at each other.

"Yeah," he said, shaking his head slightly. "Just, lost in thought, I guess."

"Well," said Radda, "there are worse things to get lost in." When Fox didn't answer, he set aside his instrument. "Why don't you head on back to the staging area? We've got a few more plans for tonight's festivities. You can watch from there." He leaned in closer and put a massive hand on Fox's shoulder. "We're not going anywhere for awhile, so don't you fret. I'm here if you've any more questions. Just go enjoy yourself."

Fox nodded mutely and wound his way back through the Shavid camp in a haze. But he did not go back to the staging area. Instead, he slid through the crowd like a ghost, barely noticed. He wandered back to the Five Sides almost without thinking and flopped onto the bench across from Father.

"You look like I feel," said Father gruffly, shuffling through a stack of papers. "How about we sneak another piece of pie later?"

Fox made a non-committal grunt and stared out the window without really seeing. The rest of the afternoon passed slowly, despite the constant shifting of crowds in and out of the tavern. Fox did his best to be helpful to Father, helping sort through trade goods and occasionally running back into the kitchen to grab them something to eat, but his mind kept drifting back to Radda's story. He could still feel the phantom goddess's ice-cold lips on his.

When the Shavid came to the Five Sides for dinner, they put on a dazzling show. Radda played a rowdy song that made everyone cheer and throw coins at him, but Fox secretly longed for him to play the little tune with the butterflies again. Two of the girls did a southern country jig on one of the tables, and the juggler with the golden orbs finished the night with a spectacular act, appearing to juggle live, flaming birds. And then they all sat and ate a hearty meal with the Thiccans, everyone laughing and swapping stories, just like in the dark hours of winter. Except this time, they weren't just stories, they were adventures. The Shavid were excited to learn the Thiccan tales, just as the valley folk were clamoring to hear the wanderers' stories. Everything was suddenly new and fresh, even the songs that Fox had heard a hundred times before.

There was something there for him, with the Shavid. Something he needed, something that he'd never known he was missing, until now.

Chapter Four
Neil

The celebration at the Five Sides ran late into the night. By the time the last song was sung, the fireplace along the far wall had burned completely dark, and the firepit at the center of the room held only the hint of flickering embers. By the whispers of light from the tabletop candles, Fox could see that many of the Thiccans and Shavid alike were choosing to sleep right where they were, curled up near the hearth or sprawled out on a bench. Father had fallen asleep hours before, sitting upright against the wall with his feet propped up on the table.

Fox stretched out on the neighboring bench, closing his eyes gratefully. He felt he had never been so tired, and yet he'd been determined to hear everything the Shavid had to offer that night. And now, though his body was aching for sleep, his brain was wide awake and humming with the stories of the night. He tried to remember the names of strange places and cursed princes, and wondered how many roads one would have to travel to gather so many tales. Pieces of a dozen different legends flittered through his head as he finally drifted into a half sleep.

Every so often throughout the night, a Thiccan would drag himself up and make his way home, forsaking the immediate comfort of the common room for the warmth of his own bed. Each time one of them opened the front door, a chill would settle on the room, making Fox pull his cloak tighter around his shoulders before letting himself sink back into the swirl of strange dreams keeping him company. Half awake and half asleep, he wasn't quite sure how much time passed before the smell of something coming from the kitchen woke him totally and completely.

He sat up, rubbing at a cramp in his neck and stretching. The common room was full of the heavy, even breathing of deepest sleep, but Fox's nose told him that Picck was already up and hard at work. Fox slipped from his bench and crept across the common room, carefully stepping over and around sleeping shadows. He ducked gratefully into the warm kitchen and blinked, his eyes adjusting to the glowing firelight.

"You're up early," said Picck through a yawn. He was sitting cross-legged on the counter top, wrestling a spoon through a bowl of some sticky kind of dough.

"Can I help with anything?" said Fox, stifling a yawn of his own.

"Potatoes in that basket over there. Start peeling."

Soon, the two were sitting by the fire, retelling moments of their favorite stories from last night. As they talked, Picck dropped spoonfuls of dough onto the long, flat rock that sat near the front of the fireplace. Soon, the shapeless masses would be delicious corn cakes that were perfect for breakfast, or even for saving to snack on later in the mines.

"I wonder what they eat on pirate ships," said Fox, watching the dough flatten and brown in front of him.

"Like Captain Lorello's crew in the Shavid song?"

"Yeah. I mean, you can't have fires on a wooden ship, can you? It could burn the whole thing down. You couldn't make things like this."

Picck began flipping the corn cakes over to cook on their other sides. "I suppose you could make plenty before you left, and then just save them. These things keep pretty well."

"But for an entire crew? And they're gone for who knows how long?"

Picck shrugged. "Maybe that Radda will know. He's the one who sang the song." He stared into the fire for a moment. "Wonder if he's ever been on a ship like that. Fighting off sea monsters and escaping from island witches and the High King's navy." He sprang to his feet suddenly, brandishing the doughy spoon at Fox like a sword. "Have at you, scurvy dog!"

Fox jumped up from his perch on the hearth and scrambled backwards, running his hands along the counter top to find something to defend himself with. His fingers found a rolling pin and he braced himself, holding his weapon in front of him with both hands. "In the name of the king, I hereby declare you under arrest!"

"I'll throw you to the sirens, you yellow-bellied land-lubber! Ah HA!" Picck lunged, dough flying from the tip of his spoon. Fox beat the spoon away and swung madly with his own makeshift sword. And then they were off, Picck chasing him all around the kitchen until Fox finally clambered up onto the cutting table, making himself almost as tall as his opponent.

"I'll see you hang for this, Lorello!" Fox launched in with a fresh attack and then danced away across the tabletop, just out of reach of Picck's spoon. "No one fishes in the king's harbor and gets away with it!"

Picck dropped his stance and raised an eyebrow. "Fishing? Of all the dastardly pirate crimes I could have committed, you picked fishing?"

"Well, what would you have preferred?"

Picck's face lit up. "Robbing the castle armory!"

"And your weapon of choice was a spoon?"

Picck brandished his spoon with a flourish. "Scoff not, Sir Navy Scum! This weapon is mighty, and shall be your downfall, you ... twit!"

Fox laughed at Picck's fumbling banter, but he wasn't the only one. A female giggle glistened through the kitchen briefly before the boys whipped around, and the beautiful young woman standing in the doorway covered her mouth quickly with her hand.

"Rose!" said Picck, arm still raised. "What are you ... when?"

"Oh no, don't stop!" she said. "That was *wonderful!*" She clasped her hands in front of her in genuine delight.

Fox leapt nimbly from the tabletop. "Yes, well, we're thinking of submitting our play to the Shavid. We'll call it, 'The Kitchen Wars.'"

Rose's gaze slid from Fox to Picck, and her smile seemed much shyer all of a sudden. "I'd watch it." And then she turned away, stripping off her snow-flecked cloak and exchanging it for one of the aprons hanging on a hook by the doorway.

Rose Beckweed was considered by all to be the prettiest of the Five Sides kitchen girls. Merchants passing through were always offering her presents and buying her drinks, and every Thiccan boy of marrying age seemed to be wooing her. As she started about her morning chores, Fox turned to tease Picck, but then he stopped. Before his eyes, the kitchen boy was beginning to transform. He stood up straighter and ran his fingers through his hair, making it lie somewhat tidier on his head. And then, in a voice much deeper than his own, he said calmly, "Long night last night. Did you stick around for any of the festivities?"

"Some," said Rose. "I danced a bit. Traded some needlework for a piece of pretty for my mother."

"Sweet of you," said Picck. "But she's already got the prettiest thing in town." And then, when Rose turned to look, he winked. A completely and entirely un-Picck-like thing to do, in Fox's mind. And Fox, suddenly feeling quite sure that he'd intruded on something very personal and intimate, stood up quickly.

"Air," he said. "Fresh air. I'm going to step out and get ... yes."

"Feed the old biddies too, while you're at it," said Picck, without so much as a glance at Fox. But Fox scooped up the bucket of potato peels obediently and slipped out the back door into the kitchen courtyard, closing the door gratefully behind him.

Picck? Flirting? With a *girl?* Fox couldn't make sense of it. He had always seen Picck as that funny, gangly youth who lived in the Five Sides kitchen and made the best bread in the valley, not the charming young man who'd just been confidently talking to the most desired girl in four towns. And for Rose to be flirting back? Fox simply didn't understand women. Maybe someday he would, when he was older, but for now they were entirely baffling to him.

He shifted his grip on the bucket, putting the mysteries of women out of his mind for the moment as he made his way across the courtyard. Nestled into one of the oddly-shaped corners of the building was a small hut that the Five Sides employed as a stable. Fox slid the door open with his foot and said, "Good morning, girls."

The "old biddies," as Picck had called them, were the Five Sides' two she goats, Aly and Fermia. They were slumbering near the center of the hut, but both roused and came eagerly to Fox when he entered, pressing their muzzles against him and nosing around the bucket. Fox scooted past them and dumped the potato peels into their feeding trough, then turned the empty bucket on its end and sat down while the goats munched happily on their breakfast. Above them, the messenger birds that nested in the rafters began to shift and ruffle their feathers, shedding a light featherfall down onto the goats.

Fox had heard once from a visiting merchant that goats farther south were much, much smaller than the goats in Sovesta, but Fox couldn't imagine that such beasts would be very useful. The valley goats were not just used for their milk, though one udder-full was enough to keep the tavern in cheese for two days, but as beasts of labor as well. As tall as a pony, and much sturdier, many of them were used by farmers as plow animals. They pulled wagons and carts, and they were better than guard dogs when it came to warding off unwelcome predators. Fox reached up and fondly rubbed Fermia's neck. He'd spent many summer days milking and grooming these goats, as well as churning their rich milk into butter with Lai. "Eat up, lovelies," he said. "You know what they say: 'With Springtime sun comes the end of the fun.'"

The goats gave no sign that they heard him, and Fox stood up, yawning. The valley saying was more than true. Livestock and Thiccans alike would be working themselves to the bone as soon as the Homecoming ended. And so Fox left the goats to finish their breakfast in peace. As the frigid morning air bit his nose, he caught a whiff of smoke drifting over from the Shavid camp. He turned to look. Sure enough, from here he could just see a faint haze of grey and a flickering light illuminating the front of the stage wagon. A breakfast fire, he was sure. He itched to go over and investigate. He wondered who was there so early in the morning. Who had stayed behind from the festivities last night, or else abandoned the warmth of the Five Sides before dawn?

The distant firelight called to him, a promise of more stories. He supposed he should get back into the kitchen to finish with breakfast ... but surely that chore could wait? His feet seemed to agree with his heart, and they began to carry him across the courtyard toward the tantalizing glow. But before he had gotten very far, the back kitchen door was thrown open with a bang, and Fox was shaken from his trance.

"Kill me," said Picck, leaning against the doorframe and taking in huge gulps of cold air.

"What's wrong?" asked Fox, taking a carful step towards him.

"She –" Picck gestured wildly into the kitchen. "And I –" He buried his face in his hands and let out a muffled yell. Then he slumped down the doorframe and sat back on his heels. "She is the most beautiful woman in the whole world. How can I even ...?"

"You two seemed to be getting on just fine," said Fox, biting back a smile.

Picck laughed humorlessly. "Do you know how long it took me to practice talking like that?"

Fox couldn't help it. The image of Picck practicing his smooth talk alone in the kitchen sent him into a fit of quickly stifled giggles.

Picck shot him a glare. "Oh ha, ha. I'm sure Lai can tell you the stories if you ask her. She's walked in on me more than once, making a fool out of myself. Trying out lines on the morning dough ..." At this, even Picck began to smile. "I suppose I did look rather stupid."

"You have no idea how much I would have paid to see that," said Fox truthfully.

Picck chuckled. "I could have made a fortune." Then he shook his head and sighed deeply. "Sometimes, when it's just her and me in the kitchen, I forget that we're so different."

"Different?"

"She's like this beautiful little flower that floats around the kitchen. She's sunlight, and music and fresh apple pie. And I'm this ... this bumbling, big-eared ... " He clenched his hands in frustration, as though trying to catch the right word with his flour-powdered fingers.

"Mossweed?" Fox supplied helpfully.

Picck snorted, pulling at a strand of his unruly hair, which they often joked about resembling the riverside plant. "Exactly. She has every eligible miner in town fighting for her hand. How can I compete?"

For this, Fox had no answer. He wasn't courting anyone himself, but he'd seen enough of the valley marriages to know that women were keen on strong men who could protect them. And Picck, while kind-hearted and plenty talented in his own ways, was nobody's idea of a protector.

BREAKFAST WAS A NOISY affair that morning. Fox and Lai were kept busy, running back and forth delivering plates of ham and cinnamon bread to the common room. The room seemed to have divided itself into smaller groups, all sitting around swapping stories. Not adventure stories and legends like the night before, but more everyday tales. Thiccans were telling the Shavid what it was like to work in the mines, while Shavid in return were detailing the layout of a merchant's boat, or else telling stories about the time one of them had to escape from an angry king who didn't like his music. As Fox slipped into one group by the fireplace, platter of eggs in hand, he heard one of the waresmen telling everyone about this year's caravan.

"... swear the streets at the Eastmarket haven't been that crowded in five years! Not since the Royal Tour, and that's when the High King himself was passing through town! But now, all of these little vendors sprung up like weeds. Wasn't really a concern for us until we realized, that *one* of them," he held up a large, meaty finger to emphasize, "had stolen our prime spot!"

The crowd around him cried out in shock. One of the Shavid players said, "What did you do?"

The waresman smiled. "Not what I did, lad. What *he* did." He pointed across the room to where Father sat, already conducting business in his corner booth. "Timic Foxglove goes right up to this vendor – weasely little man he was, too – and says, kind as you please, 'Excuse me, sir, but I believe this spot is ours.' Man looks at him and says, 'I got here first, so why don't you just —' Well, it's not appropriate for mixed company what he said next." A laugh rippled through the little crowd. "But Timic, he gets right in the vendor's face. He says 'Son, you must be new around here. So I'm only going to say this once. I come from a land where the winters claim more souls than the battlefields, and young men can throw boulders heavier than you without flinching. Now, we have a gentlemen's understanding with the rest of the merchants here, regarding who sets up shop and where they do it. But believe me when I say that if you do not honor that understanding, nothing about what follows will be gentleman-like.'"

The listening crowd cheered, some shouting praises to Father, who smiled in acknowledgment before turning back to his business. Over the applause and laughter, another merchant in the crowd said, "You should have seen that little man scurry! Left half of his wares behind when he cleared out!"

Fox left the eggs with the storyteller, and then slipped out of the group again. He was used to hearing stories about Father, but he never got tired of them. The caravan tales always excited him, making him eager to get on the road himself and start trying to live up to the Foxglove legend.

As he looked around the common room, he noticed how many of the Shavid were still there, and his mind was pulled back to the breakfast fire at the campsite. Who was missing? Why weren't they here? Fox ducked back into the kitchen, still thinking when he was handed a fresh plate of ham. But instead of heading back out into the common room, Fox turned right around and hurried out the back door, grabbing three hot sticky rolls on his way out and adding them to the plate.

His feet carried him to the edge of the kitchen courtyard where he clambered over the low wall, still balancing the plate, careful not to drop anything. As he left the noise of the Five Sides behind, he could hear something else floating on the morning breeze. A pipe of some kind. And its player, Fox was almost positive, would be sitting at the Shavid campfire.

The tune was simple, but beautiful. As Fox drew nearer, he could see someone seated on the edge of the stage, half illuminated by the rising sun. A boy, a few years older than Fox by the look of it. If he'd had to guess, Fox would have placed him at about sixteen. He didn't so much as glance up as Fox approached, but kept on playing. By the time the boy was finished, Fox was standing right next to him. "That was a lovely song," Fox said.

The boy laughed humorlessly, a single sharp note. "You've heard Radda play?"

"Yes."

"Then my song wasn't lovely. It was just a song." He turned to look at Fox, tucking the pipe into his vest pocket. "So then, who are you? What brings you here?"

Fox gestured to the small fire. "Everybody seems to be eating breakfast at the inn, but I saw the smoke, so I figured —" He held out the plate.

They scrutinized each other for a moment. Now that Fox got a closer look at the boy, he could only find one word to describe him: shadowy. He had black hair and grey eyes, and his skin was a smooth, rich brown. Something about his look made Fox feel that this dark young man could disappear into a crowd without anyone taking notice. In fact, Fox couldn't remember seeing him at all during his brief tour of the Shavid camp the day before. Even his clothes were nondescript, nothing at all like the bright costumes the rest of the Shavid wore. Instead, simple grey breeches and shirt with a black vest.

At last, the boy held out his hand. "Neil."

"Fox." They shook, and Neil patted the empty piece of stage beside him, wordlessly offering Fox a seat. He took it, handing the plate over as he sat.

"So," said Neil after a moment. "You're a kitchen boy?"

"No, I just help out." He shifted in his seat, rubbing his hands together to warm them. "I'm a trapper, actually." When Neil cast him a disbelieving look over a handful of bread, Fox corrected himself. "Going to be. My father is, anyway, and I'm training. And what about you? You're one of the musicians?"

For a brief moment, a look crossed Neil's face. Was it sadness? Anger? But then it disappeared, replaced by a crooked smile. "I'm flattered, but no." He tossed his crust of bread into the fire and dusted the crumbs from his hands.

"A player then? Or a dancer? I only saw women dancing last night, but I heard at the inn that sometimes men join them. A storyteller?"

Neil laughed. "Slow down, little trapper. Those are all very good guesses, but no. Actually, I'm not even one of the Shavid." He hopped down from the stage and bent down beside the fire, poking at the embers with a stick and throwing off sparks. "I'm what they call a Dervish. Someone who is adopted into a Shavid company, but has no real Blessings. Like a stowaway on a ship, allowed to become part of the crew. If they're lucky."

"But why?" said Fox. "Where were you before?"

Neil's back was to him, but Fox could hear something in his voice as he spoke next. Something painful, like an old wound that still stung. "Very, very far away from here." Fox waited, and Neil stood up, turning around and shoving his hands in his pockets. "I'm not a storyteller. I can't do what they do, make you see places and feel things."

"It's still a story," said Fox.

"But why would you want to hear *my* story? With just words?"

Fox was confused. Why should it matter so much? Neil was a stranger to this town, and fascinating as well. Allowed to travel with the Shavid, even though he wasn't one of them? Fox was just as interested in this boy as he was in Radda and Otter. So why should it matter that his story would have no magic to it? Fox didn't mind, but it seemed that Neil did. "I'm interested," Fox said at last. "A good story doesn't need all that. All the pictures and feelings and such."

"Try playing to the emperor's court without them," said Neil with a laugh. But he settled himself back down on the stage beside Fox, took a deep breath, and began.

"It wasn't a bad life, what I was living before. I was a candle boy at the university at Maradwell. I made sure the students had plenty of light, and I ran messages and supplies and helped stack books back on their shelves. My father was a professor, so we lived at the university. Just me and him, since my mother died. We took meals in the mess hall with everyone else, and I was sneaking into classes and listening to lectures before I was six." He smiled reminiscently. "One of the professors who didn't like me much always tried to punish me when he caught me, but I somehow managed to talk my way out of trouble. Father and I were very close with the emperor's family , and that got me a lot of special treatment.

"As I got older, it became clear that I was going to be a scholar. Maybe even a professor, like my father, and my grandfather. I got the highest marks in my classes. I spent every free minute in the library or helping my friends with their studies. And then, four years ago, everything changed.

"I was eleven. My eleventh birthday, actually. That's the day the emperor was murdered in his bed, before dawn." Neil was looking off toward the distant peaks, but not as though he really saw them. It was as if he were trying to look into the past, to see the murderer's face. "I don't know how he got in. The emperor's chambers are protected. Guarded by his most loyal warriors, and every entrance is magicked. A bird couldn't fly through his bedchamber window without the palace mages being alerted. But no one ... no one heard him. Or saw him. And they never found him. "

Neil shook himself back into the present and continued. "They tried to keep it quiet at first. Only the advisors knew, and the emperor's children. Four daughters, and Adil. My closest friend, and heir to the throne. He was only ten years old, and scared. So he came to us, looking for help. Advice. Anything. But by nightfall, the whole city knew. And while we watched from the palace walls, it began to tear itself apart.

"You have to understand," said Neil, turning to look Fox square in the eyes, "Maradwell was an unstable city at the heart of an unstable nation. Adil's father, Emperor Oazhe, was the only thing holding it together. He brought peace and prosperity back to our people, and he was a gifted and beloved leader. But there was always this ... this hunger in the land. Family grudges and property wars were pushed aside when Oazhe took the throne, but they didn't die. If anything, they festered and grew during the peaceful days, and the emperor's death seemed to be just what our people needed to fall back into their old ways. Everyone with a drop of royal blood seemed to think they had claim to the throne. Within two days, there were five separate assassination attempts made on Adil and his sisters. And while we increased security around the palace, we ... we failed. Two of Adil's younger sisters were killed, another kidnapped. His older sister, who would have been first in line for the throne if Adil were to die, was taken into hiding at the temple of Phiira. That left just Adil to protect, and war was erupting all around us."

Neil ran his fingers distractedly through his hair, staring into the dying embers of the morning fire. "Everyone always said me and Adil could have been brothers, we looked that much alike. And no one would notice the son of a scholar ... just a candle boy. I don't remember whose idea it was, but we made the switch. Father took Adil away and hid him in our rooms at the university. And I, in turn, waited at the palace. Besides Father, only one other person knew: Thabet, Adil's personal bodyguard. For a week he stayed by my side, distracting me from the war with books and stories. He knew how much I liked to read. We moved rooms every few hours, sneaking from place to place, using secret passageways and deserted hallways to avoid detection.

"Thabet explained to me that we couldn't trust anyone. The palace guards had divided, loyalties split. Each fighting for their own cause now. And within that week, nine different emperors claimed the throne. The longest holding his place for just over a day, the shortest for only one hour.

"Finally, a man named Li-Kamen came forward. Through a combination of brute force and sorcery, he won the throne and named himself emperor. Fighting continued in the city, and civil war continued to sweep through the nation, but the palace remained untouched. It was the perfect time to make our escape."

"How did you do it?" asked Fox.

"It wasn't easy. Li-Kamen had men scouring the palace and the grounds, looking for Adil. Word was, he wouldn't stop until the heir was dead. We didn't want to risk him somehow discovering that Adil was still alive and safe, so we decided the best plan was to give him a dead heir. Or, at least, someone who looked like him."

"You faked your death?" said Fox excitedly. One of Radda's heros in the songs from last night had escaped from a wicked queen by pretending to be dead.

Neil smiled, apparently pleased by Fox's interest in his story. "There was a spell I'd come across in one of my books. Dangerous, even for a skilled magician. Thabet only had the barest knowledge of his own Blessing, whereas I had no Blessings at all. But we decided it was worth the risk." He rubbed his fingers together, as though his hands itched to be around the spell book as he tried to explain. "When used properly, this spell aids the deep sleep required for some of the more intense meditative arts. But in Thabet's untrained hands, it knocked me out for a full two weeks. I looked dead to all the world, including Li-Kamen. And Thabet, claiming that he wanted to bury the emperor's son in the proper way, was allowed to take my body from the palace without question. He then managed to sneak us aboard a merchant ship and buy the captain's silence and cooperation.

"When I awoke, we were at sea. And by the time our journey ended, we had become very close with a group of traveling Shavid. Radda's players. We were on the run, and had nowhere in particular to go, so we tagged along for awhile. Then awhile turned into a year, and then two. But Thabet was always looking for word on the war back home. Keeping up with news of Li-Kamen. Looking for a way to spirit Adil out of Maradwell, until he was old enough to fight and reclaim his throne. Last I heard, that was still Thabet's plan."

"Last you heard?" asked Fox.

"He left," said Neil, shrugging as though it didn't matter, but Fox could see that he was pained by the memory. "His first priority was always Adil. A little over a year ago, he returned to Maradwell, intent on gathering followers and building an army to reclaim the country, and the throne, for its rightful emperor. And I ... well, I've made my place here. Learning and living with the Shavid."

Fox frowned, letting the information sink in. "But," he said finally, "if the plan was to get you, or rather Adil, out ... why did you have to switch places at all? Now he's left behind in the capital, in danger of people finding out who he really is. Isn't that so much riskier?"

Neil seemed to have been prepared for this. He answered as readily as though it was an argument he had been having with himself for years. "Adil was raised to be strong. He was, and is, almost aggressively *good*. Even at ten, he refused to abandon his people. He believed, with a righteous conviction that bordered on dangerous, that his life belonged to Maradwell. He didn't want to die, but he didn't want to run either. He wanted to stay close, and come of age quietly hidden in plain sight. Close to the people who might be able to rally around him one day as their emperor."

"I can't imagine he was too happy letting you run away in his place."

Neil chuckled darkly. "He came very near *ordering* me to stay. But in the end, we convinced him it was for the best. Safest, if Adil insisted on remaining in Maradwell."

"And your father?" said Fox. "What about him?"

Now, there was definite pain in Neil's voice, though he tried hard to hide it behind a forced, lopsided smile. "Raised Adil like a son. From the few messages we've managed to pass on ... he seems to be doing just fine." From the way he said it, it was clear to Fox that he was done talking about it. Whatever feelings he had toward his father and the boy who'd become his father's son, he was keeping them to himself.

A light snow had begun to fall. After a moment's silence, Fox said, "I liked your story."

Neil grunted in acknowledgment.

"And I liked your song."

For a moment they sat there in silence. Then, Neil stood again and offered a hand to Fox, pulling him down from the stage. "Come on," he said. "I'll show you around the place. You can help me with my chores if you'd like."

Fox's sheer joy and excitement must have shown on his face, because Neil began to laugh. A full, hearty laugh that Fox would not have believed possible from the same sullen young man who was so worried about the quality of his songs and his stories.

Chapter Five

The Contests

It seemed that Neil was rather eager to tell his stories, now that he had a captive audience. He answered Fox's constant stream of questions with enthusiasm and a dramatic flair that showed him to be a player at heart, no matter his brooding exterior. As they went through a roster of early-morning chores, Neil chattered on about the incredible places he'd traveled with the Shavid.

"The Candlewood at Elvador, have you heard of it?" They were stationed at the river, setting out fishing traps and digging up edible roots.

Fox nodded. "Where lost souls are trapped on their way to the After Realms."

"'And the trees were alight with a thousand lonely spirits, whispering their secrets to the weary wanderer,'" said Neil, quoting an ancient poem. "I can't begin to describe ... The lights, the flitting breezes that constantly play at the leaves ... it was beautiful and dark and treacherous all at once."

"Where else?" said Fox, nearly breathless with fascination.

Neil shook his head, a wry smile pulling at the corners of his mouth. "How can I even keep count anymore? We've fished in the Red Harbor and sailed the Gossamer Sea. We've passed through the Gates of Eldrock and taken dinner with the High King in Athilior. And the hanging gardens at Lamanti? What a sight to behold."

"Wow," breathed Fox. "And they just let you go anywhere with them?"

"I've been named an honorary Shavid. I have none of their talents or magical Blessings, but I'm welcome to the same privileges and sanctuaries that they might enjoy."

For a moment, Fox let his imagination wander, dreaming about what it might be like to be welcomed in foreign courts and distant lands. Then he sighed and turned back to the cold, hard earth he was scraping away at. "Traveling with them must be incredible," he said.

Neil tugged at one of the traps, adjusting its position in the river. "It does have its moments," he said. "But this kind of life ... it wasn't meant for folks like us."

"What do you mean?"

For a moment Neil didn't answer, focusing instead on his work. Then, he secured the trap into place with a rope anchored to a nearby stone. "I mean ... you say 'traveling,' but the Shavid don't travel. They wander. There's no rhyme or reason to it, at least none that *we* can tell. They hear things, or feel things in the air, and they just ... change course. And sometimes, two Shavid will hear very different things, even standing side-by-side." He fiddled distractedly with the hem of his vest. "There used to be another in our group. A girl. She was like ... like someone out of one of Radda's stories. A legend come to life, beautiful and passionate and kind ..."

"What happened to her?"

"She left. Heard a different call. The wind spoke to her, and she followed it to Rhin only knows where." He stared up at the cloudy sky, almost as if he were trying to see her, wherever she was. "She left in the middle of the night. Packed her things, and vanished with only the quickest of goodbyes." They sat in silence for a moment, until finally Neil cleared his throat and turned back to Fox. "We can't hear the wind, you and I. And we'll never truly understand the way the Shavid live. I may be a part of their group, but I am not one of them. Don't confuse the two."

Fox didn't say anything as they finished up on the riverbank and headed back to the campsite. They might not understand the rambling lifestyle that the Shavid lived, but it was clear that Neil wanted to know. And so did Fox.

BY THE TIME THE BOYS returned to camp, the Shavid had begun trickling back to their tents and wagons, beginning their own morning routines. A handful of women settled themselves in front of one of the tents, sewing and laughing. Two men and a beautiful young woman were rehearsing on the stage. As they paused to watch, Fox distinctly heard the younger of the two men say, "But I don't want to play a girl *again*! It's your turn!"

Neil chuckled. "This is an almost daily argument. Poor Merrick, his voice just hasn't dropped enough yet." He gave a sharp whistle, and the girl turned. "For your mother," he said, tossing her the bag of roots they'd gathered.

The girl caught them easily and sniffed at the bag. "Perfect! She'll be thrilled."

"Anything else?" asked Neil.

"I think Mindi needed some help. You might want to check in on her."

They moved on, Fox craning his head to catch every little thing. To him, the day-to-day affairs of the Shavid were just as fascinating as their performances. He would have stopped just to watch Otter re-stringing his instrument if Neil hadn't dragged him along, pointing ahead to the dancing pavilion he'd seen the night before.

Inside, a young girl was perched on top of what looked like a tribal drum. She was focusing intently on stringing tiny, shimmering beads onto a line. This, he supposed, was Mindi. She was a little scrap of a girl with a long, golden-red braid running down her back. She glanced up at their approach.

"Mary sent us," said Neil. "What is it this time?"

Mindi turned back to her work, biting her lip in concentration. "I need scales."

Neil raised an eyebrow. "Scales? From a fish?"

"For Daddy's new play," said Mindi, as though that answered everything. When Neil continued to stare, she sighed and turned to look at him. "For the Water Witch's mask! You get them for me, I'll worry about the rest."

"But," said Fox as the girl turned back to her beads, "you can't do anything with fish skin, can you?"

"She can," said Neil. "Delicate touch and all that, she can sew them into a leather mask without tearing them, no problem."

"What about the smell?" said Fox. He was thinking of the baskets of fish heads and insides he so often took to throw out for the birds. If you left them inside too long, the whole house started to smell like the underside of a river rock.

"No problem," said Mindi, finishing her beadwork and holding up the line to examine it. It shimmered gently, throwing off sparks of light where the sun hit it.

"Mindi's the only one in our group who has any *practical* Blessing. She has a knack for the little things, like keeping the fires going and making light. And sometimes, some of the not-so-little things, like making someone forget she was there, or brewing up fog."

And then, as Fox watched, Mindi released the beaded string in midair, and it floated, swaying gently like river grass in slow current. Then, Mindi gestured with one finger and the shimmering line darted off, dancing around the tent like an airborne snake. Fox dropped to the cold grass, startled and unsure what this strange little magic might do, and Mindi and Neil both laughed. Finally, Mindi raised her hand and the beads came to a stop, wrapping several times around her wrist and laying there innocently, just a bracelet.

Mindi leapt nimbly down from the drum as Fox stood, brushing dirt and grass from his knees. "She's also a bit of a show-off," said Neil, but Mindi ignored him. She was making her way toward Fox, staring at him with large, un-blinking, blue eyes. Somehow, this made him more nervous than the flying bracelet. When she reached him, she stretched out her hand.

He hesitated for a moment, then took it. "F - Fox," he stammered, and she smiled at him.

"Mindi."

"Yes ... yes, so he said." Fox tried to let go, but Mindi held tight, continuing to smile at him.

"There you are!" said a female voice, and Mindi turned, dropping Fox's hand at last.

It was Lai, breathless and pink-cheeked. She leaned briefly against one of the pavilion supports to catch her breath. "The games start soon, and the suitors from Hatcher Valley and Edgewood are arriving."

"Oh!" said Fox. "Of course, I'll be right there."

"Suitors?" asked Mindi. Fox couldn't help but notice that the smile had been replaced with a pouting glare the moment that Lai had entered the pavilion.

"For the Courter's Contest," said Lai. It happens every year at the end of Homecoming. Young men who've been courting young women prove themselves with wrestling and mining games, all sorts of things. It's always exciting!"

"Everyone's welcome to come," said Fox to the two Shavid.

Neil shrugged. "It's worth a visit, I suppose."

Lai grinned at him and darted forward, grabbing Fox's hand and dragging him along. As they left, Neil tagging along behind them, Fox caught a glimpse of Mindi's face. And he was quite sure that if, at that moment, the girl could have set Lai on fire, she would have.

THE COURTER'S CONTESTS were just as Lai had said: a yearly tradition dating back before anyone in the valley could remember. It was a series of contests and games that symbolized the end of the Homecoming and the start of a fresh new spring. Its key purpose was to solidify potential unions between courting youths. Men showed off their skills and fought for the hands of their chosen brides, and parents wagered on their children, swapping promises and dowries. It was a chance for a young man to prove that he had what it took to protect his wife through the brutal winter, and it was a tradition which Fox could never truly take part in.

Even as a child Fox had always known that he'd never be able to participate in most of the contests. It was meant for the miners and farmers, men built for hard labor. And Fox, though he may have grown slightly taller over the past winter, would never be strong enough to throw boulders and haul great wheelbarrows of ore. When his time came, he would have to limit his marketable skills to archery and the hope that he would be as successful a trapper as his father.

As they reached the center of town, they could see colored flags being raised in the distance, marking out racecourses and finish lines on the proving grounds. Just ahead, two goat-drawn carts were parked outside the Five

Sides. The first was empty, with its goat tethered to a nearby stake. The second, by the looks of it, had just pulled up. A tall, burly young man was climbing down from it, dusting snow from his coat.

"Which one is this?" asked Fox.

"Trent, from Edgewood," said Lai. "The two boys from Hatcher are already inside, but I didn't catch their names." They continued to watch the newcomer as they made their way to the tavern, Lai chattering away all the while. "One of the Hatcher boys and this one here are the only suitors in line for their brides. But I heard the *other* boy is fighting for the same girl as Larr Bracken."

"Your dad's going to be up to his ears in bets," said Fox. "Did we send anyone away this year?"

"Not that I know of," said Lai. As they slipped into the tavern and took seats beneath a window, Lai explained the custom to Neil. "When people marry here in the Highborns, the man goes to live in his wife's village. So if someone's wooing a bride in another town, he follows *their* rules of courtship."

"So these men are here for your contests," said Neil.

"Exactly." She elbowed Fox and pointed to the great fireplace across the room. "Look! There they are."

The two boys from Hatcher were already the center of a loud and curious group. The shorter of the two seemed surly and not at all interested in talking to anyone. But the taller was all smiles and hearty laughs.

"Which one's going in against Larr?" asked Fox

"The tall one," said Lai.

Fox sized him up. Larr Bracken was one of the biggest, sturdiest miners in town. At seventeen he was just as tall as Borric, and almost as wide. In any other case, Fox would have thought that no one would be a threat to Larr. From the whispers he heard and early bets being placed, the rest of the valley felt the same. But now, watching this smiling stranger, Fox thought they might all be wrong. While he didn't have the bulk that Larr did, he matched him inch for inch in height, and he was all lean muscle. To Fox, it was like comparing a bear and a great mountain cat. Larr, as the bear, might have the obvious advantage, but Fox was sure that in a fair fight the cat's speed and agility would tip the scales.

Trent, the suitor from Edgewood, came bursting into the tavern a moment later, drawing every eye to the door. "A drink!" he bellowed, stomping across the floor and slamming a coin down on the bar. "Hot. And I'll need someone to take care of my cart." No one moved or spoke for a moment. And then Trent turned and glared at one of the younger boys at the bar, who jumped and scrambled outside. Slowly, talk returned to normal, but the eyes of the Thiccans were constantly flicking back and forth among the three suitors. An excited buzz filled with wagering and predictions filled the air, until finally the bells in the square rang out, and the tavern erupted in cheers. Borric's voice could be heard even above all the clamor, directing suitors to the proving grounds and taking last-minute bets. Fox and his companions slipped outside quickly, joining the eager crowd of youth all flocking to the grounds.

The afternoon was spent enjoyably by all, including the many Shavid who had come to watch. Some of them even participated in the contests that were allowed for non-suitors. Fox enjoyed watching Radda best some of the Thiccan men in knife-throwing, and Fox himself took part in several rounds of Flap, a game rather like a seated, two-man, tug-of-war. Lai was busy taking bets for her father, leaving the boys to wander around on their own for most of the day. They watched the hammer toss and pick-throwing games. They stood on the sidelines and cheered as the competing suitors ran wheelbarrow races. And they, along with the rest of the valley, watched in fascination as the competition heated up between Larr Bracken and the tall stranger from Hatcher Valley.

The woman they were fighting for was Filia Beckweed, Rose's oldest sister. She sat watching the proceedings surrounded by half-a-dozen other young women, all smiling and laughing and cheering for the contenders. As the day wore on, Neil kept watching her, a slight frown on his face. Finally he said, "Which one do you think she wants?"

Fox tore his eyes away from the wooden pen where Larr was busy tying the back legs of a struggling goat. "What do you mean?" he asked.

"The girl those two are fighting for. She's been watching them both all day, but she doesn't seem to care *which* one of them wins her."

Fox followed Neil's gaze to where Filia was sitting. She was wearing the traditional "dowry dress," a simple cotton gown with long sleeves. Hers was an earthy reddish-brown, with a darker red sash tied around the waist. Filia had added a handful of matching red ribbons to the cascades of coal-black hair she'd let fall loosely down her shoulders. She was fiddling with the end of one of them and watching Larr in the goat pen. The longer Fox looked, the clearer he saw what Neil had meant. Other brides who were being wooed by more than one suitor tended to have a clear favorite. One they were hoping could best the others and earn her hand, where he had already earned her heart. But Filia watched Larr with the same look she had given the charming stranger: like he was a mildly interesting toy. One she would quickly bore of before moving on to something else. She watched the entire contest like it was simply a game, and not the course of her entire future.

The crowd around him cheered, pulling Fox back to the games. Larr had successfully wrestled his goat into submission, tying its front and back legs and pinning it to the ground. Now, he stood over it and raised his arms triumphantly over his head with a primal roar, earning another enthusiastic round of applause from his audience. As the goat was untied and led back to its stable, Lai elbowed her way to Neil and Fox through the crowd.

"Odds on Larr for the win!" she said. "No one's ever pinned their goat that fast! That suitor didn't come close! People are already placing bets on how fast Larr will pin *him*!" She pointed across the field to where Farmer Beckweed and his wife were deep in conversation with Larr's parents, the Brackens. "They've practically already settled on terms for the marriage."

"Hey, Lai," said Fox, nodding toward Filia. "Which one do you think *she* wants to win her?"

Lai glanced at Filia and wrinkled her nose in disgust. "I head Rose talking about her, back in the kitchen. She says her sister doesn't even care, she just wants a roof over her head, until someday some foreign trader-merchant will pass through town and sweep her away to far-off kingdoms." She rolled her eyes. "That's her plan, anyway." Throwing one last, irritated look at Filia, she added, "Someone can sweep her off *tomorrow*, and that would be just fine by me."

Neil elbowed Fox and nodded at the goat pen. Two young men were now vaulting the low fence and stripping off their shirts. "Wrestling?" he asked.

"It's the last game," said Fox. "For most of the suitors today, it's just a formality, since they're all courting unopposed. But for Filia's boys, it's the final deciding factor." As the first match began, Fox glanced at Neil. The older boy was watching the game with an almost hungry expression in his eyes. "You should try it," said Fox. "Wrestling's open to anyone."

Neil didn't answer. Instead, he watched the next five matches with keen, calculating eyes. Then, Fire Merchant Terric climbed into the ring for the start of the next round, welcomed by tumultuous applause from the crowd. He smiled broadly and stripped off his shirt, stretching and pacing around the ring, daring anyone to oppose him.

"He's undefeated," Lai explained to Neil. "He never loses a match. Last year when he won his bride, he broke his opponent's arm, nose, *and* the other guy still walks with a limp. No one dares to go up against him now."

The crowd was getting restless, which only made Terric smile more confidently. And then, Neil started forward. He stripped off his shirt as he went, revealing himself to be shockingly muscular. An excited hum filled the air, and then a rhythmic stomping of feet on the ground, and hands pounding on the wooden beams of the ring. In disbelief, Fox turned to Lai, but at the expression on her face he lost his words. She was looking at Neil with the same fluttery, girlish expression he saw on lovestruck young brides. He stared at her for a moment, stunned into silence. And then he punched her lightly on the arm, pulling her out of her trance. "Enjoy the view while you can. Terric's going to kill him."

Lai stuck her tongue out at him and shoved him playfully in the chest. Then they both hurried forward, fighting their way closer to the front for a better view.

Neil had swung himself easily over the enclosure wall, and now the opponents paced along opposite ends of the pen, sizing each other up. Terric's brazen smile widened as he casually rolled his neck and shoulders, preparing for the fight. All around them, bets and wagers started to punctuate the excited hum. The Shavid would go down in under a minute. In three moves. In one kick. Terric would break five of his bones. The Shavid might hold his own for awhile, but in the end the victory was inevitable.

But Fox, watching Neil, was not so sure. While Terric stood confidently at ease, every inch of Neil was poised to pounce. He wasn't tense with fear, but with the sureness of a predator knowing its prey was unaware.

As Terric lunged, Neil darted away so quickly that the crowd gasped. Fox and Lai cheered as Terric, surprised, tried to recover. But Neil was there, so fast no one quite saw what happened. In an instant he had swept Terric's feet out from under him, and then casually strode away, back to the far end of the pen. Terric scrambled to his feet, his smile gone, replaced by a look of confused fury. He attacked again, and was just as easily thrown off. But instead of finishing him, Neil backed away for a second time.

"He's toying with him," said Lai in awe. "He knows he can win, he's just making a good show."

"He's a Player," said Fox. "He's putting on an act for applause, just like the Shavid. Instead of on a stage, or with music, he's doing it with combat."

As the match went on, it became ever clearer that Fox was right. Neil proved time and time again that he was the stronger fighter, but he always let Terric recover, rather than finishing him off. The whole match was a series of intense bouts, where Neil dazzled everyone with combat styles they had never seen before, punctuated by moments of calm where Neil leaned casually against the enclosure walls and Terric fought to regain his footing and composure. Meanwhile, most of the crowd seemed to have transferred their affections to the shadowy young Shavid. And he played right into their eager hands, flashing a smile every time he pulled off a spectacular kick, and holding a hand to his ear as the crowd began to chant for him.

Finally, as the audience's palpable excitement appeared ready to burst, Neil seemed to decide it was time to end the match. Rolling his shoulders and neck in an exaggerated mockery of Terric's opening stretches, he then leaped forward and attacked, all flying fists and footwork. Terric fought back wildly, but within just a few minutes he was face-first on the hard ground, with Neil's knee pressed into his lower back.

Fox was sure that his own mother, sitting at home all the way across the valley, could have heard the explosion of cheers and hollers that followed. As Neil helped Terric back to his feet with a smile, the Thiccans went absolutely mad. People calling for their wagers to be paid, hot-blooded young men challenging Neil to a match to prove themselves, and the empty shouts of excited onlookers who simply enjoyed the show all filled the air. Fox hurried forward to the enclosure wall to meet Neil as he climbed back over it. He grinned and clapped his Shavid friend excitedly on the shoulder, then jerked his thumb toward the edge of the crowd, signaling that they should escape before Neil was swarmed with admirers. Already, those who were nearest were fighting for Neil's attention, but instead he waved them off with a charming smile and followed Fox to the outskirts of the proving grounds, where the crowd was much thinner.

"That was fantastic!" Fox said breathlessly as Neil pulled his shirt back on. "Where did you ever –"

"You learn a lot on the road," Neil explained, running a hand through his sweaty hair. "It comes in handy, let me tell you."

"Do you think ..." Fox coughed and tried again. "Maybe, while you're here..."

Neil laughed and punched Fox lightly on the shoulder. "Yeah, I could teach you a bit. But right now, I'm *starving*. Let's hit the tavern before the rest of the valley."

Behind them, the fight everyone had been waiting for was beginning: Larr and the suitor. "You don't want to watch?" asked Fox, and Neil shook his head.

"I can't stand to watch them fight so hard over someone who doesn't care about either of them," he answered. He cast one last, disapproving look at Filia, then shoved his hands in his pockets and started off toward the Five Sides, Fox close behind him.

Chapter Six
Picck

The Five Sides was almost completely empty, with most of Thicca Valley eagerly stationed at the Contests. The only other customer was Moss, the goat-breeder's weathered old father-in-law. He sat in the farthest corner of the room, nursing a bowl of stew, and didn't so much as glance up when Neil and Fox entered. The boys settled themselves across the room, pulling two chairs up to the hearth of the fireplace and propping their feet up to warm.

"Piiicck-ling!" shouted Fox. "You've got customers, you lazy dog!"

There was no answer from the kitchen, and after a few minutes Picck still didn't emerge. "Maybe he's out with the goats," said Fox. "I'll go check."

But Fox didn't make it that far. As he cut through the kitchen on his way to the back courtyard, he stopped dead. There, sitting together on the counter top, were Rose and Picck. Fox fell back to watch, hidden in the doorway. They were filling pie crusts with some dark kind of berry that Fox couldn't place from this far away. Rose's apron was stained violet from where she'd wiped her hands, and every so often she would tuck a stray hair behind her ear, leaving a violet streak along her skin.

And Picck, it seemed, was being completely himself. His hair was a mess, and he wasn't using his fake, deep voice. He was just Picck. The odd and lanky kitchen boy. And Rose was smiling at him with more genuine affection than her sister had shown either of her suitors. As Fox watched, she planted a berry-juice handprint right on Picck's face, making him sputter and scramble off the counter as she laughed with delight. Smiling to himself, Fox carefully slipped back out of the kitchen.

"No luck?" said Neil.

"Oh, I had plenty of luck," said Fox mischievously. "Just not with food."

When Neil raised an inquisitive eyebrow, Fox lowered his voice conspiratorially and told him the whole story. Of the other morning, when he'd discovered Picck's feelings for Rose, and watching them together now. "It's perfect," he said. "They must have worked here together every day for a year by now, and I never noticed it before. But he makes her laugh, and she ... well, she was looking at him like my mum looks at Father when he gets home off a trapping trip."

"So what's stopping them?" asked Neil. "Besides your friend Picck being entirely unaware, from the sound of it."

"I'm not quite sure," admitted Fox. But after a moment, he thought better of it. "Well, actually ..." He pulled his feet up onto his chair, leaning his chin on his knees in thought. "It's the Contests. They're for miners and farmers, and even some of the waresmen ... strong types. Without having some other skill to recommend him, it will be so much harder to win her hand. To prove to her, and her parents, that he can take care of her."

Neil glanced around at the empty tavern. "The Contests aren't over yet. I'm sure there's something he could —"

Fox shook his head. "Wrestling's the last bit. And after the Contests, life in the valley starts up again. He wouldn't *have* to wait until next year, but most farmers don't want to be bothered with little things during the planting and growing seasons. He'd be hard-pressed to bring it up to her father any time before harvest. Besides, what could he offer? He's a younger son."

"And she's a younger daughter," said Neil. "What of it?"

"That's just it," said Fox. "She'll have no dowry, he'll have no family money to recommend him, and no prospects ..." And then it hit him. It was so simple, he couldn't believe that none of them had ever thought of it before. He scrambled to his feet so quickly that it made Neil jump.

"What's wrong?" asked Neil, but Fox ignored him.

"Moss!" he called across the room, making the old man at his table look up. "Do you know where Borric is?"

"Storeroom," grunted Moss.

With a quick thanks, Fox hurried downstairs, Neil close on his heels.

They found Borric re-arranging barrels of dry goods. "Oh, perfect!" he said. "You, Shavid. Help me move that," he said, pointing to a crate settled against the far wall.

As Neil hurried forward to help, hefting one end of the box, Fox said, "Borric, I've got an idea that I need your help with."

"Go on," grunted Borric as he and Neil hauled their load across the room.

"It's about Picck, and Rose."

Borric chuckled as they set down the crate. "You mean the courting couple that doesn't realize they're courting?"

Fox smiled. "Sounds about right. But listen, Picck needs something to offer. He's got to be able to provide for her, and he's got to be able to do it now. The Contests are almost over, and let's face it. If he has to wait until next year, she'll be off the market. With Filia married off, Rose is the last daughter that Farmer Beckweed has to worry about."

"Well he's a cursed fine cook, I'll tell you that," said Borric, sitting down on the crate. "That should be enough for a younger daughter."

"Yes," said Fox carefully, "he is an *excellent* cook. One you might want to keep on here?"

"Of course I will!" said Borric. "He's family! Besides which, he can keep that kitchen running with his eyes shut. That's more than enough to make him a worthy suitor."

Fox ran his fingers through his hair in nervous frustration. He was very close to Borric, because of Lai, but he felt that at this particular moment, he might be interfering a bit too much in the family's personal life. And then, just as Fox opened his mouth, unsure of exactly what he was going to say, Neil stepped in.

"Doesn't he live in the kitchen?" he asked casually.

"Yep," said Borric. "Slept there ever since he was ..." And then it hit him. The boys watched as the realization dawned on his face. Then he leaned back with a satisfied smile on his face. "You want me to give him a room."

"And make him your official heir," said Fox. "You're already training him to run the place anyway! They could both live here, and she already knows her way around."

Above them, they could hear the heavy footsteps of guests beginning to trickle back into the Five Sides. Fox waited, silently pleading with Borric, careful not to push too hard.

Then Borric clapped his hands together. "It's perfect!" As Fox breathed a sigh of relief, Borric said, "We'll give them one of the bigger rooms at the far end. Much more space, and a little privacy as well." He stood, the crate beneath him creaking with the relief of his bulk. "Fox, run on up and tell Picck I'd like to see him. Then find Beckweed, tell him we've got an offer in mind for his daughter." As Fox sprang to do as he was told, Borric called up the stairs after him. "And tell Lai she'll have to take care of the wagers for awhile! Just until I'm finished with this!"

But the bit about Lai proved unnecessary. As Fox stepped back into the rapidly-filling common room, he found her perched on top of the bar, calmly managing the hoards clamoring for their payouts. Neil clapped Fox on the shoulder and said, "I'll get Picck. You find the farmer."

They parted ways, Neil disappearing into the kitchen and Fox scanning the crowd for Rose's father. All around him, he could hear snatches of conversation about the Contests. The final wrestling match, it seemed, had been an incredible bout. In fact, talk appeared split evenly between Filia's suitors and Neil's fight. Pausing briefly in his search for Farmer Beckweed, Fox listened in on an intense discussion between two Thiccans, trying to determine from their excited talk who finally won Filia's hand. But their conversation gave away nothing, and just as Fox leaned in to ask one of them outright, the tavern door swung open again, rendering both his questions about Filia and his search for her father unnecessary.

Farmer Beckweed came in smiling and talking loudly, with Filia on his arm. On his other side was the charming stranger from Hatcher Valley, looking tired but pleased with himself. "Drinks!" shouted Beckweed. "A hot spice for me and my newest son!" The tavern cheered in welcome, and Beckweed led his small party to seats by the fire. Now was the best time, with Beckweed in a cheerful and gracious mood. As Beckweed made his way across the common room, Fox wound his way through the crowd to intercept him. He ducked briefly behind the counter to grab a basket of bread. As he passed Lai he said, "Pay you back for these! I'll explain later!" And then, with his plan only half-formed and the full awareness that this might be Picck's one chance at getting the girl of his dreams, Fox presented himself to Farmer Beckweed.

"Fresh sticky buns!" he said confidently, offering the basket to Beckweed. "Compliments of the kitchen. And congratulations on the wonderful match of your daughter, sir!"

"Yes, it is wonderful isn't it?" said Beckweed, clapping his new son-in-law on the shoulder. "Fine young man he is, and just in time! My Filia here was one long winter away from running off with the next passing waresman!" He laughed heartily, the company around him joining in. And Fox, glancing over at Filia, was startled. The beautiful, regal young woman was staring at the back of her father's head with nothing short of loathing. But in a moment, her face changed again, and she laughed politely with everyone else and tossed her dark hair elegantly over her shoulders.

"Well, I thank the kitchen for these," said Beckweed, moving to settle himself by the fire, but Fox cut in quickly.

"Before you get too comfortable, sir," he said, "would you mind following me? The tavern master has something to discuss with you." When Beckweed frowned slightly, Fox added, "A proposition. Something to benefit you both, I think. I promise, we'll have you back to the fire and celebrating your triumph in no time!"

Beckweed sighed and shrugged. "Where's the harm?" He turned to his companions and said "But when I return, a full account of the fight that won my daughter's hand! Eh?" All those in earshot cheered, and Beckweed followed Fox back across the tavern and down into the storerooms. Borric was waiting for him, along with a terrified and thoroughly confused-looking Picck.

"So what's this about a proposition then?" said Beckweed. Borric glanced over the farmer's shoulder at Fox and gestured with his head, signaling he should wait outside. Fox obliged, retreating back to the stairwell as Neil, who Fox hadn't even noticed, detached himself from the shadows to join him. They sat in silence for a moment, listening to the muffled voices behind the storeroom door.

"What if the farmer says no?" asked Neil.

"Then they don't marry," said Fox.

"Just like that? Rose has no say?"

Fox settled himself on a stair, thinking. "I guess she *does*," he said, "but no one in the valley goes against the father's wishes. The few times it does happen, the rebellious child is cut off. The parents don't help with building the new house, or give them any marriage gifts ... It's rare. And it's dangerous. New couples usually can't survive here without a little help."

Neil sat beside Fox and stretched his long legs out with a groan. "People have such odd customs. Everywhere I go, they're different." He chuckled softly to himself. "There's a small town in Lidiom where each woman catches a fish and feeds it her ring, then releases it back into the lake. And all the suitors catch a fish, gut it, and whoever's ring they find is their bride." When Fox shook his head, Neil laughed even harder. "Of course when *we* passed through town, Otter thought it would be funny to feed one of the fish about nine rings, and watch the townsfolk argue over which was which. Oh, what a day that was."

Fox laughed, imagining the confusion. And then he asked a question that had been on his mind for a good part of the day. "How do the Shavid decide who they marry?"

"It's not so complicated," said Neil. "They fall in love. Just like your Picck and Rose. It's not so much about connections or joining families together. They travel with the wind, following their instincts and their passions. You can't put a price on love, so they don't try." He leaned back, propping his head on a higher step. "Radda met his wife when he was traveling with another company and stole her heart away from the man who *had* been courting her. To this day, Radda swears the wind took him there just so he could meet her." And they lapsed back into silence, punctuated every so often by the sound of what Fox hoped was friendly negotiating.

Soon, he'd be at the age where fathers started to size him up, and daughters started to decide if he was worthy of their attention. He was expected to start courting somebody, and proving that his skills were enough to recommend him as a husband. He'd seen all sorts of marriages in the valley. Some strong and happy, like his parents or Fire Merchant Terric and his new wife. And he was sure that if Picck and Rose were given Beckweed's blessing, they would be positively blissful. But then there were the wives who simply tolerated their husbands. Women like Filia, who were set up merely to be comfortable. Fox couldn't imagine being stuck in a marriage like that. He'd much rather not be married at all.

The storeroom door swung open suddenly, and Fox scrambled to his feet. Then Beckweed and Borric emerged, laughing and shaking hands, with Picck right behind them, looking rather dazed. The whole group made their way upstairs to the common room, where Beckweed called for order and attention.

"It seems that today is a day for celebrating!" he said, once the room had quieted. "To all those happy matches made in today's contests, I say hurrah!"

"Hurrah!" the tavern echoed, and applause broke out briefly before Beckweed silenced them again with a raise of his hand.

"And a special welcome to the newcomers to our humble valley. Go on, stand up boys. Trent Fillwater from Edgewood." A polite applause for the hulking and moody Trent. "And to the young men from Hatcher Valley, Ennit and my new son Rale!" Louder applause for these two. The Hatcher suitors seemed much nicer than Trent, and they both seemed happy to be there. "We say welcome to the family of our valley! We hope you'll be right at home!" And then he smiled cheerfully. "But one more announcement! It seems that today is not only the day that I pair off my daughter Filia, but the day I make a match for my youngest! Rose! Where are you, girl?"

Rose had been leaning against the kitchen doorframe, watching her father's speech. But now, as every eye in the tavern turned to her, she straightened up, adjusting her apron nervously and tucking a stray hair behind her ear.

"Come here!" As Rose edged uneasily forward to her father's open arms, Beckweed said, "Tonight, I celebrate the end of a father's duties! I pair off my last child, my youngest daughter! And we celebrate the happy union of Rose and Borric's heir, Picck Blackroot!"

All of Rose's nervousness seemed to vanish at once, and her face lit up with pure delight. As the tavern cheered, she threw herself into Picck's arms and kissed him full on the mouth. Laugher and even more applause filled the air, and Beckweed chuckled and made his way back to his spot by the fire, ordering even more drinks. As singing began to fill the common room, Fox watched the newly betrothed couple, locked in a passionate embrace.

That's how it should be, he thought. Not like Filia, only waiting for something better to come along. But like Picck and Rose, oblivious to the world. Happier than anything with just each other.

He caught a glimpse of Lai, perched on the counter top and singing with the rest of the crowd, and she waved at him. He waved back and gestured to her, silently asking if she needed help. Her smile and the shake of her head said no, he should go enjoy himself. As he and Neil settled in for the night around the center fire pit, Fox put his own marriage out of his mind. It was years away. And besides, who would ever want to marry him?

Chapter Seven
Shivers

Neil became something of a fascination that night. Young women kept coming up to him, praising his performance in his match against Terric and batting their eyelashes. Even Kimic Lillywhite stopped by, ignoring Fox completely and instead clinging to Neil's arm and brazenly running her fingers through his hair. Fox shook his head at it all, a small part of him jealous of the older boy's skill and strength.

"I could teach you, you know," said Neil during one of the brief moments they were left to themselves.

"Teach me?"

"To fight. As long as I'm here, I could show you a few tricks. If you're interested."

Fox perked up, imagining thrashing one of the bigger boys, and smiled. "When? Now?"

Neil chuckled. "Come by the camp in the morning if you'd like. If your folks can spare you, that is."

Tomorrow was the start of the planting season in Thicca Valley. Work began before the sun was even up. But for Fox and Father, things were a bit different. The bulk of their work came later, during the summer when the game was bigger. Springtime was for routine cleaning and trap maintenance, as well as helping Mother in their small garden. But Fox himself was often free to pursue any chores he himself felt were necessary. In fact, in early spring when his parents were enjoying each other's company after the long winter apart, Fox was encouraged to spend his time elsewhere.

He smiled. "I'll be there!"

The rest of the evening passed enjoyably, but ended early. Farmers and miners headed home to get to sleep, preparing for the start of the working months. With the tavern mostly empty, the Shavid also returned to their campsite, with the exception of Radda, who sat talking in a corner with Borric for a long while. Finally, as Neil excused himself for the night, Fox wandered back into the kitchen to help clean up.

Picck and Rose were saying their goodbyes at the courtyard door, Picck kissing Rose gently on the forehead before sending her off home. He watched her go, leaning against the doorframe as Fox quietly joined Lai in mopping up the floor. Then, finally, he backed into the kitchen and shut the door with a contented sigh. He turned, a stupid grin spread across his face, and Fox couldn't even bring himself to tease him. Instead, the three of them tidied up the kitchen and talked over some of their favorite moments of the contests. They got as far as arguing over who would win a fight, Neil or Rale the Hatcher champion, when Fox stopped mid-sentence. A sudden chill passed over him that had nothing to do with the cold.

"Fox?" Lai was watching him, a slight concerned frown on her face. "Everything alright?"

"Yeah," grunted Fox, shaking himself. He was quiet for awhile after that, listening to Lai and Picck's argument but not adding anything himself. Twice more as he worked, he felt an odd shiver. But the feeling that passed over his skin was not the cold of a drafty kitchen in winter, but of something else entirely. Ever so briefly, it was the cold of being naked in the snow. Intense and painful, and completely exposed. After the third time this happened, Fox excused himself, saying he wasn't feeling well and he'd better head home to bed. He could feel Lai watching him as he left, and so he didn't stop until he was halfway home. Then, on his way up the hill leading toward his family's property, he paused for a moment, waiting to see if it would happen again. He breathed deeply, standing perfectly still in the darkness. And then, as a chill breeze wound its way around him, Fox felt it again. A bone-numbing shiver, accompanied by a dozen different smells that weren't from Thicca Valley. Charred wood and ash. He could almost taste a thick, heavy smoke on his tongue, his eyes watering. He started to cough and shake, wracked with a cold much sharper than the mild spring air around him.

Somewhere to the north, something terrible was happening. In the same way that he could smell the snow, and the same way he knew when the caravan would arrive, he could feel something in the air. A fire, in some town a day or so away. And there was a hint of fear in the air, the wild panic of a trapped animal before the slaughter.

And then the feeling passed, leaving Fox flat on his back on the frozen ground. He couldn't even remember falling down. For a moment he lay still, breathing deep. The air in Thicca Valley was clear and clean, filled with the comforting smells of hearth fires and fresh berries. He waited until he was calmer, then pulled himself to his feet and trudged the rest of the way home. His parents were already asleep. He crept quietly up to his nook without waking them and slipped into bed, his mind racing.

Whatever had just happened, he didn't know how to explain it. Or who to talk to. Should he just keep it to himself? The answer came to him in an instant: Lai. She knew his other "secret," the fact that he'd predicted the arrival of the caravan. And this, if it was anything other than sheer madness, was so much more than that. He would tell her, and no one else.

But Lai was as busy as any farmer for the next few days, running around town on her father's errands and helping with the wedding plans for Rose and Picck. And so Fox kept himself busy, doing his best to ignore the nagging feeling in his chest that something wasn't right. He spent his mornings at the Shavid camp, learning how to throw simple punches and practicing sparring with the musicians. He fished with the players and some of the valley sons, those too young to work in the mines. He mended traps, hunted smaller game and traded their pelts with Shavid and Thiccans alike. But everywhere he went, he found himself looking over his shoulder for an unknown danger. He was constantly restless, sleeping very little, and he often found himself spending his nights in the stable with Cobb. He groomed the pony over and over again, singing quietly and listening to the sounds of the sleeping valley.

And he waited. Sure that something was coming, and just as sure that he couldn't stop it. Why, of all people, was *he* the one who could feel it? And why was he so afraid of telling anyone?

IT WAS JUST PAST DAWN, five days after the Contests. Fox was eating breakfast at the camp with Neil and Merrick, the poor young apprentice who was always forced to play a woman. Merrick was a friendly youth, with tightly curled red-gold hair and an uncanny gift for bird calls. He was only silent when he was eating, and even then he carried on talking between each bite. He would start into one story, stuff his face with bread, and then pick an entirely different tale to tell when he'd swallowed. Fox rather enjoyed having him around though, scattered as he was.

As they finished eating, Neil stretched and stood, dusting crumbs from his hands. "Well, James and Donlan want me to scribe for them this morning."

"What are they working on?" asked Merrick through a mouthful of ham.

Neil shrugged. "James told me, but honestly I wasn't really listening." The boys chuckled, and Neil headed off, leaving Fox and Merrick to finish their breakfast.

"Scribe?" Fox asked.

Merrick swallowed. "For the plays. Sometimes we need someone to write down what we're doing, in case there's something really good and we forget." He took another bite and continued, trying not to spray his food across the fire. "Plays are half instinct, and half rehearsed. And having Neil around has really helped us with the rehearsed part."

"So, do many of the Shavid troupes have Dervishes? Like Neil?"

"It's rare," said Merrick, shaking his head and swallowing again. "But sometimes you get an Unblessed sha in a group." Fox didn't even get a chance to ask the question before Merrick launched into an explanation. "They're born into a Shavid family, but they don't have any Blessings or special talents, so they usually tag along, just learning the skills and doing what Neil does. Sometimes they leave and settle down in some town like a normal person. But sometimes this life is all they know, so they follow their troupe, or their mate, or their family forever." Merrick's eye fell on the half-eaten roll in Fox's hand. "You gonna eat that?"

Fox tossed the unfinished piece to Merrick and stretched out on the ground by the breakfast fire, staring up at the sky. His muscles were sore from the training Neil was putting him through, but it was a comfortable kind of pain. One that the cold ground eased somewhat. He'd discovered that the morning practice sessions were the only thing that truly relaxed him and kept his mind off its worries. And so he pushed himself harder, begging to learn something new every day.

He closed his eyes, half-listening to the musician's continued ramblings. He let his mind wander, thinking about the chores he had to do that day, and how much he'd rather be at the Shavid camp. The more time he spent with them, the harder it was to tear himself away to everyday life. He found himself humming Radda's songs as he worked, always eager to get back to the camp for their songs and performances at sundown. How lucky Neil was, to be allowed to wander with them. For a moment, Fox breathed deep, taking in the exotic smells of the camp. Saddle polish and ink, new spices. A clean, sharp scent that might have been soap. The strings of the Shavid instruments, even the paint on the wagons smelled of adventure and a thousand different places.

And then, just as Fox started to take another breath, an unwelcome but frighteningly familiar scent hit him, making him sit straight up and cough wildly. His eyes watered, but he ignored them, waving off Merrick's worried "Are you alright?" Instead, he scanned the horizon. Somewhere, a messenger bird was flying in from the burned city. He could smell it, and almost feel the beat of its wings against his face.

There. A flash of color, a fabric scrap tied around the leg of a bird winging its way toward the Five Sides. It was bigger and darker than most Thiccan messenger birds, and it was drawing attention from the Shavid. As it flapped even closer, Fox was nearly drowning in its smell on the wind. A smell of charcoal and smoke. A smell of fear.

He stood, watching as the bird dropped low behind the tavern and disappeared. He turned to catch Merrick's eye, and found the musician already staring at him. He looked perplexed, eyeing Fox like a puzzle he was trying to work out. Finally, he said quietly, "You could smell it, couldn't you?"

Fox hesitated, then nodded slowly.

Merrick stared at him for a moment, eyes growing wider by the second. Then he scrambled to his feet, mouthing silently, for once at a loss for words.

"I do that, sometimes," said Fox quietly. "Father calls it a hunter's instincts. But he's a hunter himself, and I've got a better nose even then him. I smelled you all coming ... and I smelled the fire. The one that bird's come to warn us about."

The valley bells began to toll, ringing three times in succession and then pausing for several moments before starting up again. A Council Call, summoning the most influential and aged Thiccans to the Five Sides. Whatever message the bird had brought, it wasn't good news.

Fox kept talking. It seemed that now he'd started to spill his secret, his mouth wouldn't be still. "It's stronger sometimes than others, and I don't know how it works exactly. But I've been able to do it all my life. Only now, recently ... sometimes I even smell things I'm not trying to. Like the fire. I knew about it days ago. It's somewhere to the north ..."

"Spirit's Mercy," whispered Merrick. "You knew for *days*?"

Fox nodded, suddenly very aware of how dry his tongue was. He swallowed, and the valley bells fell silent. For a moment, the two boys simply stared at each other. Then Merrick took a step back, then another. And then he turned and ran through the camp, shouting for Radda.

Fox didn't wait to see what would happen next. He was already running in the opposite direction, heading straight for the Five Sides. At the start of the main road, he turned and darted around the backs of the buildings, finally leaping over the low courtyard wall and coming to a halt just inside the back door. As he leaned against the doorframe, catching his breath, he could hear the deep hum of a dozen male voices in the common room. He crept to the kitchen doorway, careful not to make a sound. There, he edged his way into the common room, just enough to hear more clearly and see who was there. He'd only just started scanning the room, picking out the faces of those who'd deemed themselves important enough to answer the Council Call, when a sharp tug on the hem of his breeches made him drop to his knees. He found himself face-to-face with Lai, crouched on all fours and gesturing to him to stay silent. She beckoned with her head and he followed her. They crawled along behind the bar, just as they used to when they were younger and wanted to listen to stories long after they'd been sent to bed. Now, the sounds filling the common room were not those of fireside tales and songs, but what sounded instead like the beginnings of an argument. As Lai and Fox stationed themselves at the far end of the bar, just beside the wall, they could hear someone say, "I don't understand what *he's* doing here."

It was dark by the wall, and Fox and Lai were able to see the whole common room without being discovered. The "he" in question appeared to be Moss, who growled from his usual table, "*He* has got just as much right to be here as any, you fat-fed tub of worm's waste. And more right than some!"

The man who'd spoken first stood, gripping the head of the ore-pick on his belt. Fox recognized him as Armac Flint, quarrymaster and head of the miners' guild. He prided himself on being part of the only "pure" family in Thicca Valley. From the very first of his ancestors, all the way down to his own sons, the Flint family were miners. No one changed professions, and no one married outside the mining community. Consequently, he was the undisputed leader of the valley miners, though from what Fox had heard, Armac had let the power go to his head in the last few years.

Borric raised his hands, stepping forward to intercept the miner before he and Moss came to blows. "There's more important things to worry about now. We're all friends here, but whoever raises a hand against another member of this council will be asked to leave." For a moment he and Armac stared each other down. Armac was big, but Borric was much bigger. Finally, grudgingly, Armac sat heavily back at his table, crossing his arms over his chest. The tension in the room released somewhat, replaced instead by the fidgeting of restless men.

"What are we still waiting for, Borric?" asked one of the farmers. "We answered the call. We're all here, now what's this about?"

"Not all," said Borric. "This news is bigger than us. I've sent Picck out to fetch the last member of our group. When he arrives, then we'll talk."

The common room filled with an uncomfortable buzzing again, but no one spoke out against Borric. Fox shifted slightly, making sure to stay as hidden as possible, and Lai whispered in his ear.

"Father had me take the bird out to the hut, and let it rest with the others. But it was so agitated, it sent all the other birds and even the goats into a frenzy. I had to sing them all quiet, and by the time I got back everyone was here."

"You don't know what the note said?" whispered Fox.

She shook her head.

"I've been trying to talk to you for days," said Fox, dropping his voice even lower. "Something happened, on the last night of the Contests. I left early, remember?"

Lai nodded and frowned. "You were sick."

And just as Fox opened his mouth to finally tell her all of it, about the strange fits of cold and shivers, about the fire to the north, about Merrick's strange reaction to his gift, the door opened and the common room fell silent.

Picck had returned. Fox's vision was partially obscured by the forest of chair and table legs, and for a moment he could only see several pairs of boots in the doorway. Then the party stepped over the threshold, and Fox shrank back into the side of the bar, trying to make himself inseparable from the wood. It was Radda, along with Otter and two more Shavid that Fox hadn't met. He knew the tall one was called Donlan, and he was one of the Players. And the other stranger was a woman. Fox recognized her as one of the dancers, and he was fairly certain she was married to someone else in the company. He didn't know her name, but he was shocked that Radda had brought her. The Council was a man's duty, he must have known that.

Some of the men seemed to be thinking along the same lines. Talk grew louder, until the farmer who'd spoken earlier raised his voice above everyone else's. "This is no place for strangers. And it's certainly no place for a woman."

"And a dancer's private tent is no place for a man," the woman said calmly. "But you had no problem drunkenly stumbling in there two nights past."

A smattering of chuckles danced through the room, and Lai whispered, "I *like* her!"

"Enough," said Borric before the farmer could reply. "There's things on the horizon that affect us *all*, strangers and Shavid included. I invited Radda Southwick to join us, and whomever he chooses to join him in council is his business." He gestured to a nearby table, and Radda and his company sat, while Picck made his way back to the kitchen. Just before the door, Borric caught his nephew by the arm and said, so quietly that Fox and Lai could barely catch it, "Take the day with your pretty lady. This doesn't concern you."

Picck looked uneasily confused, but nodded and disappeared into the kitchen. When he'd gone, Borric turned and took his place at the head of the room, with his back to the fireplace. Fox and Lai shrank back even farther into their hiding place, and the room fell silent.

For a moment Borric didn't speak. He pulled the scrap of parchment message out of his pocket and smoothed it between his fingers. Finally, he said, "There's been a fire. In Hammon, only a few days northwest of us. It's not a big town, but it was prosperous. Now, it's scarcely more than rubble and ash."

"That's all very tragic," growled Armac. "But what's it got to do with us?"

Borric worried the edges of the message over and over again with his fingertips. The more Fox watched, the more he realized that Borric's face was lined with an emotion that Fox had never seen on him before: fear. Big, laughing Borric was afraid of something. And that, more than anything else, terrified Fox.

"The fire," said Borric after a moment, "is not the problem. The fire is the outcome. The result. The end of a gruesome and bloody raid, at the hands of the Desolata."

What little sound that had filled the room vanished. Breathing was muted, shuffling feet were stilled all at once. Even the merry and comforting crackling of the fire seemed to be swallowed in the abrupt and terrible silence that swept over the tavern.

Nobody spoke. There was simply nothing to say. After a few moments, Borric continued, and even his low and quiet voice seemed far too loud in the empty air. "The survivors are few, and scattered. Seeking refuge in the neighboring towns and valleys. Should some of them make it this far, we should be prepared to take them in. There is no obligation to any of you, of course. Times are tough for all, but I ask you to think on how you'd like to be treated under such a crisis."

"Does this mean they're on the move?" asked one of the waresmen. His voice was barely above a whisper, but it could be clearly heard across the entire room.

"Yes," said Borric simply. It was just one word, but it brought despair to the faces of every man in the room. Except the Shavid.

"Not to intrude," said Radda, "but might I ask ... who are they? These Desolata?"

"They're men," said Borric. "They live to the far west —"

"They're not men," rumbled Moss. All eyes turned to him, hunched over his cold soup at his table. "They used to be. Hundreds of years ago, before the curse, they were. Then Sovesta's wealth and beauty were taken from her. We became a barren wasteland in most parts, and the worst of it was the Avet Region in the west, now called the Desolate. Once a series of beautiful farmlands. But fruit began to rot on the trees, and calves died in their mothers' wombs. The region tore itself apart from the inside out, but somehow the survivors grew stronger. And they strengthened with each generation. Now, they are the Desolata. The Desolate bandits."

A collective shudder went around the room. Even Fox had known from a very young age about the Desolate, and the wild men that lived there. It was because of them that the caravan had to leave when it did every year. Too late in the season, and the Tessoc Pass would have closed with snow. Other than that, the only other open road led straight through the Desolate.

"They're not men," Moss repeated. "Men have mercy. Men have souls. Men can be brought down by the stinging cold of a harsh winter, but *they* survive it in scarcely more than rags and bare skin. They feel no pain, and have no fear. And they feast on the flesh of their victims."

"And now," said Borric, "they're moving. They've never come this far east before. Usually they stay confined to the ruins of the Desolate, preying on travelers. Sometimes we get a report from the towns nearest the Desolate that they've started raiding, but it's always over quickly. They never stray far from their homeland."

"So what's different now?" asked Radda.

"Does it matter?" said Borric. "The point is, this affects all of Sovesta. And that includes you and your company. No one is safe, least of all those who wander the road as you do, so take heed. I don't know when you plan to leave us, but until then I encourage you to seek shelter within friendly houses here, instead of sleeping in your tents outside. I can offer you a handful of rooms at the inn, if you're interested."

Radda waved off the suggestion. "We can discuss lodging later. What about the survivors of the raided town, and the people here? What protection can we offer?"

"We need none of your protection," said Armac, apparently no longer content with sitting quietly. "We survive the bitterest winters here, and we are men of strength and survival in this valley."

"Every able man can help," said Farmer Bracken. "We've never had to defend ourselves from any invasion in Thicca."

"What of the survivors?" said another miner. "Those who will come here seeking aid? How many can we truly take in before we run out of food ourselves?"

Every man had his opinion, and now they seemed determined to have them heard. Half in turn, half shouting over each other, each of them voiced his own concerns or ideas about this new threat. Someone wanted to set guards out around the valley perimeters, but what farmer could spare an able-bodied young man? Especially around this time of year? Others wanted to barricade the whole valley's population within the mines and wait out the raids. Armac spoke out emphatically against this one, saying that while the mines were certainly safer than the open air, they had no way of knowing how long the Desolata would be on the move. Work could not be disrupted for any lengthy period of time. And besides, who knew if the Desolata would even come this way?

"There's nothing for them here," Armac said.

"Nothing for them?" spat back Moss. "There's human flesh and houses to burn. They care nothing for wealth or goods. *Any* town, valley, or city is a target, no matter how small."

"So," said Armac, his voice raising again. "What do *you* suggest? We live our lives in fear, waiting for an attack that may or may not come? And hide away from the work that *must* be done for our valley to survive?"

"Easy for you to say," broke in one of the younger farmers. "You and your people are safe in the mountain! But us? We who work in the open fields?"

"Ha," said Armac. "A pansy profession anyway, *farming*."

Every farmer in the room stood at that point, half of them starting in toward the miner, who gripped his ore pick again and pulled it free.

"Enough!" shouted Borric, in a voice that set the rafters shaking. "If you want to attack each other, you do it on your own time! Not under my roof!" He seemed to have grown even taller in his anger. "This is a threat to all of us! Farmers, miners, waresmen ... *all* of us! And our wives and children! And if one faction of Thiccan life goes down, we all do." He glared around the room at them, and even Fox, hidden as he was, could feel the heat of his gaze and shrank away from it. "Fighting in a Council. Grown men, acting like a bunch of boys with winter fever."

Slowly, and looking ashamed with themselves, the men sat back in their places, avoiding eye contact with Borric. In the uncomfortable quiet that filled the common room, they could hear the wind picking up outside, rattling the windows. Finally, Borric spoke again, the quiet in his voice almost more frightening than the rage.

"We have no right to demand anything of each other. But our valley has survived this long with family and community strong at its heart. Whether you choose to take in the wandering survivors or barricade yourselves in your homes, this inn and tavern will do as it's always done. My doors will be open."

The wind outside was growing stronger. Fox could hear it whistling through the frozen grasses outside, sharp and icy. He shivered. Talk in the Five Sides picked up again as the council started discussing strategies and plans, but to Fox they sounded as though their voices came from a great distance. It was growing colder, despite the roaring fire mere feet from him. He watched the mouths of the council men moving and talking, but every time he tried to hear what they said it seemed that their words were torn away from him on the wind. He shivered again.

The Desolata were on the move. They hadn't stayed long in the ruins of their latest conquest. Now, smelling of charcoal and dried blood, they were heading south. Tracking the survivors of Hammon Town. They would catch up with the injured first, and then ...

The injured. Three collapsed near the river road but not dead. Hidden away by the tall grasses and terrified. One more almost frozen to death in the woods, pressed up against an ancient tree. And somewhere, the last storm of winter was gathering strength to strike. It would rip apart the survivors and tear its way through the mountain valleys. A panic filled the air. The sick, reckless fear brought on by hopelessness.

Someone was smoothing Fox's sweaty hair away from his brow and saying, "Hush, boy. It's alright." And then, to someone else, "He needs water."

He didn't need water. He needed to throw up. Fox tried to speak but no words came out. Instead he blindly pushed away at the massive hand and rolled onto all fours, vomiting until he was empty. He was vaguely aware that his hands were not resting on the hard wood of the Five Sides floor, but instead on a fresh layer of snow. His face was stinging, pelted with wet flakes and darts of ice. As he finished, coughing raggedly, someone pulled him back and propped him up against what felt like a stone wall.

His awareness began to return, and he realized he was sitting up against the back wall of the kitchen. Just beyond the roof overhang, a thick snowfall was being whipped back and forth by the wind, blurring the kitchen courtyard in a haze of grey and white. A handful of faces swam into focus before him. Radda, crouched beside him and his two Shavid companions standing behind. Lai. Picck, bearing a cup of water and looking frightened.

"You're fine now?" asked Radda. It had been his voice Fox had heard earlier.

Fox nodded.

"I saw young miss Lai helping you outside, sneaking through the kitchen," said Radda. "It seemed like something was wrong. When the opportunity arose, we excused ourselves from the council and came to find you."

Fox wanted to ask why they had followed, but he couldn't just yet. He'd met Lai's gaze, and he couldn't look away. She hadn't said a word. She just sat, a foot or so away, staring at him. And she was furious with him. But a slight shake of her head indicated that now wasn't the time to talk about it. And so Fox tore his eyes from hers and looked up at Radda. The time to keep his secrets was over.

"There are survivors, injured," he said quickly. "A little ways from Hammon. Three by the river, one in the woods. Someone fast enough might save them before the storm gets really bad. And the Desolata are moving.

They've already left the town behind and they're headed south. Not directly for us yet, but things could change. And the storm ... by sunset in two days."

Radda and Donlan exchanged the briefest of glances, but Radda didn't question it. Instead, he said, "How big of a storm?"

"You won't want to be sleeping outside," said Fox simply.

"And two days?" said the woman. "You're sure?" Fox nodded, and she sighed. "Looks like Merrick was right."

"Later," said Radda, standing and massaging the back of his neck. "First things first." He turned to Donlan. "Don, it's your choice. No one will make you go, but if you do, be sure you're back in time. This valley will be sealed off with snow and ice if you wait too long."

Donlan said nothing, but nodded sharply.

"Good," said Radda. "Take Anthem, he's the fastest. We'll see you in two days."

And with that Donlan was gone, striding away toward the Shavid camp with his hood pulled up against the snow.

"What's going on here?" asked Picck quietly. "Where's he going? And Fox ... how did ..."

"Donlan has gone to search for the survivors and bring them aid," said Radda. "And as for young Master Fox ..." he turned his gaze on Fox and offered a hand. Fox took it, letting himself be pulled to his feet. "I daresay there's more to this young one than meets the eye."

"Merrick told you I could smell them, didn't he?" said Fox.

"He may have mentioned it," said Radda.

"He's scared of me now," said Fox. And then, quietly voicing the fear that had been on his mind for so long, he said, "Just like everyone else will be."

They could hear raised voices. Someone in the council had started shouting again. Radda gestured with his head, and his female companion slipped back into the tavern through the kitchen door. Once she had gone, Radda said, "I think it's time we talked. We both have questions, I'm sure."

Picck laughed nervously. "*You* have questions? *I* have some questions, sir!"

"Weren't you supposed to be with Rose today?" asked Fox.

"I had to come back and fetch her scarf," he answered. "She left it in the kitchen. And anyway, if I'd have known there would be *so much fun* happening here, I mightn't have left at all!" He poured the untouched water out onto the snow and then tossed the wooden cup unceremoniously back into the kitchen. "Now, if *someone* would be so kind, as to tell me what in Dream's reach is going on?!"

"The Desolata are on the move," said Fox. "They've attacked a village, and they're going to attack more. And I knew. Even before the message arrived, I knew there was a fire and that something was coming."

"How?" said Picck. "How could you possibly have known?"

"Because I'm cursed!" shouted Fox, the words escaping before he could stop himself. "Because I know things and hear things and smell things I shouldn't! I always thought it was something special, instinct ... but it's a curse. And now everyone will know!"

"Woah there!" said Radda, but Fox kept going.

"That's what happened to the Desolata. They can do things that others can't. They can survive in the cold!"

"Now now," said Radda. "Hold!" And as Fox opened his mouth to continue, he picked Fox up and hoisted him over his shoulder like a sack of flour, carrying him over to the goat barn with Picck and Lai following behind. Inside, Radda dropped Fox onto a barrel where he sat, wiping the beginnings of tears away from his eyes.

"Now, calm down," said Radda. "Breathe. And stop yapping like a baby monkey. I can't hear myself think."

Fox took a deep shaky breath. It was warm in the goat barn. The messenger birds in the rafters fluttered and shifted at the new company, but seemed too comfortable to move much more than that. Fermia and Ally came trotting over to meet him, nuzzling fondly at the toes of Fox's boots as his feet dangled from his barrel seat. After a moment, he said, "What's a monkey?"

Radda chuckled. "Not important right now." Then he sighed, running his fingers through his hair and pacing around the small barn. Finally, he said, "The Shavid have very ... unique magical gifts. Our Blessings are subtle and complex, and often give us a special connection to the wind itself. We hear things we shouldn't, sometimes. We smell things. Sometimes even changes in the weather. Little things, but things that nevertheless make life on the road much, much easier." He looked Fox right in the eye. "I knew something was coming. We all did. Just like we can all feel the storm on the horizon. But *none* of us could have told you exactly when it would arrive. Not the strongest or most Blessed among us." He shook his head. "Sunset, in two days. That, my young friend, is not a curse. It is a *gift*. It is a Blessing."

"No," said Fox weakly. "Sovesta doesn't have Blessings."

"When you say smell things," said Picck, "what do you mean, exactly?"

"Just what I say," answered Radda, shifting his gaze to the kitchen boy. "Why do you ask?"

"Because this one here," Picck said, nodding to Fox, "can pick out any smell in my kitchen. And he always knows when the snow's coming. But it's just a good nose on him, isn't it?"

"Could be," said Radda, shrugging. "But that's not all he can do. Is it?"

Every gaze in the room was turned on Fox now. He could have sworn even the birds were watching him, waiting for his answer. Lai still hadn't said a word, but she was watching him with a fierce intensity. Slowly, tremulously, he shook his head.

Radda smiled. Not a grin, or a kind-hearted laugh, but the self-satisfied smile of a man who has just found something he was looking for.

"I've been seeing things," said Fox, and every word seemed to punch through the air like hailstones. "I've always had a good nose, and a sense for weather. But lately ..." How could he explain it to them when he couldn't even explain it to himself? But he tried. "The first time I felt something different, it was like I was feeling what the people of Hammond felt. I was scared, and cold, and I could smell things burning."

"And today?" asked Radda.

"I could feel the Desolata moving. I could almost see them, even." He shuddered, feeling sick again. Then he looked up at Radda, staring squarely at him. "What's wrong with me? What's happening?"

"I assure you, young Master Fox," said Radda. "Nothing is wrong with you. You have a magical gift, nothing more. And it's growing stronger."

"Impossible," said Fox. "Sovesta was cursed. There's no more magic left in her."

"There is a rare flower," said Radda, "that grows in the deserts of Agazard. There is no reason it *should* be there, in such a harsh environment. But it is, and it is nearly impossible to uproot when it appears." He placed a hand on either side of Fox's barrel and leaned in, as though staring into Fox's very soul. "And sometimes the strongest magic blooms where there should be none at all. You have been Blessed, Forric Foxglove. You are one of the Windkissed, those who are Shavid by nature and power, not by birth. And you are beginning to bloom."

Fox's eyes slid past Radda's to see his friends, standing still by the barn door. Picck was still looking at him with an almost comical expression of dumb confusion. But Lai ... her face had changed. She was no longer angry. Instead, every inch of her radiated one emotion only: terror.

Chapter Eight
Windkissed

Lai was afraid of him. The one person he hadn't thought twice about. The one person he didn't see coming. Fox walked home that afternoon in a daze, full to bursting with everything that had happened since dawn. The council, the news about the Desolata. Finally telling his secrets to someone. And then, there was the issue of the magic.

Radda said he needed more time with Fox, to discover what his "blooming potentials" truly were. But not until this crisis had passed. Until then, Fox was to go about business as usual. But how could he? Danger loomed on the horizon not once, but twice. With the coming storm and the Desolata, Thicca Valley could be overwhelmed at any moment. But to Fox, none of that was important. At least, not for now. His gift could be *magic!* And not a curse, but a Blessing! Something worth celebrating, something to be proud of!

And Lai was afraid of it. Fox had spent so long worrying that the Thiccans would look at him differently. That his parents would look at him differently. He worried that his strange instincts might make him unfit for normal life in the valley, or even that his family and friends would be scared of them, of him. Not even for a second had he visited the possibility that the one person he could always count on wouldn't be on his side.

Lai had excused herself from the goat barn while Radda was still talking, making it impossible for Fox to follow her. Instead, he sat perched on his barrel seat, listening as Radda went on and on about discovering his talents and how Fox must have been the reason that they were brought here in the first place. Fox tried to pay attention, but in his mind he was chasing after Lai.

He had tried to find her after Radda was done with him, but with no luck. Now, he trudged up the hill to his family's home, all at once restless and exhausted. His parents weren't home, so he went up into his nook and collapsed into bed. He passed most of the afternoon like that, listening to the distant sounds of the valley and his own thoughts. His parents returned soon, and just after that Farmer Bracken arrived. Fox listened to the grown-ups talking in the kitchen. It seemed as though Bracken, along with many of the other valley farmers, was offering lodging in his home for the Shavid, as well as any refugees who might come through town. Fox heard him say, "Seems worth the price of the extra stomachs to fill, to have more arms on our side."

There was a constant flow of visitors at the Foxglove house after that. People looking to trade, or else conferring on the situation with the Desolata. Many came to buy traps, hoping to fortify their homes. Fox could hear them, the kitchen conversations echoing up through the floorboards and up the stairs. Every now and then one of his parents would come up the stairs to get something, but they usually passed right by the bedroom and into the small storage room at the end of the hall. That suited Fox just fine. He was in no mood to be discovered right now, and certainly didn't want to talk to anyone.

The first of the refugees arrived just before sundown. Fox overheard one of the Thiccans telling Father that there were four of them. In bad shape, but they'd already been taken in by one of the farmer families. Mother left shortly after, saying she'd like to offer her services as an herbalist, hoping she could help. Father went too, taking his guests down to the Five Sides where the valley was once again gathering for the evening. And then, Fox was alone again.

He rolled over, turning his face to the window. The moon was just visible, half-tucked behind a dark, heavy cloud. He lay like that for some time, drifting in and out of sleep until finally he awoke completely, unable to lay still any longer. It was full dark outside now, and his parents were asleep in their bed below. As much out of habit as restlessness, Fox made his way out to the stable to groom Cobb.

The pony seemed just as anxious as the rest of the valley. He stomped in place and tossed his head in agitation, clearly aware that something was not right. Fox sang to him, stroking Cobb's nose until he calmed. Fox continued to sing as he brushed every inch of the pony over and over again. He sang a valley children's rhyme about playing in the mud, and then a tavern song that was a favorite of the miners'. And then he found himself singing one of Radda's songs. It was a haunting melody, about a lonely wanderer who was the last of his people. He began brushing Cobb in rhythm with the music, slowly and deliberately working over the hills of every muscle.

Turn after turn
My feet set 'cross the stone
Through wood and glade
To find my waiting home

Through winter's walk
And summer's shining haze
Alone to be
A lost one all my days

He sang verse after verse, his tools and fingers tracing the lines of Cobb's back as though they were the trails in the song. As the last verse came to a close, a voice spoke.

"That's not one of our songs."

Lai detached herself from the shadows, but only just. She was twisting the bottom of one of her braids nervously, and stayed half-hidden in the dark corner of the stable.

"It was Radda's," said Fox. "I heard it at the camp a few days ago."

"You've been spending a lot of time there lately."

"Yes," said Fox. He stood, not sure of what to do or say. After a moment, he said quietly, "You don't have to be afraid of me. I'm not dangerous ... and I'm still me."

Lai took a step forward, into the light. There was something strange about her eyes. It took a moment, but Fox realized that she had been crying. He had never seen Lai cry, not in his entire life. He found himself wanting to go to her, to hold her like he sometimes saw Father hold Mother when she was upset. But he didn't know how. He tried to take a step toward her, but Lai slipped back into the shadows and was gone.

Fox didn't bother trying to chase after her. He wanted to run away himself. A world without Lai as his friend seemed unimaginable. Of course, so did a world where he could have magic.

As dawn painted the horizon, Fox wandered over to the Shavid camp, hoping to find Neil. But the camp was already awake and buzzing with activity as the Shavid prepared to move into the Five Sides and some of the valley houses. Fox tried to help, but he found himself constantly in the way. And so he headed for the Five Sides, where he could already see chimney smoke coming from the kitchen.

Picck and Rose were both hard at work already, and Lai was nowhere to be seen. Here, at least, Fox wasn't in the way. Picck put him to work immediately, pointing him to a cauldron of porridge that needed stirring. "And then the bread and beans should be ready," he said as Fox stirred. "There's already people filling up the common room, and I heard more survivors arrived late last night."

"Where are they staying?" asked Fox.

"All over," said Picck. "There's two families staying here already, and we've promised rooms to a handful of the Shavid."

"I know of at least one person staying with the Lillywhites," said Rose. "And Old Man Moss took in *three*."

By Picck's reckoning, it seemed that there were twelve Hammon survivors scattered throughout the valley. And when Fox ducked out into the common room to deliver hot loaves of bread, he found all of them. Twelve new faces, dotted in among the familiar Thiccan patrons and Shavid visitors. Fox took them all in as he went from table to table, in and out of the kitchen with platters of food. They ranged from young to old, the youngest looking to be about five. A little boy, clinging to his mother's leg under their table and not speaking. His mother looked tired but grateful to her host family, while a handful of the refugees looked entirely mistrustful and angry. Four of them sat in the farthest corner, away from the fire and not making eye contact with anyone. The rest seemed to be lost. They sat quietly with their host families, or else alone at their tables, looking misplaced and ragged.

Kimic Lillywhite was sitting next to the young woman her family had taken in. She seemed to be trying to encourage the girl to eat a sticky bun, with no success. When Fox came out of the kitchen next, he took a small crock of hot beans over to their table, setting it down in front of the young woman with a smile. Kimic looked at him gratefully as the refugee finally started to eat. She mouthed her thanks, and Fox headed back to the kitchen with a nod.

No one seemed to want to leave the tavern that day. The whole valley seemed to be waiting. Waiting for the rest of the refugees, or else waiting for an attack from the Desolata. The common room was crowded, but quiet. Whispered conversations flitted through the room, and every head turned whenever the front door opened. Back in the kitchen, Picck and Fox were left alone as Rose went out to milk the goats.

"So," said Picck after a few minutes of silence. "This storm that's coming." He didn't look up, but kept wiping the same bowl clean, over and over.

"It'll be the last big one of the season," said Fox.

"And you know it," said Picck. "You shouldn't, but you do."

"Yes," said Fox.

Picck sat quiet for a moment. Then he smiled. And then he laughed, full and hearty like his uncle. "Spirit's shackles, boy! Always knew there was something about that nose of yours!" He laughed so hard tears ran down his face, and he mopped them up with his cleaning rag. "Shame you don't bite, you've got a better sense of smell on you than any guard dog!"

Fox shook his head, amused and grateful for Picck's reaction. "I'd bite you if the occasion called for it," he said teasingly.

Picck laughed even harder, swaying so much he threatened to fall from his perch on the counter top. Once he'd calmed himself, he said, "So then, what now? Are you going to learn all the great mysteries of the Shavid?"

Fox hadn't admitted it to anyone, but that was exactly what he was hoping for. He imagined his summer days filled with lessons in magic and trapping with Father. Wild fantasies filled his head, about using his Blessing to bring home the biggest, richest game the valley had ever known. He was the Blessed boy from Thicca Valley! The end to the Sovesta curse! The rebirth of magic back into the land!

But he simply shrugged, and said, "Maybe. Haven't really had time to think about it." And then, because he couldn't keep it in any longer, he said, "Lai's afraid of me."

To his surprise, Picck chuckled. "You really are a badger brain, you know that? She's not afraid *of* you, she's afraid *for* you."

"Afraid of what? What about me?" asked Fox, entirely confused.

"Afraid you'll leave," said Picck. "You're her best friend. Sometimes, you're her *only* friend. And now you've got this special gift, and Radda's talking about how you might be one of them, one of the Shavid ... and she's worried they'll take you away. Away to a world she doesn't understand, and isn't a part of."

A part of Fox's brain latched on to this idea with hope. She wasn't afraid of him? It made sense, after all. In a way, he was just as afraid of losing her. "Did she tell you this?" he asked.

"Didn't have to," said Picck. "I may not always understand women, but I know my family. I know her."

Rose returned to the kitchen, hauling two buckets brimming with fresh goat milk. There were flecks of snow in her hair. As Picck went to help her, Fox excused himself and slipped past them, out through the back door and into the kitchen courtyard. His feet carried him without thinking to the Shavid camp, where he found Borric and Radda in discussion about rooms for the night. "Don't know how much longer we'll be in the area, truthfully," Radda was saying. "But we can pay for the lodging, that's no trouble."

Borric shook his head in reply. "Never mind the payment, I'll take you in as my guests."

They took no notice of Fox, and he left them discussing terms. Finally, he found Neil, packing the last tent into a tight roll. "Need any help?" he asked.

Neil looked up, and an expression flickered briefly across his face. It wasn't quite jealousy. More like fierce protectiveness, and it made Fox want to take a step back. But then, the older boy's face cleared, and he said, "Thanks, but I'm finished."

"So you're staying at the inn?" asked Fox.

"Some of us," said Neil. "A few of the families in the area wanted to take us in, too. Actually," he said, smiling slightly, "quite a few of them offered to take *me* in. Seems like they think my fighting skills would come in handy in an attack."

"So where will you be staying?" asked Fox.

Neil shrugged. "At the inn, most likely. It'll be crowded, but still ... better than staying with a stranger's family."

"You could stay with us," offered Fox at once.

Neil laughed humorlessly, but did not answer. "I heard about your gift. The Windkissed ... it's a rare Blessing. I assume that means you'll be looking for a new mentor then," he said. "A *real* Shavid." He spat out the phrase like it was poison.

Fox stared at him. "Why?" he asked. "And even if I did, a mentor isn't the same as a friend." He shrugged. "I'm not in the business of trading friends."

Neil smiled and ruffled Fox's hair in a brotherly manner. "If you insist. Come on now, tell me about this discovery of yours. I'm fair upset that I had to hear about it all from Merrick."

"I blame James," said Fox. "He's the one who kept you busy scribing all morning!"

"Fair enough." As Fox helped Neil take his things up the hill to his home, he caught the older boy up on everything. When he got to the part about Lai, Neil shook his head. "Any idea where she is now?"

"No," said Fox. "But she'll turn up. She always does. And I know she's mad at me for not telling her what was happening ... but she was busy! It's not my fault things happened the way they did ... I didn't ask for any of this!"

"Don't try to question women's tempers," Neil advised. "She'll come around when she's ready. And she has every right to be scared. Having a Blessing ... it sets you apart. You never know what you might become. And being the only Blessed one in a cursed nation is a big responsibility."

"How?" asked Fox.

"Well," said Neil carefully, "what's so different about you? Is it luck? Did the gods truly smile on you? Magic isn't an exact science. I should know, I've studied it for years. Why one person is Blessed and another is not ..." He shook his head and hefted his bag higher onto his shoulder. "Forget it. You'll have plenty of time. Right now, we all just need to survive the week."

The snow was beginning to fall thicker now. A little over a day remained until the valley was hit by the promised storm. And Fox, who was tired of sitting around waiting for something to happen, decided that he was going to make the most of that day.

HE WOKE UP LONG BEFORE dawn and crept downstairs. He was careful not to wake Neil, asleep by the fire pit. His parents had no objections to letting the boy stay, and Mother had even recruited him to help make dinner last night. Now, Fox slunk silently past the kitchen and through Father's workshop, out through the side door and into the frigid night.

There was something he wanted to try. A theory he'd been working out in his head without even realizing it. There was a chill breeze whipping its way around the valley. That was good, he would need that. He climbed over the little fence that ran along the back of the Foxglove property and headed out, away from the valley and toward the thick forest in the distance. Halfway there, separate from any of the usual valley sounds and smells, he stopped.

He stood very still, breathing carefully and slowly. He could hear the soft, muffled sound of snowfall and the distant hooting of owls in the forest, but all else was silent. He took one more slow, steadying breath, then closed his eyes and breathed deep.

It was like a hoard of smells and emotions had been waiting for him to let them in. They all clamored for his attention, making his head pound until he was gasping for breath and tugging his scarf away from his throat, choking on it. He slowed his breathing again, taking in deep gulps through his mouth. After a few moments his head cleared, and he carefully closed his eyes again. Slowly and deliberately, he took a deep breath through his nose.

This time, he was ready for the onslaught of smells. He sorted through them, looking for something. There, that peculiar scent of death and anger and cold. The Desolata. He focused on that smell, tracing it almost as if he could see it. He could hear them coming, running through the snow like wild beasts, effortless and untiring. They had hit two more towns, leaving no survivors. And now, they were coming. They were following in the storm's wake, and they would be here soon. He could hear their rattling breath, almost feel it on his neck. They were chasing something, and they wouldn't stop until it was found.

Fox opened his eyes and collapsed into the snow, vomiting spectacularly. Then he stood, shaking but determined. He hurried back down toward the valley, his surefootedness quickly catching up to him again. As he went, whispers of wind kept bringing him smells and sounds. It was almost as if the wind itself were telling him what he already knew, and begging him to stop it.

He burst through the door of the Five Sides and sprinted upstairs. Left at the first hallway, then three doors down on the right. That was where Radda was staying, Fox could smell it. He pounded on the Shavid's door, ignoring his freezing hand's protest at the hard surface. Finally, the door swung open. Radda frowned at him, but Fox spoke before the Shavid leader could.

"I know where they are," panted Fox. "And I know what they want."

"The Desolata?" said Radda. In the room behind him, his wife and daughters were whispering to each other. Mindi pulled herself quickly out of bed and came to her father's side, watching Fox with her huge, blue eyes.

"I know what they want," Fox repeated. "It's me. They're coming for me."

Chapter Nine
Storm

Radda welcomed Fox into his family's room without a word. After a few moments of bustling activity, the room was lit and warmed by a small fire in the grate, and Fox was wrapped in a thick blanket and seated at the foot of the bed. Nobody asked him if he was sure, or how he knew. Instead, they jumped into action.

Radda had three daughters. Mary, the oldest, was sent to wake up the others. She wrapped herself quickly in a patchwork dressing gown and was gone. Once she had left, Radda's wife asked, "Have we any news from Donlan?"

"Nothing yet," said Radda heavily. As Fox watched their exchange, Radda explained quietly, "Donlan and my eldest are betrothed. She's been worried ever since he left to seek out the injured survivors. And if you have some news about him that hasn't reached our ears yet ... well, I wouldn't want her in the room."

Fox tried to think back, tried to remember every smell and sound that he'd been overwhelmed with. But it was impossible. "I'm sorry," he said, shaking his head. "I wasn't trying to find him, so I don't know. I didn't think —"

"Not to worry," said Radda. "I'm sure he'll be back before the storm. That's not your concern anyway. Now, what can you tell us about these Desolata?"

"They'll be here on the heels of the blizzard. Tonight. Tomorrow morning, at the latest. They can survive the cold, and they're using the storm to hide their approach and weaken their prey." He swallowed hard and tried not to think "to weaken *me*."

Radda and his wife began discussing options. How much could they fortify the town in just one day? What help could the Shavid offer? As they talked, the youngest daughter, Sarah, began quietly stoking the fire, though it was clear she was hanging on to every word.

Fox knew what he should do. What he *needed* to do. The Desolata would tear Thicca Valley apart looking for him. Not caring who else got hurt. Not caring what they destroyed.

"Don't you dare," whispered a voice in his ear.

Fox jumped and turned. Mindi was perched right next to him. "Don't what?" he said innocently.

"I can see it written all over your face," she said, keeping her voice low so as not to disturb her parents. "You're planning to run."

"What choice do I have?" whispered Fox, frustrated. "They'll kill everyone! Including you! And your family, and *my* family!"

"So you'll give yourself up?" she asked. "Just like that?"

"I can hide," said Fox. "I can hide in the forest. I can run until they lose me."

"You'll die," said Mindi flatly. "And even if you didn't, they won't stop chasing you."

Fox pulled his knees up to his chest and buried his face in them. "I know," he said weakly. "I just don't know *why*. I'm nothing special." But even as he said it, Fox knew it wasn't true. The only Blessed in a country that was cursed. And the Desolata were the very embodiment of that curse. "That's how they can feel me," he said, almost to himself. "Just like I can feel them." He looked at Mindi excitedly. "It's magic. They're the magic gone bad, but it's still magic!"

"So?" said Mindi. "What are you going to do?"

Fox smiled. "I'm going to let them catch me."

MOTHER DIDN'T LIKE the plan. Fox could hear her and Father arguing in the workshop, but he tried not to listen. Instead, he and Neil were in the kitchen, bundling up in their warmest winter clothes.

"You know you don't have to come with me," said Fox.

"And let you have all the fun?" said Neil. "Not on your life." He was tucking his breeches tightly into his boots. "Besides, who else is going to save your neck if you get in too deep out there?"

The yelling from the back finally stopped, and after a few moments, Mother went sweeping past the kitchen and straight upstairs without a word. She didn't even glance at them. Fox wished he could have said something to comfort her, but there was nothing. This wasn't like going off with a merchant caravan, surrounded by a group and taking only the well-laid highway. This was something entirely different, and much more dangerous.

"Don't worry," said Neil quietly, "I'll get you back to her."

Fox nodded, but didn't reply. That was a promise that Neil couldn't make. No one could. Fox finished lacing his boots in silence, and then made his way down the hallway to where Father still waited in the workshop.

During the summer, the workshop would be filled with the smell of fresh hide. By the end of the season, before the caravan left, there would be packages of furs and gloves and hats, ready to trade. But now, as winter melted into spring, it was mostly just tools and traps that needed mending. However, Father did hold one small scrap of fur in his hand. It was a bright, sharp green pelt, a color that put Fox in mind of the garish paints on the Shavid wagons. Perhaps it was a trick of the light, but as Father ran it back and forth in his hands, the fur seemed almost to shimmer.

At a gesture from Father, Fox sat beside him on a long bench beside the fire. After a moment, Father held the scrap of fur up.

"Do you know, these are the most valuable skins I trade?" He reached out and offered it to Fox, who carefully ran his hand along it.

"Oh," he said, surprised. "It's so warm."

"Hibbins," said Father simply. "Even after they've been skinned, the furs stay bright and warm for years after their original wearer is gone."

"So they're for winter clothes, then," said Fox.

"Yes," said Father, "but only small ones. Gloves, hats. Sometimes linings for slippers. But these are rare, tricky creatures to catch. And the natural heat and color ... the biggest one I ever caught was only about two hands long. A single pair of hibbin gloves alone could keep this valley in fine wax candles for two years. Can you imagine how expensive it would be to line coats with these furs? Or make rugs?" He sighed and stroked the fur with the back of his hand. "Even the rich have their limits, Fox."

For a moment, Fox simply watched the firelight play across the little fur, imagining what it would be like to have enough gold to make a whole hibbin rug. Then, as a shimmer danced its way across the fur's surface, Fox asked, "What makes it do that?"

"They say the hibbins used to be precious jewels," said Father. "Legend tells us that Yavic, the Great Gods' jester, stole them from Farran, the pirate god, and hid them deep in the mountains where he'd never find them. But a priestess of the pirate god's temple heard Yavic laughing about his plan and told her master. Farran came here to the Highborns and searched for a hundred years, and while he was looking, the seas and the fishermen knew peace."

The wind was beginning to pick up outside. Fox could hear the branches of the nearby woods creaking in protest as Father continued. "He did find them eventually, but when he touched them, they turned into these little creatures and scattered away so that he could never find them again." Father chuckled as he began to smooth the skin in his lap. "They also say that Farran spent the *next* hundred years chasing Yavic around the heavens, trying to make him pay for the nasty little trick he played."

The two men laughed quietly for a moment. Then Father reached over and tucked the scrap of fur into the folds of Fox's scarf. "May it keep you warm," he said gravely.

"I'll be fine," said Fox, with much more confidence than he felt.

"I know you will," said Father. "You're a Foxglove. And even with these new ... things that are happening to you ..." He clapped his son on the shoulder. "You've got good instincts. Use them. And remember, every trap is only as strong as its bait. The greediest predator won't look twice at fish bones."

"Well I'd like to think I'm a bit heartier than fish bones," said Fox, attempting to joke. He laughed nervously, then covered it with a cough.

"You've got everything?" asked Father. "That cabin is fully stocked, and if you make it in time you should be able to wait out the storm. But you have extra flint? Some firestones?"

"Yes, and yes," said Fox.

There was a knock at the open workshop door, and Radda poked his head around the doorframe. "Sorry to interrupt," he said, "but if this is going to work, the boys best be off."

And with that, they were on their way. There were no goodbyes, no final words of wisdom. But that was Father's way. He walked out to the front porch with them, and then he and Radda fell back to talk as Neil and Fox started down the hill. Though the men kept their voices quiet, the wind carried their conversation to Fox's ears.

"If my son gets hurt out there ..." Father said harshly.

"This wasn't my idea, Foxglove," said Radda. "You raised a good boy, and he just wants to do what's right."

"Easy for you to say," said Father. "He's just a new toy to you people."

"Watch it," said Radda, his voice growing firmer and more confrontational. "If he fails, my people die too. We're still here, aren't we? We'll be on the front lines, fighting alongside you."

"Then you'd best pray to your gods that he pulls this off," growled Father. "Because if I lose my boy, you'll wish the Desolata had torn *you* apart."

The conversation stopped. Fox could hear Radda jogging to catch up to them, and after a moment the musician was keeping pace. "Armac and his people are moving folks into the mines as we speak," he said. "Then most of the miners will be joining us. They've done their best, gathering whatever weapons they could find, but it's mostly a collection of pickaxes and shovels, to be honest."

"Well," said Neil, "you're certainly inspiring us with confidence. Will there even be a valley to come back to?"

Radda smacked Neil lightly across the back of the head and said, "Hush up and do your job. Let me worry about the valley."

In theory, the Desolata should change their course to follow Fox, wherever he might go. And if he left the valley, it should remain untouched. But there was no way of knowing if they would take the bait. And so, a small militia of strong men, Shavid and Thiccans and even a handful of the refugees, stood ready to defend the valley. Fox had been against this part of the plan. He was much more comfortable with the idea of everyone hiding in the mines, Father included. But it was pointed out to him that even if every Thiccan survived, their lives would mean nothing if they all lost their homes. The farms, the Five Sides, the shops ... they were all worth defending.

The group stopped just before the valley square. "They need me at the tavern," said Radda. "It's headquarters, such as it is."

There was so much Fox wanted to say. He wanted to say something comforting, or even to *hear* something comforting. He wanted to ask Radda to look for Lai, and to give her a message. But since he wasn't quite sure what that message would be, he said nothing. Instead, he reached out to shake Radda's massive hand. Briefly, Radda pulled him into a rough hug before releasing him with a firm pat on the back. And with that, they parted ways. Fox turned northeast, heading toward the deep woods that he and Father often trapped in, with Neil at his heels.

THE WOODS WERE THICK with snow. It muffled their footsteps and wrapped them in a frozen silence, where nothing moved and every breath was swallowed by the trees. Roots and rabbit holes were hidden from view, and while Neil was not quite as sure-footed as Fox, he was keeping up rather well.

Even without Fox's abilities, he could easily navigate the hidden forest paths. They were heading toward one of Father's trapping cabins, and Fox had been there so many times he could make the trip in his sleep. The boys moved as quickly as possible, keeping their voices low whenever they spoke. Mostly, they were silent.

Fox wondered if Donlan had found the injured Hammon survivors. And then if he had made it back to the valley yet. What if the storm arrived early? What if the Desolata attacked *during* the blizzard, not after it? His whole plan was built on "ifs," and with nothing else to focus on, uncertainties pelted him like frozen rain. The plan was simple in theory: lure the Desolata away from the valley, trap them in some of Father's larger game snares. The thrown-together militia back in Thicca Valley would be waiting out the storm at the tavern rather than the mines, ready to defend their homes should the Desolata not be drawn away. And Neil ... well, Neil was good company, and an extra pair of eyes. Fox would have preferred to carry out his mission alone, and had even convinced Father to stay behind, insisting that the valley fighters needed him more. And besides, what good would it do Mother if they were both killed? But as they traveled, even Fox had to admit that it was comforting having Neil around.

Father had several cabin outposts scattered throughout his trapping territory. Three of them were within a day's journey on foot. This one was nearest. As the afternoon began to close into evening, they found the little hut tucked away carefully in the side of a small hill. Here, beneath an ancient canopy of forest, the snowfall was lighter, simply dusting the cabin and its grounds, rather than covering it. But even without the snow, Fox knew Neil couldn't see it. After all, he didn't know what to look for.

Neil would only see a hillside. Thick, twisting tree roots snaking across the ground. Rocky outcroppings and decaying, fallen logs overgrown with moss and late winter mushrooms. But if he looked carefully, he might begin to notice a pattern at the heart of the tree roots. An archway, almost like a door. And from there, the rest of the cabin might begin to come into focus, as it had for Fox so many years ago, on his first trip with Father. The gentle curve of the earth, creating a natural roof. The stone overhang that jutted out over the front door, and a second one to the left, just where a kitchen window might be. Once you saw it, you simply couldn't *un*-see it. The thick moss like a welcome mat, the outdoor workbench that was a simple, stone slab. Even the fallen logs started to look like wood-post fences once you noticed it.

There was a thick knot on one of the archway roots, just where a doorknob should be. Fox reached out and pressed his hand to it, then pushed hard until it sank all the way into the earth behind it. And then he grabbed hold of the root and pulled, swinging open the hidden cabin door and slipping inside, Neil right behind him.

The cabin was full of a soft, warm glow from a handful of firestones embedded in the ceiling. In the half-light, it was clear that they were directly inside the hill. The ceiling dipped and rose in unlikely places, and twisting tree roots wove in and out of sight along the walls. Storage niches had been carved out, just like at home, and the single room sprawled back quite a ways to accommodate the many traps and supplies Father had stored there.

But Fox didn't have time to take inventory. He already knew what he was looking for.

Father didn't catch bears often. The pelts were difficult to move across country, and they took up valuable space in the caravan packs. But every now and then, when he had the time and the resources, he could provide Thicca Valley and the surrounding areas with bearskins for rugs and cloaks. Fox's own parents had a massive bearskin blanket on their bed.

There were five bear traps hanging on massive hooks along the back wall. Huge, metal jaws that Father had collected over the years. They were deadly and powerful, just like the beasts they captured. In fact, the traps could be just as dangerous to the trapper as to the prey if they weren't handled correctly. And so, last summer when Father taught Fox how to use them, he made sure his son was drilled in trap safety over and over. Now, Fox could set them in his sleep.

But it was Neil who had to carry the heavy traps back out into the forest. Fox simply wasn't strong enough to do it on his own. Instead, he led Neil a little ways out from the cabin as the snow began to fall thicker around them. He could smell the Desolata all the time now, even without trying to. They were coming faster, and he knew exactly which direction they'd be coming from.

Fox could almost see their path in his mind. It was like a hunter's trail. Wolves or bears, or even him and Father. Every predator tracked its prey, and could be tracked in return. No matter how strong or barbarous the Desolata were, they were still predators. And Fox was the one prey who knew they were coming. All five traps were set quickly and quietly, with Neil placing them where he was told and Fox doing the actual rigging. He didn't bother covering them with leaves and earth as he normally would; the snow was already beginning to hide them perfectly. Instead, he set them as fast as he could while still being extremely careful. And then, backing away from the trap sites, he turned and headed straight back to the cabin for more supplies. He wasn't taking any chances.

With Neil watching in amazement, Fox began to fill the woods around them with traps. Nets, rigged to haul their prey high up into the trees. Snares to break legs and deadfalls that would bring heavy logs crashing down on them, snapping the necks and spines of whatever was below. Neil helped as best he could, but mostly he stayed out of the way. Fox barely noticed him as his instincts took over. By the time night was fully upon them, the wind was whipping shards of ice into his face, and each of his traps were hidden by snowfall. He scampered back to the safety of the cabin, expertly avoiding his own traps, and slammed the cabin door tightly shut, locking them both in for the night.

"And now?" asked Neil.

"Now," said Fox, "we wait."

The cabin was built for waiting. Waiting for a catch, weathering out a storm. And once, several summers ago, waiting for Mother to let Father come home again after a fairly tempestuous fight. Fox had waited along with Father during hunting trips, and once during a heavy rain. He'd even headed out to the cabin while Father was isolated, lending him some company while they waited for Mother to start speaking to him again. But never had Fox thought he might be waiting out his own death.

And so, with nothing else to do but wait, he and Neil talked. As the storm worsened outside, they sat by the fire and swapped stories. Neil told him all about his childhood in the desert, and Fox clung to every word. Father had never traveled that far before, and Fox was fascinated. He interrupted almost every five minutes with a question, and Neil answered them happily. In return, Fox told him more about life in Thicca Valley. The more they talked, the easier it was to forget about the Desolata, and ignore the howling winds outside. They might have been safe at the Five Sides during deep winter. In fact, it was easy to imagine that any minute, Borric would come thundering in, offering to refill everyone's drinks. Fox could almost picture Lai skipping through the common room, clearing tables and singing along with the fireside songs, her long black braids bouncing off her back. He could almost smell Picck's cooking, and feel the warmth of a dozen other bodies pressed around him, all waiting out the dark winter.

That image got him through two days. Two days of talk and simple chores to pass the time. Two days of whittling and tending the fire, careful to ration the supply of firewood stacked along the wall. He taught Neil some of the lighter trap maintenance and repair, and they fell asleep late each night when their voices were raw. And always, on the edge of Fox's senses, were the Desolata. Their smells were mostly almost hidden in the smells and sounds of the raging storm, but he knew they were there.

It was during their third night that Fox suddenly awoke, completely alert. The fire had burned to embers, and the winds outside had slowed. He could hear the trees moaning, protesting the weight of the snow and ice. He could hear Neil's light snores as he slept on, and the creak of the roots that surrounded the cabin. But there was something else. Footsteps racing through a heavy snow. Tree branches being snapped and pushed aside as a predator hunted. No, as nine predators hunted.

He could smell them all now ... they were close enough. He could pick each one's scent out of the group, distinct but all deadly. Fox scuttled across the cabin floor, pressing his back against the wall. He pulled his hunting knife out of its boot sheath with one hand and gripped it tightly, holding it close. He breathed as slowly and quietly as he could, but even those breaths sounded like roaring winds. He wished his heart would beat quieter. He was sure the Desolata could hear it pounding as clear as a miner's hammer.

He wished Neil would wake up, just so he would have someone to talk to. But he couldn't bring himself to make any sound that might wake the older boy, sure that the Desolata would be able to hear him. And so he sat, waiting.

His fingers found the hibbin fur that Father had sent with him. With his free hand, he began to fiddle with it, clutching it tightly and rubbing his thumb up and down the soft, warm surface. He remembered the story Father had told, about the pirate god Farran. And with Neil asleep, and no one else to talk to, Fox found himself whispering quietly into the darkness.

"You're the god I heard my father mention most recently," he said. "I don't know exactly how this works, but the way I figure it, mentioning is about as close as you get to worshiping in our parts. What with no temple and all. So I'm asking you to help me, Sir Farran. Help me make it through this. And if I get out alive, well, then I'll start mentioning you too."

And then, he heard it. The snap of metal jaws and the inhuman, raging shriek of a trapped creature. The bear traps were a ways away from the cabin itself, but Fox could hear the sounds of the struggle as though they were sharing his fireside. Five sets of steel teeth clamped onto five pairs of running legs, bringing the trapped Desolata crashing to the ground. If they didn't manage to free themselves, that was five down. Four to go.

Fox pressed himself as far back into the wall as he could go, wishing to simply disappear into the earth. He closed his eyes, listening harder than he'd ever listened in his life. Tracing the footfalls of the remaining four, hoping they didn't change course. Praying they stayed on their path, where more traps were lying in wait.

Two of them were caught in the net trap. He could hear them shrieking their anger and gnawing at the ropes, but he knew it would be nearly impossible for them to tear their way through one of those nets. He'd woven them himself, using some of the finest, most stubborn greenery in the whole Highborn range. A knife couldn't cut through it without dulling the blade to beyond useless.

The last two seemed to have slowed almost to a stop. Fox held his breath, trying to make himself as silent as possible. *Don't turn,* he thought desperately. *Don't change course. Just come and get me.* After a moment, there was an angry cry that almost sounded human for a moment. Fox shuddered. The deadfall. It was meant to crush the skull of waiting prey, killing it instantly. But from the primal cries now echoing through the woods, Fox was sure that the creature trapped beneath it wasn't dead. Not yet.

That left only one. As Fox took a deep breath, trying to smell him out, he was sure that the Desolata was doing the same. It was the leader, he knew it. While the others had all smelled like death and fear, this one still smelled like a man. Tainted with death, yes, but he wasn't all beast. He could still reason, and he was being careful now. Careful, and silent.

Fox couldn't smell him anymore. Nor hear him. He felt blind and helpless, sitting in the dark cabin, waiting to be caught. Every now and then he could still hear an anguished cry from one of the trapped, injured Desolata, but try as he might, he couldn't hear the footfalls of the leader.

And then the cabin door was hit with such a force that it shook the frame. Neil jerked awake and scrambled to his feet, looking around wildly. The force struck again, and Fox tightened his grip on his knife. Neil ran to his side, pulling him to his feet and whipping out his own weapon, a curved desert short sword. The glow of the firestones washed it in a shining, reddish light, making Neil look like a warrior from legends.

Another crash at the door. It sounded like the Desolata leader was throwing himself at it, determined to break it down. The cabin had withheld winter storms and summer rains, but even the strength of the earth had its limits. And then, as dust and dirt began to shake loose from the ceiling, Fox broke away from the wall, rushing toward the door. Neil tried to grab him, but Fox dodged away. He slid to his knees several feet into the center of the room, and dug his knife directly into one of the floorboards, levering it out of place and throwing it away. There, tucked safely in a secret floor nook, was Father's spare bow. It gleamed softly in the firestone glow as Fox pulled it from the hillside and dug around for spare bowstrings. He found one, fraying but serviceable, wrapped in an otterskin pouch.

As he began to string the massive bow, Neil understood. "Arrows!" he called.

"Five boards to the left from the fireplace!"

The bow was taller than Fox was, and stiff from disuse. He could hear Neil tearing out the floorboards behind him as he grunted, summoning all his strength to string the massive weapon. His own bow he could string and have aimed in an instant, but this one took more work. He didn't have any idea *how* he managed it, only that it was done. And Neil was by his side, handing him two arrows.

Fox looked up at him desperately.

"These were the last two," said Neil as another crash shook the whole cabin. And with a look, they knew. Neil was stronger, but Fox was the better shot. Fox grabbed one of the arrows and put it to the string, took a deep breath, and then raised the bow, aiming it at the door.

They waited, each crash a little louder as the Desolata leader flung himself at the door over and over. Fox's arms began to shake with the effort and sweat began to trickle down his face. He shook his head, trying to keep it out of his eyes, and in that moment a gap splintered in the doorway. Without thinking, Fox released his arrow, straight through the hole. A cry told him that he'd struck home, and for a moment he breathed. But then a hand clawed at the opening, tearing chunks off the door in fury. He grabbed the second arrow, strung, and raised the bow again, his arms on fire from the weight. Beside him, Neil was poised and ready, sword drawn in a fighter's stance. He was muttering what sounded like a prayer in his native tongue.

Words Fox couldn't quite understand, though he caught what might be a name of one of the desert gods Neil had told him about. And, sending his own desperate prayer skyward, Fox said, "Farran, give me strength!"

The Desolata had torn an opening big enough for his torso, and Fox could see the shadowy form fighting his way inside. But still he held off. He needed a clearer shot. Neil seemed to know what he was waiting for, and he sprang forward with a warcry, drawing the creature's attention for just long enough. Fox pulled back on the string, drawing it past his ear, and as he did, his arms suddenly steadied. His head was clear, and he held the weapon with a strength and sureness that was not his own. And then, with a slow exhale, he released.

The Desolata's cry was cut off abruptly as the arrow shot clean through its throat. It collapsed in the doorway, hanging half in and half out of the gaping hole it had battered. And Fox, his temporary strength sapped from him as quickly as it had come, sank to the floor, letting the bow slip from his shaking fingers and clatter beside him.

There were still several hours until daybreak, when they could get a closer look at the damage. Until then, Fox simply wanted to curl up by the fireplace and sleep. But he couldn't, not yet. They still had to deal with the Desolata corpse, which Fox happily left to Neil. The older boy shoved the body out with the blunt edge of his sword, and then began sealing up the hole it had made with the ripped up floorboards. Fox wasn't much help there either. His muscles screamed with every pound of the hammer, and Neil ended up doing most of the work himself. Finally, they both lay down again, trying to sleep, and ignore the anguished cries of the wounded still echoing through the woods.

It was then that the wolves came.

Fox had been taught his entire life to fear wolves. Father always said, "I spend all summer hunting them. But when winter sets in, rest assured, they start hunting *me*." But as Fox had lain warm and safe in his nook so many winter nights, listening to them howling at the edges of the valley, he'd always found it hard to believe that something that made such a beautiful sound could be bad. Their songs had always comforted and thrilled him, rather than frightening him.

And now, their songs were filling the woods. Echoing through the icy trees and intermingling eerily with the pained shrieks of the Desolata. It sounded like more than a dozen of them. An entire pack, and a big one at that. The Desolata began to scream louder, each of them struggling to free themselves from their traps. And then, their cries turned into something else. They were the cries of a prey fighting with all their might to escape. Snarling growls punctuated the wolfsong, and Fox knew once again without seeing what was happening outside the cabin walls.

"They're attacking," he whispered. "They're attacking the Desolata."

A quick and vicious battle raged outside, and then one by one the barbaric raiders were silenced. But the wolves remained, pacing around the perimeter of the cabin, throwing their victory song to the sky.

"Do you have wolves, where you're from?" asked Fox.

"No," said Neil. "I've heard them, some nights. In places we've traveled. But never so many, or so close." He shifted, seemingly trying to get comfortable enough to catch some sleep. "I thank them for taking care of our little friends out there, but I hope they're gone by morning. It would be a shame to survive tonight only to be picked off by a bunch of dogs."

But as Fox settled in himself, adjusting on his thin sleeping mat, he couldn't bring himself to fear the wolves. Their beautiful voices still held a sense of comfort for him. And for the first time in three nights, Fox went to sleep feeling perfectly safe.

Chapter Ten
The Mudlock

They packed quickly the next morning. Fox in particular was eager to leave the battlefield behind him, and was ready and waiting before Neil had even laced his boots. Finally, as Neil threw his cloak over his shoulders, Fox wrenched open the cabin door and let in a flood of bright, cold sunlight.

It was as though the devastation of the storm had been perfectly frozen. Shattered tree trunks were blanketed in snow, and tree limbs hung low with ice. It was as though some great beast had come through the forest, taking whole bites out of the landscape.

Fox tried not to look at the Desolata corpse just outside the door, but he couldn't avoid it. And once he looked, he couldn't tear his eyes away. At first glance, he might have just been a man, with an arrow shot clean through his throat. But the longer Fox looked, the more the Desolata simply seemed ... wrong. His limbs were oddly stretched, like the bones had started to grow longer than the skin would allow. His joints seemed to be trying to escape from his very body, and Fox couldn't imagine what daily pain that kind of bone structure would cause. He was bald, but ragged scars criss-crossed along his scalp. He wore nothing but a pair of frayed, short breeches, and Fox was amazed that every inch of his skin wasn't black with frostbite.

"No shoes," said Neil. "No coat, or even a shirt. How do they live like that?"

Fox shivered, and it had nothing to do with the cold. He turned his back to the cabin, and the corpse, and headed down the path. He kept his gaze away from the other Desolata, dead in their traps. He would let Father take care of them. That was a man's job, and Fox felt he had spent enough time playing at being a man lately. For now, he just wanted to be home, warm and safe in Thicca Valley. Whatever might be left of it.

The wolves followed them all the way, keeping just out of sight. But Fox knew they were there. He kept it to himself, not wanting to worry Neil. Instead, he smiled a little to himself. Father was right about many things, but it seemed he was wrong about wolves.

Fox had no idea how they made it back to the valley so quickly. But soon enough, he could smell the familiar scents of the outlying farms. And then, quite suddenly, he stopped, scared to step through the treeline. Terrified of what he might see. His plan had been built on guesses, and he had no way of knowing if all of the Desolata had been drawn away. The storm had probably taken its toll as well, and while he couldn't be held responsible for the weather, it *was* his fault that the Desolata had come this way in the first place.

Neil seemed to know his thoughts. He placed a comforting hand on Fox's shoulder and said quietly, "What's done is done. We survived, and that's the important thing. Take everything else one step at a time."

Fox could smell smoke, and blood. And fear. He wanted to turn, to run back into the forest and live with the wolves. But instead, he took a deep breath and made himself stand a little taller. It seemed he wasn't quite done being a man yet. And with one shaky step after another, he led the way out of the trees, leaving their silent guards behind.

The late afternoon sun washed over the valley, making the snow shine red as if with blood, and casting a harsh light on the valley's destruction. Whole sides ripped from houses, doors torn from their hinges, and broken glass like jagged teeth growling from the windows. A haze of smoke had settled over the western end of town, and the smell of death hung in the air. Numbly, Fox let his feet take him forward, down into the heart of the valley. He passed new-fallen trees and broken fences as he went, until finally he reached the main road, and the valley square.

Here, women and children were cleaning rubble from the streets and wading through hip-deep snow to retrieve scraps of wood and stone. Men were shoveling great heaps of snow, cutting an easier pathway through town. It might have been his imagination, but Fox thought the Thiccans were looking at him differently. They mostly kept their eyes on their work, but every so often their gazes would briefly shift to him and then back, as though they were trying too hard *not* to look at him. Trying not to notice, Fox kept moving until he came to the Five Sides.

The common room was empty and dark, but the quiet thud of a knife on wood told Fox that someone was in the kitchen. There, he found Picck, slowly and deliberately chopping vegetables. Not just enough for a crock of stew, it seemed, but every vegetable in the valley. Potatoes, mushrooms, carrots ... the kitchen was filled with heaps of them, spilling over the countertops and onto the floor, and some towers reaching up even past Fox's shoulder. It was like a mountain range of food, and when Fox looked closer, he realized they weren't all vegetables. Herbs and smoked meats had made their way into the piles, as well as what seemed to be several loaves of bread.

"What happened?" asked Fox quietly.

Picck looked up. His eyes said he hadn't slept in days. The smile that always seemed to play around the edges of his mouth was gone, and for a moment he stared at Fox as though he was looking right through him. Then he blinked, and finally looked as though he could actually see the two boys in the doorway. "Oh," he said dully. "Hello. I see you're alive. Good, that's good." And he turned back to his chopping.

"Picck?" said Fox, taking a careful step farther into the room. "Picck, are you alright?"

The chopping continued, but slower now. Finally, after about a minute, Picck spoke. "I can't fight, you know," he said. "I'm not a strong man. I've never entered the contests. But ... I didn't want to go into the mines. I didn't want to hide, while my family was defending the valley. I begged them to let me stay." He spoke as though he had to fight to remember how.

As though every word was a struggle. "It was Uncle Borric who convinced the men to find a place for me. And since headquarters was here, everyone agreed that I should just stay in the kitchen. With the extra supplies and food, everything that wasn't moved into the mines."

He looked up, turning haunted eyes onto Fox. "That was my only job. Watch the back door. And I did, and the storm picked up, and I could hear the goats crying from the stable. So I went out to bring them in." It was then that Fox noticed the goat curled up in the corner of the room. Fermia, her head down, looking just as melancholy as Picck.

"What happened to Aly?" asked Fox.

Picck went back to chopping his vegetables. "Radda had this idea," he said. "Something to do with his magic. He said he could hide the valley. Make it disappear, to anyone who was looking for it. Or appear as something else, a target that wouldn't be as appealing to the Desolata. But it was a powerful magic he said, and he would need to focus. So we let him be. He sat for two days, in the corner by the fire, playing his music with barely a pause. Sometimes we could hear it over the storm, and sometimes we could just hear the wind. But it was beautiful. And we all stayed quiet, keeping out of his way. And if people needed to talk, they brought their conversations in here.

"And then Aly started going stir-crazy. Two days into the storm, she started trying to beat down the door, and I couldn't calm her. She was making so much racket that Emmend Fisher came into the kitchen and told me to silence her or else ... and that's when they came."

"How many?" asked Neil.

"Only four," said Picck. "We got lucky, I suppose ... but four was enough. Four was even too much. Of the twenty-eight men we had here, we lost twelve." He looked up again, a tortured expression twisting his face. "They're just so *fast,* Fox! And they wouldn't die! And they were tall, and horrible. And they have no mercy."

Fox didn't know whether he wanted to throw up or just sit down until his legs stopped shaking. Twelve dead, and all because of him.

"It's not your fault," said Neil. But he wasn't speaking to Fox, he was speaking to Picck.

"I broke Radda's concentration," said Picck. "I let them find us. And Emmend was the first to die ... one of the Desolata came in through the kitchen window while we were trying to get that cursed goat to shut up."

"Shavid magic is powerful but flighty," said Neil. "Just like the wind herself. You don't know that Radda would have been able to keep it going much longer. You can't blame yourself. Every man here chose to stay behind and fight, just as you did. And even you did your part."

"He did more than his part," said a quiet voice from the doorway. Borric had slipped in unnoticed. "He killed one of them. And he saved my life." He strode over and grasped his nephew in a tight, fierce hug. "We will bury the dead. The widows will mourn. And then, we will begin to rebuild. There is nothing to be ashamed of." He pulled away and took Picck by the shoulders. "Now, hold your head high. And be proud. You saw battle and came out a new man. You survived. And because of you, some of us can live another day." And with that, Borric was gone. Fox wanted to follow him, to ask about the rest of the valley. His parents. Lai. He cast a worried look at Picck, who had gone back to silently chopping vegetables. Then he and Neil exchanged a quick, wordless glance, and Fox knew that Neil would take care of him. He turned and hurried out of the kitchen, catching up with Borric as he made his way down to the storage rooms.

"You've been a busy little mite," said Borric when he caught sight of Fox.

"Yes sir," said Fox.

"How many came after you?" asked Borric.

Fox didn't wonder that Borric seemed to know the whole plan. Father would have told him for sure. "Nine."

"Spirit's Shackles," said Borric, running a massive hand across his forehead. "It's a miracle you survived at all, let alone in such good condition."

"Sometimes there's more damage than just wounds," said Fox, thinking of Picck.

"You know you saved the valley, Fox," said Borric seriously. "With the number we lost as it is ... if more had come for us? They would have torn us apart. Yes, there were casualties. But just as they're not Picck's fault, they're also not yours."

Fox nodded, but didn't say anything. He knew Borric was trying to help, but nothing anyone could say would rid him of the gnawing guilt. After all, he was still the reason the Desolata came.

"Go home," said Borric finally. "See your mother, let her know you're safe."

"What about —" Fox started to ask, but Borric answered before he could even finish.

"Your dad is out taking care of the Desolata corpses with some of the other men. Radda is upstairs, sleeping off the exhaustion of keeping so much magic up for so long. And Lai is with Picck's family. I'll be sure to tell her you're alright." He sighed heavily and sent Fox on his way, calling after him, "Funeral's tonight. She'll be wanting to see you."

WHEN FOX WALKED INTO his family's kitchen, Mother shrieked and hugged him so tightly he began to cough. She began tearing off his outer layers, wet from the snow, and sat him down at the fire pit with a hot bowl of broth. Within minutes he was wearing fresh, dry socks and had a blanket wrapped around his shoulders. His boots and cloak were hanging on a rack by the fire to dry, and Mother was talking his ear off. Half scolding, half thanking all the gods that he was alright. Finally, when she'd calmed down, Fox was able to tell her the whole story. Or most of it, at any rate. He left out the details of the Desolata leader's attack, thinking that she might never let him out of the house again if he told her. Finally, she kissed him on the forehead and said, "It sounds like my little man is all grown up." She smoothed his hair back and took his now empty bowl. Then she sent him up to bed, promising to wake him at nightfall.

He slept fitfully, and all too soon Mother's voice floated up the stairs, calling for him to get up. He groggily pulled his spare boots from their shelf and began to tie them on. Father wouldn't be joining the funeral proceedings, he knew. Then, he slid easily down his ladder and went to the window, looking out at the valley.

Every window was dark. No fires burned in their grates during a funeral. Instead, little pockets of soft, green light could be seen gathering like fireflies, making their way out to the mines. Here and there a handful of glowing lights would appear out of a darkened building, and join the larger group. When Fox finally joined Mother downstairs, dressed for warmth, she silently handed him his own softly glowing stone. A lymstone.

Lymstones were the rarest and most mysterious gems that came from the Highborn mines. When held in the hand, they glowed green. Casting light but no heat. But when worn around the neck, they gave light only to the wearer. They allowed miners to see even in the deepest trenches, and women to sew even during the darkest of Deep Winter. When used too much, however, they caused headaches and dizzy spells, and some who wore them too often started to lose the power of speech. But for every funeral, they lit up the valley streets as the only light in town.

Fox and Mother made their way silently to the center of town, their glowing stones joining the larger group. No one spoke. Even the wind was silent, leaving the valley in deadly hush. They followed the glow of lymstones all the way up into the mountains. But where the miners would normally turn right to head off to work, everyone turned left. Down a rarely-used path, winding between high walls of pale grey stone. And then, the path opened up into a stone clearing, and the men began to sing.

Those who had been carrying the bodies of the fallen were in front. As the crowd parted, spreading themselves around the clearing in a wide circle, Fox could see the twelve corpses being laid out in a row. He ticked off their names in his head, making note of everyone he had killed, every life that had been lost because of him. As the song swelled, magnified by the rock, the dead mens' widows came forward. Some with their children, some alone. Fox could see their faces, streaked with tears or else numbly blank, and he knew he could never forget a one of them. They each said their last goodbyes, and then slipped back into the crowd.

Someone's hand found his, and squeezed. He didn't need to look to know that it was Lai. He always knew when it was her. Together, they watched as the funeral pyre was lit, glowing green with lymstone powder. Emerald flames swelled and enveloped the bodies, illuminating the high stone walls and dappling them with stretched shadows. For several minutes, the valley stood watching the fire grow, throwing its sparks to the heavens like green stars. Finally, as the last verse of the funeral melody began, one by one the Thiccans stepped forward. Each took a branch from the fire, flaming like a torch, to respark their own homefires. Tonight, every fire in the valley would burn green.

As Fox turned his back on the fire, starting to follow Mother home with her green torch leading the way, Lai still didn't let go of his hand. All the way back up the path, out of the side of the mountain and back down into the valley. And as they went, Fox caught another light out of the corner of his eye. Far out, across the fields and near the distant treeline, a solitary red fire flickered. Tonight, the Desolata were burned without honor. With no songs to guide them into the After Realms. Their souls would wander forever, unable to rest, stuck between worlds. But Fox, thinking back on the harsh angles of their bones and the pain it must have caused, wondered if it would even matter. For a cursed life, any death would be a welcome relief. Wouldn't it?

Lai left him at the Five Sides, with a quick squeeze of his hand before she slipped away. And Fox, the last week finally catching up to him, let his feet carry him home without thinking. Exhausted, he pulled off his boots in the kitchen and undressed as he climbed the stairs. His last memory before falling asleep was of Mother lighting the bedroom fire with the funeral torch, and bathing the room in glowing green.

DAYS PASSED, WITH FOX only vaguely aware of his parents occasionally waking him up to eat something. He would force down some soup or bread before falling back into a deep but troubled sleep. By the time Fox fully awoke, the snows had all but melted. Spring was truly upon them, and with it came the Mudlock.

The Mudlock didn't happen every year. Sometimes, the spring thaw was gradual. The days would begin to warm slowly over the course of several weeks. The trees would dry, the snow would melt, and the earth would soften enough for heavy farming. But sometimes, it all happened at once. The sun would come out with a vengeance, melting everything it touched in only a day or so, leaving the valley wet and filthy for quite some time. The last Mudlock Fox could remember had lasted almost two weeks. The rivers had flooded, the valley was a uniform brown, and more than one pair of boots was claimed by the ankle-deep mud that permeated the land.

But despite the unpleasantness of never being properly dry, it seemed as though the Thiccans were determined to have the valley rebuilt as quickly as possible. From his window Fox could see two fresh new structures being raised to the west, undoubtably replacing those that had been burned down. Anxious to learn what he'd missed while he'd been sleeping, Fox dressed quickly and hurried through the lunch Mother made him eat. When she finally agreed to let him go, on the promise that he would take it easy, Fox was out the door and down the front path in an instant.

The valley square was a bustling hub of activity. Long wooden planks had been set atop the worst of the mud in the streets, giving people a drier path to walk. Store fronts were being repainted and doors repaired. Children ran barefoot from place to place, carrying notes and messages for their parents. And outside of the inn, a long line of goats was tethered where visiting horses were usually tied.

"Several fences in town were destroyed with the storm," said Borric when Fox went inside to ask. "Most of them have been fixed by now, but Farmer Ballard was one of those killed, and his young widow hasn't a clue what to do with the goats. Told her I'd keep an eye on them for awhile, until someone can get out there to help her."

"I could mend a fence," said Fox helpfully.

"Oh no, boy, I've had a messenger bird from your mother already. I'm not to let you overtax yourself. Not after the week you've had. It's straight to the kitchen with you, and you can help Picck."

Normally, Fox wouldn't mind staying at the Five Sides, listening to the talk and gossip pass through the common room and making jokes with Picck. But as he sat and pounded dough, he couldn't help feeling useless. He wanted to do *something* to help repair the damage that he had done.

It went on like that for two days. Two days of mundane chores, while the rest of the town worked to rebuild and carry on after the tragedy. And Fox, his restlessness almost too much to stand, found himself cleaning every inch of the common room over and over again. He scrubbed mud from the floors and listened to every scrap of news that floated by. News of the finished buildings and Farmer Bracken being in the market for a new plough animal. The story of how the Shavid Donlan had arrived just before the storm, with the injured Hammon survivors riding in behind him on deer, as easily as though they were horses. Even the seemingly ordinary pieces of information, like the baker painting his new shop door bright yellow, Fox drank in eagerly.

And then, always humming at the back of his mind, there were the Shavid. They were busy doing their part in the valley, happy to help with the repairs. But Fox wanted nothing more than to follow Radda around town, dogging his steps until the company leader made good on his promise, helping Fox to discover the true nature of his Blessing.

It was Mindi who finally came to Fox. She found him grooming Fermia for the fifth time that day. No matter how much he scrubbed, the mud clung stubbornly to her coat and hooves. She watched him work for a moment, before she said, "The town's looking nice again."

"Yeah," said Fox.

"Things got fixed real quick."

"Mmm."

After another few moments, Mindi said, "I'm glad you're alive, you know." Fox glanced up to find Mindi smiling at him, those giant blue eyes staring. "Would have been a shame for the cutest boy in the whole valley to die before courting age. I'm sure all the ladies would have been disappointed." Fox tried to think of a clever retort, but his mind was blank. Mindi smirked at his obvious discomfort, and finally she said, "Daddy wants to see you."

Fox didn't waste another moment. He tethered Fermia to a post in the kitchen courtyard and followed Mindi upstairs to her family's room at the Five Sides. Radda was waiting, along with the dancer woman he'd brought to the council. James the player was also there, as well as the juggler Fox had seen on the Shavids' first day in the valley. Mindi was dismissed, and Radda began making introductions.

"James you probably already know," said Radda, gesturing to the young player. James bowed with a flourish, making the woman roll her eyes.

"He's a show-off and a lazy lout," she said, "but a decent player, I'll give him that." She offered her hand. "Belle. We weren't properly introduced before."

They shook hands, and Radda said, "And that's Tallac, our Acrobat Extraordinaire! He juggles, he tumbles, he climbs things ..."

"They just keep me around for the food," the juggler said, shaking Fox's hand as well. "Best cook in the company, and they all know it."

Radda laughed and waved off the comment. Then he clapped his hands together and said, "Now! To business." He motioned for Fox to sit in an empty chair and continued. "When Shavid children are growing up, they are exposed to a wide set of skills. Sooner or later, their Blessing will manifest itself. They'll start showing proficiencies at one or more talents. But with the Windkissed, it can be much more complicated. They can come to us at any age. And with you in particular, exposed to no specific Shavid gift in your lifetime, we have no way of knowing where your talents lie. And so, it's our job to find out. Assuming you'd still like to learn?"

"Yes!" said Fox at once. "Yes, of course!"

Radda laughed at his clear enthusiasm and said, "Well then, so we begin."

They started Fox with the most common gifts. They let him play around with some of Radda's instruments: the flute, the lyre, and even one of the small drums. And whereas he wasn't terrible, and even Radda agreed he might learn them one day, none of them seemed to be his forte. And Fox felt nothing other than awkward confusion as he tried to play each one in turn.

Next, Belle taught him a simple dance routine. It was nothing like the dances they did in Thicca Valley, and Fox found himself stumbling over his own feet. In the corner of the room, James tried to hide his laugh in his hands. When it was James' turn, he determined at once that the stage was *not* Fox's Blessing, without even a trial. The others did not ask how James knew, but they seemed to accept it without question.

Tallac tried Fox in several different skills. He was impressed at Fox's surefootedness, and with the amount of flexibility and strength he'd picked up from the morning training sessions with Neil. He even admitted that someday, Fox might have a great talent for combat. But as a tumbler, he was nowhere near the skill of the Blessed.

But Radda was not discouraged. He arranged for new tests every day. He would send Mindi or he would come and find Fox himself, stealing him away from his chores and running him through every Shavid skill he could think of. He tried painting with Radda's wife, Adelai. Mask-making and storytelling with Donlan. Even Mindi tested him, looking for signs of the simple household magics. And with every failed or rejected skill, Radda became more and more excited.

"Don't you see?" said Radda. "It's in there, somewhere. We just have to find it! And we've tested all of the common Shavid skills."

"So?" asked Fox, trying not to feel disheartened. "What does that mean?"

"It *means*," said Radda, with the air of a child excited to play with a new trinket, "that your gift must be more *un*common! Your Blessing is rare, and that could mean great things for you!"

"If we ever figure out what it is," said Fox gloomily. And then, after a moment, he voiced a concern that had been nagging at him for several days. "What if I'm not Windkissed after all? What if it's just like Father says ... a tracker's nose and a hunter's instinct?"

Radda shook his head. "I've seen magic in all its forms, little one," he said. "And you've got it." He put his arm around Fox's shoulders in a fatherly manner. "I can see it in you! I can *feel* it!" When Fox was still unconvinced, Radda said, "This land still has magic. But nobody has the ability to harness it! Except *you*."

As Fox trudged back to his chores, waiting for Radda to find yet another test for him, he thought about it. Was that so impossible to believe? Could that be the real curse of Sovesta, that magic still lived and breathed in the air and the earth, but nobody could use it anymore? Neil would know. He had studied magic theory, and he could explain it to Fox. For now, Neil was busy helping with the cleanup of the valley, but when he had a chance, Fox intended to ask him.

But that chance was torn away that very night. Fox awoke from a deep sleep, suddenly and completely. He was dressing and hurrying silently out of the house before he even realized what he was doing. His feet took him running along the main road to the Shavid camp, where the wagons stood, being loaded up. They had been repainted and the damages from the storm had been repaired. Horses were being hitched up as Fox watched.

Neil found him first. Before he could speak, Fox said dazedly, "You're leaving?"

His friend nodded. "That's the way of the wind. Radda woke us all, said our time here was done."

Fox was seized by a sudden urge to stow away in one of the wagons. To go with them, wherever they were heading. Not for the first time, Neil seemed to know Fox's thoughts. "Radda says it's not time."

"I can find him," said Fox desperately. "I can ask ... maybe my parents will let me ..."

Neil held up his hand, silencing Fox's panicked spouting. "He says soon, but not now."

There was a whistle from the camp. The last crates were being loaded into the wagons, and Neil was being summoned. "I have to go," he said quickly. And for a moment, he looked like he wanted to say more. But he pulled Fox into a rough hug, and ruffled his hair. Almost like a brother might. And then he left, calling over his shoulder, "Look for us when the wind changes!"

And then they were gone. Fox watched as the wagons rolled out of town, out past the farmlands and north, deeper into Sovesta. He watched until he could no longer see their garish wheels, no longer hear the jangle of bells on the harnesses. And then, he closed his eyes, breathed deep, and felt them leaving. The scent of foreign spices and ink drifting away, and the sound of their distant travel songs disappearing into the night.

Chapter Eleven

Dreamed

The days grew warmer. The Mudlock finally ended, and warm sunshine greeted Fox each morning as he settled into the season's routine. From now until late summer, the whole valley would be buzzing with activity from sunup to sundown. Farmers tended their fields and goat-herders could be found on the upper hills with their charges. The Five Sides was constantly busy with passing trade. Father spent the early spring rigging up fresh snares in the outer forest and helping Mother with their small garden. And Fox, more than happy to keep himself busy, spent his days running all over Thicca Valley, taking over the trading end of Father's business while his parents enjoyed each other's company.

This year, more than ever, Fox was eager to stay occupied. The sudden absence of the Shavid in his life had left him with a strange sense of discomfort. He constantly felt as though he was forgetting to do something important. He found himself performing the same chores over and over, and looking for things he hadn't actually lost.

Neil said they'd be back. They *had* to come back. And "soon." But when was soon? At first, Fox looked for them every morning at sunup, and every night before he headed home again. Searching for a sign of them on the horizon, and listening for their distant melodies. But eventually, as the days wore on with no hint on the wind of the Shavid's return, Fox made himself focus instead on the springtime. This was *his* year, after all. This was the time to prove to Father that he would be ready for the caravan, and to take his place with the waresmen.

Not everything had been traded away during the Homecoming. And there were always leftover pelts from the caravan. Some mornings, Fox would take his wares to the Five Sides and set up in the corner like Father, bartering with the out of town traders and merchants. Other times, he would go straight to the farmer's wives, taking orders and trading whatever they could spare. The women in town were always eager for the finer quality goods that the waresmen collected, and Father always managed to pull in some luxury items during the journey.

But while the valley folk were plenty cordial with Fox, he couldn't help but notice they seemed to be looking at him differently. None of them knew the whole story of the Desolata attack, but it was clear that they knew he'd been involved. Eyes shifted to him when he walked by, and whispers followed him around town.

If anyone could understand, it was Picck. With Neil gone, Fox found himself confiding more than ever in Lai's cousin. When the stares of the community would become too much to handle, he would hide away in the Five Sides kitchen.

Of course, Picck was not always the good company he used to be. He tried hard to be his old, carefree self, but Fox could tell that the storm still haunted him. Whenever the conversation lagged, or he was left alone too long with nothing to do, Picck would begin to shake. Sometimes just a subtle tremor in his hands, sometimes as bad as a spring fever. His eyes would go blank, and nothing and no one could pull him from his mood.

Except Rose. A well-timed peck on the forehead could clear his expression. Even just her voice seemed to soothe him. With her by his side, Picck regained some of his old spark and humor. Sometimes, Fox stayed in the kitchen just to watch them, feeling a strange sort of pride for his part in having brought the two together.

"They really fit, don't they?" asked Lai one morning, as they both sat by the kitchen fire, watching the happy couple from the corners of their eyes. Picck was brushing flour from Rose's cheeks with a gentle and loving hand, laughing in the way he only did when she was around.

"My parents get like that sometimes," said Fox. "After Father's been gone all winter." He smiled, remembering. "Father told me once that he'd gladly trade all the pelts in the world just to see her smile."

Lai dropped her gaze. She suddenly seemed to be very interested in the stonework of the fireplace. Fox watched her trace the grooves with her fingertips. It wasn't until Picck and Rose left, heading out together into the kitchen courtyard, that she answered Fox's unasked question. "I sometimes wonder if Daddy was ever like that. If he was the type of man who loves to see his wife at the end of a long day, like your dad. Or if he was like the miners who come here to drink sometimes, just because they don't want to go home."

Fox knew the type. Men who'd been forced into marriages where neither party was happy with the arrangement. Theirs were the wives who brought passing merchants into their homes while their husbands were out, or ran away with men from other towns, hoping to find a better life. It was hard to imagine any woman wanting to run away from Borric Blackroot. He was a loving father, and a kind-hearted man. Then again, none of them had ever seen him courting.

"We have this old loom of mama's, down in the store room," Lai continued. It was as though she was making herself talk about it, saying things she'd wanted to say before, but never could. "I sometimes like to sit down there and look at it, try to figure out the workings. But it's not like fishing or plucking the hens, or even like making pies. It doesn't come natural to me."

Fox was stunned. He had never thought of Lai as missing something. She and Borric made the perfect little family, just the way they were. But as he watched her, wiping her sooty hands on her breeches, something hit home for him. She wasn't just talking about her father. She was talking about herself. She didn't have any of the skills that made her a marketable bride. With no mother to teach her, she couldn't even mend a pair of breeches, or sew on a button. Borric taught her what she needed to survive, but he'd never thought to teach her what it meant to be a valley woman.

"Lessons?" Fox suggested hopefully. "Maybe one of the women in town could teach you how to —"

"With what spare time?" asked Lai. "Besides, I have nothing to pay anyone with. What would I trade for my schooling, free brew? That only works on the men."

Lai tried to change the subject after that, but Fox kept revisiting the conversation for days afterwards. Always wondering, as he went about his work, what he could do to help.

The answer came to him as he traded with Widow Mossgrove. Her husband and oldest son had both been killed in the Desolata attack. But as Fox sat with her on her porch, helping her peel potatoes, he was happy to discover that she wasn't looking at him like it was his fault. In fact, she didn't seem upset by the tragedy at all, instead carrying on in an entirely businesslike way.

"It's no surprise, you know," she said. "Folk in this valley lead a hard life, even without outside trouble. Cave-ins, winter fevers, accidents on icy mountain paths. There's more widows than me who have spent their whole lives prepared to be alone. I've still got the little ones at home, and who would take care of them if I let myself go to pieces? And who would look after the farm?" She shook her head, attacking the peel of a large and lumpy potato with her bone-handle knife.

Fox finished his own potato and selected another. "How are you handling it? The farm work?"

"It's not easy," said Widow Mossgrove. "I've had to sell off almost all of the goats. We've only three left now. I would have sold off the shepherding dog as well but," she cleared her throat, "she was my husband's, you know. And the children would pine after her, if she were gone." The briefest hint of a tear shone in the corner of Widow Mossgrove's eye. Fox pretended not to notice as she carried on brusquely. "We'll manage. Just got to find a way to hire out some extra hands, help tend to the animals and the land."

Before he knew what he was saying, before he was even aware that the idea had formed in his head, Fox said, "You know my friend Lai? Borric Blackroot's daughter?"

Widow Mossgrove smiled. "Course I do, she's a right pretty girl. And kind as summer sun to my little ones."

"She's very good with animals, and she can even work the land! Just as good as any boy her age."

The older woman frowned. "A bit of help here and there is all well and good, but ..."

"And she wouldn't need paying," said Fox, before Widow Mossgrove could entirely refuse. "She could work, in exchange for lessons. Lessons in women's work, like the loom and sewing and ... and whatever else women do!"

He worried for a moment that he might have gone too far. Some women in the valley, his own mother included, got very touchy about "women's work." One of the biggest fights Fox could ever remember his parents getting into was after Father, tired and cranky after an unsuccessful week on the road, suggested that women never truly worked as hard as men.

But Widow Mossgrove didn't look offended. Instead, she smiled appraisingly at Fox. "You drive a hard bargain, just like your father. He'll make a fine trader out of you."

"Thank you, ma'am," said Fox politely.

"You tell your friend I'll see her at noon, starting tomorrow. Now, are we to sit here chatting all day, or are you going to help me finish these potatoes?"

SPRING WILDFLOWERS blanketed the mountainsides. Countless shades of green dripped from the forest leaves and fresh new grasses. A blithe breeze flitted through the valley, tugging at women's dresses and children's hair like an old friend, just wanting to play. New moss crept its way across rocks and up tree trunks. Shoes were all but abandoned by the younger Thiccans, and some of the elder ones as well. The season of weddings was upon them.

It seemed almost impossible that mere weeks ago, the valley had suffered an unprecedented tragedy. Now, as Fox sat high up on a hillside, watching great wedding tents being erected in the valley below, even he found it hard to remember that he had once been trapped in a hunting cabin, facing certain death. For now, there was a celebration of new life. A wedding day, where the five new couples of Thicca Valley would begin their lives anew.

Beside him, Lai worked furiously at a hand-held loom. A smaller version of the loom Widow Mossgrove had been teaching her on. Her lessons were not coming easily, but that didn't stop her. With a determined stubbornness that Fox was amazed at, Lai spent every free moment practicing. Borric said he'd discovered her up late at night, long after she was supposed to be asleep, crouched by the dying firelight in the kitchen, trying to stitch holes in dish rags and old shirts. The times she was not learning at the widow's side, she was working. For the widow, or her father. Today, like many other days, found her watching the goats up on the eastern foothills. She was often put in charge of Widow Mossgrove's small remaining herd, as well as the sturdy little brown pony that grazed with them. She even brought Fermia out to graze with them, which seemed to perk up the old nanny goat's spirits.

"Lai," said Fox, nudging her and pointing down to the valley. "They're hanging the lanterns, look!" Normally, the wedding preparations would fascinate and excite her. Especially since her own cousin was among those to be married. But now, she didn't tear her eyes away from the knot of tangled thread in her lap.

Then, with an exasperated yell, Lai threw the loom so hard that it shattered on a nearby stone. "I can't *do* it!" she shouted, scaring the goats and making them scatter across the hillside. And then, for good measure it seemed, she stood up and grabbed the broken pieces, then hurled them even further.

Even as Fox tried to comfort her, he struggled hard not to laugh. "You'll get it," he said carefully. "And there's no rush, honest!"

But Lai didn't seem to hear him. She grabbed her shepherd's crook and started rounding the animals up again, ushering them closer to her and Fox's perch. As she worked, Fox plucked an apple from the basket lunch Picck had sent them off with and bit into it. Cold, sticky juices ran down his chin, and he wiped them off with the back of his hand as he watched the fields below coming to life with party preparations.

Fox had heard plenty of stories about other wedding traditions. Binding ceremonies from the deserts; deep jungle rituals involving live snakes; even the glorious spectacle surrounding so many royal weddings in the Central Continent. But while they all sounded fascinating, Fox preferred Thicca Valley's above them all. It was simple, a celebration more than a ceremony. All of the couples were married at once, promising their lives to each other.

Lai sat down beside him again with a thud, tossing her crook aside and then laying back on the grass. After a moment of silence, Fox said, "You know, your loom will be harder to work with in pieces like that."

In spite of herself, it seemed, Lai laughed. It was half-hearted and tired, but it was still a laugh. "I don't know why I can't manage it," she said.

"I don't know why you *care*," said Fox. "So there's one thing in the world you can't do. You're great at everything else you try! The sewing is coming along, and Widow Mossgrove says you're excellent with her children. They love having you around."

Lai tucked her hands behind her head and stared up at the thick, white clouds. "I just always pictured my mother, sitting at home weaving. Making blankets and tapestries and ... I thought if I could just do it, then maybe I'd have something in common with her." And then, before Fox had a chance to comment, she sat up on her elbows and changed the subject. "Only two days until the wedding. And then what? Rose moves in, and hopefully Pick goes back to his normal self all the time."

Fox finished his apple and tossed the naked core away. "Father's got the whole summer planned for us. Traveling to neighboring valleys and towns, learning the trading circles. It's my time to prove I have what it takes to be a Foxglove."

They watched in silence as bright banners were strung from the high tent poles, bringing the wedding pavilion to life with wind-tossed color. Then Lai said, "In a few years, it'll be us down there. My daddy will have set me up with someone, and you'll have won the hand of somebody's daughter." She shifted, absently plucking at the blades of grass beneath her. "I always used to think it was so far away, being grown up. But you're learning to be a man, and I'm practicing my womanly trades ... doesn't seem so far off now."

A lone wedding banner pulled loose from its hangings and was borne away on the wind. It danced upward, a scrap of purple like fresh brambleberry, flapping back and forth like a confused bird. Finally, the wind carried it up toward them. It drifted over their heads and then settled to earth, hidden away somewhere in the foothills.

Fox stood and grabbed Lai's hand, pulling her to her feet. "I'm not quite a man yet," he said. "A man would be polite, and let the lady get a head start." And then, he took off, running to search for the fallen flag. And Lai, laughing and calling him names, chased after him.

THE NIGHT BEFORE THE wedding was still and clear. Not a single breath of wind so much as rustled the trees. The sky was cloudless, letting the half moon bathe the town in light, casting harsh black shadows over everything. All was grey and eerily quiet.

Fox sat up late into the night at the Five Sides, helping the Blackroots prepare for the morning. Not only was Picck one of the grooms, he was also the chief baker for the party. The kitchen was filled with cakes and pies and sweet rolls. Rose was there too, laughing and singing as she helped decorate the sweets. Borric and Lai were enjoying themselves as well, but Fox could not. There was a restlessness about him that he could not shake.

He'd grown used to the feeling that he was forgetting something. He'd even found that keeping busy could help him ignore it almost completely. And then there were the nerves; the horrible, twitching feeling of waiting for something he couldn't put his finger on. That, too, could be pushed to the back of his mind. The combat practices Neil had taught him kept his mind and body occupied. The errands for Father. Even helping with the wedding. All were perfect ways to keep him from going absolutely stark-raving mad. But this was something new.

When he quietly excused himself to go home, no one seemed to notice. And when he stepped outside into the still and empty night, the feeling worsened. He ran home without knowing what he was running from, and threw himself into bed fully dressed. He pulled the blankets all the way up over his head, shutting out even the comforting glow of the firestones, and tried to force himself to sleep. Any sleep, no matter how fitful and uneasy, had to be better than this.

He was wrong.

IT WAS AS THOUGH THE dream was being pieced together around him. As though Fox had been dropped into an unfinished painting, and somewhere, an unseen artist was busily streaking colors across a wooden panel. He was sitting alone in a small wooden boat, surrounded by thick, grey fog. The boat rowed itself silently, taking Fox somewhere only it seemed to know. Bit by bit, things began to come into focus as the fog cleared. He became aware of the sea, slapping against the sides of his boat. He'd never been to the ocean, but he knew it at once from the smell and the sheer vastness of it. It was bigger than the biggest lake he'd ever seen. Bigger even than Fox could have imagined from Radda's tales of sailing adventures. On and on it went, stretching out as far as the eye could see, in every direction. Here, the sky was not just above him, framed by the mountain peaks, but all around him. He felt sure that if he kept sailing long enough, he would someday reach the place where sky and sea met.

Shadows in the distance began to take shape. Great masses of grey became islands. Enormous black smudges on the horizon revealed themselves to be cliffs. And there was something else. A tangle of shapes far ahead that the little boat seemed to be aiming for. Shapes that became clear as Fox drifted into their shadows.

Ships. Countless, abandoned ships, towering above Fox in his tiny wooden boat. Some were whole, complete masterpieces, stunning in their grandeur. Others were splintering, rotting shells. It was like the forest after a blizzard, with some trees sturdy and upright, others reduced to firewood and scrap. Fox struggled to remember the few names of ship parts he knew. Masts, the tall poles at a ship's center. And sails. And ... he stopped trying, and simply stared. Even in their ruin, the ships were beautiful. He could hear their wood creak in a lonely, abandoned way, and he longed to climb aboard one of them and explore. But his boat carried him on, through the depths of the watery graveyard, to an island deep in its heart. An island with high cliffs, and lush green rippling across the black stone peaks.

There, the boat stopped, just off the shore. Fox climbed out, wading in the shallows up to his ankles before climbing out onto the sand and looking around. The beach stretched to either side for a good number of paces, until it curved out of sight. Ahead of him, there was a ... the word that sprang to mind was "jungle," although he'd never seen one. It grew thick, filled with trees he didn't recognize, and hid the rest of the island from him. And, lounging casually in the sand, his booted feet propped up on what looked like a gigantic turtle's shell, was a man.

He sat up as Fox approached, and then sprang up, dusting sand from his bottom. "Excellent," he said. "You're finally here." And then, without so much as an inviting gesture, he turned and headed off into the forest. And Fox, without any idea of what else to do, followed.

The man was wearing colors to rival even the Shavid's costumes. His vest was deep purple with dark green trim. His breeches were a rich brown that almost seemed green when the light hit it. They were woven in with shimmering golden thread, and tucked into knee-high, supple burgundy boots. His shirt, with its billowing sleeves and decorative cuffs, was a few shades lighter green than the vest trim. A red-and-purple striped sash hung from his hip, and his long black hair was pulled back with a beaded ribbon. His colors might have been dark and earthy, but they were somehow richer than the brightest yellows and blues of the Shavid wagons. Richer even than the multi-colored hibbin furs.

"Sorry about the mess getting you here," said the man as he led them deeper into the jungle. "But you, sir, are a hard one to get in touch with."

"And why would you want to get in touch with me?" asked Fox. He struggled to keep up, fighting his way through the thick greenery, and resisting the urge to stop and look around in awe. He felt that if he fell behind, he would be lost in this strange place forever. Everything was so real, so much clearer than any dream Fox had ever had. So real, in fact, that he wasn't sure if he was even dreaming any more. Maybe he really had been transported to a faraway island, never to return home.

The man didn't answer his question. Instead he kept up a steady monologue, which confused Fox even more. "Oh, if you only knew how much trouble it took to bring you here," the man said. "I've had to call in favors, pay bribes. I've had to pull strings I shouldn't even be allowed to *touch*!" He sounded almost proud of himself. "But the wind keeps an eye on her Blessed, and you've got more watchdogs than anyone I've ever seen! You must be something special. Special indeed."

He pulled aside a curtain of vines with a flourish, exposing the great mouth of a cave set into the black rock. Fox went in first, and the man followed, letting the vines fall back into place behind him with a *hush*. And then, taking the lead once more and leading them down a wide tunnel, the man said, "If you'd come here in the waking world, you'd have to take the other way to get in. Much longer, and much more treacherous. Beautiful scenery, though."

Even in his awe and confusion, Fox couldn't help but notice the stone around him. He didn't recognize it. And the part of him that had grown up around miners his whole life was insatiably curious. The stone was black, rippled with veins of some sort of green that, upon closer inspection, seemed to be glowing faintly. And Fox knew enough about stone that he was fairly certain this tunnel was not manmade. He reached out a hand in passing and ran his fingers across the wall. It was cold to the touch, and smoother than cut stone.

"Where are we?" Fox asked.

"The only place in all the worlds where they can't find me," said the man.

They rounded a corner, and Fox stopped in his tracks. The tunnel opened up into a tremendous, open cavern, filled with color and patterned light from dozens of lanterns hanging throughout the room. A lake was tucked in the far corner, and even it seemed to be glowing from somewhere deep in its depths.

Everywhere Fox looked, treasures met his eyes. Great jeweled cups and platters. Chains of gold and silver. Open chests, spilling out coins Fox didn't recognize. There were gems he couldn't name, and furs from creatures he'd never seen. Great cushions lay scattered throughout the cavern, in colors brighter even than the Shavid's wagons. The stranger flopped down casually onto one of these, producing an apple seemingly from nowhere and biting into it.

"Make yourself at home!" he said, propping his feet up on an opulently carved, gem-encrusted chest.

Fox sat gingerly on a stack of rugs. They were softer than any weaving he'd ever seen at home, with intricate patterns and thick, colored fringe dripping from the edges.

"The riches of a thousand lifetimes," said the stranger proudly. "From every age of men. And even those who are more than men." He closed his hand around the half-naked apple core, and it vanished, as simply and silently as a traveling magician made coins disappear. Then, the stranger wiped his hands on the front of his vest and tucked them behind his head, lounging comfortably as he looked Fox up and down. "So, to business."

"You said you brought me here," said Fox. "Why?"

The man chuckled. "You get straight to the point. I like that about you, boy." He studied Fox appraisingly. "You really are a little scrap of a thing, aren't you? But, size doesn't always guarantee power. And you'll have to do." And then, before Fox could ask any questions, or even have a chance to feel properly angry over being called a "little scrap," the man said, "It's not enough. Everything you're doing now, it's not enough."

"Beg pardon?" said Fox, not sure whether to be confused or offended.

The man pulled his feet down from the chest and sat up, looking Fox straight in the eye. There was something so oddly familiar about the man's face. A close-cut beard and moustache framed his mouth like the curtains on a Shavid stage. No one in Thicca Valley ever kept their whiskers that trim, but still ... it was as if Fox had grown up his entire life with this stranger right next door, but had simply never spoken to him before now.

"It is not *enough*," the man said, slower this time. More precise. Almost as if he was trying to convey something more than just the words. "You are meant for more than weddings and spring chores, you know that." When Fox didn't answer, the man sighed and shook his head. "I can't keep you here for long, this kind of power is costing me. And if they catch me ..." He seemed to be at war with himself, fighting over choices that Fox couldn't understand. Finally, apparently coming to a decision, the man sprang over to Fox and took his head between his hands, staring the boy squarely in the face. "Listen. I'll have to spell it out for you as best I can."

Fox couldn't pull away. He was rendered completely immobile by the man's touch. And so he listened, for he had no other choice.

"You have to take what you know and *run* with it!" said the man. "Everything you need, right now, you already have. And you, of all the Blessed in the world, can not take this time for granted." He closed his eyes briefly, as though what he was about to say caused him great pain. Then he opened them again, staring straight at Fox with his astonishingly deep eyes. "There will come a time, sooner rather than later, when your gifts could save not only your life, but the lives of those you love. How much more blood do you want on your hands? You already have a lifetime's worth ahead of you."

He let go, and Fox could breathe. He pulled himself away, scrambling as far back on his pile of rugs as he could, scrubbing at his face with his hands. His jaw and ears were painfully cold where the stranger had touched him. His mind was reeling, and he didn't know what to ask first. Finally, when he regained control of his tongue, he said quietly, almost frightened of the answer, "This is real, isn't it?" And though the man did not answer, Fox knew. Then after a moment he said, "Tell me what to do."

"You are Windkissed," said the man. "So *listen to the wind.*"

As Fox began to feel himself pulled away from the dream, sure he was beginning to wake, he said, "Why do you care? About me, or my gift?"

Something of a smile played around the man's mouth, and again Fox felt that surge of familiarity. "We all have our reasons, lad," he said.

It was only when Fox awoke that he realized he'd never asked the man who he was. And then, just as he thought it, he was somehow sure that he didn't want to know.

FOX WATCHED THE WEDDING ceremony without really seeing it. He clapped when everyone else did, and came out of his reverie enough to notice that Picck and Rose seemed to be the most genuinely happy out of all five couples. He did his best to enjoy the festivities afterwards, eating whatever was handed to him, dancing with Lai. But behind his forced smile, his mind was hard at work. Reliving his dream over and over. For, unlike most dreams that melted like morning frost at sunrise, this one haunted him. He could remember every detail, every word.

And he remembered the warning. About saving those he loved. He watched Lai, dancing in the circle across from him, and felt an ice cold grip tighten around his heart. Who more might be lost because of him? And how many more tragedies were waiting in his path?

Three days after the wedding, the Foxglove men set out for the first of many hunting trips. This time, they would be heading out to the site of Fox's battle with the Desolata. Here, at least, Fox had a guide. Someone to teach him how to be a skillful trapper and woodsman. But to learn about his Blessing? He had no idea where to begin.

Chapter Twelve
Whitethorn

There was a simplicity to Father's teaching methods. You ate what you trapped. And if you couldn't trap anything, you didn't eat. "The woods are full of life," he said. "Not just the lives of the beasts, but the ability to give life to us. You learn how to use it, every piece of it, to survive."

"So, what do I do?" asked Fox.

Father settled in with his back against the hillside, his feet propped up on a stump. He pulled out his knife and began to whittle at a scrap of wood. "I guess we'll find out," he said.

That first night, Fox caught nothing larger than a squirrel. It wasn't nearly enough to keep him fed, and his stomach protested loudly, making him toss and turn all night. Father, however, seemed to have caught an entire basket of fish and a beaver while Fox was working, and ate heartily.

The next day, Fox was a bit more careful. He blamed his initial excitement at finally being treated like a man, as well as the constant distraction of the island dream, for his abysmal performance the previous evening. Today, he took his time in setting traps, and then settled himself down at the river's edge, about a mile from the cabin, and began hunting for mussels. When, in the late afternoon, he returned to Father's side with his pockets full of mussels and two large grey weasels hanging over his shoulder, Father looked him up and down, and nodded in approval.

Fox had helped Father with the trapping countless times. He'd grown up tagging along on the shorter trapping trips, and clinging to the doorframe of Father's workshop long after he was supposed to be in bed, watching him work. The care and maintenance of the traps fell to him during the winter months, and Fox felt he was more than qualified as an apprentice. But then, it had always been at Father's bidding. They laid traps where Father said, and Fox was merely an assistant. Now, it was up to Fox to make the calls. And Father watched silently. He made repairs on the cabin or whittled or took long naps in the sun while Fox set a cooking fire and began to skin his weasels.

It was early on the morning of the third day, as Fox went out to check the snares, that an idea occurred to him. An idea so strangely simple, he couldn't believe he hadn't thought of it before. He picked up his pace and hurried off deeper into the woods, until finally he stopped in the center of a small ring of trees. It was right near the heart of this piece of trapping territory. Fox sat on the sun-dappled forest floor and closed his eyes. He breathed slowly and carefully, taking in every little noise of the forest around him. He could hear the river not far away, gurgling and splashing over rocks as it wound through the trees. Buzzing insects filled the air around him, enjoying the spring blooms. He could hear clearly the things that were close. And then, he breathed deep.

There it was. The now-familiar and overwhelming cascade of smells and sounds. They made his head ring, but he focused hard. And the pieces became clearer. From a mile north, a family of otters playing on the riverbank. Two miles to the east, a buck scraping his antlers against a tree, shaking leaves to the ground in a shower of fresh green. Father, back at the cabin, chopping wood.

When Fox opened his eyes, he was flat on his back. He sat up, rubbing the back of his head tenderly. If that was going to keep happening every time he experimented with his powers, he would have to start doing so lying down. Then he scrambled to his feet, dusting off the grass and leaves that clung to his clothes, and set off north. While the buck was a tempting find, the otters would be much easier to bring back to the cabin on his own. As he hiked, he smiled to himself. How fine would it be to hunt after a sure thing, rather than always looking for tracks and signs and waiting?

Father looked stunned when Fox came strutting back into view just before midday with not only three otters hanging across his shoulders, but holding a large rabbit proudly by its hind legs, its ears dragging on the ground. Fox tried not to look too pleased with himself as he started skinning the day's catch. Then, for the first time since their arrival at the cabin, Father began to help. He set the fire and began tending it as Fox carefully began slitting the first otter along its stomach. And then, Father began to talk. He talked, Fox was interested to note, not as a father would to a son, but as a man would to a fellow trapper. He did not give direct advice, but instead talked as he might to an equal. However, there were gems of wisdom tucked into his conversation, and Fox stored them away in his mind. He adjusted his technique as Father talked, taking in the unsolicited but extremely welcome tips on how to keep the meat from spoiling, or how to get the most use from a pelt.

They worked as long as the light held out, scraping clean the four hides together. Then they hung the pelts to dry and feasted on a stew Father had made from the hare meat. All the while, the otter meat was smoked on a line over the fire, sending tantalizing scents out into the trees and making Fox's mouth water. And he wasn't the only one. He could feel the wolves growing closer. Through smell or sound, he wasn't sure, but he knew they were there. Just outside the cabin's line of vision. But once again, Fox was not afraid of them. And he kept their presence to himself. But before they turned in for the night, Fox was careful to drop a handful of otter strips on the ground outside the cabin. It was his own private thank you to the wolves, for their help in disposing of the Desolata.

That night, after Father had fallen asleep, Fox rummaged silently around in the cabin gear for something to write on. He found a scrap of old parchment wrapping, the type Father sometimes used to package up his smaller wares before the caravan. Fox crawled back to the fireside where he slept, and rescued a small, charcoal-blackened stick from the fireplace. Then, he started to scribble down everything he knew about his Blessing.

He was one of the few children in Thicca Valley who could read. He'd picked it up quickly as a young boy, scanning the notes on Father's trading papers. Lists of what people wanted, and who was willing to pay. Mother said it was uncanny how fast Fox managed to learn sometimes. Father said it was the gift of a natural trapper.

Fox wrote quickly, scratching out a few simple sentences. He wrote everything he could remember about his recent experiences with breathing. And, he supposed, with the wind. Then he sat back and re-read his scrap of parchment. His own personal learning text. Then he folded it up and tucked it carefully inside his vest, right next to the green hibbin fur he still carried. And somewhere, he knew, the strange man from his dream was smiling with satisfaction.

TWO MORE HUNTING TRIPS followed, each one taking them farther out into Father's trapping territory. And Fox, practicing more and more with his gifts to find game, was bringing in more each day than Father had ever expected.

He allowed himself to swell with pride a bit as Father said this winter would be their best caravan in years. And as they talked each evening while they smoked deer meat and settled into the long, messy process of tanning hides, Fox clung to the advice that Father spouted off, often cleverly disguised as stories. By the end of their third trip, the news had spread to the whole valley: the young Foxglove would be joining his Father on the caravan this year. He was becoming a man.

"Of course you are," said Lai when he told her. "I *knew* you'd be allowed to go this year!"

They were sitting in the back kitchen garden, shelling peas and letting Fermia nuzzle at their feet. Since the wedding, it had been increasingly difficult to find time together. Lai was kept busy with Widow Mossgrove, and Fox was out on the trails and in the woods. But whenever they caught a moment, they would fall eagerly back to their old habits. They helped out at the Five Sides or else spent all day up to their knees in the river, fishing and digging up mussels and roots.

Fox was partial to hanging out at the tavern these days. Not only because it made him feel at home, but because he loved to watch Picck and Rose. They had settled wonderfully into their new life together. Picck no longer slept on a mat beside the fireplace, but instead in their new suite of rooms upstairs, at the far corner of the Five Sides. He was smiling again, and you could often hear him and Rose singing from the kitchen as they worked. The sound of their mingled voices made Fox feel warm as summer midday. Today was no different. The back kitchen door was propped open, and they could hear Rose and Picck talking and laughing, and every now and then they caught a whirl of color as the couple danced across the room.

They were every bit as playful and loving as they had been on the wedding day.

"You know," said Fox thoughtfully, "it's a good thing Picck never was a miner. I don't believe that woman could survive a whole hour without him."

Lai giggled, and then added, "Dream save us if he ever became a *waresman*! All winter apart?"

Fox rolled his eyes. "There'd be more weeping than in one of Radda's tragic plays."

They laughed over this for awhile, and then Lai said, "Speaking of the winter, how's your mum taking it? Both her men being gone for the caravan?"

Fox shrugged. "She's not. She says she doesn't have to worry about it for another four months. But I expect she'll be a mess." Then he smiled and said, "But then, I won't be here to have to worry about it!" And, putting on a fake, overly-proper voice like some of the older women in town spoke in, he said, "Be a dear and pop in on her for me, won't you?"

Lai laughed and threw a handful of peas at him. "I hope they sell you for room and board" she said. "It'd serve you right."

A breeze tugged at Fox's hair and shirt collar, and he could hear talk from inside the tavern as clearly as though the speakers were sitting beside him. He listened for a moment as a traveling waresman exchanged news with the Hatcher suitor who had won Filia Beckweed. He could hear their conversation long enough to gather that they knew each other, before the wind whipped the sound away from his ear again. He shook his head to clear it, and noticed Lai watching him.

"What was it this time?" she asked.

"Talk from inside. One of the new ones, Filia's husband."

"Rale," Lai supplied helpfully.

"Yes," said Fox. "And a waresman. From his voice, it sounded like the man who came in selling that fancy wine. Sounds like they might be from the same parts." He hesitated, then voiced a concern that had been on his mind quite a lot lately. "What if it's going to be like this forever? Just bits and pieces of things on the wind I can't control?"

He had told Lai all about his experiments with using his gifts. "Listening to the wind," as the dream stranger had suggested. She'd seen Fox's little scrap of parchment where he took notes, and though she couldn't read it, she knew he was taking his studies very seriously. Fox had not, however, told her about the dream itself. Instead, he made it sound like he'd simply decided to take on his own learning. To discover how to work his gift, with or without the Shavid. Perhaps even to figure out *what* his Blessing truly was.

Lai frowned slightly. "Well, would it be so bad? I mean, it's dead useful, right?"

"When it works," said Fox. He'd discovered that, through no change in his own behavior, there were times when his gift was stronger than others. Times when he could smell and hear only within the reach of his normal, albeit heightened, senses. And other times when he could *feel* things from miles away. Other cities, other towns. And no matter how many notes he took on the matter, there seemed to be no rhyme or reason to it.

Perhaps it was, as Neil had suggested, just the wind. He remembered the older boy commenting on the Shavid way of life. It was, just like the magic itself, unstable. There was often no telling where you'd be going or when, or how long you'd stay. That was the way of the wind. Fox could no more control his Blessing than he could tell the breeze to blow north. And without the Shavid to guide him, he had no way of knowing if they all experienced this. Or if it was just him. Set apart, once again, and different than all the rest.

But, Fox's determination never wavered. And while wind-borne rushes of sound and smell didn't truly disappear, Fox became more adept at ignoring them. Or paying them only the slightest bit of attention while focusing only on the ones that mattered; a fleeting sense of when or where his prey was going to be. Or the coming rain that might trap him and Father out in the middle of the woods.

Fox spent his fifteenth birthday in the valley, preparing for his first journey to a neighboring town for trade. It was two weeks into the summer, and he sat in the wide open doorway of his family's stable, barefooted with his breeches rolled up over his knee. He was making repairs on the family cart, and painting "Foxglove's Fine Furs" on the side, in fancy lettering like he'd seen on one of the Shavid wagons. He smelled Lai coming up the hill long before he saw her, and smiled. She had such a distinctive scent that he always knew it was her. Even when his senses weren't heightened. It was almost flowery, but not any kind of flower he'd ever smelled in the valley. And there was something else ... some warm and familiar scent he'd never been able to place.

When she reached him, she flopped down beside him and wrapped her arms in a tight hug about his neck, making him choke and sputter even as he laughed. When she let go, she said, "Happy birthday, you useless weed snake."

Fox shoved her playfully and thanked her, rubbing his neck where she'd squeezed him. Then Lai continued.

"Papa's got a special birthday dessert basket all set for you, only you'll have to go down to the inn and get it. The happy couple's got a gift for you as well, and they said you could pick it up whenever you come down. But I wanted to come up and give you *this.*" She pulled out a lumpy little bundle from the pocket of her dress and held it out eagerly.

It was some sort of woven cloth. Fox took it and began to lay it out flat. It was a scarf, clearly made by Lai's own hand. It was uneven and knotted in places, without any real semblance of a pattern, but it was clear that she was experimenting with changing colors. Fox counted no less than seven different shades. Green and brown and orange ... Lai was watching him carefully, and Fox beamed at her and wrapped it around his neck. It was surprisingly soft. "I love it," he said. And as he tossed the long end over his shoulder, something fell out of the folds of wool and hit the ground with a thud.

It was a book. A small, leatherbound volume. Fox bent to pick it up, dusting off the soft, dark walnut cover. He looked at Lai curiously, then flipped through it. The pages were blank.

"It's for all your writing," she said, almost shyly. "After you told me what you were trying to do, I traded for it. First chance I got."

Fox looked up at his best friend, seized almost overwhelmingly with the urge to tell her every bit of his dream. But though he still remembered each detail with a surreal perfection, he couldn't bring himself to do it. He did not want to see the look in her eyes when he told her that his path ahead, apparently, was filled with death and bloodshed. That his choices might save or condemn the people he loved. People like her.

Instead, Fox tucked the little brown book into his pocket and hugged her. Long and tight, more than he normally would have. He let her unique smells fill his nose before pulling away with a quiet thanks. Then, he got silently back to work. By the time Lai picked up a paintbrush and began to help, the moment had passed.

BORRIC'S BASKET OF treats was enough to last Fox for several days. There were sticky buns and little cakes, candies, bite-sized pies and Fox's favorite rosemary bread. Picck said he'd of course helped with the baking as well, but that he and Rose had their own gift to give him. It was wrapped in fine paper on the cutting table, and Fox opened it excitedly. And then he stopped in awe. Tucked inside the wrapping was the most beautiful set of hunting knives Fox had ever seen. They had black stone handles and thin, dark blades. There were four of them, and Fox lovingly hefted each of them in turn. One small, almost dainty-looking knife, perfect for skinning tricky little pelts. One that looked more like a dagger than anything. One dangerously curved knife with a thicker blade, almost like a small hatchet with a hooked end. And one large, clearly deadly weapon that looked as if it could cut straight through bone as effortlessly as a kitchen knife through bread.

Rose and Picck were smiling at him. And when Fox opened his mouth to thank them, Rose swooped in and kissed him on the cheek. "We owe you more than you can possibly know," she said quietly. "And we feel we can never truly repay you, but this is a start."

As Fox was climbing into his bed nook that night, warm and happy from his parents' birthday dinner, his gifts all laid out on top of his trunk, Fox could almost hear the man from his dreams, speaking to him. Reminding him of all the people he could lose if he didn't work harder. And Fox, sure he was already doing everything he could, slipped into a miserable and restless sleep.

FOX HAD SPENT HIS ENTIRE life in Thicca Valley and the surrounding woods. His farthest journey from home, before tracking with Father, had been one trip years ago, up onto the mountain road and into the untamed rock that surrounded it. The trip had not exactly been sanctioned by either of his parents. He hadn't gotten lost; he was never lost. But he *had* been keen on exploring as a small child, and hadn't given a scrap of thought to how his parents might react when they woke up in the morning to find him missing. It took them more than half a day to find him, happily climbing on and around the rock formations that he'd deemed his "castle." After that, the Foxglove parents kept a much closer eye on their son, until it seemed that he'd finally outgrown that dangerous phase of his life.

But it was with the eyes of a small child that Fox viewed the city of Whitethorn, his first true excursion into the world of trade. He wanted to look everywhere at once. He saw shops and inns and eating houses all crammed together like suckling piglets. So many he could not keep count. Colors blurred before his eyes as he tried to catch a glimpse inside shop windows. He kept one hand on the side of Cobb's harness to keep from getting lost in the crowds flooding the streets, but he was fighting the urge to simply run off and *touch* everything! He wanted to run his hands along the stone walls and feel the fine fabrics of ladies skirts. He wanted to taste the rich meats and fruit he smelled, and press his cheek against the cool glass of the tavern windows. And he wanted to climb, all the way up to the highest rooftop of the highest building in the city, look down upon the streets and the people and declare, "This is *mine*."

Father led them to one of the six inns that Fox had counted so far. It was a small, off-white building with a sign dubbing it "The Hatted Goat." Father left a coin with the proprietor, a short, plump little man who smiled jovially and welcomed them in. A stable boy was sent for to take care of Cobb, and then the innkeeper himself showed them to a tidy little room in the back.

There were two small beds, a washing station tucked in the corner, and a simple but sizable fireplace along the wall. Father took stock of the room, then set to work unpacking his bags.

"We'll send for the rest of the things from the wagon," he said as Fox drifted casually toward the window, trying to peek out at the city beyond.

"I'd like to get set up in the common room by supper, that's usually my best hours. Shame this city doesn't have a Nightmarket like Athilior or Sibica or ..." He trailed off, and Fox started, feeling guilty for being distracted during such an important part of his apprenticeship. But Father was smiling slightly. Then he sighed in resignation, although there was clear amusement in his attitude. "Or," he said, "since I'll be busy setting up here, you might take awhile and get to know the lay of the land. On a strictly professional level, of course."

Fox was out the door in an instant, pausing briefly to hug his laughing father. And then, as the room door clicked shut behind him, Fox scampered down the hall, through the common room, and out into the crowded, foreign streets of Whitethorn.

At every turn there was something new and exciting to see. Fox let his feet carry him where they liked, in and out of shops and down twisting alleys with drying laundry strung between buildings. He found shops that sold fine candles, and another devoted only to fabric. To think, there was a city so big and glamorous just five days from Thicca Valley. And the idea that there were even *grander* places farther south! In other countries, on *other* continents! There was a tingle along the back of Fox's neck, and a strange quickening in his heart. It was longing. Longing for a life on the road, with the wind as his guide. He stood in a shop window, watching all of the people milling about, and wondered how many of them had ever left their city. Then again, how many Thiccans had ever left theirs?

He wandered until the streets began to smell of suppertime. The late afternoon sun washed the city in orange and gold, and Fox found himself heading away from the bustling hub of the city, and into some of the quieter corners. He drifted past cozy little farmhouses and pastures. These, at least, were familiar to Fox. The goats might have been straight from Thicca Valley. The snug little cottages were surely built for hard winters. They might not have the same storms here in the flatlands as they had in the mountains – Fox wasn't sure of their weather patterns – but they were definitely sturdy, and made for warmth.

Fox chuckled to himself slightly, thinking of one of the Thiccan miners' jokes, describing their amply built wives in much the same way. It was a joke he had not understood as a young child, but in recent months he'd come to revel in the humor of men. He was, after all, going to be on the road with them each winter for the rest of his life. And the time when he would be considered their equal was, perhaps, not far off.

He started to make his way back to The Hatted Goat. As much as he would have loved to run all through the countryside, exploring each and every back alley and goat barn, he knew he was here to learn. He belonged at Father's side for now, learning to become the trader that everyone was so sure he could be. And so, turning his back on the farm-splattered flatlands, he returned to the heart of the city.

The streets had emptied considerably. Lanterns were being lit all down the main road, giving the shop fronts a comfortable glow. Fox watched as boys not much younger than himself scurried from post to post, climbing up on collapsible footstools or else on each other's shoulders to bring life to the rippling glass cases, taking care to light each individual wick until the lantern was full of dancing light. Fox's eyes followed one of the boys as he ran back down the street, crowing taunts to his fellows. Apparently, *his* lanterns had all been lit the quickest. The others called childish curses at him and quickened their own pace, and Fox's eye was caught by the littlest of the lamplighters. A small, mousy boy who often rode on a taller boy's shoulders to get his job done. Fox could tell that even with the footstool and the long stick with a flame on the end, this boy would simply be too small to reach.

He was a pale boy, with straw-colored hair and a thin dusting of freckles across his cheeks and forehead. As Fox watched, he stood with his bare feet perched easily on his companion's shoulders. He balanced expertly and lit the final lantern, then dropped to the ground like a cat, landing briefly on all fours before coming to his feet. The taller boy who'd been acting as his ladder waved a farewell and started off, presumably heading home for dinner. Two more boys joined him, leaving only the smaller boy. None of them seemed to have noticed Fox, tucked into the shadows of a glove-maker's doorway.

He watched as the straw-haired boy went off on his own, carrying the long pole over his shoulder and whistling carelessly. But after a moment, the boy turned back to watch his companions depart. Once they were out of sight, he quickly disappeared down a side alley and re-appeared moments later without his lighting stick. He glanced up and down the street, rubbing his nose with the back of his hand, and then scurried across the road to a well-lit bakery window. He pressed his nose to the glass. Fox could see that beautiful cakes and sweet rolls were displayed in the window, and even he found himself licking his lips at the sight of them. Then the boy sidled up to the door of the shop and knocked quietly. When no one answered, he knocked again, loud enough this time that Fox could hear it from his spot in the shadows, several buildings away. When again there was no answer, the boy carefully opened the door, just wide enough to slip in. He disappeared briefly into the bakery, and then hurried back out, closing the door quickly behind him. The front of his shirt bulged, as though he was hiding something beneath it. From the smell, drifting to Fox on a playful little breeze, it was bread. Simple, hearty bread.

The little thief scurried back across the street with many quick glances around him, and Fox watched as he made his way back into the little alley where he'd apparently stashed his lamplighting tools. The alley where, Fox was almost certain, the boy would be sleeping tonight.

Lawkeeping was a very loose practice in Thicca Valley. Oftentimes, bargains were struck between the wrongdoers and those they'd wronged. But usually, Thiccans helped each other to survive. Everyone was family, everyone pulled their weight. But here, in such a large city, Fox was sure that the little thief was risking much more than an isolated shift in the deep mines, or the midnight watch during wolf season. He'd heard of places, more civilized than his own humble home, where children were hanged for stealing. Or shipped away to be slave to some rich lord, or work on a distant island harvesting expensive spices and fruit.

Fox watched the alley mouth for several more minutes, but the straw-haired boy did not reappear. Finally, torn between the adult, law-abiding idea of turning the boy in and his own natural instinct to let him be, Fox returned to the inn. But all through the dinner rush back at The Hatted Goat, where Fox sat dutifully at Father's side, his mind wandered back to the little thief. Something about him nagged at Fox's mind, tickling the back of his thoughts like a spring breeze playing at his hair.

THE ART OF TRADING did not come as easily as trapping. Fox often found himself letting expensive items go for much less than they were worth. A mistake he wouldn't have made back in the valley, where everything was only as estimable as its ability to keep one alive. But here, in the grander world of trade and commerce, Fox found himself constantly stumbling. Father would slip in every so often with a gentle reminder or correction on a price. He'd ask quietly if Fox was *sure* that was his best offer, or wonder out loud if that gentleman wasn't equipped to pay *more* than the price he'd walked away with.

But Fox was stubborn and determined to catch on. He began to learn how to pick up on what Father called "barter language." The way someone acted when they desperately wanted what a merchant had to offer, as opposed to when they had only a passing interest. Tricks to tell when a customer was bluffing, and how one might act if he really could just walk away. And, after a few frustrating days that felt like an eternity, Fox began to get the hang of it.

By the end of the week, Fox was running many of the trades himself. Father watched him from the other side of the common room at The Hatted Goat, ready to step in if a deal went sour. But with the exception of one rather belligerent gentleman who "won't take orders from a pox-ridden little *child*!" Father never had to intervene. And while he never voiced aloud his pride at Fox's success, Fox could see it on his face. As clearly as though it had been painted there with a brush.

They ventured out into the city on occasion, going door-to-door around the finer establishments. Offering to sell their pelts to milliners and cloak makers. And every evening, just as it began to grow dark, Fox made his excuses and slipped away from Father's side. He would claim to need fresh air, or offer to run an errand. And he would watch the lamplighters. And he would look for the straw-haired boy.

It didn't take him long to figure out that none of the other lamplighters knew that their smallest companion was fending for himself. When the rest of them would cheerfully head off for supper at the end of their chore, the small one made sure to wait until they were out of sight before he disappeared into his alley. Sometimes, if the other boys were hanging around longer than normal, the urchin would make a show of heading off in the opposite direction, as if he were simply heading home. Then, he'd double back when he was sure the coast was clear. Fox watched as, night after night, the boy crept through the empty streets, looking for empty shops to steal from. Never the same shop two nights in a row. And always, Fox noted, small items that seemingly wouldn't be missed. He did not steal fancy foods and fine linens, but instead rough and simple things. Fraying shoes from the secondhand shop. Short, yellow candles of the cheapest fat. Plain bread and fruit. Just enough to get by, it seemed.

One evening about ten days into their stay in Whitethorn, Fox was watching the boy hover uncertainly in the street, as if deciding where he could do his thieving tonight. The streets were empty save for an occasional straggler. It seemed that supper time truly was the best chance for a little thief to do his best work. The shops weren't closed up for the night yet, simply empty. The boy didn't have to pick locks or fumble around in the dark. He would just take advantage of the brief times when storekeeps disappeared into the back to enjoy a solitary meal. Or else joined their families in upstairs quarters. Most of the shops didn't have apprentices to keep watch while the proprietors were away, and those that did the little thief avoided.

The boy seemed to make up his mind, and Fox followed at a distance as the urchin moved through the empty streets, keeping an eye out for anyone who might take notice of him. But Fox was far too good at keeping to the shadows to be discovered. He followed the boy all the way to the far end of the market district, where the smell of fresh mutton met Fox's nose. And he knew at once that the thief was about to make a mistake.

The meat stall was perched prominently between a leather store and a great, sprawling laundry house. The butcher was a large, loud, beast of a man who often frequented some of the rougher taverns in town. Fox could hear him singing drunkenly in the streets late at night sometimes. His great leather apron was permanently stained with blood and smoke, and the whole street could often hear him roar his disapproval if someone couldn't pay. He sold fresh slabs of beef and goat. Smoked pork. Great links of sausage. Spiced and dried meats hung from the rafters of his simple wooden stall, making his piece of the market district a feasting haven for scavenging birds. Great black crows would perch on the surrounding roofs, waiting for a dropped scrap.

The butcher had no apprentice. He had a son, a scrawny lad who would lurk in the streets, waiting for his father to call on him to tend the stall if he had to leave. But he rarely did. It was not a place to look for handouts or, Fox was sure, to be caught stealing so much as a chunk of gristle. One didn't have to be in Whitethorn long to know who to steer clear of, and "Meat Man Mallard" was definitely on the top of the list.

But tonight, his stall was empty. Fox watched as the straw-haired lamplighter scampered over to it and clambered up onto one of the support beams, reaching for a hanging bundle of sausage links. The smallest, least-noticeable one, of course. And for a brief moment, as the boy stood triumphantly with his hand clasped around his prize, it seemed as though he'd get away with it.

But then a hand reached from the darkness, grabbing the boy by the wrist and hauling him up into the air in one swift motion. Meat Man Mallard, red-faced with fury, detached himself from the shadows of the small street that wound behind his stall, right between the laundry and leather shop. He held the boy up to his eye level and shook him, screaming wildly.

"Step away for a drink and you come crawling in, little vermin, planning to take my wares!" He snatched the meat in question from the boy's hand and tossed it unceremoniously back onto his chopping table. Then, still dangling the poor thief by the wrist, he took his other hand and twisted the boy's ear, making him cry out. "You know what they do in the islands, *boy*?" he spat. "When they catch a little rat like you with his hand in a hard-working man's wages." And here he lowered his voice dangerously, but Fox could still hear him from his place across the street. "It is common practice to *remove* the offending limb. And I've got just the chopper that would do it, too."

Fox had no plan. But his feet carried him forward anyway, and words spilled from his mouth before he could stop them. "You will unhand my apprentice, sir!"

His voice came out much more confident than he was actually feeling. He sounded almost like a man, instead of a scared little boy probably not much older than the one he was trying to save. But Mallard looked up anyway, and turned his evil gaze on Fox.

"You wanna be next?" he growled. "I've got more than enough knife to go around. Could take a hand from each."

Fox held his ground. He let his chest swell with a false authority and said, "This boy is apprenticed to the Foxglove traders, and is therefore protected under Merchant Law." He crossed his arms over his chest and planted his feet wide, a stance he'd seen Father take sometimes when dealing with a particularly hostile customer. "And I will ask you again, un*hand* him sir!"

Mallard's face contorted with irritation, but he dropped the boy anyway. The lamplighter landed on his rump with a yelp, but stayed there, looking up at the confrontation in apparent terror.

"This little thief was *stealing* fine meats from *my* stall!" spat the butcher. "If you don't intent to punish your so-called *apprentice,* then I will!"

"Stealing?" said Fox evenly. "Nonsense. I sent him out to run my errands. I *assume* that upon discovering your empty stall, he decided to instead leave the payment for you to discover upon your return."

Mallard's eyes did a quick scan of his stall, and then he glared at Fox again. "I see no coin."

In an instant, Fox went to the chopping table and, using a sleight-of-hand trick that Tallac the Shavid juggler had taught him, produced a fat silver coin. "Right here on the table, as it should have been." He tossed the silver piece to Mallard, who caught it greedily. "And that," said Fox, "should be more than enough." He glanced down at the discarded sausages, mashed and bruised where the butcher had handled them. "These are unacceptable. You will get us fresh ones, as well as a rasher of smoked ham. And your best hare, for the damages you did to the boy."

Mallard looked fit to kill, but something about Fox's tone must have made it clear that there would be no haggling these points. And so, grudgingly, the meat man wrapped up the purchases and thrust them into Fox's chest, then spat on the ground dangerously close to Fox's boots.

Grabbing the boy by the back of his shirt, Fox marched away. It wasn't until they were out of sight of the meat stall that the boy began to struggle against Fox's hold. "Mister, please don't take me back there! I don't know who you been sent by and I thank you for saving me but please mister!"

"Calm down," said Fox, amused. He had brought them back to the alley where the little boy constantly disappeared. "I've brought you home is all."

The boy stopped fighting and looked around. Then his shoulders sagged slightly. "I thought no one in town knew."

Fox shrugged. "Well," he said, shrugging, "I'm not from town. So you're not entirely wrong."

For a moment, the boys simply looked at each other. Then, the lamplighter said, "Do you wanna come up?"

And Fox followed him all the way to the back end of the alley, which was closed off by a stone wall. A stone wall with grooves in just the right places for a skilled climber to work his way up. And they did, heading straight to the very rooftops of Whitethorn.

One roof over from the alley entry, there was an odd dip in the angle of the shingles. The boy slid lightly down out of sight, followed closely by a fascinated Fox. And what he found was ... well, quite simply, it was a nest. A nest tucked into the strange flaws of the rooftop, beside a slightly-smoking chimney. There was a great expanse of perfectly flat roof, hidden from sight unless you were right on top of it. Even from the other roofs, Fox had not seen it. And the boy seemed to have made himself well at home. He'd built a crude overhang that seemed as though it might keep him dry in all but the cruelest rains. Ragged blankets of varying colors were laid out neatly along the "floor" of his little home, and he'd found a handful of discarded chair cushions somewhere. It was on one of these that he now sat, and motioned for Fox to do the same.

He did, pulling out the packet of sausages and tearing one off for his host.

"So," said Fox, "what's your name?"

"They call me Topper, sir," said the boy. "On account of I got all this straw on top of my head. And also, on account of my unnatural way for climbing on top of things." Topper smiled proudly. "They tells me I was climbing before I could crawl."

Fox laughed. "And how'd you wind up here, Topper?"

At this, Topper's smile faded. "My parents got sick, sir. And then ..." He hesitated, looking uncomfortable. Then he said, "You're not from Callad, are you?"

Fox shook his head. And then, hoping it might go one step further in earning the boy's trust, he held out his hand and said, "Forric Foxglove, from Thicca Valley. Fox."

Topper shook the offered hand carefully, and then seemed to give in. "I got sent to the temple in Callad. Sent to be raised and taught as a shrine boy. And I hated the life, sir, I hated it! Locked up inside all the time, made to clean and dust and change candles. And so I ran away. And I don't mean to steal, sir, promise! I always mean to replace what I took. But I've got no prospects, so I'm not looking likely to be paying back my debts any time soon." Then he cocked his head curiously at Fox. "You planning on keeping me indebted in return for the saving of my hand and life sir?"

Fox tore open the packet of salted pork and handed a piece to Topper. "I'm only passing through. As far as I'm concerned, your life is your own."

The boy's face broke into a wide grin, rounding out his cheeks and stretching his mouth to show two missing teeth. They ate their way through the rest of the pork, talking and laughing like two old friends. And when Topper began the long process of smoking the hare over the chimney, bubbling his thanks all the while, Fox returned to The Hatted Goat. Supper had long-since ended, and the common room was filled with late-night drinkers and song. Fox briefly checked in with Father and then turned in early, suddenly exhausted from his adventure. He thought of Topper, orphaned but independent, living in the shadows of the city. He didn't know why he'd felt so inclined to befriend the young urchin. But something in his heart told him it was the right thing to do. And as Fox fell into a heavy sleep, he heard a familiar voice, as if from a distance. The stranger from his dream.

"Yes, he'll do just fine."

THERE WASN'T A SCRAP of hide or pelt left for the Foxglove men to trade. The trip was over and, by all accounts, a success. Father gave Fox a handful of coins and the day to himself as reward for such a fine job. Fox went and found Topper, and the boy followed him all around town as he shopped for gifts for Mother and Lai. They picked out a fine silver necklace for Mother and, in a little shop that sold knickknacks, a beautiful carved statue of a sparrow for Lai.

There was one piece of Whitethorn that Fox hadn't yet visited. Off to the north, past the market district. But when he suggested they explore, determined to have seen every inch of Whitethorn before they left in the morning, Topper suddenly got flustered and nervous and excused himself. He scampered away and out of sight, leaving Fox to wander on his own.

The crowds were much more sparse at this end of the city. The streets were not kept up as well, and shops were smaller and set farther apart. Trees popped up here and there, giving the place a wilder look than the clean, groomed city proper. Wildflowers and weeds grew out of cracks in buildings and up along the sides of the road. The path began to twist, curving around a small, crumbling fountain. A great stone deer graced the center of the fountain, antlers held high. Around the cracked and overgrown rim, stone rabbits were perched. Water lay still at the fountain's heart, and Fox was sure it had not run in years.

He passed small thatched huts that looked entirely abandoned. He crossed over a bridge that spanned a wide piece of river, and traced the water's path with his eyes. To his left, it stretched out across the plains, disappearing into the tall, wild grass. And to his right ... it twisted into a small, dark patch of woods. But there was something else there, something nestled within the trees. Fox could feel it more than see it. There was something tucked inside those woods that was different from the rest of the city. Something new.

He picked up his pace, the tingle of exploration and adventure quickening his feet. Here, the path broke apart completely, giving way to tangled weeds and bright sprigs of wildflowers. Dark, bare tree trunks stretched several feet into the air before they filled out, blocking most of the sun with their thick branches and soft needles of green. Fresh sap glistened in ridges on the bark, and the whole wood smelled sweet.

And then, Fox's feet found stone. He tore his eyes away from the trees and looked ahead. A walkway of carved, grey marble stepping stones stretched out before him, leading to someplace hidden in the shadows.

As he followed it, his eyes picked out a ghostly pale shape in the dappled gloom. It looked like a great boulder at first, but as Fox drew closer, he realized he was wrong. The shape was spiky and twisted in odd places, and Fox was startled and intrigued when he realized that it was, in fact, a building of some kind. A building designed to look like a large, domed bramble of thorns and great briar stems. It wasn't exactly white, Fox decided. More of a pale, creamy grey. The color of elk antlers and bone. It did not look man-made, but instead it seemed as though it had grown right out of the ground, and man had simply inhabited it.

A set of polished oak double doors was propped open in welcome, and from within Fox could smell dozens of curious things. And, somewhere buried among them, he caught a smell that was strangely familiar. He couldn't put his finger on it, but as he wandered up the wide, flat steps to the entrance, Fox was sure that there was something inside that he *knew*.

His eyes adjusted quickly to the dimly lit interior. It was like stepping into a great tangle of vines, all twisted and gnarled, with a great open center where a handful of people milled about. Above him, thick knots of colored glass were tucked into each crack and hollow of the great arched ceiling, casting smears of tinted light over the entire room. Fox imagined this was what it would feel like to be trapped inside a giant butterfly wing.

Where there was no colored glass, there were candles. They flickered and winked from dark crevices in the walls, illuminating tall carved shapes that stood around the edges of the room. Statues, larger-than-life figures of men and women dressed in glorious things. Holding scepters and harps. Or books. Here and there, people knelt at the statues' great feet. And Fox realized where he must be. This was a temple.

He'd never seen one before, but he'd heard of them. Father talked often of temples in the south, where people went to worship and pray to their gods. They left offerings and sacrifices for success in their homes or business. Some gods even had entire temples dedicated just to them. But Fox, looking around at all the differing statues, knew that this was a common temple. There seemed to be more than a dozen different gods represented, each statue made to look just like its corresponding deity.

He began to wander between them, taking in every detail. Each shrine had a little plaque, labeling the god it depicted. Here was Corda, god of innkeepers and barmen. Fox looked up at his genial, stone-carved face, and smiled. This would be Borric's god, then. A grinning, chubby man, raising a tankard as if proposing a toast. And here was the god of herders, with the legs of a goat and wild curls on his head. Phiira, goddess of seers. Her eyes were draped in cloth, and Fox marveled at the detail these statues expressed with only stone. He walked all around the room, taking in every carved inch of every shrine. He watched people carefully placing offerings at their gods' feet. They left little trinkets or lit candles, and bowed their heads in prayer.

There were women here in robes. Attendants for the god-shrines. Priestesses, Fox recalled. They were tending to the candles and sweeping the rosewood floors. One of them was tidying up the base of one of the statues, dusting off the stone feet and rearranging the collection of gifts left there by worshipers. Some statues clearly saw more attention than others. The very walls around them were draped in gifts, and tiny rolled scraps of parchment were tucked into the vine-like creases. Prayers, written down and left for the gods to answer if and when they chose to. The herder god seemed to be especially popular here.

There was one statue that caught his attention. One that held his gaze more than all the others, from its stone-carved boots all the way to its hair, pulled back in a tail. It was situated near the back of the room, tucked into a rather deep alcove. There was a book propped open on a stand just before the statue. Candlelight illuminated the displayed page, revealing it to be some sort of map. Elegant text across the top dubbed it "The Gossamer Sea and Her Lands," and Fox's eyes lingered curiously over it for a moment before he looked back up at the stone. The god depicted in the shrine was tall, with boots that went up almost to his knees. One hand held a long spyglass, raised and pointed off to the distance. The other hand gripped the drawstring of a bag, which seemed to be bulging with something. Ropes of pearls and jewels were spilling out of it. A cocky smile shaped the man's mouth, which was perfectly framed by a trim beard. A beard that may have been white stone here, but that Fox knew to be raven-feather black. As his eyes fell to the plaque at the bottom of the shrine, Fox could hear the man from his dream chuckle as though he were there. "Farran, the Pirate God."

In the entirely sensible part of his mind, Fox realized that the very thought that a god would take interest in his little, insignificant life, was near-madness. Then again, the idea that he was magically Blessed had seemed just as impossible not so long ago. And so, when the familiar voice spoke from somewhere in the shadows, Fox wasn't nearly as surprised as he should have been.

"Not my *best* angle," said Farran. He was leaning casually against one of the viney protrusions just behind his statue, looking appraisingly up at his own stone figure. "Truly, the work of an amateur. But, for these provincial parts, I suppose it will do."

He was dressed quite differently than he'd been in Fox's dream. He wore a long, high-collared coat in a style that Fox had never seen before. It was deep green, with gold buttons running down the front, all the way to the waist, where the whole thing flared open, revealing rich violet pants tucked into black boots. And it might have been a trick of the light, but it seemed to Fox as though he wasn't always entirely there. He almost seemed to *flicker*, like a guttering candle at times. Appearing entirely solid one moment, and half lost in the shadows the next. Even as he peeled himself away from the alcove wall, Farran didn't quite seem to have a tangible form.

"This isn't another dream," said Fox.

"If it is," said Farran, "then you have an extraordinarily dull mind. Most little boys dream of great battles and pretty women, don't they? Not many dream of hinterland temples." He smiled, seemingly amused at his own sense of humor.

"You're a god," said Fox. Again, it was not a question, merely a statement of fact. His voice sounded oddly calm and at ease with the whole situation, even to himself. "An actual, straight-from-legend god."

"Observant little kit, aren't you?" Farran bent briefly to pluck an offering from his own statue's feet. It was a little satchel of some sort, and Farran sniffed at it dubiously. "Lavender," he said scornfully. "A rather boring scent, if you ask me. Of all the fine spices and weeds the Known World could offer, people insist on leaving me lavender." He dropped the satchel back to the stone and dusted off his hands. "And, not that you bothered to ask, I'd much prefer a bottle of Ordasian wine or a fine opal pendant."

"Why don't you tell them yourself," said Fox, gesturing at the worshipers and priestesses. "Give them a complete list of all the offerings you deem worthy."

Farran didn't seem the slightest bit offended by Fox's tone. Instead, he chuckled in amusement. "I must say, I admire the way you handle yourself. Never miss a trick, even among the very gods." Then he sighed dramatically. "But, alas, I cannot inform the uneducated masses on my likes and dislikes at present. *They* can neither see nor hear me. Only you."

And then, Farran threw back his head and sang, the jolly sea tune filling the silence of the temple from wall to twisted wall.

Come sail with me on the rolling sea,
Where the fish are swell and the air is free.
We'll take a ship down the old Black Way,
And marry tomorrow in the ocean spray!

Nobody noticed. Not a single head turned to find the owner of the booming voice now making the candles shudder in their niches. As the echos of Farran's song faded at last, Fox said dryly, "Lucky me."

Farran laughed heartily and took Fox by the shoulder. "Come," he said. "Take a walk with me. We'll get to know each other a bit better before you're off back to your father."

Fox let himself be steered deep into the darkness at the far end of the temple. As they walked, no one's eyes so much as flickered in their direction. It seemed that Farran was right; no one knew he was there.

"Can they see me?" Fox asked curiously. For not even the priestesses acknowledged him as he passed.

"For the moment, no," said Farran. "And I'd prefer it stay that way. People, even temple folk, sometimes get uncomfortable if they know a god is sniffing about. Especially one such as me. No need to cause a panic. Not yet, at any rate."

He led Fox down a winding, earthy staircase tucked so far into the shadows that Fox didn't see it until he stood on the top step. They went down, deep beneath the temple until the passageway opened up into a wide, sprawling room. It was dimly lit by great hanging globes that glowed from within. And Fox, watching the light curiously, thought that it wasn't candles that illuminated the globes. The soft, milky light was much more similar to the steady glow of lymnstone.

When he finally tore his eyes away from the strange lights and looked about the rest of the room, he found himself staring about in wonder. They were standing in a great, underground garden. The walls were overgrown by flowering vines as far as he could see. Pockets and rows and hillocks of flowers carpeted the floor, with small stone pathways winding here and there among them. He stepped out, away from the stairwell and into the green. Plants he had never seen grew wild and free, wrapping around the vine-like walls, fighting for space with the patches of moss. There was even a small tree gracing the approximate center of the room, its long green limbs dipping to form a curtain of growth, affording some privacy for whoever felt the need to sit at the tree's base.

There was a purple flower that seemed to grow in abundance here. Fox could smell its subtle tones, wrapping through the scent of every other plant almost playfully. It was a weedy sort of flower, twisting through the exposed roots of other blossoms and springing up unexpectedly in dark corners and rival flower patches. Fox found its smell strangely comforting, and curiously familiar.

"Where are we?" he asked finally.

"Every temple has somewhere ... safe." Farran was a few steps behind him, running the tips of his fingers along a line of soft yellow petals. For a moment, it seemed as though the flowers were trying to wrap around his hand, but Fox blinked and they were still again. "Somewhere for the priests and priestesses to commune with their gods. It's called the sanctuary."

"Is it normal for you to pop up in places like this?" asked Fox.

Something of a darkness passed over Farran's face as he said, "Not these days." And then his expression cleared as he said, "But for you, I make a special exception. I thought it was important that we meet in person, sooner or later. Luckily, it was sooner. And I bless the winds that brought you here today. Saved me the trouble of having to brew up another dream. A thing like that takes *power*, don't you know. And to spirit you away without anyone noticing ... quieting the wind so she wouldn't catch on ... I owe a lot of people rather big favors." He laughed almost nervously.

"And why is it so important that you meet me?" said Fox. "I have done what you said. I've started practicing, learning. But why? And why do you take such an interest?"

For a moment, it looked as if Farran wouldn't answer. And then he said quietly, "You prayed to me. And sometimes, you get exactly what you ask for."

Fox thought back to that long night in the cabin, waiting for the Desolata. He remembered asking the Pirate God Farran, the last god he'd heard his father talk about, to get him through the ordeal safely. And then ...

"The wolves," he said. "You sent the wolves to me."

"A life for a life," said Farran. "I saved two of you that night, and helped you save the valley you love so dearly. In any ledger in the world, that makes you in my debt."

"But I'm only fifteen," said Fox warily. "What could I possibly have that you'd want as payment?"

"I told you before," said Farran, plucking a deep red flower from the earth and running it through his fingers. "I have my reasons. And it's not for you to know. But a god like me takes great pains to stay unnoticed, and there are certain favors you might owe me."

"For how long?" said Fox. He may not have understood the ways of gods, but he certainly understood the ways of debt. Father had been careful to explain it to him from a young age, telling him stories of waresmen and traders who made costly mistakes and ended up forever enslaved to the people who helped them get back on their feet.

"That remains to be seen," said Farran. He crushed the head of the flower in his palm and let the broken pieces fall back to the ground. "Think of it more as ... an agreement between friends. You help me, and I help you. Don't underestimate the benefits of having a god on your side. Especially in your line of business."

"Father doesn't have a god looking over his shoulder, and he does just fine."

"Then I'm not talking about trapping, am I?" said Farran. He began to wander deeper into the underground garden, and Fox watched him from a cautious distance. "I told you that you were meant for more. And as for my interest ... even a master craftsman needs tools."

"Do I have a choice?" asked Fox, a hint of irritation creeping into his voice.

"Of course you do," said the god smoothly. "Just like I had a *choice* to save your life, or to let you be gutted by a bare Desolata hand."

"You said my path ahead was filled with blood," said Fox quickly. His bluntness seemed to take the god by surprise, and Fox hurried on before he lost his nerve. "Can you stop the people I care about getting hurt?"

Here, Farran paused for a long while. They stood boy and god, among the flowers, staring each other down until, finally, Farran spoke again. "Some things cannot be changed. And the future isn't always clear, even to us." And then, quite suddenly, Farran froze. He cocked his head to the side, as if listening intently to something only he could hear. Then he said, "They'll be looking for me soon."

"Who — " Fox began, but Farran cut him off.

"Listen, there are things more important than you. Or even me. You have to *trust* me when I say that you'll want me in your corner one day. And another thing ... " He hesitated for a moment, and then drew closer to Fox. "We both share someone ... very important. You *might* think about how all this will affect *her*."

As Fox wracked his brain, trying to think of who he and Farran might have in common, he suddenly realized he could smell the pirate god's scent, in a way he'd never been able to in his dream. It, like the purple flowers, was strangely familiar. Comforting, in a homey sort of way. Like he'd smelled it every day for his entire life. And as Fox breathed deep, a picture came to mind. And he knew at once who Farran meant.

"Why do you smell like her?" he asked in a whisper, almost terrified to know the answer. "Why do you smell just like Lai?"

There was something like regret on Farran's face. "I can't protect her the way I would have wished. Not with things the way they are."

"What things?" demanded Fox. "Why do you need to protect her? What's she to you?"

Farran's form began to flicker again, and Fox knew the god was about to disappear completely. But as he faded, Farran said quietly, "Borric's a good man, taking care of her as he has all these years. But some day, it won't be enough. Her lineage, her *true* lineage, will catch up to her. And he might regret ever taking them in." By now, Farran had disappeared completely, and just his voice remained, echoing around the strange garden. "She looks just like her mother, you know."

Chapter Thirteen
Maps

The journey home was pleasant enough. Fox mentioned nothing of his strange encounter with Farran, and he and Father chatted easily. But while Fox smiled and joked gaily, his mind was far down the road. It was miles over the horizon, in Thicca Valley with Lai. And, even more than that, with Borric. A friend, a second father ... a liar.

Farran had said Borric "took her in." He said Lai's "true lineage." The implications were so enormous, Fox couldn't quite wrap his head around them. But by the time their cart looked down into Thicca Valley once more, he'd come to terms with the general upshot of it all: Lai was the daughter of a god.

When Lai herself came to greet him that night, wanting to hear all about his first successful outing, Fox kept a warm smile stretched across his face. He answered all her eager questions, and was rewarded with an ecstatic hug when he presented her with the gift he'd bought. The little carved bird. And when she left well after dark, his eyes followed her home. Back to the Five Sides, and Borric Blackroot.

He slept poorly that night, tossing and turning in his nook until almost dawn, when a dreamless sleep finally washed over him. When he awoke a few scant hours later, he had made up his mind. He might not be ready to talk to Lai about any of this, but by Spirit's shackles, he was going to find out the truth from Borric.

Fox waited until Lai was out for the day, stationed out on the hillside with Widow Mossgrove's goats. And then, he slipped through the Five Sides and found Borric sitting in the empty common room, polishing tankards with his feet propped up on a table. Fox slid silently onto the bench across from him and didn't speak. He simply sat, unsure of exactly how to start.

After a moment, Borric said genially, "Something on your mind, my boy?"

"I've just ... been thinking," said Fox carefully. He felt that anything he said might come off as much more accusatory than he meant. But finally, he took a deep breath and said, "There's a certain trust that comes with friendship. And Lai is my best friend. I'd never want to hurt her."

Borric lowered his tankard and rag to the table. "I know it," he said slowly. "What's this about, lad?"

"Borric," said Fox, "I want to know about Lai's real parents." The words came out calm and evenly, much more steady than Fox himself was feeling.

To his surprise, Borric seemed unshaken. In fact, he seemed more relieved than anything. He ran his fingers through his bushy black hair and said, "How did you find out?"

"I met someone," said Fox. "Someone ... important. He seems to have taken a personal interest in her."

Borric chuckled darkly. "I should have known it would be him. Gods never know when to keep out of it." He cast a glance at the kitchen door, then shifted in his seat, stretching out his legs along the bench and propping his back against a wooden beam. Then he said, "I don't know everything, but I'll tell you what I can."

He nodded at the stairway that led downstairs, to the storage rooms. "It was just down there that I met her. A young woman called Adella, pregnant full to bursting. And sick. Sick enough I was worried that childbirth might kill her."

"Why was she there?" asked Fox.

"Hiding out from the winter," said Borric. "Her family had put her out, ashamed that she was pregnant with no husband. She was traveling south, looking to start a new life when she got caught in the storms. I took pity on her, and took her in. Cared for her in the last few months of her pregnancy. I grew rather fond of her. She was excellent company when she was having her healthy days. She was bright and witty, and spun the most beautiful stories and songs ..." He smiled softly at the memory. "And clever to a fault. I see a little more of her in Lai every day.

"I married her in secret, a quiet ceremony in Deep Winter when no one was around. By the time Lai was born, the rumors had been spread that I'd been married. And since no one knew exactly when, it was perfectly reasonable to assume that I was Lai's rightful father."

"Did you know who it was?" asked Fox.

"Not at first," said Borric. "And I didn't ask. It was a painful subject, and neither of us seemed eager to bring it up. But Adella began to fade. She stopped laughing, she stopped smiling. She forgot to feed Lai, or watch after her. She simply sat, staring out the window, singing old sea songs for hours. Days. And she told me who he was. And when your heart and soul belong to a god, sometimes there's no turning back. Every part of her wanted, *needed*, to go and find him.

"When she left, I played the mourning husband. I told everyone she'd died in an accident, so Lai wouldn't have to grow up knowing the truth. But I wasn't surprised. I'd known for months that Adella couldn't stay. She belonged to Farran."

For a moment, Fox let it sink in. Then he asked, "So what does that make Lai?"

"There are many children of gods, scattered through the known world," answered Borric. "Half gods, demi gods. She may be entirely mortal. Or she may discover, one day, that she is something *more* than mortal." His eyes met Fox's. "Like you."

"I'm not a god," said Fox at once.

"But you *are* truly Blessed," said Borric. "You have something in you the rest of us can only dream to understand. You are meant for more."

"You sound just like *him*," said Fox dryly.

Borric chuckled. "How was it, meeting the great Captain Farran, terror of the seas?"

Fox sighed. Once again, life was moving far too fast for his age, and he felt he was talking man to man rather than boy to barkeep. "Raised far more questions than it answered," he said. "Why, have you met him?"

"A handful of times since Adella left," said Borric. "He likes to check in. But he prefers to do it in dreams, rather than hauling his godly self all the way down here."

"Yes, I've noticed," said Fox, sure that he could expect even more of the strange dream visits, now that he and Farran were in "agreement."

For a moment, the two sat in silence. And then, Borric said, "I love her more than my own life. She is *my* daughter, no matter her bloodline." There was a fierceness in his voice that Fox had never heard. A protectiveness that made Fox shiver. "And the truth would break her very spirit." They locked eyes, and Fox held his chin up.

"It's not my secret to tell," he said. "She'll always be your daughter, as far as I'm concerned. I just want to keep her safe."

Borric bobbed his head respectfully, almost a bow. "Then we are on the same side."

Fox left the Five Sides a little while later and headed home. He was exhausted. He wanted nothing more than to take a nap, and not wake up until all of this made sense. But instead, he made himself useful in the kitchen, helping Mother set out a hearty dinner. He listened as Father talked over plans for their next hunting trip, and joined in as they counted down the weeks until summer ended. But his mind was haunted by one clear, painful thought: Lai had been abandoned.

OVER THE NEXT FEW WEEKS, Fox found himself watching Lai more closely than ever before, looking for any hint of god-like behavior. Any clue that her true lineage might be leaking through. He wasn't sure quite *what* to look for, but was convinced he would know it when he saw it. He started to become irrationally concerned if she came down with the slightest hint of the sniffles, worried about what might happen if a mortal were afflicted by a divine illness. After two weeks of well-concealed terror, Fox resolved to track down a book that might help him better understand the nature of the gods at the first opportunity.

But Lai remained ever herself, stubborn and lively and bright, and Fox's one true confidant. For while his parents, Borric, and Picck might know bits and pieces of what Fox was going through, Lai was the first one he went to whenever he made a new discovery. When his Blessing began to manifest itself more strongly, or if he found he could do something new. The two of them would sit together on the hillside among the goats; Lai with her loom or needlework, Fox with his rapidly-filling book of scribbles. And they would talk over everything.

Midsummer morning was no exception. Fox was sprawled out on the grass, nose buried deep in his own notes. "It feels like there's something I'm missing," he said. "I may be Windkissed, but I don't seem to have connections to *any* Shavid power I've ever heard of."

Lai tore her focus away from the little wooden goat she was carving. A gift for one of the Mossgrove boys. "Well that's not true," she said easily. "Music and dance isn't all they do. They're connected to the wind, aren't they? And so are you." She began to tick off on her fingers, lightly tapping the tips of each with her whittling knife as she counted. "You can smell the weather coming, sometimes even from days away. You hear and smell and even *see* things that are happening somewhere else, all because you can sense them on the wind. And, there's the wolves."

Fox ignored her, pretending to be engrossed in his own scratchy handwriting. He had, of course, told her about the role the wolves had played in the destruction of the Desolata. And how he felt they'd been watching after him ever since, silent watchdogs in the shadows. What he had *not* told her was how Farran had sent them to his aid. In fact, he'd been especially careful not to mention a word about the pirate god to anyone but Borric.

Who he *really* longed to talk to, above anyone else, was Neil. Apart from being Fox's friend, he was a scholar. He knew the ways of magic better than Fox could ever hope to, and Fox wished more than anything that he could work through all of this with Neil by his side. To help him understand, and puzzle it out. But instead of brooding over the mysterious whereabouts of the Shavid, Fox decided to distract himself by practicing his newly discovered power.

It had happened a week before, when Fox was tracking a particularly crafty bunch of quail. He'd been testing the direction of the wind, making sure the animals couldn't catch his scent. He'd held up a handful of forest debris. Dead leaves, grass, dirt. And he'd released them slowly into the wind, watching them float away and shifting his position in frustration, for he'd been tired and just wanted to head home. And then, mere moments later, the birds had come waddling up to him as easily as though they were begging to be caught.

Now, Fox crouched low to the earth and plucked a few blades of grass, holding them carefully between his fingers. He aimed himself at the small herd of goats, and thought long and hard about how much he wanted them to come. And he released his handful, watching the green scraps float across the hillside. The goats' heads perked up, and they came trotting obediently over. And Lai, grinning broadly, began to scratch one of them behind the ears.

Again and again they did this, releasing the goats to wander the hillside and calling them back again with Fox's trick of the wind. Lai tried it once, with no luck, and instead watched Fox with amazement and joy painted all over her face. He practiced until he no longer needed the grass. He could simply feel the wind's path through the air, and whispered his thoughts into it.

"How are you doing it?" asked Lai finally as they let the goats be.

"I can only guess," said Fox, closing his journal and sprawling out on the grass beside her. "I think the wind can tell them what to do. And since I can talk to the wind, I can ... manipulate that, somehow." His head hurt from so many tries in a row, and he rubbed his eyes. "I don't know how far I can reach, or who else might accidentally hear. For all I know, I could use the wrong trail and tell the Desolata themselves to show up at my door."

"Trail?" asked Lai.

"Oh," said Fox sheepishly. "Yeah ... that's how I see the wind, sometimes. Like hundreds of little paths through the woods, all crammed together. And I just have to pick the right one."

Lai frowned slightly. "Doesn't that get exhausting? Seeing everything, all the time?"

"A little," admitted Fox. "But I think I'm learning to control it. Watch." He sat up straighter and closed his eyes, taking a deep breath, letting the sounds and smells of the valley come crashing in on him. But instead of overwhelming his mind and senses, Fox sorted through them carefully, like spices on a shelf. Arranging them in his mind, keeping them all in a row, acknowledging them on *his* terms. "There's a handful of children playing in the mud at the riverbank. Three ... no, four of them. And a miner is taking a bite to eat outside in the fresh air. Smells like berry corn cakes, but not Picck's." He sorted through the images and feelings again, looking for specific things and people this time. "My father is in his workshop, packaging our newest beaver pelts for our trip next week. Mother is making pheasant for dinner. *Your* father is chopping wood for the bonfire tonight, and Picck and Rose are having a late-morning picnic, just a few hillsides away. And ..." He opened his eyes. He wasn't breathless, or flat on his back on the earth like he used to find himself after so much wind-reading. Instead, he was calm and upright, as though he'd merely been describing pictures on a parchment page. Except, there was one thing he'd sensed that he hadn't counted on. He turned to Lai, momentarily speechless. Then he said, "Rose is pregnant."

"ARE YOU SURE?" ASKED Lai. They were crouched in the back kitchen door of the Five Sides later that afternoon, secretly watching the happy couple go about their work.

"Positive," whispered Fox. "But it's so new, even *she* may not know." He watched as Picck swept Rose up into a playful embrace, kissing her on the forehead before releasing her again to her duties. Then Fox backed slowly out of the kitchen doorway, and he and Lai sat with their backs against the outside wall. "Why can I smell *that*?" he asked. "Are all Shavid that sensitive?"

"They'll come back someday," said Lai reassuringly. "You'll be able to ask them everything then."

"And until they do?" said Fox, running his hands through his hair irritably. "Do I just keep *sitting* here, discovering little bits and pieces on the way and never truly knowing what to do with them all?" He pounded his fist into the earth in frustration. Then he said quietly, "Why did they have to leave? Why did *all* of them have to disappear just when I started to learn? Why couldn't someone have stayed behind to help with ... all of this?"

Lai leaned into him, wrapping one arm around his shoulders. "Sometimes, we have to figure things out on our own. Maybe it will make you stronger, in the end."

"I hope you're right," said Fox moodily.

But before he could start feeling too sorry for himself, there was a disturbance out front. They could hear someone arriving at the Five Sides, and Fox sat up a little straighter. They could hear a muffled but unfamiliar voice briefly conversing with Borric's deep, resonant boom. And then both voices disappeared into the tavern, and Fox and Lai scrambled to their feet. They made their way around to the main entrance instead of cutting easily through the kitchen, so as not to disturb Picck and Rose.

Visitors were always exciting in the valley. They brought news of far-off places, or else stories from neighboring cities scattered through the Highborns. This one, Fox could already tell, was not a local. The man himself might be inside, but one glance at his horse and wagon told anyone walking by that he was clearly foreign.

His horse was a rather serene, dappled mare, hitched to the strangest little wagon Fox had ever seen. Very different from the great, boxy carts that the waresmen used to tote their goods, or even the painted wagons the Shavid traveled in. This piece of wood and wheel was tall rather than long, with a great padded driver's seat built right into the front. There were two massive wheels that, if Fox had to guess, probably doubled as makeshift steps up to the perch. The seat itself was cushioned like a massive throne in soft, gold velvet that contrasted elegantly with the smooth, polished black of the wagon. The whole unit swooped into a graceful curve in the back, stretching out a bit into a warped "L" shape that ended in an elegantly stamped "B.B." Every bit of the wagon was sealed tight, leaving Fox's imagination to run wild about what might be inside.

The two of them exchanged curious glances, and Lai shrugged. "We weren't expecting anybody."

Fox led the way inside eagerly, and his eyes fell upon the gentleman exchanging coins over the bar with Borric. He was a flamboyant weed of a man, with tight sandy curls and round, gold spectacles perched on the end of his thin nose. He wore a pale brown jacket cropped at the hip, and matching riding gloves. A bright green scrap of silk was knotted at his neck and tucked into the collar of his jacket.

"And that's for just the three nights?" the man was asking, and Borric nodded.

"If you decide to stay any longer, we can re-negotiate the terms," said Borric. He then noticed Lai and Fox, and said, "My daughter, Lai, will be around if you have any special requests."

The man spun around to greet them and dipped into a low bow, sweeping the hem of his jacket behind him with one hand, and offering the other one forward grandly. "Bartrum Bookmonger, at your service!" Then he drew himself straight again and flashed them an impossibly white grin. "Reading and writing instructor, and purveyor of fine paper goods!"

He had a thick, almost comical accent. As if he stretched his mouth too far when he spoke. Lai threw her father a raised-eyebrow, and Borric shrugged. "He's a bit of a character, I'll admit. But I'd like to keep him around, and see if the miners have him killed." He glanced apologetically at Bartrum with a wry, lopsided smile. "We're starved for entertainment here in Sovesta. Something you might have thought of before you ventured this far from home."

Bartrum laughed nervously and adjusted his glasses. "Well, I admit, I may have wandered a *bit* farther north than I originally intended. However!" And he sprang back to his attitude of player-like splendor. "Somewhere deep inside, something *spoke* to my soul and said, 'Bartrum, someone out there needs you! *Someone* out there is waiting for you and your *books*!' And so I took to the road!"

The scattered patrons throughout the tavern were watching Bartrum with various levels of amusement on their faces. Some of the more rugged miners were openly laughing and exchanging low whispers about him, and Fox remembered Borric's comment about the miners having him killed. It may have been half a joke, but Fox found himself hoping that Bartrum Bookmonger would double-lock his doors at night.

"So!" said Bartrum, rubbing his hands together, apparently oblivious to the mildly threatening looks being thrown in his direction. "If someone might show me to my room? I'd like to freshen up before I get down to business."

"I will!" said Lai, rather more quickly than Fox would have expected. As the two disappeared upstairs, Borric finally let loose the laughter he'd clearly been keeping bottled up out of respect for his guest. The room filled with great roars and guffaws from every corner as not only Borric, but most of his customers, gave in to their amusement.

But Fox did not laugh. True, he found the man's whole persona wildly ridiculous, especially considering how obviously out of place he was, but Fox was thinking about what Bartrum had said about someone *needing* his services. And didn't Fox truly need a book, right now?

But he decided to wait until later to approach the book-seller. Let the man settle in a bit. And so he retreated to Father's workshop until sundown, when the whole valley came together for the Midsummer bonfire. And then, he made his way back to the Five Sides, slipped in through the kitchen, and looked for Bartrum Bookmonger.

He was easy to spot, alone in the otherwise deserted tavern. Everyone was out on the proving grounds, where an enormous beacon of flame had been erected. Unlike the Homecoming, or even the grand Harvestmast festival that was just a short ways away, Midsummer was a simple affair. It was a mountain tradition, as old as the Highborns themselves. A prayer to the gods for a successful harvest season, and a plea that winter would hold off until the crops were all brought in. The bonfire was kindled by a plant from each farming household, and sparked by each miner's finest flint. It marked the halfway point of the growing season, and it was a call for everyone to pull together and start preparing for the harsher months to come.

Bartrum was wise to stay away from the ritual. Outsiders were not welcome at such a sacred event. Instead, the man sat at a table by himself, scratching away at a long roll of parchment with an extravagantly plumed quill. Fox approached cautiously, not wanting to startle him, and cleared his throat when he was inches away from the table.

Bartrum jumped slightly and looked up, startled, but managing not to spoil his writing. "Hello young master," he said exuberantly. "Come for a simple chat? Or did you desire, perchance, to browse my fine wares? Or have you come for lessons in reading and writing, like your little friend?"

"Thank you sir, but I already read and write," said Fox politely. And then, "What friend?"

Bartrum brushed the question away with his quill, as though trying to dust away the very words Fox had spoken. "Never you mind! So, you've come for something else then! Parchment, quills? A fine business ledger?"

Fox was feeling strangely nervous now. He'd never owned a book before, and he didn't have a clue how much one might cost. "I was actually hoping ... maybe I could look at your books?"

"Oh, but I have so much more than simply *books*, my fine young scholar!" said Bartrum, practically leaping from his seat and taking Fox by the shoulders. "Come. Take a journey with me!"

He led Fox out and around the back, into the kitchen courtyard and to the rebuilt goat barn. "Your innkeeper was kind enough to let me anchor my little traveling store in your stables," said Bartrum, flinging open the doors and sweeping inside, Fox at his heels. Lanterns were lit quickly, illuminating the cozy little barn and waking a very cranky Fermia. She bleated at them and retreated farther into the corner of her stall as Bartrum rubbed his hands together in anticipation.

The wagon was parked right in the center of the room, great blocks wedged under its wheels to keep it in place. The wagon's horse was housed in an empty stall, looking just as calm as ever. She'd have to be, thought Fox, to be able to tolerate her owner's exuberant energy all the time. And then Bartrum began to open his wagon, and every other thought flew from Fox's mind.

It seemed that only Bartrum himself knew how to open every drawer, cupboard, and sliding hatch, but as Fox watched, he was amazed to discover that the entire wagon seemed to be made up of just that. The whole back panel, with the "B.B." stamped into it, pulled out into one massive drawer, filled with great tomes and leatherbound volumes. A door halfway up slid open to reveal shelves of colored ink, rolls of parchment and scrolls. And a little pocket in the side of that same cupboard held not only quills, but a series of finely carved pens that Fox had only seen once before, used by a particularly wealthy merchant passing through the valley years ago. Doors opened up on both sides of the wagon as well, and there was even a small hidden shelf that extended from the bottom and hung beneath the wheels.

Bartrum ran his fingers fondly along the spine of one of his books. "Tales of daring from across the seas. Biographies of kings. Histories of war and succession. I've got them all, right here, for your enjoyment and edification." And then he took a step back, gesturing for Fox to come take a look for himself.

By the dim light of the rafter-hung lanterns, the book titles seemed to flicker and shimmer on their spines. Fox brushed his fingertips along each one in turn, pausing here and there to pull one from its housing and flip it open. Here was a beautifully illustrated picture of a woman with leaves woven into her hair, playing a lap harp that seemed to be made of so many live branches. There was a poem on the opposite page, telling the sad tale of a woman who waited in the woods for her lover to find her. She sang and played to bring him to where she sat, but he never appeared. And as she faded into illness and drew close to death, the spirits of the forest who heard her lovely voice took pity on her. They transformed her into a weeping willow, keeping her forever alive and protecting her from heartbreak. According to the poem, her voice and harp could still be heard if you stood beneath the willow branches on a breezy day.

Another book was full of nothing but highly detailed accounts of ancient battles. There were lists of ships and their crew, cataloguing who was killed, injured, or lost at sea. Personal tales of the front lines from captains and commanders, on land and ocean combat alike. And beside that one, a book that was all in some strange language Fox didn't recognize. There were books of all sizes, balanced and stacked inexplicably in this moving library. Fox grinned. How Neil would love to see this.

And then, as he wandered around to look at the books tucked into the left-side shelf, something caught his eye. A thin, black volume with emerald green lettering on the spine. The title was one word: "Asynthum." Fox plucked the book curiously from its spot, and was surprised to find it was much heavier than it looked. As he opened it, he marveled at how thin the pages were. Impossibly thin, making him worry he might tear them straight out of the book if he so much as turned a page.

"They're stronger than you think," said Bartrum, in a much calmer voice than he'd used before now. He was leaning against a wooden beam, one foot propped up and his arms crossed over his chest. "It would take more than your sharpest knife to cut those pages from *that* book."

"What are they made of?" said Fox. "This isn't parchment." The pages were an opal-esque, creamy white that seemed like it should have been so thin that the ink would bleed straight through it. But instead the fine, flawless lettering on each page was clean and even, and even its shadows did not show through on the back. It seemed impossible.

Bartrum winked. "Trade secret," he said.

Fox began to flip through the book, not daring to ask how much it would cost him. And as he read, he felt a strange chill. This was the book he'd been looking for. Even silently *asking* for. A book about the gods. Stories, tales, legends, drawings ... Gods from every country. Demi-gods who went on to become heroes. It was an entire university course on the divine, tucked neatly into one slight tome. And there, not one third of the way through the book, was Farran.

Even in his black-and-white ink portrait, Farran looked cocky and highly amused with something. Fox glared down at the page, resisting the childish urge to stick his tongue out at it. He continued to browse through the pirate god's section of the book, and came across a map very similar to the one that had been on display in the Whitethorn temple. In fact, upon closer inspection, Fox found that it was indeed the very same. It laid out, in a series of tiny lines and great shapeless things that Fox assumed were supposed to be countries, the course of Farran's infamous raiding days on the high seas. Fox had only glimpsed pieces of these stories, but it seemed that there was a time when those sailing the Gossamer Sea had to be very wary of crossing Farran's ship. Fox's curiosity and hunger for learning screamed at him from within, wanting to know more about everything from the journeys of the ship to the color of the paint on its hull. He reached out and ran a single fingertip along a line that was labeled "The Hydra Route," smiling to himself as he imagined the thrill of sailing on a real pirate ship.

It happened as he traced the route with his finger. He could see it as clearly as though he had been there: Farran standing on the rail of his ship, holding himself steady with a rope tied to one of the sails. His red cloak was billowing behind him as he shouted orders, and all around him, his crew were launching themselves over the edge of their ship, landing on the deck of the smaller boat helplessly tethered to their side. The captured ship was boarded, looted, and any sailors who put up a fight were run through at once. Fox could smell something burning, and hear the relentless crash of the sea behind the screams of fallen men and the shouts of triumph from Farran's crew. And he could see Farran himself, smiling his wolfish smile.

Fox ripped his hand away from the page, and the vision disappeared. He looked shakily over at Bartrum, who was watching him curiously. Then Fox wiped his now-sweating palms hastily on his pants and closed the book with a thud.

After a moment of heavy silence, Bartrum spoke. “I stock my roving warehouse with books of all types. Many of them I even write myself. The biographies especially are a project of mine.” He smiled. Not the toothy, winning smile he’d flashed before, but a soothing sort of friendly smile. “I make it my business to have something here for everyone, and I price accordingly.”

There wasn’t a doubt in Fox’s mind that this book was the one he’d be taking home. And now, to find out how much he’d have to pay for it.

Bartrum stepped away from his pillar and moved in closer to Fox. He picked the book up, held it out, and wrapped Fox’s fingers tightly around it. Then he said quietly, “To be collected at a later date.” And with that, he began closing up his wagon again. Their business, for now at least, was done. Fox mumbled a quick thank you, and slipped out of the barn.

The valley streets were still empty, and Fox could see the glowing light of the bonfire in the distance. A faint hint of song drifted toward him on the warm breeze, and Fox recognized it as a farmer’s prayer. He kept moving, back up the hill to his deserted house, straight upstairs into his firestone-lit cubby, where he changed into his night things and crawled into bed. There, he propped the book open on his knees and began to read, starting with the very first page.

HE SPENT EVERY SPARE moment reading his new book. He took it with him to the stable in the mornings, grooming Cobb absently with one hand while he held the book open in the other. He read late into the night and continued before dawn each day. And no matter how many pages he read, there always seemed to be so many more ahead of him. But this did not bother Fox. In fact, he would have been happy if the book never ran out of pages. For every inch of them was covered in more information than he’d ever hoped to learn, and it was exhilarating.

The gods, he'd realized, were not very unlike mortals. Prone to the same feelings of love, or anger, or even jealousy. As he read story after story, he was fascinated by how much the gods were once a part of people's lives. And he took note, somewhat anxiously, of how often those people seemed to come to sticky ends. He read lineage charts of which gods were related to which. He found Radda's story about the creation of the Shavid, and the wind god Rhin. He found detailed illustrations of many of the deities, though whether they were actual representations or how the artist imagined them, Fox couldn't tell. And there were maps. Dozens of them, scattered throughout the book, depicting which lands payed tribute to which god. Or where certain notable god-shrines were located. These pages, Fox avoided touching. Even days later, his head still buzzed from his encounter with the black ink "Hydra Route" and the visions it caused.

Fox had no idea what it was about the map that had done it. Was it the fact that it was Farran's page? Or was it something else? The one person he wanted to ask was miles away, the gods only knew where. And so, eventually, he settled on the second best person. And he found him, two days after his initial arrival, sitting up on the hillside with Lai, poring over a small portable desk with a scroll of parchment stretched across it.

Bartrum Bookmonger looked up when Fox approached them, and grinned broadly. "Welcome, youngling! Come, have a seat, won't you?"

Fox looked down at the parchment they were studying, and then turned a questioning face to Lai. It appeared to be a simple chart laying out all the letters of the common alphabet. "Bartrum's teaching me how to read and write," explained Lai sheepishly.

The gentleman's earlier comment about Fox's "friend" suddenly made sense, and Fox smiled at her. "That's excellent!" he said cheerfully. He flopped down easily onto the grass on Bartrum's other side and said, "I could help you too, if you want!"

Lai shook her head, smiling. "Thanks, but you've got enough going on. Bartrum's agreed to stay on the rest of the summer and tutor me. Father's paying him."

"I also teach mathematics and business," said Bartrum genially, all teeth and hinting eyebrows. "For a fee, of course."

"Maybe later," said Fox. "Listen, I wanted to ... talk about something with you." He glanced at Lai, who raised an eyebrow in silent question. "Something I can't quite figure out, and I'm wondering if it's your book, or ... or me."

Bartrum's player air was beginning to dissipate somewhat, as it had back in the goat barn. He grew quiet and calmer, and sat up a little straighter. "Ask away," he said. "And I shall do my best to oblige."

Fox spread the book open on the grass, never worrying that it might get dirty. He'd discovered very quickly that the book was impervious to dirt, water, and even food stains. Now, he flipped to a random map entitled "The Oracle's Mountain," depicting the hard-to-reach pathways to various temples of Phiira, goddess of seers. Fox had been very careful not to select a map that had *anything* to do with Farran.

"What is that?" asked Lai, scooting in closer to look.

"Just some reading for fun," said Fox quickly. Then he turned to Bartrum. "These maps," he said. "Have people been known to ... see things, when they touch them?"

Bartrum raised one perfect eyebrow and adjusted the position of his glasses. "See *what*, might I ask?"

Fox took a deep breath, and placed his finger on the spot labeled "The Gates of Agaath." Again, it was as if he had been there himself. He spoke as the vision came to him. "There is a great tree that's always in bloom, growing in the heart of a round pool. A pool with rose-colored stonework. And there is a winding path you cannot see with your eyes, it blends so perfectly into the stone. Only those who close their eyes and stop trusting in what their sight tells them will be able to hear the echoes leading them up, up the side of the mountain. But the earth at the gates is dead, from generations of pilgrims' feet trampling the grass as they wander hopelessly, looking only with their eyes."

Fox pulled his hand away, trying to ignore the sharp, sudden headache that came with the abrupt sights and smells. Even now, he felt the lingering scent of that faraway mountain tickling his nose. He looked Bartrum straight in the eyes. "I've never been there before," he said. "I'd never even heard of it. Why can I see it? What are these pages made of?"

Bartrum looked stunned. And, for what Fox felt certain was the first time in the excitable man's life, speechless. He pulled his glasses off with a trembling hand and pulled the book close. "These pages," he said finally, "have a very specific kind of magic. They allow for a lot of information in a limited amount of space. They stay clean, and whole. They are meant for hard study, and for texts that should not be easily lost. But they cannot make you see things. That is not their power." He looked up, replacing his glasses once more. "Show me again," he said. And he held out the book.

Fox turned to a different page this time. A map that showed the capital city of the Central Continent: Athilior. It was said to be a chosen city, favored of many of the Great Gods. That's why its map was included. Fox had heard many stories of the city from Father, but of course he'd never been there. Breathing deep again, Fox closed his eyes and touched a random piece of the map. "The market district is wide and sprawling. Every season has its goods, and every trader knows his place. I can smell saddle oils and soaps from the islands. There is a kennel on the west end of the market, with the finest hunting dogs in the city. And a mews that shares the kennel courtyard, where the city's best hawks are raised. Streets of grey stone. Fireproofing balm on every wooden beam in the district since the Market Fire eight years ago, which claimed the lives of over three hundred citizens."

This time, Fox had to *pull* his hand away from the map. His finger seemed to want to stay put, and Fox felt dizzy when he opened his eyes. It was almost as if the information was clattering to get to him, and he'd cut it off like a dam in a river. He settled himself before looking at either of them, and then his gaze locked with Lai's. "It's maps," he said, only to her. Bartrum was all but forgotten. "That's what I can do. I can see them, Lai. I can see everything." He knew as he said it that it was true. Just as he could feel the snow. The Desolata. Just as he could see the wind laid out before him, he *knew*. "It's the maps."

A great gust of wind swept up the hill toward them and settled on their little group, almost knocking them over. Bartrum clutched his glasses to his face, and Lai grasped at the parchment before it flew away. But Fox stood, spreading his arms wide and letting the wind wrap around him, taking in all it had to say. And when it finally slowed, he grinned.

"It's the Shavid," he said breathlessly. "They're coming back."

Chapter Fourteen
Departure

The Foxgloves' next trading expedition took them to a little hamlet called Doff. It was even smaller than Thicca Valley, and tucked far up in the mountains. Their people were primarily fire merchants, specializing in candles, firestones, and even a specific strain of lymnstone. In any other circumstance, Fox would have found their whole culture fascinating. But now, he found it hard to focus on anything.

The Shavid were coming back. He had no idea where they were, or how long it would take them, but they were on their way! He was even more anxious than when they'd first left, checking the horizon regularly for signs of a colored flag or listening for a measure of song. It was only when Father cuffed him over the head and said he was acting like an incompetent child that Fox began trying to put his excitement out of mind. It might take months for them to meander back to him from wherever they might be. For all Fox knew, they could be far across the sea, past the Magistrate's Harbor to the east.

And so he fell to his usual routine, cramming his life full with anything and everything he could to keep his thoughts in the here and now. Only this time, he did it with a certain renewed fervor, determined to show the Shavid how much he'd grown in their absence.

He started up a morning training class with many of the valley boys once he returned home. All the techniques and tricks Neil had shown him were dusted off and put to good use again as he and the boys sparred and practiced in the early dawn. As the weeks progressed, many of the men started to join them, and even a handful of the women. As one of the widows pointed out, those who couldn't fight were more likely to be murdered by those who could.

Each morning after the training group dispersed, Fox would head out to the woods to put his newly honed tracking skills to work. There was no game in all the forests in all the world that was a match for him now. With a growing instinct so powerful it almost frightened him, Fox could track even the cleverest elk with barely a hint of a trail. In fact, he found he had to be very careful to limit his daily haul, or else the woods would be completely barren of animal life by the end of the summer. It was a careful balance between bringing in enough pelts to satisfy Father, and letting the bulk of the animals be, so they could continue to reproduce.

And then, Fox would turn his attentions to his own personal practice. It was this part of his day that Bartrum Bookmonger was particularly interested in. As Fox began to delve deeper into the maps, Bartrum seemed to assign himself to be Fox's personal tutor. He was always there, eager to help and ecstatic to answer any question he could. Fox noticed that the man lost a bit of his flamboyant air whenever he was deeply involved in teaching, and he asked about it one day as the two sat in Bartrum's room at the Five Sides.

"My apprenticeship was rather ... unorthodox," the man said reminiscently. "My master was a lady bookbinder. The only woman in a predominantly male trade. But she turned it to her advantage." He sighed almost dreamily. "That woman could sell pages to an eyeless illiterate. In any case, I kept to myself for the most part. I was a scholar at heart, and being around the books and letters felt *right*. I wanted nothing more than a calm, comfortable life. I kept my head down, stayed out of trouble, and followed her rules to the letter.

"But the dear lady Life, it seemed, had other ideas," said Bartrum. "And I began to discover I had a gift for making paper that even my dear mistress could never hope to emulate. *My* paper was stronger. Sturdier. Smoother. It sold for more; it was requested by the regulars. And my mistress began to see me as a threat, rather than an asset. Long before my apprenticeship was up, she threw me out. Left to my own devices, with but the one marketable skill, I tried to sell my wares on my own.

"I quickly learned, however, that a quality product will only get you so far. And so, I became this," he said, gesturing almost ruefully at himself. "People react better to a cheerful smile and a jolly laugh." Bartrum chuckled softly and shook his head. "For twenty years I have been living as *him*. The florid book man, with his fine clothes and fancy speech. It is most of who I am now. But every so often, the quiet scholar from the back of the bookbinder's shop comes up for air. And I welcome him like an old friend."

Not for the first time, Fox was strongly reminded of Neil. A scholar, trapped in a player's world. And as he and Bartrum went about the days' studies, Fox found himself hoping the two would meet someday. Perhaps Bartrum would still be in town by the time the Shavid once more rode in over the horizon.

Fox discovered quickly that he rather liked Bartrum. Not only as a teacher, but as a friend. He was exceptionally helpful to have around, an extra mind to help work out why Fox's powers behaved as they did. He'd also begun to test Fox, putting him and his Blessing through an ongoing series of trials to see how powerful Fox truly was.

"And to *stretch* your gifts, as it were," Bartrum would explain. For just as he made Lai practice her reading and writing, he expected Fox to practice using his magic at every opportunity.

And so, the summer passed far too quickly. The days spent in a haze of chores, work, and lessons, the nights spent in pleasant companionship at the Five Sides. Trade caravans from farther north began to pass through town, and there was a sense of agreeable tension in the air. New songs began to circulate around the farming community, and the nights slowly began to grow cool. Autumn came early to the mountains, and with it the caravan.

THE START OF SEPTEMBER found Fox and Bartrum perched high up on the goat hills, with Lai and her herd nothing but tiny smudges below. Fox had been gone on several trade and trapping journeys in a row, and it seemed Bartrum was determined to make up for lost time. He'd compiled a whole list of experiments he was eager to try, and he was practically bouncing with excitement as he spoke.

"Now, *focus*," Bartrum said, rubbing his hands together in anticipation. "We know you can call the goats from a short distance, but try it from *here*."

It was almost too easy for Fox. His instinct took over, and within moments the small herd was running up the hill toward them. Bartrum giggled excitedly and fluttered his hand. "Back, back, send them back now!"

With a quick scratch behind the ears, Fox carefully whispered to each that they should head back to their grazing. Once they returned to Lai, Bartrum said, "Now, let's see if we can't call *one* at a time."

This, too, was painfully easy. Fermia came trotting eagerly up to him when he called, and Fox wrapped his arms around her soft, strong neck.

The next test was more difficult. He had to call them without actually *looking* at them. The first few tries were messy and unsuccessful. He accidentally ended up summoning an entire flock of geese, and once Lai said *she* felt inclined to go racing up the hill. But eventually, Fox managed it. And Bartrum was beside himself.

"This is magic unlike anything I've ever *seen*!" he said joyously. "When your Shavid friends return, oh what a tale we'll have to tell them!"

But as September wore on, Fox couldn't spend as much time on lessons as either he or Bartrum would have liked. The caravan was mere weeks away, and that meant every waking moment was dedicated to intense preparations. Repairs had to be made to the gear and the cart. Meat had to be smoked, to make portable rations for the journey. Pelts were stretched on frames to make them easier to display to potential buyers.

And every waresman in town had their own routine. Thicca Valley was never truly calm during the end of the summer, which only added to the restlessness already plaguing Fox. The wind still taunted him with hints of the approaching Shavid, but he could never tell how close they might be. He even attempted in vain to reach out to them *with* the wind, but he wasn't hopeful. It seemed all he could do was wait.

But waiting, he'd discovered, truly did not come naturally to him. He knew it now more than ever: his restlessness was a product of the wind. Just another strange quirk that came with his particular Blessing. Just as the wind could not sit still, neither could he. He began to keep a whittling knife and a block of wood in his pockets at all times, just in case he found himself caught with nothing to do. By the time the final preparations for the caravan were in place, he'd carved enough wooden pieces to fill his entire windowsill.

Departure was a week away, and with it came the Harvestmast. The two rituals went hand-in-hand, as the harvest festival filled the day and night, leading up to the dawn commencement of the caravan the following morning. Bartrum Bookmonger was thrilled to be witnessing what he called "these pleasant little mountain ceremonies." In the days leading up to the two events, he could be seen dogging the heels of anyone preparing for the festivities, asking them questions with a little book and pen held out before him, ready to take notes on the proceedings. Many of the Thiccans had begun to tolerate him by now, and some even seemed to enjoy having someone take such an interest in their humble lives. Fox watched Bartrum conduct many an interview at his favorite table at the Five Sides. It was also from here that Bartrum could sometimes be seen commanding the attention of the entire room, as he read passionately from his beloved books. A great number of Thiccans enjoyed his animated speeches and performances, just as they'd enjoyed the Shavid. And Fox, watching Bartrum grandly deliver a tale with one foot on his bench and one foot on the table, found that it was unfortunate that the book man wouldn't be staying in the valley through the winter. His contract as tutor was up, and he would be traveling back to the south with the protection of the caravan.

The day before Harvestmast, the entire valley woke to a blanket of frost on the ground. And even those who did not possess Fox's heightened senses could smell it: fall was here. Excitement filled the air, and the same anxious energy that preceded the Homecoming months before now settled over Thicca Valley again. Homes were cleaned from top to bottom. Rugs were beaten out, over and over again. Even Lai was grooming the goats so often they began to protest.

But why? Fox wondered to himself as he sat on the hillside with her, watching her pick stones that weren't there out of Fermia's hooves. Lai had never given in to the valley's nervous little quirks before. And why would she? No one she cared about ever left on the caravan. None of her family were waresmen. She never had to watch a father or brother leave for the entire winter, always wondering when and *if* he'd be coming home. And as Lai finally released the goat back to its grazing, Fox realized. It was him. He was leaving, for the very first time. And that made this year different.

Fox had been so wrapped up in his own preparations. With the excitement of the returning Shavid, and the responsibility that came with finally becoming a man, he hadn't even thought about how his absence would affect the people left in the valley. Mother, alone for the first winter since Fox was born. Lai, with hardly a friend in the valley, losing both her tutor and her closest companion all in one day. Even Picck might find himself wishing for Fox's company in the kitchen this winter.

He suddenly felt strangely guilty for abandoning them all, and tried to shake the feeling away. This was how life was in the valley. He'd never begrudged Father for being gone all winter. It was the way things were. Father *had* to leave for his family to survive. And the whole of Thicca Valley depended on the business of trade, Fox knew that. But even so, as he looked at Lai absently running her fingers through her hair, he was visited by a strange sense of discomfort. And he knew, somehow, that things would never be the same between them once he returned.

THE STREETS CLEARED early that afternoon, as waresmen and trader families enjoyed each other's company one last time. Fox stayed away from his own cabin, knowing that his parents preferred to be alone right before Father left. Instead, he chose to spend his last free evening with the Blackroots. They all sat together in the empty common room, eating thick and flavorful rabbit stew and playing cards. Bartrum was invited to join them, and he gladly accepted.

As the skies grew darker outside and the fires were lit, Fox watched Picck and Rose, wondering if they knew about the baby. Wondering if he should tell them. He put off making the decision by throwing himself into a lively game of dice with the group. A game at which Bartrum failed spectacularly. The poor man ended up losing two of his fancy scarves to Rose, and an exceptionally nice cloak to Picck. When Borric collected *his* winnings from Bartrum, he joked that none of the stick-man's clothes would fit him, so he settled instead for hard coin. But despite his constant losses, poor Bartrum continued to play.

"I'm *sure* I can figure this game out!" he said after Lai teasingly suggested they play something else. "I am a scholar after all, young madam! And there is no strategy to be had that can elude me! I have studied it all!"

After losing three more rounds, Bartrum finally admitted defeat. He stood and adjusted his glasses. "Perhaps I should have graciously stepped away from the table when it was first suggested," he said with a wry smile. And then he sighed and patted Fox on the shoulder. "Come on then, I suppose I ought to let you claim your profits."

Fox followed him out to the traveling library, still tucked cozily in the goat barn. He didn't want any of Bartrum's clothes or money, but he had agreed to take his winnings out in paper goods. He sifted eagerly through the books tucked into the wagon, and even leafed through the fancy sheets of parchment. In the end, he selected one of the fancy pens and a bottle of rich black ink. But as he stepped back to let Bartrum close up the wagon doors once more, a handful of rolled-up papers tucked into a corner caught his eye. At a glance, they looked like a crude map, and he was intrigued.

"Oh, those," said Bartrum, noticing Fox's gaze. "One of the tradesmen was so kind as to show me the path we'll be taking back down to the southern lands. Here," he said, pulling the papers free, eager to share his knowledge with Fox. He tugged at yet another secret panel in his miraculous wagon, producing an attached table at just the right height for he and Fox to spread the map upon it and read.

It was a strange, sketched map of the Merchant's Highway. Simple squares marked certain cities and waypoints on the journey, and a thick line symbolized the general placement of the road. There were notes here and there, saying things like "Left Fork at the Lowest Cavern" and "Keep Away from Townsfolk at Garrindor!"

"I found it rather fascinating," said Bartrum in his usual, excitable tone. "Your people have no notion of the proper mapmaking techniques, but you've gone on for generations making this journey every year. With only the barest, rudimentary charts. And, well, instinct, I suppose."

Fox smiled to himself. The idea that someone who'd seen as much of the world as Bartrum, had read all the books that he had, could find the Thiccans fascinating. Absently, Fox ran his fingers along the trade route, as he had done so many times before with the maps in his precious book.

It happened in an instant. A cold, crushing pressure wrapped around his chest, and he was drowning in a freezing cold terror. He heard himself screaming as if from a great distance, but he couldn't seem to stop himself. Or maybe it wasn't him screaming. Perhaps it was the very earth, crying out in pain. He could hear something thundering, making his head pound. His vision was all at once white and dark and blinding.

And then someone was pulling his hand free of the map, and Fox doubled over, trying with all his might not to collapse onto the goat barn floor. The thundering stopped, and the pressure released as quickly as it had come. But the deep, cold feeling, the feeling of standing naked in the snow, did not go away.

There was a hole in the map, just where his finger had been. A charred, jagged hole, right in the center of the block marked "Tessoc Pass." For a moment, Fox simply stared at it, trying to force his breathing to slow through the stabbing pain in his ribs. And then he ran. Back through the empty valley streets, back up the hill to his cabin and his parents. And when he burst through the front door, breathless, he found Father sitting by the glowing embers of the long-dead kitchen fire.

"You can't go," said Fox at once. "It's the pass ... it'll kill you. It'll kill us all." He stared his father directly in the eyes, unflinching and unapologetic. Man-to-man. And when Father did not respond, he said it again. "You can't go."

There was a look in Father's eyes, only just visible in the emberglow. It was a look Fox had never seen before. An ever-so-quick glimmer of fear. But then, the look vanished, to be replaced by one of fatherly comfort. "Come," he said. "Sit."

Fox joined him at the fireside, and there was silence in the kitchen. For several minutes, father and son sat quietly. Then Father said, "I don't presume to know *how* you know this ... but you do, don't you?"

Fox nodded, and after a moment Father continued.

"You're a very clever boy, Fox. You always were. And now, with these new things happening to you, you're growing up so fast that I fear I might miss it." Then he sighed deeply and went on. "You're practically a young man. But because of your maturity, I know you'll understand me when I say this: *not* going is never an option."

Fox opened his mouth to protest. To say he *knew* it wasn't an option, but this year it *had* to be. But Father held up his hand and went on.

"The lives of everyone I hold dear depend that caravan. You, your mother, this valley ... they are all worth the risk. And there is always risk. But we are prepared to meet those risks head on." He put his arm around Fox, as he had so many times when Fox was a little boy. Times when he would tell Fox stories of the caravan. Stories that Fox would cling to and dream about. Now, Father said, "You'll see. Right by my side, we'll take on the whole Merchant's Highway."

But Fox pulled away. "You don't understand," he said. "This is bigger than just a bad winter storm, or a highway bandit. There is something happening out there!"

Father sighed and rubbed his temples. "Go to bed, Fox."

"But –" said Fox angrily.

"Go," said Father sternly, "to bed."

The conversation was over, and Fox knew it. Father's word was final. And Fox, feeling defeated and lost, climbed the stairs angrily and disappeared into his cubby. He buried himself in his blankets, hoping to ward off some of the cold that still wrapped itself around him, but he did not sleep. He listened to Mother's light snores from down below, and the sounds of Father tinkering away in his workroom. Late into the night Father worked, and Fox lay awake. Thinking. Praying. And by the time he finally drifted off into a fitful half-sleep, dawn was beginning to brighten the sky, and Father was still downstairs.

"BUT IT'S NOT JUST *them*," Lai was saying. "It's not *them* who will be killed if they go, it's *you!* You're one of them this year!"

"I know," said Fox bitterly, "but that doesn't mean they'll listen to me. And Father's right! Even if I could convince every one of them that death was waiting, they'd still go. They're Thiccans, after all. They face death every day just by living here."

They were sitting on the roof of the Five Sides, looking down on the rapidly-filling valley streets. Harvestmast was upon them. Fox should have been celebrating with everybody else, but he couldn't bring himself to enjoy the festival. Too much was happening, and everywhere he looked, he saw one more life that might be affected by what he knew. A wareman's wife. A trader's daughter. And over and over in Fox's mind, he relived that one moment with Farran. *How much more blood do you want on your hands? You already have a lifetime's worth ahead of you.*

He could never forget the faces of the widows he'd made. The women whose husbands had fallen defending the valley against the Desolata. A threat that had only been chasing Fox. He couldn't stand the idea of making even more by letting the caravan leave. The plan was simple, and began to grow in his mind as the valley prepared for the last festival of the year. When the sun was at its peak, the valley bells rang out, and everyone flocked toward the valley square. Music and dancing broke out, and the streets filled with the smells of delicious morsels. But Fox made his way against the tide of valley folk, back to his home.

For a moment he stood in his deserted house, in the doorway of Father's workshop. He looked around at the neatly packaged pelts and furs, ready to be loaded into the cart later that very night. The plan was, indeed, simple. If Father didn't go, perhaps the rest of them would follow. He was one of the caravan leaders. He was respected.

Fox took his whittling knife from its place on his belt and held it tight. And then, he began to slice. He tore into the packages, ripping through them and slashing the very furs within. He cut pelts from their frames and threw the frames themselves into the workroom fire pit, causing the embers to reignite into a blaze. He sliced a bear skin into unusable scraps, mentally calculating how much he'd need to destroy to stop Father leaving. It made sense, even as he threw a full package of otter pelts into the growing flame. With nothing to trade, there was no need to leave. But as Fox reached out to tear open a tightly bundled packet of tanned deer hide, he stopped. Father was watching him from the doorway. And this time, the look in his eyes was not fear, or fatherly concern. It was pure, paralyzing disappointment.

Fox let both knife and hide slip from his hands. He searched for something to say. Anything that would make Father stop looking at him like that. But no words came. It was Father who finally spoke.

"I have been looking forward to sharing this journey with my son. A strong, intelligent young man. For a long time, I've wanted to take him on the caravan with me, as my apprentice." His voice was empty of any emotion, but his eyes still rang with that absolute disappointment. "Perhaps I was mistaken. I haven't got a young man for a son. He is just a little boy. And little boys stay home for the winter."

Fox's voice caught up with him again. "What are you saying?" he asked.

In that moment, Father seemed to grow taller. His voice deepened as he said, "You are no longer invited on the caravan. You no longer have apprentice status in this valley, or in my home. You will stay home, and think about what it means to truly be a man." And then, as he turned to leave Fox standing in the wreckage of the workroom, he said quietly, "I hope to Spirit that you figure it out."

Fox did not join in the Harvestmast festivities. He took to the woods instead, hunting to keep his mind off what he had done. But he could hear and smell pieces of the celebration on the wind at times. A scrap of Borric's pies, or a hint of a dancing tune. And it wasn't long before he realized he was not alone. The wolves were keeping their distance, but he could see them tucked in the shadows, and hear them roaming behind the trees.

They kept him company all night. As he hunted small game and set traps for larger prizes. They lounged just out of reach when he sat high up on a grassy ridge, watching the lights from the Harvestmast. And they began to howl their haunting songs as dawn brushed the mountaintops, and the caravan pulled out of town.

Chapter Fifteen
Doff

Change was in the air. The change of seasons, with summer's end melting into the chill of autumn. Colors changed, as bright green grasses faded into yellow and brown. Leaves turned deep red and orange and copper, and frost greeted every farmer when he woke before dawn each morning. And in the midst of it all, there was the change that only came from the whispering hints of rumors.

Fox heard them all. Theories about why he hadn't joined the caravan this year, as everyone knew he should have. Some believed he was going to be married off to a daughter in another town, and he'd be learning her father's trade. Others touched on the truth, though they didn't know the full story, when they said that the Foxglove men had a falling out. But there were a select few who could be heard saying that young Forric Foxglove simply didn't have what it took to be a trapper. That he'd been left at home because he was a disgrace to the fur trade, and would never be the man his father was. Fox could feel them watching him every time he set foot outside his house. Every eye in the valley was turned to him, waiting for something. Just as they'd watched him after the destruction of the valley, so many months ago.

He began spending more and more time in the woods, even staying some nights in Father's nearby trapping cabin. He caught his own meals, and ventured deeper and deeper into the wild with each journey.

"Doesn't that upset your mother?" asked Lai. They were sitting by the river during one of the brief moments they had to spare together. Lai had been helping Widow Mossgrove with the harvest every day, working just as hard as any of the farm hands. And with Fox doing his best to avoid the

Thiccan's stares, the two had hardly seen each other since the caravan's departure. Now, they sat on the riverbank, skipping stones across the water.

"Not really," admitted Fox. "Truth is, she's not too happy with me right now. She says my 'childish tantrum' might have cut his profits for this year almost in half." He threw his next stone with such force, it shattered when it hit a boulder across the river. "She's been depressed since he left. Figured it was best for her if I didn't … if I wasn't around to remind her what I'd done."

They stood in silence for awhile, skipping handful after handful of smooth, flat river rocks. Then Lai said cheerfully, "Rose knows she's pregnant now. She and Picck announced it just yesterday." She grinned. "Can you imagine? Picck, a father?" She giggled and tossed her next stone.

"They'll make good parents," said Fox, smiling a bit. There, at least, was one thing he'd done right lately.

Lai kept him company for a bit longer, then said she was needed at home to help with the dinner rush. After a halfhearted invitation to join in, which they both knew he'd refuse, Lai headed back to the Five Sides. And Fox sat for a long while, skipping rocks and floating dried leaves in the current. He waited until well after dark, when he knew Mother would already be asleep, before he crept back into his cubby and began packing his things. Short journeys to and from the cabin weren't enough anymore. It was time he tried trading on his own.

DOFF WAS A SOLID THREE-day journey on foot. At least, it had been when Fox traveled there with Father. But his instincts told him to take different paths. Cut through different parts of the mountain. And by the time he'd reached the rough stone pillar marked "Doff," it had only been just over a day and a half.

He'd been too distracted on his last journey to take in much of the scenery of Doff. Now, he looked around with a wanderer's fascination. He admired the way the village was arranged, up and down the mountainside, as if everything was perched on a great stone shelf. And he discovered quickly that, in its own way, rough and provincial Doff was just as interesting as the sprawling Whitethorn. Perhaps even more.

The whole little town looked as if it had been carved directly out of the mountainside. Everywhere Fox looked, he saw rough stone. House fronts looked like cave mouths fitted with doors. Their roofs were angular and uneven, sometimes nothing more than natural rocky outcroppings. Great boulders had been carved and shaped into little gardens, with oddly-shaped shelves and pockets overgrown with herbs.

For a bit, Fox simply wandered. Taking it all in. Enjoying the new sights and sounds and smells. There was wax in the air, and flint. In everything there was a hint of charcoal, even the very stone. Natural chimneys protruded from every stone-cut house, and smoke curled from every one in the late-afternoon chill. It was as though the whole village was steaming. He breathed deep, his senses delighting in the fresh excitement of a strange place. And then he hitched his bags higher onto his shoulders and set off to the public house.

Even if he hadn't remembered it from his and Father's last visit, the smells would have drawn him straight to the little cavern. It was two levels up, at approximately the heart of this strange village, hidden within a long, deep crevice in the wall of the stone. In fact, it was the sort of place you almost couldn't find if you didn't already know what to look for. The entrance looked like nothing more than a low, jagged shelf in the rock. But as Fox dipped low and slid beneath it, warmth settled upon him. Here, tucked safely behind the face of the mountain, its narrow entryway protecting it from the harsh mountain winters, was the pub.

It was a dark, sprawling cave with low ceilings. Tables and benches were scattered throughout the room, sometimes disappearing into the darker corners. Torches cast their glow from rough brackets on the walls, and deep veins of unharvested firestone ran through the walls. The soft crackle of the flames echoed strangely against the stone, and voices all through the room were kept low. Smells of ale and hearty stews met Fox's nose, making him suddenly very aware of his stomach. He'd only snacked on bread and scraps of smoked elk on his trip, and now he was ravenously hungry.

There was a long slab of stone that took up a large portion of the right side of the cavern. Fox made his way up to it and waited until the surly-looking bartender behind the slab took notice of him. "You're that trader's kid," the man said after a moment. His voice was low and grunting, and his face was mostly in shadow from the bulk of his protruding forehead. He was busy wiping down a strange piece of crockery. It was almost a deep, wide bowl, but with a bulbous handle on either side.

"You remembered," said Fox, somewhat surprised.

"Don't get many visitors around here," the man grunted. "New faces always stick out." He slapped the now-clean dish down in front of Fox and said, "What'll you have? Goat? Eggs? You look too young for hard ale, but for the right coin I won't ask any questions."

There was no kitchen in this pub. Everything was cooked out in the open, over and around a series of fires throughout the room. Fox could smell some kind of rabbit stew bubbling over one of these, and it made his mouth water agreeably. "Got anything with rabbit?" he asked.

"Take your dish and find a seat in the back. Someone will be with you."

Fox did as he was told, gripping the dish to his chest. He found a long, rough wooden table tucked deep in the shadows by a cooking fire, and selected a seat at the end. He let his bags slip from his shoulders and fall to the ground as he looked curiously about the room. From his seated position, he watched a handful of men a few tables away playing a quiet game of cards. They seemed to be gambling with chunks of stone. Their table made up half of the overall population of the pub, but Fox knew business would pick up soon. Evenings were always the busiest times for any tavern.

Fox noticed that everyone seemed to have the same sort of dish he'd been given. It didn't seem to matter if they'd been served soup, bread, or drink, the dishes appeared to be all-purpose. A man sitting by himself by one of the torches was drinking deeply from his, gripping both handles and tipping the whole thing back, letting streams of liquid run down his beard and drip onto his massive chest.

It wasn't long before Fox's meal was delivered. A heavyset woman brought a small cauldron right to his table and ladled stew into his dish. Thick curls of steam rose up and obscured Fox's vision, and by the time it cleared she had moved on to another table. Fox dove in hungrily, savoring every bite. There was a great pile of bread at the center of every table, and Fox helped himself to several large chunks. He used them like spoons, scooping and soaking up every last drop of the thick, hearty stew until his dish was clean once more. Then he sat back, enjoying the comfortable warmth of a full belly.

More villagers were starting to come in now. Most of them were miners, by the looks of them. Strong, sturdy men and women, with stone powder on their clothes and clinging to their hair. Fox longed to join one of their tables. To ask questions about life here in Doff. Instead, he simply watched. And he kept quiet when a group of villagers sat down at the other end of his table.

"Got himself into a whole host of trouble with the wick weaver," one of them was saying. A woman, tall and impossibly muscular. "Wouldn't be surprised if bits of that poor idiot show up in the next batch of candles."

Her companions laughed, and another one replied with, "But no one wants to smell that unwashed buffoon all day. That's one scent that won't sell."

So, these were candlemakers. They smelled of fine wax and their clothes were free of stone dust. For a moment, Fox watched them out of the corner of his eye. And then, something caught his attention. Someone in their group who wasn't quite one of them. Someone with straw-colored hair, and a spatter of freckles across his cheeks and forehead.

"Topper?" Fox said in amazement.

The stone bounced his voice farther than Fox had expected, and the group of candlemakers turned to look. Including the smallest of them all, a little boy tucked between the tall woman and a dark, slender gentleman. The boy leaned forward to get a closer look at Fox, and his eyes widened.

"Fox!" he shouted happily and scrambled to his feet. He raced down the table and threw his arms around Fox's shoulders in a shockingly crushing embrace for someone his size. Then he pulled back, a grin stretching his face so far it looked almost painful.

"It *is* you, Topper!" said Fox joyfully. "What in Spirit's name are you doing here?"

The candlemakers were watching the two boys curiously, but Topper didn't seem to notice. "I live here now!" he said cheerfully. "Seems I got a natural instinct for fire, what with spending so long working the lamps back in Whitethorn."

"But when..." said Fox. "How?"

Topper shrugged. "Meat Man Mallard had it out for me after you left. Started telling everyone around town how I was a rotten little thief. Made for a right hard few weeks. So I skipped town. Took myself off with a merchant group, stowed and hitched my way down until I settled here." And then he blushed slightly. "Truthfully, I was looking for you. Thought, seeing as how nice you were to me, you might be able to help me get settled. But I guess I missed your town somewhere, and ended up here in Doff." And then his grin returned in full force, and he looked back at his companions. "And it's the best that could have happened! Come on, I'll introduce you."

And with that, Fox was dragged to the other end of the table, where he was seated right in the middle of the group. Topper quickly related the story of how he and Fox met, and Fox was surprised to find how much of a hero Topper really thought he was. The candlemakers certainly seemed to agree, as they welcomed Fox into their little group enthusiastically. Names and titles flew at him so quickly he had trouble keeping up, but one of them stood out.

The muscular woman reached across the table to clasp Fox's hand with a certain air of dignity. There was an attitude in her firm handshake that said she was somebody important. "Kaldora Flintstock," she said smoothly. "Master Craftsman, and first *female* master, of the Fire Merchant's Guild."

Fox returned her handshake just as firmly, trying not to appear as outwardly nervous as he felt. But he was sure this woman could kill him with a loaf of bread. She was at least a head taller than all the men at the table, or indeed in the whole public house. Fox wouldn't have been surprised if her yellow-blonde hair, pulled back in its severe braid, brushed the ceiling each time she stood. Every bit of her looked chiseled and stone-cut, like the carved statues in the Whitethorn temple. In fact, Fox half expected her hand to be cold as marble when he touched it.

She was watching him more intensely than the rest of her group, and it wasn't long before Fox realized why. When Topper sat down beside her again, she ruffled his hair affectionately and said, "Well then, will your friend be staying with us?"

"Oh yes please, ma'am!" said Topper excitedly. "You will stay, won't you Fox?" he asked, joyous pleading in his eyes. And when Fox nodded, Topper sprang to his feet again and came around the table to grab Fox's wrist. He pulled him to his feet and said, "Come on! I'll show you the town!"

As Fox let himself be dragged back to the entrance, he laughed at Topper's enthusiasm. It was good to see the boy smile, and good to know he wasn't sleeping on rooftops anymore. But as they reached the crevice that led back outside, Fox put his hand out and gripped the wall to stop their rapid progress. "It's after dark," he said. "We'll never be able to see it all at night. Why don't we wait until the sun is back up, so I can get the proper tour."

And then a sly grin slid across Topper's face. "Fox," he said, "this is a city of *fire*! Nighttime is only the *best* time to see it."

They dipped into the low, narrow crevice, and back out into the village, where Fox stopped and stared, absolutely breathless. Doff was indeed a city of fire. And at night, it *glowed.*

It was as though the whole mountain was made of dying embers. Stone that had appeared ordinary by the light of day now shimmered with veins and rivers of richest orange. Raw firestone, just like the walls of the pub. And woven in among these veins were thinner, spider-web fine shocks of dark blue. Doff shone to rival the starlight, its glow at once entrancing and unattainable. It seemed impossible that a place so charmingly strange and beautiful as this might exist, and Fox found himself longing to reach out and touch every shimmering beacon in the darkness.

As Topper took them farther up the mountain, Fox followed without truly noticing where he was being led. His eyes were darting here and there across the village, catching every spark of light and making new discoveries everywhere he looked. Even after dark, Doff was wide awake. Doors were propped open, and Fox could see people working inside their little cavern homes and workshops. Here, a blacksmith was hammering out iron cages that Fox assumed were meant to be lanterns. A little farther up, a group of miners were heading back down into the mountain through a wide cave entrance set with shaped, polished firestones.

"How long have you been here?" asked Fox once he found his voice again.

Topper had been kind enough to stay quiet up until now, leaving Fox to look about without interruption. Now, words spilled from him like a broken dam. "Just over two months! But it feels like a lifetime already. Lady Kaldora took me in! Said she'd always wanted a son, but never settled down enough to get married."

"How did you find her?" asked Fox.

"She found me!" Topper said. "Found me hiding out in the nests, and she took pity on me. Wasn't until a few days later that she found out how good I was with fire, and started training me up to be a fire merchant."

"The nests?" said Fox curiously.

Topper's grin returned, like he was about to let Fox in on some incredible secret. "This way," he said.

Their next turn took them on a strange pathway. Whereas before they'd been winding around the outside of the mountain in a constant, upward spiral, now they cut straight in. The path wound tighter and tighter toward the heart of the mountain, with stone rising high on either side of them. Cutting out all but a slice of the star-strewn sky overhead. And then, the path spat them out onto an open ledge, and Fox caught his breath.

Great, black birds were everywhere. Perched in stone pockets that pitted the glowing walls. Soaring back and forth in the semi-dark. Huge birds with long necks and sharp, cruel beaks, their silhouettes like black paint darkening the starlight.

"They're called eborills," said Topper, looking fondly on them. "They're our hunting birds. They can reach places on the mountain that we just can't."

As they watched, a handful of the birds flew from their nests, winging their way out into the open air. By the blue and orange glow, Fox could make out great, angled wings and fierce talons. The birds looked more skeletal than sturdy, and despite their size, Fox was sure they couldn't handle the weight of more than the smallest game.

He was wrong. As the birds disappeared into the night sky, another eborill was returning. It carried something huge in its claws, and as it dipped down to drop its prize on a great, round stone at the center of the nests, Fox took a quick step back. A full-grown mountain goat, even bigger than those they raised in Thicca Valley, crashed to the stone. The eborill landed beside the carcass and began to preen itself. Standing, it looked like it came up to about Fox's waist.

Topper went right up to the bird's head and rubbed its beak affectionately, but Fox stayed back. The eborills looked entirely vicious, and even Topper standing so close to one made him nervous. The bird was almost as tall as the boy. But the eborill simply crooned, a strange trill that made the hairs on the back of Fox's neck stand up. A few moments later, a rather beefy man shouldered his way past Fox and over to Topper and the bird.

"Ho, there, little one!" the man called, and Topper waved.

"Hullo, Lugor!" said Topper.

"Getting cold out here," said the man Lugor. "Better be heading home, you and your friend."

With a quick goodbye to both the man and the bird, Topper scampered back over to Fox and led him back down the mountain. So many questions plagued Fox's mind, he didn't know which to ask first. About the birds, about the firestone trade ... if there was so much to know about such a little village, how could Fox ever learn all he needed about the rest of the world?

But his questions would have to wait until morning. As Fox was brought into Topper's new home, exhaustion swept over him. Kaldora welcomed them warmly, and a sleeping pad was rolled out for Fox on the floor of Topper's little cave room. Even here, the walls glowed with fine orange and blue veins. It was strangely comforting, and within moments Fox was deeply and entirely asleep.

Chapter Sixteen
Deep Winter

The people of Doff were very welcoming to Fox when they discovered he was Topper's friend. The little urchin was very beloved in this cozy hamlet. And when the story of Fox's rescuing Topper back in Whitethorn began to circulate, Fox was treated like a local hero. He was welcomed eagerly into homes and shops, where he was able to trade the small but valuable pelts he'd brought with him. He found himself helping to skin the day's catches from the eborill nests, and was happy to share some of his trapper's knowledge on the subject. But his best trades came from the traps.

He'd always been good with traps. Most of Father's most accurate snares were Fox's design, and Fox could make them almost unnaturally quickly. And while the Doffians were incredibly skilled fire merchants and miners, their hunting craft was rather lacking in some respects. As Fox began to make more and more business acquaintances in the village, he started taking special orders for traps. The owner of the pub wanted rabbit traps, as he said rabbit was a rare but popular delicacy. For just two simple snares, Fox was given enough credit to eat for free at the public house for the rest of his trip.

And others were just as eager to barter with him. Miner's wives who did much of their own trapping; they wanted better fishing nets to help them get all they could from the tricky mountain rivers. The rocky gardens were outfitted with snares to catch scavenging little creatures who might try and steal the growing herbs. Even the candlemakers sought his help. He helped them bring in turtles, as their shells were very useful molds for pouring wax.

When he wasn't at work, Fox was learning. He was allowed down into the mines on his sixth day, someplace he'd never been in his own valley. With an ancient but unexpectedly spry old miner as their guide, he and

Topper were welcomed down, into the very heart of the village. As they traveled down a long series of wooden ramps and carved stone stairways, Topper leaned in close and whispered conspiratorially, "Mum Kaldora says I might be able to work here someday. She says I'm well on my way to becoming a Master Fire Merchant!" And then he giggled slightly, as if the thought was so ridiculously wonderful he simply couldn't hold it in.

"What's that mean?" asked Fox, just as quietly.

"Means I'm specialized in everything! Some folks just are candlemakers or wick weavers, and some folks only work in the mines. Masters can do it all! It's the highest honor in the whole of Doff! The Grand Master is the head of the entire village, and Mum Kaldora hopes to get there someday."

If anybody could do it, thought Fox, *that* woman could. And then he shuddered, but it was not from the mere cold of being under the mountain. It was her. While he'd been welcomed into her home, Kaldora made him nervous. And it hadn't taken him long to figure out why.

She was a severe woman, and was regarded all throughout the village with the highest respect. He'd known right from the start not to cross her, but it was more than that. No, it was in the way she looked at Topper. Her face broke into a smile that made him forget how intimidating she was. Her hardened features vanished into a face that was purely beautiful. It was written over every inch of her body that she loved this little boy like he was her own flesh and blood. And that, more than anything in the world, made Fox edgy. Farran's prediction of his future, that it was filled with blood and danger, buzzed in the back of Fox's mind like an angry swarm of wasps. And just as he worried about ever having to report to Borric about Lai's safety, so too he now worried about reporting about Topper to Kaldora.

But she was put quickly out of his mind when they turned through a tight passageway and came out into the mines. Not for the first time since his arrival in Doff, Fox was amazed at how many incredible secrets the little village held. Now, he looked around in awe as he watched men and women pulling great chunks of glowing ore from the very earth.

They appeared to be standing at the base of an enormous trench. A labyrinth of bridges and ladders and planks criss-crossed from one end to the other, and up the shimmering walls and down into even deeper pits. Ropes and pulleys carried tools and pails of harvested ore up and down the mine, and high overhead great glowing stalactites served as natural lanterns. Everywhere Fox looked, there were whirlwinds of movement. Miners hard at work. Great turning water wheels. Rope pulleys hauling their loads up and down the face of the rock. The firestone veins and the strange blue shimmers were even brighter here, and they shifted and glowed like so much snowfall catching the firelight. The mines simply crawled with life, and it was as though the mountain itself were truly a living creature.

As the small group wound their way through workers and equipment and jagged mounds of uncut stone, Fox asked, "What is the blue? I know the orange glow is firestone, but what –"

"You've got lymnstone where you come from?" said the old miner.

"Yes," said Fox.

"It's a very specific strand of the same," the miner explained.

Fox remembered hearing something about a peculiar type of lymnstone on his first journey to the village. Now he asked, "What's so special about it?"

"The question should be," said the old miner, smiling with the few teeth he had left, "what *isn't* so special about it."

"It's only the most powerful and lasting ore they've ever found down here," jumped in Topper excitedly. "We use it in light baubles that don't use fire. And its powder can be mixed into the candle wax for a brighter glow!"

"We're discovering new things to do with it every year," said the old miner. "It's stronger than your ordinary green lymnstone, and in many ways still a mystery. Even to us. But it saved our village a decade or so back, so we welcome the challenge."

After the tour of the mines, Fox positively itched to know more about this new, blue lymnstone. Maybe not on this trip, but he definitely planned to visit Doff again in the future. For just as his father had certain cities and towns on his regular trade route, now Fox had his first. And as they emerged again into the fresh mountain air, Topper still chattering on about all you could do with the blue stone, Fox thought that he couldn't have found a more worthwhile town in all of Sovesta.

THERE WAS SNOW IN THE air. Fox could smell it when he awoke, and it tickled his senses as he went about his business in the village. All morning, he felt it drawing nearer. And by mid-afternoon, he knew it would be his last day in Doff. He had to get home before the storms began.

"Just one more night," he told Topper. "And I'll have to be off first thing in the morning." When Topper's face fell, Fox said quickly, "But I'll be back! I promise!" He laid a hand on the younger boy's shoulder and looked him square in the eyes. "You and your village have been good to me. Like a second home. And traders always return home."

This made Topper smile. "We'll at least have a proper send-off then! Tonight, we celebrate!"

And he meant it. When they entered the public house for dinner late that evening, the stone cavern echoed with cheers and whoops. Fox felt himself blush, and grinned to hide his embarrassment and joy. And then he was pulled to a table near the center of the room, and surrounded by many of the fire merchants he had come to call friends. There was a stout young girl about Topper's age, who was already working down in the mines. She had a wonderful gift for finding exactly which veins of firestone and lymnstone would produce the most ore. And there was Kaldora's younger brother, Topper's adopted uncle, who was called Wick. A handful of candlemakers whose names were all very similar, and Fox could never quite keep them straight. But he *thought* the boys were called Malla, Dalla, Dari and Denn. Either way, he found he got along with them splendidly.

Dinner was a raucous affair, with everyone talking and laughing and raising their dishes in toasts. An entire roasted goat was slid out on a board right in front of Fox, and he was asked to cut the first piece. Renewed cheers shook the stone walls when he did, and then Wick jumped to his feet and started the music.

Music was very different here in Doff. Fox had heard little pieces of song and instruments every so often in passing, but never quite like this. There were great hollowed stones with skins stretched across them, making for fascinatingly strange drums that echoed like thunder. Everything was done in rhythmic beats, from wild and savage dancing tunes to somber, even pounding. Now, Wick began to clap his hands in an even rhythm, and two of the men produced the stone drums and began to beat along with him. As they did, Wick started to sing.

Heart, heart
Heart of the stone
That woman of mine
Who left me alone
Heart, heart
Heart dark and cold
I hope you survive on your own!

After a few verses, even Fox was able to join in on the chorus. And he did, with a great gusto that was rewarded by many a cheer and clap on the shoulder from the people at his table. All night this went on, until finally the last song of the evening was sung. A slow, steady song of farewell. And then the crowd began to clear, to head back to work or to their beds. Out into the glowing stone night they went, and Fox looked out on Doff with a certain pang of sorrow. He'd grown so quickly attached to such a little place, it would be difficult to leave it behind. It would most likely be spring before he could visit again.

His packs were full of candles and firestone totems and blue lymnstone. His head was full of songs and wondrous memories. And with the dawn next morning, Fox was gone. He would just beat the first snowfall home, but he wasn't worried. His first trip on his own had gone better than he had ever imagined. And for the first time since the caravan departed, Fox felt like a man.

THE FEELING WAS SHORT-lived. He ambled back through his kitchen door in Thicca Valley just after dawn, and Mother's reaction to his absence made him feel very much like a little boy again. She vacillated between holding him tight and crying that she'd been so worried, and raging at him with a face of sheer fury, calling him things he'd only heard her call Father when she made him sleep in his trapping cabin.

The note Fox had left explaining the reasons for his disappearance and telling her not to worry did not seem to have had much of an effect. In fact, when Fox mentioned it in an attempt to defend himself, Mother produced it, crumpled and worried-over, from her apron pocket and brandished it in his face.

"And suppose I'd never seen you again?" she shouted. "Suppose you'd died in a snowstorm or been tracked down by the Desolata, and all I had to remember you by was *this?*"

When Fox opened his mouth to protest, she sent him upstairs. He was sentenced to isolation in his cubby, to be lifted when Mother saw fit. And so, feeling chastised and too guilty to refuse, Fox dragged his things behind him, all the way upstairs where he crawled up into his room and sat cross-legged, unpacking. He could hear Mother angrily cleaning downstairs; scrubbing more roughly than normal, putting things aside with heavy thuds and half-formed curses.

Fox spent all morning tucked in his cubby, arranging the goods he had so proudly traded for in their own little nooks and crannies. Then he pulled his writing supplies from his trunk, sprawled out on his stomach, and flopped his journal open to an empty page. He began to scribble away furiously about everything he remembered from Doff. Trying to capture in words what it had looked like, and felt like. He was pleased to discover not only how much he *could* remember in perfect detail, but also that the new pen he'd received from Bartrum Bookmonger had such a fine tip, he could cram rather a lot of words onto one page. And then a thought came to him as he wrote.

He blew on the page to help the last few words dry. Then he turned the page and, careful not to use the back of the still slightly wet sheet, he began to draw. At first, it was just a rough sketch of Doff, as it might be seen by the eborills soaring overhead, and slightly to the north. But the more he worked, the clearer it became. He began to etch in tiny details with the tip of his pen. Not mere blocks and X's like the map he'd seen of the merchant's highway, but roofs of certain buildings and the exact shape of the rock gardens. He even drew shadowy smudges that looked like eborills, soaring over the whole mountain.

Morning wore into afternoon as he worked, and the skies outside the window grew darker as heavy snow clouds rolled into the valley. Still, Fox continued to draw, trying to perfect every inch of the village, all that he could remember. Not from straight on, not flattened from above like the maps he saw in his book of the gods, but at an angle. Taking in every shape and every road. The last piece was the stone pillar that marked the village entrance, with its primitive build and "Doff" carved roughly into it.

Then, smiling to himself, Fox pulled from his pocket Topper's special gift to him: a pouch of fine lymnstone powder. Scooping a handful from the pouch and holding it over the wet map, Fox began to sprinkle it across the page until every inch of ink was covered. Then he lifted the book to his lips and blew carefully, so that the excess powder drifted away, leaving only that which was stuck to the ink. And then Fox smiled and retreated farther into his cubby, to the darkest corner. He propped the book up on his knees and watched the map of Doff begin to glow.

SNOW WAS FALLING THICKLY outside when Mother finally released him from his punishment, just in time for a late dinner. She seemed to have calmed down quite a bit since his arrival that morning, and now she started asking questions about where he'd been. They sat on the wide stones around the fire pit, and as Fox told story after story of his time in Doff, Mother began to smile.

"Your father used to talk just like that when I met him," she said reminiscently. "He'd go on and on about the places and the people. Bored me to death at times, but in the beginning that's what I fell in love with. His passion."

Fox stirred his soup absently. "You miss him when he's gone," he said.

"I miss him even when he's here," said Mother, her face turned to the window, watching the snow. "I listen to him tell his stories, and I miss the part of him that's still off on the road, because I can never go there with him." And then her smile fell somewhat, and she looked back at Fox. "I can't protect him, out there. I can't ..." Her voice trailed off. She clasped her hands tighter around her bowl, and Fox noticed they were shaking.

"Mother?" he asked. And again when she didn't answer, "Mum?"

"You said he was going to die," she said finally. "You said he was going to die, and then you disappeared. You went off and did this wonderful thing, where you were on your own. You made choices and survived, and you were a man, not a boy. And that was his reason for making you stay, he told me." She began to speak more quickly now, as though she'd been planning all day what to say and she was in a hurry to get it out. "He told me your visions or feelings might have just been a tantrum. That he would be careful, that you had no way of knowing. But you haven't acted like a boy. I hear you talking like a young man ... and I know you are your father's son."

She took a long, shaking breath, tears shimmering in her lashes, but she set her jaw stubbornly and refused to let them fall. She looked Fox straight in the eyes and said, calmly and directly, "Is he already dead?"

"No," said Fox at once. Mother's question had taken him by surprise, but he knew the answer with an impossibly steady certainty. "I would know. I would have felt it." When Mother did not look consoled, Fox reached across the space between them and clasped her hands, squeezing them tightly. "Don't you think I have been listening, *feeling* with all my strength, every day? For now, they are all safe."

"For now," said Mother dejectedly. "But you know they might not be."

For a moment they sat in silence. And then, Mother looked up at him with pleading in her eyes, and Fox answered her unasked question with a heavy heart. "I did consider following them. But what good would it have done? If Father didn't believe me then, there's no reason he would believe me now. And the Tessoc Pass will already be sealed tight for the winter."

"So all we can do is wait?" asked Mother. And when Fox nodded, Mother pulled her hands from his grip. She turned her full attention back to her meal, scraping the bottom of her bowl clean with a crust of bread. Then she said firmly, "You'll tell me when it happens."

It was not a request, it was a demand. And Fox, lost for words and lacking anything more helpful to say, answered with a simple "Yes."

THE SHAVID WERE GETTING closer. Fox could feel it. He woke up many mornings with the smell of painted wagons fresh on his nose, and he could often hear little pieces of their songs dancing about like snow flurries on the wind. He began to reach out to them, as he had with the goats and sometimes Lai during his lessons with Bartrum Bookmonger. He let his words and thoughts float on the breezes like leaves on a river, hoping they would find the Shavid. Hoping they would find Radda.

He'd said "soon." When the Shavid left so many months ago, Fox had wanted to go with them. And Neil had known his thoughts, and said "Radda says it's not time. He says soon, but not now."

I'm ready, he kept thinking. *Come back and find me, I'm ready now.*

But he wasn't granted much time to dwell on the approaching Shavid. He soon discovered that Mother wasn't the only person upset with him for his abrupt disappearance.

"At least you left her a *note*!" Lai shrieked at him on the morning after his return. She'd found him up on the cabin rooftop, where he was busy repairing cracks in the thin but sturdy stone shingles. She'd climbed up right beside him and, without so much as a cursory "hello," had started screaming. "I didn't even get that! No goodbye, *no* warning? How could you?"

"Look," said Fox in exasperation, "if you're going to keep yelling, at least give me a hand with this?" He nudged the bucket of thick caulking paste with his toe, and Lai glared at him. Finally, with a grudging snort, she plucked an extra brush from the goo and began to help with the repairs. They worked in silence for a time, until finally Lai seemed to calm down enough to carry on a simple conversation.

"How was it?" she asked. "Wherever you went?"

"Amazing," said Fox reminiscently. He smeared a great glop of paste onto the foot or so of tiles in front of him, using a thick-bristled brush to smooth it out and scrape it into place. As it oozed between shingles and filled cracks in the stone, Fox continued. "I was a *real* trader. Out on my own, and master of myself! But it was even more than that. The people up there..." He scooped another hearty mess of paste from the bucket and let it splatter onto the tiles with a wet *shhhhlop.* "I think, sometimes, they have it even worse than we do. It's all stone and mountainside, but they've made something so beautiful. Father always used to tell me that I never knew how big the world was, but I don't think I truly understood him until recently." Fox stopped and sat back on his rump, letting the paste dry. "Even from village to village, it's like a whole other culture. How can anyone ever see it all?"

"The Shavid do," said Lai.

Fox looked out past the valley, across the plains where the Shavid had once disappeared. Did they truly see it all? Could they really travel so wide and far, and see all there was to see in one lifetime? "Maybe so," he said out loud, to both Lai and himself. "But the most I'll ever get to see is the Merchant's Highway."

He didn't dare tell her his true thoughts. How much he longed to go with them, and how every day he hoped they'd ride over the horizon and take him on their grand adventures. It was a wish that was confusing as well as wonderful. After all, he had a home. And a life laid out before him, as a successful trapper and trader. It was in his blood, and he was cursed good at it too. As he breathed in the smells of the valley, he felt that familiar comfort of *home*. This was where he belonged ... wasn't it?

Meanwhile, the winter routine had settled upon Thicca Valley. True winter, the Deep Winter, was still more than two months away, but snowfall greeted the Thiccans almost every morning, though it cleared by the sun's highest point. Farmers were hard at work pulling in the last of the harvest, and the riverbanks were teeming with nets and lines as the valley folk caught their last fish of the season.

Soon, Deep Winter would freeze both ground and river solid, and snow would envelop the land. It was then that the cold and dark would drive the Thiccans to gather at the Five Sides for companionship and entertainment. But for now, each and every soul was hard at work, from long before dawn each morning until the hearthfires burned low every night. Home gardens were gleaned for every scrap of edible growth. Wild mushrooms were gathered, and end-of-season berries pressed into jams and preserves. The valley echoed with the sounds of firewood being chopped and cabins being repaired before the winter blizzards did irreparable damage.

Fox woke long before the sun each morning and built up the kitchen fire. By the time Mother awoke and started her day, the cabin was warm and breakfast was heating on the flat hearthstones. But Fox would already be out in the forest, checking his traps. He brought in fat beavers and plump rabbits, and set up a hearty trade at the Five Sides every few days. The many widows trying to survive their first winters without their husbands were exceptionally grateful for Fox and his fresh game. They paid him in everything from candles and sacks of potatoes to promises of firstborn goat calves in the spring. It wasn't long before Fox had a thick stack of parchment scraps scribbled over with lists and who owed him what, and notes of whom he still needed to collect from. He made himself a mental note to buy a proper ledger.

Days grew shorter, and the working light dwindled into but a few brief hours in the afternoon. The farmlands froze over, imprisoning any crops left unharvested in the earth. A fine mist of smoke and frozen breath hung over the valley like a cloud, and there was an ever-present, lingering scent of woodsmoke. As the sun hid its face for good, a silence settled over everything. Even the trees and the animals grew hushed, and the very mountains seemed to be holding their breath.

And then, the snows came.

Deep Winter crashed down on the valley. A bitter and deathly cold wind rattled every doorframe, shrieked at every window, and bit viciously at exposed skin. Blizzards shook every foundation, and the mountains groaned under the weight of the snow and ice. It was always dark, with even midday no brighter than a moonlit evening. Ice and hailstones pelted the rooftops, thundering like a thousand tiny drums. It was as if a hundred great white bears had taken over the valley, roaring across the skies and tearing at every building with their claws of ice.

But while the rest of the valley cozied up in their homes, keeping warm and waiting for the storms to calm enough to let them outside, Fox was in agony. The angry gale brought with it such a hailstorm of smells and sounds and visions that he couldn't get a moment's peace. Shivers racked his body, and smells came and went so quickly that it made him dizzy. Within two days he was physically ill. He lay curled in a ball by the kitchen fire, wrapped in heavy furs and incapable of eating.

During the Deep Winter, he and Mother always slept by the fire pit. It conserved firewood and contained all the heat in one room. They only ventured upstairs if they needed something, and even then they made it a quick trip, eager to get back to the warmth and light of the kitchen. It was a comfortable enough place to stay, with all the furs and blankets stripped from their beds and piled up around the edge of the fire. But now, Fox couldn't imagine being comfortable anywhere. Not here, nor in his bed, nor in the thawing warmth of summer.

The fifth day of the storm found him sitting huddled on his makeshift bed, a blanket of patched rabbit pelts wrapped around him like a cloak, with only his face visible. He stared determinedly into the fire, willing himself to focus on the dance of light and shadow and not on the thousands of new images battling for space in his mind. Mother was still asleep, exhausted from her own winter tradition of stitching every hole, real or imagined, in every scrap of clothing in the house. Fox could just see her silhouette through the flames, twice as large as it ordinarily should be, what with all the extra blankets. He pulled his own fur quilt tighter around him, as if that might help ward off the intense shivers constantly flooding him. But he knew they weren't from cold. They were the sounds and smells, his Blessing. And, in the heart of the storm, his curse.

Someone was in labor without a midwife. Fox could hear the screaming, and the father's soothing words. A child in the outskirt farms had already been claimed by the cold, and Fox heard the little boy's mother discover the body in the early dawn. He smelled everything cooking in every house for a brief moment, and then could smell nothing the next. Borric was keeping himself busy rearranging the store rooms, while Lai kept a very miserable Rose company. The young bride's pregnancy was beginning to truly take its toll, and Fox could hear snatches of worried talk between Pick and Lai. And somewhere, in one of the homes in the main square, a fairly annoying little girl would not stop singing the same song, over and over again.

Fox squeezed his eyes shut and breathed deep, trying to calm himself. Trying to focus, as he'd been learning to do all summer. Every thought and smell and sound that didn't belong to him, he forced into the back of his mind like a wild animal, wrestling them into a cage and slamming it shut. Then he carefully tucked himself into his bed and lay perfectly still, desperately hoping that sleep would claim him before the shivers could break free again.

This morning, for once, he was lucky. He drifted uneasily into a fitful sleep, but any rest was something these days. Nightmares and half-formed dreams that he was sure weren't his kept Fox tossing and turning, but he refused to let himself wake up. And then, suddenly, a silence fell over the cabin and he sat bolt upright, listening hard.

The storm was over. A calm, simple little breeze was all that remained of the winds that had tortured Fox for five straight days. The only sounds he heard were the dying embers of the kitchen fire and Mother's soft footsteps in the hallway. He smiled and sank back into his furs. His stomach was pinched with hunger and his head was pounding, but there was plenty of time for food later. For now, all he needed was a long, untroubled sleep.

FOX SLEPT FOR ALMOST a solid day, waking only once to shovel down a week's worth of food. He crammed corn cakes and sausages into his mouth until he could hardly breathe, gnawed on a hearty slab of smoked venison and chased the whole thing down with a miner's helping of piping hot stew. And then he collapsed, letting the warmth of food and fire carry him off to sleep again.

It was never truly daytime during Deep Winter. The Thiccans took to bed when their bodies told them to, regardless of the hour, and nights were measured by when it felt the coldest. When Fox finally woke for good, he sensed that it might have been sometime around mid-afternoon, but he had no way of being sure. He helped himself to a slice of cold bread and a chunk of roasted goose that Mother had left on the counter. There was a note beside his simple meal, scrawled hastily in trader shorthand, the only thing Mother knew how to read or write. Fox glanced at it and smiled. Then he dressed quickly in his warmest gear and left the cabin behind him, heading down to the Five Sides. Mother was waiting, and the valley would be, too.

The tavern windows were the only thing lit in the whole square. They shone with flickering firelight like a beacon, promising song and dance and laughter. Fox could hear it as he hurried through the snow, his arms crossed over his chest and his scarf pulled up to cover most of his face. There wasn't another living soul out and about, and the whole valley was crystalline, shimmering white and silver-grey in the frozen starlight. Every so often, a breeze would shake snow from a tree branch or rooftop, sending the flakes shuddering through the sky with the softest hiss. And then, Fox could smell the mouth-watering scent of roasting boar and spiced apples.

For a moment, he stood outside the front door to the Five Sides, watching the warped shadows of tavern guests through the rippled glass windows. A year ago, he'd been standing right here. As he had every year during Deep Winter. Father had just left, and Fox had been heading inside to pass the first of many frozen nights with his friends, and the valley that he considered his family. There was no talk of magic, or Blessings. There were no Shavid, no Desolata. No worries, other than if Father might take him on the caravan next year, or if the storms would hold out long enough to get some decent trapping done.

He'd been a boy back then. And it had been easy. But now? He took a deep breath, his lungs shuddering at the bite of the cold air. By the time he'd breathed out, Fox had made his decision. This would be his last winter in Thicca Valley. Whether the Shavid came for him or not, Fox would be leaving with the spring thaw. He needed to learn, from someone who knew exactly what it was to have a Blessing. And he wouldn't find it here.

"What made you so certain?" asked a smooth voice from the shadows.

Fox had given up wondering how Farran knew things, or how he decided when to show up. Instead, he simply answered. "I think I've known since Radda first told me," said Fox quietly. As he spoke, the god's figure came into clear view, leaning against the stone wall of the tavern, gazing sidelong through the window. "I knew I couldn't stay here. But that storm... I felt things. I heard things that I never want to hear again. People in pain, people dying..."

"I'm afraid you don't have a choice, my boy," said Farran. And for once, Fox heard true regret in the god's voice. "You've been chosen for a life of hearing what others can't."

"But I can control it," said Fox, tearing his own eyes from the door and looking directly into Farran's. "I can learn. You said so."

They stared at each other for a long moment. And then Farran smiled. "I knew I chose right with you."

"There's still time for me to prove you wrong," jibed Fox dryly.

Farran was gone by the time Fox pulled open the door and was welcomed in by a rush of warmth and light. Fox let himself be pulled into a group of young men playing dice, and helped himself to a heaping plate of food. He even got up on a table with Picck and sang a raucous and horrendously inappropriate chantey about barmaids and sailors. He fell asleep with his elbow in his soup, and repeated the whole process the next night. If this was to be his last Deep Winter, he was going to make it the one most worth remembering.

Chapter Seventeen
Adella

Fox weathered the next storm at the Five Sides, along with what seemed like half the valley. Borric had enough food stored away to feed a small army for months, and valley folk brought their own supplies to help supplement the stock. Deep Winter brought people together, as everyone fought the same dangers. The deadly threat of frostbite and the winter fever were both lurking in the shadows like rats, waiting to bite at unsuspecting ankles.

Not everyone could make it to the tavern. Mothers with small children and brand new babies. Farmers with livestock to care for, and the sick or elderly. For them, the journey to and from the Five Sides would have been impractical, and sleeping sprawled on the tavern floor completely impossible. But for the miners, this was their winter home. The stone paths into the mountains and mines were nothing but treacherous ice now. Work was brought to a complete standstill, and so they happily camped out at the Five Sides, some even filling their time by helping out in the kitchen or cleaning tables, simply desperate for ways to pass the hours.

As the storm rattled the tavern windows, Fox sat with the Blackroots at a table nestled up against one of the support beams. Fires were crackling in both the center pit and the great fireplace, and Armac Flint was singing a slow, mournful ballad. For such a rough and arrogant man, Fox thought he had a shockingly gentle singing voice. It was soothing and deep, and hummed through the wood and stone of the common room.

As he sang, a handful of miners hummed a quiet harmony, and one of them piped out a matching tune on a wooden flute that sounded like an owl's crooning.

In the deep
A pounding like a drum

I heard it call
And echo through my soul
A shimmer shine
Deep in the mine
Something forgotten
And left an age ago

It was one of Fox's favorite tragedies. A song about a young miner who falls in love with a woman eternally frozen in a block of solid ice. Every day the miner goes to see her, deep in her mountain cave, and he waits for her to melt. But every time he thinks she'll someday be free, winter sets in again and her icy prison grows stronger. In the end, the miner freezes to death as he waits, and eventually only his voice remains in the empty cavern, singing the story of his love.

She spoke soft
She whispered like a wind
I heard her song
And frozen wind did blow
A lady fair
With silver hair
She left me dreaming
I couldn't let her go

Rose and Picck were sitting across the table, Rose resting her head on her husband's shoulder. Their backs were turned to Fox as they watched Armac's performance, but Fox could see Picck gently kiss Rose's forehead every so often. And Rose in turn would snuggle in closer, or whisper something in his ear. Their baby was due any day now, and Rose wasn't often well enough to emerge from their rooms. But tonight, she'd managed to join in the festivities, even lending her sweet voice to the occasional song.

Lai and Borric sat on either side of Fox, Borric whittling away at a chip of stone. As the song wound though the air, Lai scooted closer to Fox, until their shoulders were pressed together. For a moment, Fox shifted uncomfortably, his arm pinched by her weight. Then he wrapped his arm around her shoulders, as he'd seen Borric do in his fatherly way a hundred times over. And, as he'd seen Picck do every day to his wife. He glanced over at Lai, but she was staring fixedly at Armac. It was nice, holding her as they listened to the song. Comfortable. His arm relaxed into place, and suddenly he wondered why they hadn't always been sitting like this.

In the deep
We lost our weary way
The days went by
And no one came to see
Two lonely souls
From long ago
But love untouched
Was waiting there for me

When the song ended, nobody spoke. It wasn't the sort of song you clapped to. Instead, the shrieking of the storm outside echoed through the room alongside the bold crackling of the fires. And then somebody started up a beat, and people sprang to dancing. It was a newer dance, a fancy and complicated jig that one of the foreign husbands brought over from his town. It had quickly become a valley favorite, and within moments men and women from all through the common room were on their feet.

With a sigh, Borric hauled his own bulk upright and stretched. "Ah well, I suppose it's the second-best cure for the love-song gloom," he said with a chortle. Then he held out his hand to Lai and pulled her to her feet with a wink. As he whisked his daughter off to dance, Fox slid quietly away from the table and went to play cards in the back of the room. Far away from the Blackroots. And far away from Lai. For the rest of the storm, though he sat with them often, Fox was careful not to put his arm around her again.

IN YEARS PAST, FOX would spend the calmer winter days playing in the snow with the rest of the valley children. Even the older youth would join in, building forts and having long and vicious snowball fights. They would skate on the frozen river and slide down the icy embankments like otters. They would all stay out until the wind grew too harsh, or until the nighttime festivities started up again at the tavern. Then they would amble inside for hot soup and to dry off by the fire.

Now, Fox spent his free days much differently. He journeyed out into Father's trapping territory, even weathering a handful of storms in the hunting cabin. Mother wasn't terribly happy about it, but she grudgingly admitted she was proud of how much he'd grown up recently. And when he was home in Thicca Valley, Fox had a steady trade going at the Five Sides. He'd dedicated several pages in his journal to the task of bookkeeping, using them as a temporary ledger for his trade records until he could purchase one. He'd sketched out lines and columns to keep everything straight, just as he'd seen Bartrum Bookmonger do. And, unknown to all, he began squirreling away his earnings, tucking them deep into the bottom of his trunk in a beaver pelt satchel. He had no idea how much it cost to live on the road, but he was certain he'd need all the help he could get.

And then, there were the days when he let it all go. Days when he allowed himself to join in the adventures of the valley youth, and came in at night half frozen and breathless from laughter. Those were the nights he slept best, whether it was home in his own bed or propped up on a bench at the Five Sides. He felt entirely alive, and free of the looming shadow of responsibility hanging over the horizon of the spring. As Deep Winter wore on, Thicca Valley wrapped itself around Fox like a frozen blanket, quietly begging him to stay. And, on the days when he wasn't hunting, he found himself wishing he could.

"Maybe you should take one of them with you," said Farran one day. The two were far on the outskirts of the territory, a good two days from home. Fox was re-setting a particularly finicky bear trap and trying to concentrate. The god had taken to appearing whenever Fox was on his solo hunting journeys, keeping him company as if they were nothing but old friends.

Fox sat back on his heels and looked up at Farran. "Take one of who?"

"A sweet young Thicca girl, from your valley. Take her as a wife, get a little company on the road." Farran plopped down lazily in the snow and laid back, staring at the black-green canopy above them.

Fox smirked viciously. "Why would I need company, when I'm *so* lucky to have the likes of you around?" He would never admit it out loud, but he found Farran to be excellent companionship. Though rather cocky and altogether infuriating, the god always kept Fox on his toes.

"Oh I'm flattered, my boy, but there's a kind of company that I can't keep. With you, in any case. There's a little problem with you being a man, is all."

Fox snorted and turned his attention back to his trap. Ever so carefully, he blew on the snow around the base, where he'd been kneeling and moving parts around. The snow swirled up in little eddies and resettled with no sign of Fox's hand imprints. He made sure to puff the snow unevenly, so it settled more to one side than another. It looked more natural that way, and one of the simplest tricks to hide a human presence.

That done, Fox stood and dusted himself off, adjusting his scarf and cloak. Farran's comment wasn't truly worth acknowledging. After all, there was only one woman he could see himself ever spending time on the road with, and she –

"There now, stop that!" said Farran, rolling up onto one elbow and pointing an accusatory finger at Fox. "I know what you're thinking, and that's enough of it."

"How often do you do that?" asked Fox irritably. "Read my thoughts?"

"I'm not reading them, I'm *feeling* them," said Farran sardonically. "And it's only when they're directly related to me. Or, in this case, my progeny." He sprang to his feet. Though he was dressed in a thin silk shirt and simple, though radically colorful, breeches, Farran didn't seem at all bothered by the cold. Or by the snow now piled in his shirt collar. "You're not allowed to think of her like that, I told you before. Lai is off-limits to you, I don't want her mixed up in your messy little future."

"I wasn't thinking of her like *anything*," spat Fox, shoving his hands into his gloves and setting off. As Farran followed, Fox tried very hard to think of anything *but* Lai, simply so Farran wouldn't be able to sense his thoughts. But the more he tried not to think of her, the more she sprang to mind. Finally, Fox glared at Farran and said, "Don't you have anything better to do than follow me around, Sir-High-and-Godly?"

"What, better than watching you squirm? Not on your life," said Farran, chuckling.

Fox forced his attention forward, to the ground and the tracks of an elk, and the promise of a hearty dinner. He let himself be drawn into the hunter's mindset, successfully drowning all other thoughts. They hunted in silence, and it took him some time to realize that Farran had disappeared again, and he was alone once more.

Well, as alone as he ever was in the woods anymore. He'd noticed it at the start of winter. Though they stayed out of sight and didn't interfere with his prey, he knew the wolves were there, his ever-watchful shadows. And with each kill, he left them an offering. A gift of thanks, and of trust. Many nights he fell asleep to the comfortable sounds of their voices, singing into the frozen woods. It was a song many feared, but Fox looked forward to. He lay in his bedroll in the cabin some nights, trying to mimic the rise and fall of their howling. There were times when he could even anticipate their warbling notes, and he hummed along quietly to himself.

He wondered if there were wolves wherever the Shavid went, and if they could sing along, too.

THE STORMS BEGAN TO last longer, and the days of relief between them shortened. It became much riskier for Fox to venture away from the valley, but he relied more and more on his instincts to tell him how far out the blizzards were. There were times when he made it back to his cabin or the Five Sides just as hail began to pelt his face, or else just before the snow thickened to the point of blindness. But he always made it.

"You're being awfully stupid, you know," said Lai one night in the tavern. Fox was at Father's old trading table in the corner, marking tallies in his makeshift ledger. At the front of the room, Borric himself was leading a massive round of "Can't Say," a storytelling game in which certain words or letters could never be said, and everyone went round offering one phrase of story at a time. "You'll get yourself killed, staying out like that!" She kept her voice low so as not to draw attention to them, but even her whispers were shaking with anger. "It's bad enough your father might not make it though this winter, but you have to put your own neck on the line as well?"

For the first time since Lai had started hissing at him like an angry cat, Fox met her eyes. "Don't talk about him," he said coldly.

Lai clamped her mouth shut, her eyes wide with silent apologies. Fox turned back to his work but kept talking.

"I know you're just worried, but I can take care of myself. Better than most people here! I have what they don't, and my Blessing keeps me safe." And then, he stopped. He let the tip of his pen grow still. "I can't sense him anymore," he said, so quietly he barely heard himself.

"For how long now?" asked Lai, just as quietly.

A cheer from those playing the story game interrupted briefly, but Fox continued. "Since the second storm or so ... I've been checking every day. And I can still smell the Shavid coming, even hear them sometimes. And they're so close I can practically *taste* their spices in the air. But Father and the caravan ... they're gone."

"Maybe they're just too far away?" supplied Lai helpfully. "We never did figure out how far your gifts could reach."

Fox placed his pen down carefully in the spine of his book, then closed the journal around it. He moved deliberately and slowly, trying to keep the shaking from his hands. "What will I tell her if he's gone?" he asked. "And forget my *own* mother, what about *theirs*?" He looked out at the Thiccans camping out at the tavern tonight. "Mothers of waresmen on that caravan. Their wives, children, sisters ..." He shut his eyes, trying not to see their faces. "I've made enough widows for one lifetime."

"You didn't *make* any of them," said Lai fiercely. She grabbed his wrists and held them tight, and he looked up into her eyes. "You're just a kid! You may act like a man, and work like a man, but unless you slit their throats with your own knife, you didn't kill *anybody*." Then she dropped his hands back to the table like they were poisonous snakes, and sat back against the wall, crossing her arms stubbornly. "So just snap out of it, Foxglove."

And when Fox didn't answer, she left. She disappeared into the kitchen, and Fox buried himself back in his work. She didn't understand. She couldn't, after all. And perhaps, in the end, Farran was absolutely right: she didn't belong in his "messy little future."

The next morning, Fox left the Five Sides well before dawn. He wasn't about to give Lai a chance to try and talk him out of his next trip. He packed lightly, figuring to make it to the trapping cabin by late afternoon, just before the storm hit. He was on the road within minutes, forsaking the valley once more for the company of the wolves.

As he hiked, Fox hummed to himself and practiced sending his thoughts out on the wind. He soon had an accidental following of little birds that he seemed to have called to himself, and that he couldn't figure out how to send back again. But he didn't mind. In fact, they made him feel like a hero in one of the Shavid songs, Zedderick Fowlfeather. A man whose strange friendship with birds drove him to try and learn how to fly. He sang a bit of Zedderick's song to the open woods, his voice swallowed up quickly in the snow.

And upon his head a hat he wore
Of feathers fine and dandy!
And though they did not help him fly,
They came in rather handy!

Fox couldn't remember the words to the last bit, where Zedderick's failed attempts to take to the sky ended up accidentally saving an entire city. So instead he bounced from tune to tune for awhile, singing everything from Shavid song to Deep Winter ballad, until all at once he stopped. He was no longer alone.

For a wild and desperate moment, he hoped it was only Farran. But he knew the smell, and it was only half the god's. He rounded on Lai.

"What are you doing here?!" he yelled, the birds finally scattering at the sound.

She detached herself sheepishly from the shadows of a nearby tree, looking properly abashed. But she recovered quickly and spat back, "I might ask you the same!"

"I have a job to do!" shouted Fox.

"A job that will get you killed?" she said. "I followed you out here to make sure you don't get yourself into any more trouble than you have to!"

Fox rolled his eyes. "No, you followed me out here because you just can't keep your nose out of it! Mind your own business, and go home!"

But a shiver ran down his spine, and he knew it was too late for that. The storm was much too close now, and she'd never make it back in time. Fox glared at her, then took her quickly by the arm and began to lead the way, quickening his speed. "Borric's going to kill me," he growled. "After he kills *you*. And then my mother will kill me." He glanced over into the trees where he knew his nearest wolf guard was keeping pace with them. "And you!" he said to the shadows. "You knew she was there, you couldn't have warned me?"

"Who are you —" started Lai.

"Don't worry about it."

Snow began to fall. Softly at first, but in thick, wet flakes. And then it grew heavier, hissing against the trees as the wind picked up. Lai couldn't move as quickly as Fox. She didn't have a tracker's steady foot, and she certainly didn't have Fox's experience in the woods. Fox began to panic. He'd always timed his journeys just so, always making it to shelter right as the storm hit. But at his pace, not at this struggling, uneven rate.

"Keep right behind me," he said urgently. "Step just where I've been, it'll be easier."

But even with him clearing the path before her, Lai was slowing down. She couldn't see as well in the dark, and she was constantly tripping over roots or getting stuck in heavy snowdrifts. Somewhere over their heads, thunder was starting to roll. It was a smooth, almost lazy sound, as if the storm itself knew they didn't stand a chance, and it was taking its time closing in.

Fox kept hold of Lai's hand so tightly their palms were sweating, despite the freezing cold. "Almost," he kept saying. "We're almost there. Just a little ways more." And then, the sky shattered, and Lai screamed.

To Fox, it was like being caught up in the very clouds. Snow wasn't falling so much as it was tearing around them in an angry whirlwind. He pulled Lai close, holding her so tightly he was sure she couldn't breathe, and they ran. Fox struggled to keep Lai upright each time she stumbled. Ice tore at their hair and faces, and the wind began to pelt at Fox's senses. He pushed it away with all his might and ran with everything he had. And then they crashed blindly into solid stone, and Fox felt blindly for the cabin door handle. He hauled the door open against the wind, and they collapsed inside, letting the door slam shut once more.

But it wasn't the familiar room of the hunting cabin that they stood in. As they caught their breath, and Lai slid down the door into an exhausted heap on the stone, Fox stared around in open shock. This *was* the hunting cabin. Even in the dark, even blind with snow and terror he knew it. His instincts and sense of direction were never wrong. He had opened the door of the cabin.

But he'd closed the door of the Whitethorn Temple. And now they were standing in the garden sanctuary, countless leagues away.

LAI SEEMED TO TAKE their sudden and inexplicable relocation rather well. After the initial shock and Fox's brief explanation of where they were, she was keen to explore. She'd never been out of Thicca Valley in her life, and now she wandered around the sanctuary with wonder painted on her face, her cheeks glowing with excitement. She brushed her nose against strange flowers and twisted her fingertips in snakey vine tendrils.

And then, she led them upstairs, taking Fox by the hand and dragging him along behind her. They emerged into the quiet, flickering darkness of the room above, and despite the strangeness of their circumstances, Fox was still amazed by the temple's beauty. It was just as he remembered it. The colors; the smells; the soft footfalls of the priestesses and the soft hiss of whispered prayers. The smears of painted light were muted now in the winter gloom, but the feeling of being trapped inside a giant butterfly wing still remained. And as Lai stepped out into the room, breathless with wonder, the colors caught on her skin and touched it with hints of blue and purple and red.

Lai looked down at their intertwined fingers, and squeezed Fox's hand tighter for a moment. Their knuckles glowed momentarily green as the light hit them just so. Then Lai said quietly, "That there are places like this all through the Known World ... it seems impossible." She turned her face up to the domed, twisted ceiling, and smiled. "It's beautiful."

And then she released his hand, and Fox watched her wander aimlessly through the temple, gazing upon each statue or candle as if it were the most wonderful thing in the world. Fox himself made his slow, steady way over to the statue of Farran. He wasn't sure exactly how worship things worked, but he felt certain that if Farran thought he was paying tribute to another god, he would never hear the end of it.

He sat down at the pirate god's stone feet, keeping one eye on Lai as he glanced around the temple. There were fewer worshipers here than before. Most of the bodies in the temple appeared to be priestesses, their robes swishing gently back and forth as they walked across the room, to and from various shrines. Many of them he recognized from his last journey to Whitethorn.

But there was one who caught his eye, and made him feel strangely uncomfortable. He found himself watching her as she re-lit candles and swept the floor. Other women in the temple might have been beautiful – this woman put them all to shame. There was not a single word that came to Fox's mind that might describe how breathtaking she was. Her hair was soft, long and impossibly black. Her skin was a perfect balance of pale and dark, he thought. Standing in the shadows one moment she would seem strangely pale and ghost-like, but then she stepped into the candlelight and her skin was a smooth, even almond. She was, to put it simply, stunning. But even so, there was something about her eyes ... they were unsettlingly empty. As though they had never, in all her years, been part of a smile.

Fox couldn't look at her for long without shivering. Even her scent, wrapping around him from afar, was all at once intoxicating and sickening. Familiar, and unknown. Finally, he stood, trying to shake off the strangeness that had settled over his shoulders and neck. He glimpsed Lai across the room, admiring the statue of Phiira the Seer Goddess, and went to join her.

"Her followers blind themselves in her honor, you know," he said quietly.

"What?" exclaimed Lai in shock, much louder than she should have. Several heads turned their way, and Fox had to stifle his laughter behind his hand. Lai dropped her voice and continued. "They really ... *what?!*"

"Not all of them!" said Fox quickly. "And they don't always *actually*, physically blind themselves. Sometimes they just veil their eyes when they're prophesying. Or sometimes, they drink a special tea that takes away their sight. It's only the truly devout that ... you know." When Lai continued to stare at him, he shrugged and said apologetically, "I read about it in a book."

From there, Fox pointed out Thalia, Goddess of the Dance, and Fyllaric, the Shepherd God. He shared little facts and stories he remembered from his wonderful book on the gods, "Asynthum." They wandered from statue to beautiful statue, and Lai listened with all the interest and wonder of a small child being told a favorite bedtime tale.

When they came to the statue of Farran, Fox hesitated. He'd been exceptionally careful never to speak of the pirate god around Lai. Somewhere, in an entirely illogical place in his mind, he thought that the very mention of Farran's name might trigger some strange god-connection in Lai, and she would figure out her whole lineage in one, horrible instant. But he knew he was being ridiculous. And so he began to regale her with stories of her true father, though he was careful to make it sound as though Farran were the greatest god in all the realms. Lai might not know she was his daughter, but Fox felt it was important that she still have a good opinion of the god.

He was just finishing the story Father had once told him, of the creation of hibbins, when the hairs suddenly stood up on the back of Fox's neck. They were no longer alone. He turned, and was face-to-face with *her*. The beautiful, unsettling woman.

"That story still rubs him raw," the woman said, half a smile on her mouth and in her voice. But the smile did not reach her empty eyes, and her voice, while beautiful, held a strange sort of sadness. "He doesn't recover well from insult."

She spoke, Fox thought, like a song played with only three notes. Musical, yes, but simply missing something. As she began to tidy up Farran's shrine, dusting off the stone with a fine piece of cloth and clearing away dead flowers, she hummed quietly. A strange little tune that reminded Fox a bit of some of the Shavid's sea chanties.

Lai didn't seem to notice anything strange about the priestess. Instead, she asked excitedly, "You actually *know* some of the gods?"

"Some more than others," she said smoothly. "My Lord Farran keeps in touch more than most, but I have had the honor of meeting a handful of other, minor deities in my time." She gazed up at the stone face of Farran, and for the first time her eyes showed something of an emotion. Longing. She then knelt down beside the statue, almost in a prayer-like position, and began to carefully dust his stone boots. And she continued to hum.

"What are they like?" asked Lai. She seemed fascinated by the whole idea of the gods. "Are there any of them here, now? How do you —" But then she trailed off. She seemed to be listening to the priestess's song with curious intensity. After a moment, she sank down beside the stone herself, propping one elbow on the statue's base and watching the priestess hum. "Your song is lovely," she said quietly.

"It is about him," said the priestess, raising her eyes to the statue's face for a moment before returning attention to her work.

"I feel like I've heard it somewhere before," said Lai. "It's so familiar ... like something from a dream." And then, as the priestess began gently, lovingly polishing the toes of Farran's stone boots, Lai began to hum along. She knew the tune well, so well that she kept time with every note. She closed her eyes and began to sing, softly and gently, as the woman continued to hum.

There's a ship with a red sail
Like sunset at sea
That e'er I did wake
Took my true love from me
There's a ship with a red sail
Like blood in my heart
That while I was sleeping
Did tear us apart

And then, Lai opened her now-misty eyes and, ever so slowly, sat up straight. She seemed to have forgotten how to speak properly. Her mouth hung open for several moments, and she gazed at the woman's face with a mixture of confusion and wonder. "I heard that song every night," she said slowly. "It sang me to sleep, and kept me calm during the worst of the storms." She was clasping her hands tightly in her lap, but even so Fox could see them shaking. "I watched you stare out the window and sing it some days, even when you wouldn't do anything else."

And then it hit Fox so completely that he couldn't breathe. The woman's smell, her face, the uncomfortable feeling of *familiarness* that made Fox shudder. Watching them sitting so close, he couldn't believe he hadn't figured it out before. And suddenly, he was painfully aware that he couldn't stop it. No matter what he did, Lai was going to find out the truth. And it would break her.

The woman didn't stop humming, nor did she look up as Lai spoke. And then Lai reached a trembling hand out, touched the woman's elbow, and said shakily, "Mother?"

The woman — Lai's mother — turned ever so slightly to look at her. She smiled again, that soft and vacant smile, but didn't speak.

Lai gripped the fabric of her mother's robe tightly and spoke again. "Mum?" And then, louder than before, in a voice that shook like a guttering flame, "You're alive?"

"Of course, my child," said her mother simply, as if it were an entirely silly question.

And then Lai flung herself forward and wrapped her arms around her mother's waist for the first time since she was three years old. She wept openly, but Adella did not hug her back. Instead, she patted Lai's head awkwardly, as though it was a gesture she'd only ever heard described and never actually seen. And then, after a moment she said, "I'm sorry child, but who are you?"

Lai pulled back, quickly wiping her eyes and nose with the back of her hand. "I'm ... Lai?" she said. "I'm your daughter."

"Oh," said Adella with a note of apology in her voice. "Yes, that's right. I did have a daughter, once."

All at once, Lai looked like nothing more than a small, lost child. Her eyes grew round with confused tears, and Fox had to make a quick decision. He slipped quietly into the conversation and said, "Her name is Adella."

Lai turned her face up to him. "How do you know?" she asked.

"Borric told me the story," Fox replied.

For a moment, their eyes locked in silent conversation. Then Lai said quietly, "It isn't a story I'm going to like, is it?"

"No."

IF FOX HAD THOUGHT it was difficult simply to *hear* the story of Lai's mother, it was even harder to tell it. "Borric found her on a winter night, pregnant with you," he began. And on he plunged, for once he began the story he didn't want to stop. He didn't want to give her the chance to ask questions, or even *think* of questions. He wanted it to be done, and then he wanted to simply run away.

And through it all, Adella continued to clean and hum. Blissfully unaware, it seemed, of her daughter. Completely oblivious to the fact that Fox was telling a personal and intimate story about her. No, she simply went about her duties.

"Borric said she started to fade," said Fox.

"I remember that," said Lai quickly. She was watching her mother now, with a sadness in her eyes that Fox had never seen before. "She would sing when she stared out the window. Days, sometimes."

"Yes," said Fox. "She was pining for the man she loved. And when she left, it was to go to him."

"And she had to leave us," said Lai quietly. "Leave *me.*"

"Borric never planned on telling you. He didn't want you to know why she'd left, and he always hoped he'd be enough for you."

And then came the question Fox had been dreading. The question he never wanted to have to answer. It came slowly as Lai tried to put the pieces together. "You said Borric *found* her. Said she left to go to the man she loved. Was that ..." She tore her eyes away from Adella at last and looked Fox straight in the eyes. "Borric isn't my father, is he?"

Fox shook his head dejectedly.

"Who?" she asked, her voice nothing more than a quiet squeak.

For this, Fox had no words. He simply looked up into Farran's laughing stone face. Lai followed his gaze upwards as the color drained from her skin, making her pale as the stone itself. And then, she stood and scrambled away from the statue as fast as she could. She backed herself into the twisted wall of the shrine alcove and began to gulp rasping, shallow breaths. "You," she said breathlessly. "They — it can't! I'm not ..."

Fox took three careful steps toward her, arms held out as though he were attempting to calm a startled animal. "It's why she left," he said calmly. "She was never leaving you, only trying to get to him. Borric said when your heart belongs to a god, there's no turning back." As he reached her, he laid a gentle hand on her shoulder. But Lai slapped it away, all tears gone, replaced by something frighteningly akin to hatred.

"Don't touch me!" she shouted. She shoved Fox hard in the chest, knocking him back. "How long have you known?" she asked. "Days? Months? All *winter*?" Her voice broke, but she didn't stop. She shoved him again, and Fox smashed into the podium, knocking the open book to the floor. "How could you keep something like this from me? From *me?* Well you can stay out here and rot with *them*!" she said viciously, glaring at Adella and the statue of her father. And before Fox could apologize, before he could even find the words to explain, Lai was gone. Fox struggled to his feet, ready to follow her, but a hand on his shoulder held him back.

"Leave her be," said Farran. "She's had more than enough trouble for one day."

"She doesn't know the way home," protested Fox, struggling to free himself, but the god's grip was bear-trap tight.

"There's a merchant wagon in town, heading out to your little valley within the hour. She'll hitch a ride, and they'll deliver her safely. I can guarantee it."

Finally, Fox shook the pirate god's hand off him and turned to face Farran. "Why did you bring us here?" he spat.

"You can't let me have even one little secret, can you?"

"No," said Fox flatly. He was not in the mood for humor today. "This is going to break her. You! And Adella! Everything, all at once ... it's too much for one person!"

Farran heaved an over-dramatic sigh. "I just saved you both, you ungrateful little barnacle," he said lazily. "So that's two you owe me, one large favor for each of you. Unless, of course, you'd rather I hadn't?"

"What do you mean, you saved us?" asked Fox nervously. "What's happened?"

"Your cabin was torn apart by the storm. Both of you would have frozen to death before you could go for help. That, or you would have been buried alive. Crushed by falling tree limbs. Eaten by an angry —"

"I get it!" said Fox sharply. And then, as Farran chuckled, he asked, "If you went through so much trouble to move us here, why couldn't you have just saved the cabin? I'm sure it would have been much less trouble."

Farran smiled and shook his head. "Don't worry your little mind with the rules of the gods. There are things we can do, and things we can't. I even broke a few major laws bringing you here in the first place, so thanks to you I'll have to keep quieter than usual for awhile."

"So sorry to have troubled you," growled Fox, rolling his eyes.

Farran's face darkened. "If you weren't so cursed irreplaceable, I *would* have let you choke to death on an icicle! And on top of that, you were traveling with my *daughter*. And even if your life wasn't worth saving, hers is."

Fox struggled for an angry reply, and when he couldn't find one, he let himself sink to the stone base of Farran's statue. As he buried his forehead in his hands, digging his fingers into his hair, he became aware that Adella was still humming placidly. He glanced over at the priestess, now lighting fresh candles in the alcove walls. "What happened to her?" he asked. "She can't have always been like this."

Here, Farran's face softened again as he looked at Adella. "There was a time when her smile could break a man's heart," he said. For a moment, he simply watched her work. And then, as she came close to them, he reached out a tender finger and brushed it down her cheek. Adella leaned into his touch, eyes closed, a contented smile on her lips. And then she moved away again, away from Farran's shrine and back into the open temple room.

"I loved having her on my ship," said Farran reminiscently, his eyes still following her. "Loved to hear her sing, and make her laugh." He smiled, almost to himself. "Oh the tales I could spin you of that woman." And, just as quickly as it had come, the smile faded again. "But there is a price of loving a god, as we've both learned. Her time away from me as she tried to raise Lai took a toll on her, and her soul began to crumble. She has never been the same."

"Is that why she didn't recognize her own daughter?" asked Fox. "And why she didn't seem to care that she even had one?"

"It is a cost that I've regretted from the bottom of my blackened soul," said Farran. "She is a shadow of the woman that was Adella DeMorrow. And for that, there are not enough penances I can pay in all the realms." He tore his eyes away from Adella and said, "She cannot see Lai for what she really is, and may never be able to again. And it would take power more than I have ever possessed to understand exactly why."

Fox watched Adella as she gathered a great goatskin rug from the herder's shrine and took it out to shake the dust from it. And then he glanced up at Farran, who was once more gazing at the mother of his child. His face was drawn and stoic, but his eyes were filled with regret. And Fox, watching him watch her, was amazed to realize that gods could truly feel love. And, more than that, he felt sure that their story would make the most beautiful tragedy ever sung.

Chapter Eighteen
The Incomparable Donovan

Fox sat outside on the low temple steps, watching night descend upon the forest. The moon hung bright and full overhead, casting jagged shadows through the needled canopy. Far off, through the trees, Fox could see the lights of the city beginning to glow. Lanterns being lit along the city streets, candles flickering merrily in shop windows. He itched to wander out into Whitethorn again, and rediscover its streets and alleys.

But Farran warned him to stay close, and so here he was. Breathing slowly and deeply, taking in everything from the sounds of the foraging hares to the long-past creaking of the merchant wagon that carried Lai away. He could almost see her when he closed his eyes, and found himself dreading the inevitable moment when they would see each other again in Thicca Valley. But Fox was in no hurry to return home. Instead, he pulled his cloak tighter around him and sank into a comfortable daze, listening to the far-off songs from the Hatted Goat flittering on the winter breeze.

After awhile, he pulled his journal and pen from an inside pocket, thinking to take some notes about Whitethorn. As he flipped through the book to find an empty page, the shimmer of lymnlight from the glowing map of Doff caught his eye, and he stopped. He smiled down at the map, and found himself missing the little mountain hamlet desperately. He ran his fingers fondly over the shimmering lines, tracing over the familiar pathways.

And then, as he slid his finger along the side of the mountain, Fox was wrung by the biggest, most intense shiver he had ever had. For a moment, he was sure he'd truly been transported away from Whitethorn. But while he could still feel himself pressed against the icy temple steps, everything he saw, heard, and smelled, was Doff.

He was on one of the winding mountain paths, with a row of rough stone gardens on his right, and a handful of haphazardly carved houses on his left. The mountain was aglow with rivers of ore, and Fox felt himself warm at the view. He heard strange and wild cries from overhead, and the part of Fox that was in Doff looked up. The night sky was full of dark, careening shadows, and Fox knew it must be mating season for the eborills. All around him, townsfolk were leaning out their windows to watch, or else sitting perched on top of their stone roofs, pointing at the airborne courtship dances. Fox's consciousness drifted lazily about on the breeze, and he caught snatches of conversation as he went.

"— old She-King might not be able to lay eggs this year! Could be a real battle for leadership."

"But she's turned out some of the finest hunters in a decade! It can't be!"

"— say there's a young one from the lower nests started fighting his way up the ranks —"

"Did you hear that, Dad? Somebody said a bird from last year's royal line's broken his wing, and can't mate this year!"

At one point, Fox found himself in Kaldora Flintstock's workshop, right alongside Topper. For a few moments, he watched as the boy hung dipped candles in the window to dry. And then, like a leaf ripped away on the wind, Fox was carried south. Unfamiliar sights and smells rushed past him in a grey-and-silver blur, and Fox knew he was no longer in Doff. Great mountain shadows rose up high above him, on every side. And then he slowed to a halt, nothing more than a jumble of senses borne on the wind.

But a deep, penetrating cold sank over him, both the body that remained in Whitethorn and the part of him that was lost in the mountains. And he could hear something whispering to him in a language he should not have been able to understand. It was a language that was not made of words, that wasn't human. Something very old was trying to speak to him, and it was in pain. Sounds and smells rushed through Fox like a storm, and he could see a dozen visions at once. But it was only when he caught a glimpse of Father, smiling and laughing at a trading tent in a crowded marketplace, that Fox understood.

When he awoke, he found himself on a cot somewhere, tucked in the corner of a tiny, windowless room. He struggled free of his blankets, gasping for breath, only to have Farran's hand on his shoulder and a quiet, "Hush, boy, you're alright."

Farran was crouched at Fox's bedside. Fox looked up into the god's face and managed to cough out, "Avalanche." He slowed his breathing and felt his heart begin to return to normal, and then he said more calmly, "I know where Father is. And I know what's going to happen to him."

Farran didn't react to this news. Instead, he simply crossed his arms over his chest and waited for Fox to elaborate.

"I was taken somewhere," Fox explained, trying to put his shiver into words. "Doff. It's a place I know well, and the map took me there. But then I got carried away, someplace else. Somewhere I didn't know, but I could *feel*." He ran his fingers through his hair in frustration, finding his experience difficult to describe. And then, realizing just how ridiculous it sounded, he said, "The mountain spoke to me. It's about to break. And my father's caravan is going to be right under it."

Farran sighed and leaned his head back to stare at the low ceiling. "I know what's coming," he said lazily.

"You have to help me get there," demanded Fox.

"Yes," said Farran, "*that's* what I knew was coming." He stood, his head nearly brushing the soot-blackened ceiling, and he rested one hand on a low-hanging beam. "It's not that I don't want to help, little one. It's just not that easy."

"You could send me there," said Fox. "You brought me and Lai here in an instant, you could do the same. I know right where he is! I saw him, and I knew!"

"You and Lai were different!" said Farran. "Both of Lai's parents were here, and there's a certain bond to be had with blood."

"But one of my parents —"

"*And*," continued Farran, cutting Fox off, "it's always been easier for me here, at a place where I'm worshiped freely and regularly. Adella makes sure of it, after all. But there are places in this world where I'm not as highly regarded as I might have been once ..." And then he waved off Fox's unasked question with a lazy hand and said, "The politics of gods, none of your concern."

For a moment there was silence in the little room. And then Fox said, quietly but firmly, "I have no choice but to be your pawn in whatever games you're playing. You've already made that perfectly clear. But for all your meddling, and for what you did to Lai today ... for an immeasurable time when I am in your service, you *owe* me." His voice did not shake, for he wasn't afraid. Fox might not be sure of everything, but he was sure that Farran needed him. "We can work together peacefully, or I can fight you every step of the way." He stared the god down, evenly and calmly, never so much as blinking.

Farran glared back for a moment, his face tight with irritation. And then, the wooden beam in his hand snapped free of its counterparts and fell in splinters to the floor. Farran dusted his hand off on his breeches and said bitterly, "Fine. But we'll have to do this the hard way, I'm afraid. As I said before, I've got to keep quiet for awhile. Big things like moving people ... it gets me noticed by people who I'd rather not be noticed by at the moment." And then he heaved another sigh, and his comically dramatic air returned. "I suppose there's no other way for it. We'll leave in the morning. I've got some things to arrange, and you ought to get some more sleep. Light may come late to the winter mountains, but our dawn is just as early."

And then he was gone, leaving a very confused Fox alone in his room.

SLEEP ELUDED FOX THAT night. He lay on his cot, staring up at the ceiling, sorting out the smells and sounds. He knew he was still in the temple, and he assumed he was underground in some sort of living or visitors quarters. The air felt closer here, tight and slightly heavy as it was in many of the underground places in the world. He had no idea how long he'd been unconscious, or what time it was now, but he was neither hungry nor tired. Every muscle was taut and expectant, like the string of a bow just before the release.

He was going to find Father! He kept saying it to himself over and over again. He was going to bring the caravan home. It wasn't too late! Finally, giving up on sleep, Fox sat up and lit a lantern on the little desk that took up much of the rest of his room. He found his small traveling bag was tucked in the corner. All the things he'd meant to take with him to the hunting cabin were safe and sound, just as he'd packed them. He rescued his journal, pen and ink from a side pocket. And then he sat, book propped open to an empty page in front of him, and began to write.

First, a letter to Mother. He would send it to Borric, and have him read it to her. This, he kept short and simple. He didn't mention Father, or the journey south, as he didn't want to get her hopes up prematurely. Instead, Fox simply wrote that he was going on an extended trapping trip, and not to worry about him. He would be safe, he promised to bring home something good, and he signed it with love. And then, tearing the journal page from its binding and setting it aside to dry, he put pen to blank page again for a second letter. This time, to Lai.

He had no idea how long he sat there, his pen poised but still. He thought of a hundred different ways to start, each feebler than the last. Finally, he put the pen aside and sat back on his seat, staring at the empty surface of the page. How could he even begin to start something like that? How could one apologize for hiding a secret that big? And how could he ever even hope to justify letting her life be upended so quickly?

At last, Fox picked up his pen once more and began to write.

To my dearest friend, Lai,

I can make no apologies that would please you, I know that. I can only hope that one day you'll understand, it was not my secret to tell. I did not go looking for your past, your past simply happened upon me. And I made a promise to Borric that I would keep his secret safe. In the end, I believe he only wanted to protect you from the heartache of the truth.

But now, in the spirit of keeping no more secrets from you, I must tell you where I am headed. I am going to bring back the caravan. Or at least, I am going to try. I know where they are now, and I know the danger that lies ahead of them. I have seen it, and by the time you get this I will already be traveling south.

Look for my return in the spring. And, if you have forgiven me, save me a dance at the Homecoming.

Fox

He carefully tore the second letter from his journal and set it aside to dry as well. And then, he filled the hours scratching out notes. Everything he remembered from his brief visions of Doff. And everything he'd seen in the Whitethorn temple. By the time a knock sounded on his door a few hours later, Fox had filled several pages with cramped, scrawling notes and small inked sketches.

He stood and stretched, then made to open the door to whomever had knocked. But as he reached out, the door sprang open and Farran bounded inside. "A fine morning for a hundred-league journey, isn't it?"

For a moment, Fox simply stared. Then he asked, "And what exactly are you supposed to be?"

Farran had forsaken his usual earthy vest and sash, and dressed himself instead in a dazzling yellow tunic, a matching pair of yellow boots and powder blue breeches. Black fur protruded from the top of the boots and trimmed the high tunic collar. Over it all, he wore a brilliant, peacock-blue cloak. Even his hair was different, curled and oiled in tight ringlets rather than pulled back in a lazy mess.

The god bowed low. "The Incomparable Donovan, at your humble service sir! Cloth merchant and purveyor of all fine linens and strings!" And then he snapped to attention, a roguish grin on his face. As Fox snorted with poorly-contained laughter, Farran went on. "I might not be as recognized as I wish, but there are still some of the common folk who know my face. So, if I'm to be roughing it across the lands and nations with mere mortals such as yourself, I need a disguise that is distinctly *un*-piratical."

Fox couldn't help it. He let his laugh free, and managed to choke through his tears of mirth, "Well we shall be careful not to muss your curls, princess!" And then he bowed extravagantly, with much gesturing of the hands as he'd seen Bartrum Bookmonger do.

Farran cuffed him lightly about the head, but he was smiling all the same. "Finish packing your things, and then meet me upstairs in front of my shrine. We'll be on our way within the hour."

But Fox was already packed. He dressed quickly as Farran left, then carefully rolled his letters into a tight bundle, and tied each of them with a thin scrap of rabbit sinew string. He would find a bird house somewhere in the city before they left, and send his messages off to Thicca Valley. Then he checked and double-checked his gear, counting the spare strings he had for his hunting bow and making sure each of his knives was sharp and clean. As he made to leave the room himself, he found that someone had put a tray of hot breakfast outside his door. A hearty slice of salted pork flank and a steaming cup of bread pudding. He ate only half of the pork, wrapping the rest of it in otter skin and stowing it with his things. The pudding he inhaled eagerly before replacing the empty cup on the tray and setting the dishes on his desk.

And then he shouldered his pack with his unstrung bow secured to the side, took one last look about to make sure he hadn't left anything, and closed the door behind him as he left.

Fox had been right in thinking he was in a living quarters. As he made his way down the long, dark hallway toward the stairway, doors on either side of him opened and closed as priestesses emerged, yawning and talking in hushed voices. It seemed Fox and Farran weren't the only ones who had an early start to their day.

Upstairs, Fox found the temple empty and quiet. Only the barest amount of candles were lit, and no light shone through the colored glass. The room was a puzzle of shadows, and Fox thanked his excellent sight as he picked his way to Farran's shrine. "Predator's eyes," Father had always called them.

And it was because of these eyes of his that Fox could see, quite clearly, the two shadows tucked in the back of Farran's shrine. As he rounded the viney corner, he suddenly stopped. Farran and Adella were there, and they appeared to be saying their goodbyes. Carefully, hoping they hadn't seen him, Fox backed away until he was hidden behind one of the statue's massive stone boots. Adella's head was buried in Farran's chest, and he was holding her and tenderly stroking her hair. Then, she pulled her head back and turned her face up to look into his.

"Safe travels, my lord," she said softly.

Farran tucked two fingers under her chin and kissed her ever so gently on the forehead. The kiss lingered for a long time, and Fox suddenly felt guilty intruding on such a private moment. And then Farran pulled away, and ran one finger down the side of her cheek. "It is always my pleasure to return to you," he said. He let his fingers tangle for a moment in her hair, and then he released her. She curtsied low, and he bowed in return. And then she left, her cloak whispering along the floor until she disappeared into the stairwell.

As Farran watched her go, Fox removed himself cautiously from the shadows and cleared his throat. Farran took a deep breath, and then said somberly, "Time to go." He bent down and plucked something from the shadows of his own statue. It was finely stitched leather gear, much larger than the bags Fox carried. Farran slung them onto his back effortlessly, then reached out in front and gripped his hand tight in midair. An elegant walking stick shimmered into being in his hand. And without another word, Farran led the way out of the temple and into the frozen forest.

They didn't speak as they made their way through the sleeping city of Whitethorn. There was a quiet resolve on Farran's face that didn't encourage talking. When they passed a little bird house on the way out of town, Fox simply gestured that he needed to stop, and Farran nodded. Quickly, Fox ducked inside the stone tower, where hundreds of birds adorned the rafters. A little girl curled up on a pillow in the corner awoke when Fox came in, and rubbed the sleep in her eyes as she came scrambling to help him. She was streaked with dirt, and there was straw caught in her flyaway blonde hair, but she smiled at him broadly as he presented her the letters. She promised to get them sent off at once, and thanked him heartily when he tossed her a fat copper coin.

Farran started walking again the moment Fox re-joined him, and he didn't speak until they reached the very edge of the city. Then Farran turned and gazed out at Whitethorn, off in the general direction of the temple. "There's something unnatural about a pirate finding a home this far from the sea," he said quietly. "And if I had it in my power, I would take us both away on a ship somewhere, until the end of her days."

"Why can't you?" asked Fox.

"That power was taken from me, long ago," said Farran. And then he smiled, but Fox could tell it wasn't real. "But this is your mission now." He turned his back on the city and held his arm wide, gesturing out at the open fields and snow-covered landscape. "Lead on, Master Foxglove."

As the sky began to lighten, a fresh breeze took Fox by the hand, and he followed. There would be plenty of time for questions on the road. Plenty of time for talk and stories. But it wasn't now. Now, Father was waiting. And Fox was coming to save him.

IT WAS EASIER TO TALK to Farran that Fox might have imagined. Once the god got away from Whitethorn, he became more of his old self again, and seemed eager to chat. He let Fox ask all sorts of questions about the gods he'd read of in *Asynthum*. He even added anecdotes of his own, and Fox was amazed at how *normal* Farran made the gods sound.

But when it came to himself and his history, Farran would change the subject. He would ask Fox questions of his own, talking about anything from Fox's past to how he was coming along in studying his Blessing. And, above all else, he wanted to know about Lai.

Over and over, Farran asked for stories about his daughter. He seemed to want to know everything, from her favorite color when she was three to how she took her eggs. He asked about her friends, what she did every day, how she'd handled growing up without a mother. These stories came easily to Fox, and he was more than happy to oblige. He spun hours of tales as they walked, telling about his earliest memories with the Blackroots and Lai's lessons with Widow Mossgrove.

"You know her well," Farran remarked at one point, as they sat together on the side of the road, eating a simple lunch.

"Maybe better than anyone," admitted Fox. And then, tearing his jerky into smaller pieces, he said, "In a way, we always only had each other." Farran raised an inquisitive eyebrow, and Fox explained. "We sort of ... found one another, when we were young. Neither of us really felt like we had a place in the valley, at least not with the other kids. Didn't matter *why* we felt it, but it was there. And it brought us together, closer than family." He absently sucked on the end of one of his shredded chunks of jerky for a moment. Then he stood, wiping snow from his backside. "We should get moving. Don't want to have to camp out in the open tonight."

Without waiting for Farran's response, Fox was on his way again.

THEY SET UP CAMP EARLY, tucking themselves into a comfortable scrap of forest. To Fox's surprise, Farran offered to set up the tent and build a fire. "You go," said Farran, waving him off. "Track us down a hearty supper, I'll take care of things here."

As Fox strung his bow and strapped his knives around his waist, he watched Farran from the corner of his eye. The god hummed to himself as he worked, stringing up ropes between thick tree trunks and anchoring loose ends to the ground with wooden stakes. By the time Fox headed out in search of game, Farran was whistling cheerfully and unrolling a great roll of tent canvas.

It didn't take long for Fox to bag three plump hares for dinner, but by the time he'd returned Farran had already built a beautifully crackling campfire. The tent was fully erected, nestled between two large pine trees, and Farran himself was lounging on a fallen log, staring up at the shadowed ceiling of branches. He glanced over lazily when Fox returned.

"Those will do nicely," he said, his eyes catching the limp carcasses strung across Fox's back.

"They'll do better if I have some help," said Fox pointedly, letting two of the hares fall to the earth while he dropped the other one onto Farran's stomach. The god coughed and sat up, chuckling slightly.

As the two began to skin the animals, Farran said, "That's quite a good shot you've got there."

Fox looked up, and found Farran inspecting the hare's eye. "Father taught me well," said Fox. "One good killing blow is better than two near misses. And if I catch them in the eye, it damages less of the pelt. Makes it easier to sell."

Farran smiled in a bemused sort of way, and turned back to his work. Once his hare was skinned and gutted, he skewered it on a sharpened branch and propped it up just beside the fire, wedging the end of the branch in between two heavy stones. As Fox finished up his own work, trussing up his two hares just as Farran had done, the god remarked thoughtfully, "Must be easier for you to catch game, now that you can just call the animals to you."

Fox looked up from adjusting one of his skewers, shocked. "I would never," he said defensively. He wasn't so much surprised at Farran's knowledge of his Blessing, but more at the insinuation that Fox could simply hunt effortlessly now. "It would be too much like cheating."

Farran chuckled. "Permission to take a moment and point out the irony of arguing cheating with a pirate."

"And if permission is denied?" asked Fox.

"I'm merely suggesting that you take advantage of the gifts you have been given," said Farran. "Why struggle to hunt and risk going hungry when you can simply command the beasts to walk up to your side?"

Fox busied himself with cleaning off every scrap of gut and fur from his knives, and for a moment he did not answer. Then, as he slid one completed blade back into its sheathe, he said quietly, "Gifts may just as easily be taken away."

Farran looked mildly surprised, as though Fox's answer had not been quite what he was expecting. But he recovered quickly. "Cheating is a way of life, my lad. It is how wars and maiden's hearts are won. Even your namesake, the cunning woodland fox, is a scavenger. Following other creatures of the forest to their hideaways and taking their food as his own."

The next knife, Fox crammed into its sheathe with more force than he'd originally planned, and a stitch popped loose from the leather. "It may be your way of life," he said firmly, "and perhaps *one* day it will be mine. But it is not yet, and I will use my Blessing as I see fit. Magic should not be a crutch, replacing a skill I already have with a quick fix. And if one day the gods see fit to take it away from me again, I will still be able to live."

A smile was playing about Farran's mouth now. A triumphant, self-satisfied smile. "For a child who has grown up in a country bereft of magic, you seem to know an awful lot about it."

"And for a god, you know an awful lot about mortal pursuits," countered Fox. He cocked his head pointedly at the crackling fire.

Farran sighed in a defeated manner and chuckled. "I suppose there's more to both of us than meets the eye."

They sat in a comfortable, lazy quietude after that, each keeping themselves entertained and taking turns checking on supper. Their little circle of trees was full of the sounds and smells of a campsite: the soft hiss of roasting meat as tongues of flame licked at the skewered hares; the soft pop and fizzle when crystals of sap caught fire and melted into the embers; a low humming and the gnawing of blade on wood as Farran whittled away at a scrap of pine; and the steady *rrrrsch* of Fox's tools as he scraped the pelts clean.

Between the two of them, they ate one and a half hares for supper. The rest, Fox wrapped carefully in parchment to save for breakfast. The fire had burned low by the time they finished, and Fox was beginning to yawn openly.

"I'll take the watch tonight," said Farran, stretching himself out on his log again. "Get your rest, you'll need it."

A part of Fox wanted to argue, if only to prove he was man enough to stand the first watch. But instead, another yawn overtook him, and he grunted a quick thanks before dragging himself to the tent and crawling inside. The exhaustion of the last few days seemed to have finally caught up with him, along with the sleepless night before. It was only as Fox laid out his bedroll and fell gratefully into it that the thought occurred to him: did gods even need sleep? But before he had time to ponder it, a dreamless unconscious washed over him.

FOX WAS AWAKENED LONG before dawn by a sharp kick to the ribs. With a painful grunt and a fit of coughing, Fox scrambled to sit upright, looking around wildly and grasping blindly for his knives.

"Oh good," said the dark shadow in the tent doorway that was Farran. "You're up. Come on, then." And he was gone, pushing back through the canvas door flap and letting a burst of freezing air rush through the tent. Fox shivered and pulled his knees to his chest, wiping sleep from his eyes with the heel of his hand. Slowly, with many grunts and muttered curses, he dressed and stumbled out into the grey haze that was not quite morning.

Farran had already brought the fire back to an even blaze, and the leftover pieces from last night's supper were laid out on flat rocks to heat. Farran himself had abandoned his merchant's costume, and looked much more like himself. In fact, he had abandoned almost everything. The pirate god had stripped down to breeches, a belted sash, and an open vest over his naked torso. He stood waiting on the other side of the fire, hands clasped behind his back.

"You spoke of skills wasting away in the presence of magic," said Farran once Fox had emerged. "And yet, you let this skill rust like an unused sword."

Fox finished tucking in the stray corners of his shirt, and glared at Farran. "Which skill do I have to sharpen before the sun is even up?"

"You were practicing combat with Neil just as early, not long ago," said Farran. "When you travel with me, you keep your skills sharp."

Dragging his feet, Fox shuffled over to join Farran across the fire. "Is there any point in wondering how you know about all that?" he asked grumpily.

A roguish grin was Farran's only answer. "Now," he said, spreading his feet in a fighting stance, "let's see what you can do with that rusty sword of yours."

By the time breakfast was ready, Fox was sore and bruised. Farran had gotten the better of him in every sparring match. And while many of the things Neil had once taught him were buried deep in his muscle memory, Fox found it harder to put into practice than he'd anticipated. He was sweating freely despite the cold, and when he sat down gingerly to help himself to breakfast, he stripped off his outer coat.

"I don't think I realized quite how long it had been," he admitted, wincing as he twisted his shoulder too far back.

"The technique is still there," said Farran. "You just need to get back at it."

Fox grunted and began shoveling warm hare into his mouth. The morning practice had made him ravenous, and meat had a way of making him not hurt quite so much. As the forest around them began to come to life with the scurrying of those animals that dared to brave Deep Winter, Farran quickly rolled up the tent canvas and tacked it securely to his bags.

Fox took charge of the ropes, which were sticky with a light glaze of sap. He wrapped and knotted them expertly, so they wouldn't get tangled and would be easy to use again tonight.

Clouds were thick across the sky, but they could feel somewhere behind them, the sun was trying to rise. They shouldered their packs and set off, Fox in the lead once more.

THEY SETTLED INTO A sort of routine as they traveled. Farran would set up camp each evening, as Fox went off in search of dinner. They chatted on occasion as they worked, and more often than not they would wind up playing a friendly game of cards. Then Farran would stand watch, and Fox would retire to his waiting bedroll.

Mornings were always heralded by combat practice. Farran drilled Fox on the things he'd learned already, putting him through his paces over and over again until he could measure "how much you've *really* learned." And then, once Fox's body began to remember what it was like to practice hand-to-hand and simple kicks and punches, Farran began to mix things up. He taught Fox tricky footwork and the basics of staff combat. Time and time again, they went through the same routines, until Farran was satisfied with Fox's technique.

Breakfast was always a quiet affair, as Fox was exhausted and only focused on his food. They would clean up camp in silence, working so seamlessly that neither tried to do the other's chores. By the time they left the campsite behind, there wouldn't be a trace that humans had set foot there.

And then, they would walk. They would keep a steady conversation, often about nothing at all, until they stopped for lunch. There, Farran started training Fox in the ways of throwing knives.

"I wouldn't *dream* of trying to teach you a thing about bows," said Farran on their second day out. They were once more taking their lunch resting just off the path. "But there are other weapons of range you could be utilizing. And I just happen to be an expert in the art of a well-placed knife."

With that, the god palmed a small blade and, with a quick flick of the wrist, sent it flying down the road to embed itself deep in the heart of a tree trunk. The first knife was hardly gone when a second one went rushing after it, and landed with a distant thud right next to the first. Once Fox was sure that Farran was finished, he went to investigate. He found both knives clustered so close together, there wasn't a hairs' breadth of a gap between their hilts. Indeed, the hilts themselves were the only things that showed. Even at such a distance, the knives had gone so deep Fox couldn't pull them free. He hurried back to Farran's side with an eagerness to learn that must have shown in his face, because Farran laughed at him.

"Easy, little pup," Farran teased. "You'll get there, I'll make sure of it. Now, for starters, let's work on your stance."

And each lunch afterwards, they focused on knives. And that, at least, came easier to Fox than any other combat practice he'd had so far. While his body may have been battered from the morning training, his mind was still clear, and his predator's eyes were keen at measuring distances. It was very much like shooting a bow, he quickly discovered. And he came to look forward to their short but fulfilling midday rests.

It should have taken more than a week to reach the foothills, even with Fox's instincts at the helm. But within five days of leaving Whitethorn, the ground began to rise beneath their feet. Their path grew steeper, and the wind whistled down at them from the mountain peaks far above. When Fox turned an inquisitive eye to Farran, the god winked and said, "I never said I had to do *everything* by a mortal's rules. And just because I can't get us there in an instant doesn't mean I won't help ... ah, speed things along a bit."

Fox grinned. "Couldn't have mentioned that at the beginning, could you?"

"And spoil my fun?" said Farran. "Come now, I can't be giving away all my secrets at once!"

With that, they began the familiar ritual of setting up camp for the night. There was a sheltering sort of dip in the earth that would tuck them neatly underneath a series of rocky ledges. The snow was thinner here, and the earth made a natural lean-to that would save them the trouble of putting up the tent for one night. They cobbled together a hearty stew of winter mushrooms and weasel meat, and as they let it heat over the fire, Fox asked a question that had been itching at his mind ever since he'd met Lai's mother.

"How did you meet her?" When Farran didn't answer at once, Fox pressed on. "A god and a mortal woman, it just seems so ... impossible."

There was a heavy, guarded quality to Farran's voice when he finally answered. "Are you asking for edification, or entertainment?"

"Both," admitted Fox.

For a moment, he was sure that Farran wouldn't answer. After all, on the road Fox had tried many times to pry bits of history from Farran, but the pirate god had cleverly eluded all of his questions, or even bluntly changed the subject. Now however, as Farran tossed scraps of kindling into the heart of the fire, he said, "Even the gods like to descend from their thrones on occasion and walk among mortals. And I – well, I have less cause to be about the divine realms than most."

Farran shifted, stretching one leg out farther in front, but Fox didn't dare to move. He didn't want to interrupt the story, or make Farran remember that he'd been actively avoiding such tales up until now.

"I was sailing with a fine and clever plundering crew," Farran continued. "We'd disguised ourselves as merchants. And she was a chancellor's daughter. A blue-blooded, fine-bred young thing. But oceans alive, did she have spirit." His voice trailed off dreamily, and he tossed another handful of scrap wood into the fire. For several minutes he simply stared ahead, his eyes reflecting the firelight. Then he shifted again, and Fox was surprised to notice discomfort in Farran' movement.

"I've never been much of a storyteller," Farran grunted finally. "And for her ... there's nothing I could say that would ever make you see her as I did. No tale I could spin that would ever truly capture Adella deMorrow." And then, he looked Fox straight in the eyes and said, "Would you like to see it?"

Fox cocked his head in curious confusion. "How —" he began.

"The Shavid may make you see visions when they sing," said Farran. "But the gods have other ways. If you would like, I can show you everything."

For a moment, Fox was torn. It was one thing hearing the story of Lai's parents, and entirely another to see it. What might be a fascinating tale was still a very private part of Lai's life, and even she didn't know it. But in the end, Fox's curiosity was stronger. He had to know.

He nodded, and Farran reached out a gentle hand. He pressed two fingers just between Fox's eyes, and said softly, "Then I'll take you to The Gossamer Sea, and the finest ship I ever sailed: the Laila."

There was the smell of saltwater and the crack of canvas sails in the wind. Winter melted away, and the sun shone brightly, bouncing off the highly polished deck of the ship. It was as though Fox were all at once gazing through Farran's eyes and watching him from afar. As the ship began to rock lazily back and forth on the swells, Fox began to lose track of who he really was. And then, he disappeared into Farran's memories.

Chapter Nineteen
The Laila

Farran dropped the last few feet to the deck and laughed triumphantly. "There's no man alive that can race the likes of me in the rigging!" he crowed. He threw his head back and laughed again, a rich and wild sound that had been known to make the very sails fill with wind, and could make mermaids sing.

With a hearty laugh of his own, Edwin came sliding down the rope after him and landed, wiping sweat from his smile-crinkled brow. "I should have known better," the man joked. "But I keep hoping one day I'll catch up to you!" He swept back the blond curls that had fallen across his eyes, running his fingers through his hair and letting the steady sea-breeze whisper through it. He was a tanned, muscular young man, with a constant boyish gleam in his wide green eyes.

Farran laughed and wrapped a jovial arm around him. "Keep trying, my friend," he said. "Perhaps if I lose a leg!"

"You know," teased Edwin lightly, "I *could* use a hand sharpening my tools later, if you happen to be around."

Farran tousled Edwin's hair and shoved him away, saying, "Planning accidents for me already, are you?"

But before Edwin could respond in kind, a bellowing shout from the quarterdeck came tearing through the air. "That'll be enough lollygagging from you Mister Farthington!" They both looked up to find the captain glaring across at them, arms crossed over his chest. Edwin hung his head like a beaten dog. "Back to work with you!"

"Yes sir," said Edwin quietly, but they both knew the captain had heard it. He heard everything. Without a backward glance, Edwin hurried below decks.

"And *you*, Mister Tallowight!" bellowed the captain. "Report to the helm at once!"

Farran bowed his head sardonically and swept up the deck to where the captain stood, surveying his ship with a critical eye.

"You shouted, sir?" said Farran.

Captain Worthright might have been intimidating to anyone else, but to Farran he was just a man. He was inch-for-inch as tall as Farran, but at least three times as broad. He had scars from a lifetime of battle rippling across every inch of him, like a map carved by each sword, knife, and shred of cannon shrapnel. The bulk of his arms so strained at any stitching that he'd taken to wearing open, sleeveless vests with no shirt. But no matter the weather, he did not seem to feel cold.

He surveyed Farran with the same sharp, calculating eye with which he took in every inch of his ship. Then he sighed and went over to the starboard railing, gesturing for Farran to follow. The captain gripped the polished teak with both hands and leaned his whole weight on it, gazing out at the open sea. As always when Captain Worthright applied his bulk to something, Farran was inwardly surprised that the wood didn't simply give way. He himself leaned on his elbows beside the captain and waited. He knew the captain would speak when and if he saw fit.

"You couldn't let him win just *once*," said Worthright gruffly after a few minutes.

Farran shrugged apologetically. "He's got his strengths, rig-racing just isn't one of them."

"Strengths be hanged," said Worthright, shaking his head and turning to look at Farran. "Make him look *good* in front of the men! Boost his confidence a bit!"

"No disrespect, sir," said Farran, "but the men *do* like him. He's friendly and much beloved around here. I know you can't see it —"

"I see *that* alright. But love does not always command respect! They need to see him as a leader!"

"You still plan on making him your successor, then?" asked Farran.

Captain Worthright heaved an almighty sigh and turned to look down the railing. Edwin had reemerged from below, and was now hanging off the starboard bow, busily repairing some of the woodwork. "They boy's a damned fine carpenter, no arguing that," he admitted. "But every time I look at him ... there's so much of his mother in him, that I want something more for his future. Something ... *grand!* Impressive."

"Not everyone is meant to be a captain," said Farran calmly. "I know he's your son, but that doesn't mean he has to fall in line for the throne!"

Worthright glared sidelong at Farran. And then, he appeared to give in, if only by an inch. He sighed in frustration and turned to lean his backside against the railing, arms crossed commandingly once more. "If he could *just* win one of your bloody races, *once!*"

"Oh come now, sir," jibed Farran. "Would that really be all it takes?"

Worthright chuckled slightly. "I suppose not." He clapped Farran on the shoulder and said, "You're a good man, Tal. And a ruddy fine sailor. But it's a big prize we're after tonight. Just ... keep an eye on him."

"I always do, sir," Farran said. He and the captain clasped hands firmly, and Farran tapped his forehead in a respectful gesture. "If there's nothing else, I'll be back to work."

And as he made his way down the quarterdeck, the captain called after him, "Shame you're not a captain yourself, lad!"

And Farran called back over his shoulder, "Perhaps someday I will be!" And then, he leaped the last few steps from quarterdeck to main, and within moments was pulling himself back up into the rigging, with a hearty crow and the start of a song. The crew joined in, raising their voices to the sky and making the wood hum.

They only knew him by the name "Tallowight," or "Tal." To them, he was merely a fisherman's boy who longed for a life of riches and adventure. He was the trickster, the womanizer. The captain's pet. And the men adored him. They never had a clue that when they prayed to the pirate god Farran, asking for a successful hunt or fair winds, he was standing right with them, watching over all. And while Farran certainly enjoyed being worshiped as much as the next god, there was a blissful sort of peace to be had in the mortal labors of the sea. A peace he could only find on the deck of a well-formed ship, being rocked and tossed on the waves like a great salty cradle.

And so, he happily let his shipmates believe that he was simply one of them. And, on the rare occasion that someone remarked upon his resemblance to the pirate god Farran, he simply laughed it off, saying that it must have been written in his destiny to be a pirate.

Now, Farran settled himself in high above the deck, lounging comfortably on the foretop. Below him and tucked in the rigging all about him, the men still sang. Their voices made the very ropes vibrate. Surely even the whales could hear them. And Farran smiled lazily, gazing out across the sea to where their quarry sailed, blissfully unaware that they were being hunted. Far enough away that they couldn't hear the men singing. In fact, anyone but Farran would have needed a spyglass to catch a glimpse of them. Four of them, flanking one great flagship in the middle. But even had they been closer, even had they known that the seemingly harmless ship on their tail was planning to take them as a prize, it wouldn't have done them a mite of good. Farran's grin spread wolfishly at the thought: no matter how they tried, they didn't have the gods on their crew.

THE SUN BEGAN TO SINK, staining the clouds a brilliant red. A palpable tension hovered on the salty breeze as the men grew eager. Wolves who had caught scent of a wounded beast. With the sun perched on the horizon like a great flaming egg, a quiet settled over the deck as the men disappeared below for a hearty supper. Farran could hear the muted clanking of dishes and the incoherent thrum of voices, but did not join them. And neither did Edwin.

The captain's son was still hard at work, making repairs to every damaged splinter of wood, real or imagined. He was just starting to apply a fresh coat of paint to the figurehead when Farran decided to join him. Edwin was perched on a swing, anchored at just the right level for him to work alongside the magnificent figurehead, and Farran shimmied down the rope pulleys to reach him. Then he sat himself down, casually straddling the wooden plank that made up the seat of the swing. For a moment, the whole contraption twisted in midair at the added weight, and Edwin stopped his work. But then the swing settled into stillness once more, and Edwin put brush to wood and continued to paint.

"I just thought she could use a bit more blue," Edwin said quietly. He was carefully edging the blue-and-gold scales of their figurehead, and Farran glanced over at the elegantly carved woman gracing the bow of their ship. While many in these waters had women as their figureheads, or even mermaids, the Laila was different. She was a siren.

Beautiful, dangerous, and a sailor's worst nightmare. Their songs drove many sailors mad, and the appearance of one meant certain doom for a crew. This one was carved with ample curves and a playful tail that disappeared into the body of the ship, in fact very reminiscent of a mermaid. But mermaids did not have wings, or great sharp spines like a sea snake's running down their backs. Laila, the name granted to both the ship and the siren, was all at once stunning and deadly. Farran gazed fondly on her, taking in the long, flowing wooden tresses that had been detailed with scale and feather patterns.

"It's fitting, isn't it?" asked Farran. "It's one of the reasons I like this ship so much."

"It's almost too fitting," said Edwin. He paused for a moment to look at Farran, pulling his brush away from Laila's painted form. "Why haven't they seen us for what we are? No law-abiding, self-respecting merchant vessel is going to have a siren as their figurehead. Can't they see it?"

"It's really not that hard to justify," said Farran, "if you think about it. Captain's been a very careful man. Careful not to let the wrong people see us, so we can't be recognized. We are nothing but a rumor on the wind, a shadow that eats unsuspecting children in the dead of night. We are a ghost story. We attack from out of nowhere, we disappear into the darkness. They could no more recognize our figurehead than our crew."

"Then why is tonight different?" asked Edwin.

"Ah, *tonight*!" said Farran theatrically. "Tonight is our grand lady's debut! After tonight, everyone will know her face."

Edwin sighed and returned to his work. "I suppose I should touch up her gilding as well, then." He painted in silence for a few moments as Farran gazed out to sea, watching their quarry sail unconcernedly ahead. "I think ... perhaps there's a great deal about piracy I still don't understand," Edwin admitted after a time. "I don't see why we should reveal ourselves at all, if we're getting along so well in the shadows. And on such an important take!"

"We've gone after big fish before," Farran reminded him.

"But the *king's navy?!*" said Edwin, dropping his voice to a passionate whisper. "This could get us moved to the top of every hangman's list in Linnat! Not to mention Fernaphia, Mirius and every other country they're in allegiance with. We'll be running for the rest of our lives after this, and for what? The captain's pride?"

To an untrained eye like Edwin's, it might have seemed like a fool's errand. Even Farran knew the risks of taking on kings and emperors. The Laila and her crew had been marauding for close to five years now, though Farran had only been sailing with them for three. And in all that time, they'd never been caught. Never suspected.

"It's not pride," said Farran finally. "Not *exclusively*, at any rate. But the Captain knows, I suspect, that it's only a matter of time before someone catches up to us. They'll find out who we are. At least now, we do it on his terms. And by the rolling seas, we will make a show out of it!" There was a fervor of excitement in Farran's own voice as he went on. "Our figurehead will strike fear into the hearts of even the boldest of sea dogs! And the shadows of our sails on the horizon will be a warning, let those who dare to oppose us come forth! But we fall to *no* man!"

Edwin had stopped painting. He watched Farran with an anxious thrill dripping all across his face, his eyes shimmering with the barest hint of the fire that pirates felt before taking a prize. It may have just been a spark, but it was there for a lingering moment. Until, far too quickly, it faded, and his boyish face was etched with concern once more. He turned back to the siren figurehead, raised his brush as if to continue, but did not paint. And then, so quietly it was almost drowned by the sound of the sea slapping against the hull, Edwin said, "He's going to make me his successor no matter what, isn't he."

"He does seem rather intent upon it," admitted Farran.

"Tonight," said Edwin gloomily. "Of all nights, tonight he had to put me in charge of something real. And I'll butcher it up, and then all the men will see I'm not cut out for leadership."

"Would that be so wrong?" asked Farran. "Not everyone needs to be a leader. Maybe he'll finally see that."

Edwin rolled his eyes and dropped his brush back into the bucket of paint, apparently giving up on even the appearance of work. "You think he'll let it go at that, do you? As long as I'm on this ship, I'll be groomed to be a leader."

"You could always leave," suggested Farran. "Take your share of the prize money and head off when we get to port. You could make a decent life as a carpenter."

Edwin laughed humorlessly, and Farran found it was a rather hollow sound. He was used to Edwin's laughs being full and playful. His mortal friend was usually so carefree. "You know I can't," Edwin said. "Four sisters, remember? And my mother always wished for a better life. For all of us."

"Maybe they can marry rich," teased Farran pensively, and this time at least, Edwin's watery chuckle was genuine.

"I'm sure Meladrie could," Edwin mused. "But the rest of them don't have her looks, much as I love them all." He chuckled again and began to tug on the rope pulleys, lowering their swing down closer to the water. "If they're not careful ... if *I'm* not taking care of them, they'll go the same way as Mother. Five children, by five different fathers."

"Oh good sir!" said Farran, mockingly appalled, "How dare you speak of your mother so?" For he knew what every man aboard The Laila knew: Captain Worthright had only been with Edwin's mother for one night, but that's all it had taken.

"Oh, surely my mother deserved every slanderous name she was ever given," said Edwin jovially, beginning to return somewhat to himself. "But she was still my mother, and I must honor her dying wishes." He wrapped his hand about one of the hanging ropes to anchor himself and bent low, dipping his paint brushes into the water to clean them, then tucked the dripping brushes into a pocket and hauled them back up again.

It was true that Edwin's mother had been less than chaste in her life. She'd made a living of it. Farran had heard many times from Captain Worthright the story of his night in Port Carraway, and his visit to Madame Petal's. There, he had met Hattie Farthington, and Edwin had been conceived after a night of drink, dancing, and passion.

He had circled the world before finding her again, and once he had, he'd been welcomed with the wondrous news that he was a father. Well he and, by that time, one other man of her acquaintance. And while the fathers of Hattie's daughters would always remain absent in their lives, Captain Worthright had taken something of a shine to the idea of having a son. He checked in on them each time he found himself harbored in their city, and once Edwin came of age, he'd offered the boy a place on his ship.

But now, the Captain's own fatherly instincts seemed to be blinding him to the hard truths about his son: Edwin Farthington was not a leader.

THERE WAS AN ALMOST painful excitement in the air as the sun finally disappeared, and darkness descended upon the Gossamer Sea. The sky was cloudless, and the moon shone bright like a lighthouse beacon. Stars filled every inch of sky, as though the gods had sprinkled great handfuls of gemstone onto the black velvet that was the heavens. The lights were mirrored in the dark waters, like countless white and silver fish darting through the sea.

As the men on board the Laila made their final preparations, Farran glanced up at the traitorously bright sky. *That's enough of you,* he thought. And, with a casual wave of his hand, a thin, grey layer of clouds stretched themselves across the moon and many of the stars, muting their light. Their plans would go much smoother in the darkness. That done, Farran reported to Captain Worthright's side on the quarterdeck.

They stood in silence, watching the flickering lantern lights on the convoy far ahead of them. They were closer now than they had been that evening, but still the five ships sailed carelessly on.

"Blind sheep," muttered Worthright. His hands were clasped behind his back, and he gazed upon the ships ahead with a fierce hunger. "Is everything in place?" he asked.

"Tivaas is readying the men now," answered Farran.

"And Edwin?"

"Throwing up over the port bow, last I checked," said Farran honestly. "But he'll pull himself together alright. He knows how important this is."

"And you're sure the medicine is on board the flagship?"

"Aye, sir," said Farran.

The underlying reason for their attack on this particular group of ships was a close-kept secret. In fact, only Farran and Edwin were privy to the captain's true intentions. While a castle's-worth of foreign medicines might not seem like a worthy prize to an average buccaneer, Captain Worthright came from a different place than most of them. A cold place. A cursed place. His family, and his people, lived in a frozen and destitute town in Northern Sovesta. Every sickness had the potential to be a death sentence, and money was not so important as food and shelter. And so, when Farran brought rumors of the ship's hidden value to Captain Worthright, the captain had simply asked if the financial compensation would be enough to satisfy his men. When Farran assured him it would be far more than enough, Captain Worthright hadn't spared a second thought.

Farran tucked his hands carefully out of sight behind him, then pulled two tankards of rum from nowhere and handed one to the captain. "A toast," Farran said, raising his drink. "To Laila. May she remain ever beautiful, and devour the souls of those in our way."

Worthright raised a silent glass in answer, and they both drank deeply. And then, Mister Tivaas came scrambling up onto the quarterdeck and bowed low.

"We're all in place, Cap'n!" said Tivaas excitedly.

"Then let us begin," said Worthright. And then, bellowing so the whole ship might hear him, "Curtains up, lads!"

There was a splash behind them as something heavy was dropped into the water, and all three of the men ran to the other railing to look. There, tethered to the ship so it might not float too far away, was a small rowboat outfitted with mast and sails. One of the men sat at its bow, awaiting his next orders.

"Let's disappear!" shouted Worthright.

Chapter Twenty

The Beneath

Fox came back to himself with a painful chill. All at once, he became aware of the deathly cold of a Sovestan night, a world away from the Gossammer Sea. Gone were the creaks and wails of ship timber, to be replaced by the gentle crackling of a merry cookfire. The smells of the foothills came crashing down on him, crowding the sharp bite of salty sea air aside and replacing it with fresh pine, woodsmoke, and stewing meat.

Farran was rubbing his hands together, wincing slightly. "Haven't done that in awhile," he admitted. "I always forget how much it takes out of me." He shook his hand vigorously as he asked, "You alright, little one?"

For a moment, Fox wasn't quite sure. He was seeing everything through somewhat of a foggy haze, and his skull was throbbing where Farran had touched him. But then the discomfort passed, and he grunted, "'Yeah, just fine."

Still massaging his hand, Farran said, "Sorry I can't show it to you all at once. But it's a rather long story. And waking dreams take a toll on the average mortal mind. We'll continue this later then, shall we?" And then, almost too nonchalantly, he added, "If you'd like, that is. If it's still of some interest to you."

"Of course!" said Fox eagerly, sounding more like an overly excited little boy than he would have cared to. But there was something in Farran's smile as he went to stir their supper that made him think: perhaps the god was truly enjoying having his story told. Mealtime was filled with talk as Fox peppered Farran with questions, all about Edwin and Captain Worthright and life aboard a ship. And that night, he fell asleep dreaming of the high seas.

ANOTHER STORM WAS THICKENING nearby as they wound their way deeper into the mountains. They traveled without speaking, picking up their pace and only stopping as much as was absolutely necessary. For three and a half days they twisted and climbed, and their campsites were reduced to the barest essentials: a fire, a latrine, and blankets. There was no time for stories these nights. Fox himself slept as little as he could, insisting that Farran wake him long before dawn every morning. If Fox's instincts were right, and they'd never failed him so far, they would reach Doff with just over an hour to spare.

As worried as he was about not reaching Father in time, or their race against the gathering storms, Fox warmed inside and out just thinking about seeing the little hamlet again. For that was where he'd determined they must go. He could feel it in the glowing map each time he touched it, that somewhere deep in those mountain mines, there was a safe path to the south. A safe, avalanche-free path to Father and back again. In times of quiet or times when he had trouble falling asleep, Fox found himself opening his book to the lymnstone-powdered page and tracing its shimmering lines with his fingertips, just to enjoy the thrill of being swept through its stone pathways once more.

He practically ran the last hundred lengths up the road to the carved town marker, leaving Farran behind. The god let him go, and Fox trusted that Farran, still disguised as "The Incomparable Donovan," was quite capable of catching up when and if he pleased. And so, making not so much as a shred of effort to hide his enthusiasm, Fox hurried through town and straight to the public house, where the breeze told him crowds were gathering for the usual evening meal and festivities.

He'd barely ducked beneath the long, low doorway when no fewer than a dozen souls recognized him. A hearty cheer echoed through the room and caused the torches to shake in their brackets, and something tackled Fox with the force of a small boulder. Laughing, Fox caught Topper around the chest in brotherly embrace and then let himself be dragged back to the candlemakers' table. There, familiar faces jumped out at him like words in a favorite song, and he offered handshakes and greetings all around. Even the formidable Kaldora Flintstock seemed pleased to see him, sliding over to make room for him on her bench.

"So what brings you back to us?" asked Topper eagerly, once the salutations were done with and Fox had been treated to a heaping pile of goat-stuffed fish. "Trade business?"

"Personal business," Fox managed to spit out through a mouthful of supper. He made himself take the time to swallow properly before continuing, "I've got to make it down south to see my Father, and the mountain passes will all be icelocked."

"What's so important it can't wait until spring?" asked Wick from across the table. Kaldora's younger brother was helping himself to a third serving of bread, and was constantly fending off his neighbors' attempts to help themselves to his share, jabbing them playfully with his elbows. "Got to be dangerous, traveling all that way by yourself."

"I've got a friend," said Fox. "Dangerous it might be, but the payoff is worth more." When his dinner companions simply looked at him curiously, Fox said, "The lives of many good men depend on me. Including my father's."

A hush fell over the candlemakers' table. Many of them suddenly became very interested in their food, or else in the sleeves of their shirts and the hems of their winter coats. It was Kaldora who finally spoke.

"I think we all find it difficult to believe that one young man carries the fate of so many," she said quietly. Her words may have been a bit harsh, but Fox sensed an almost motherly concern in her voice.

"I have trouble believing it myself sometimes," admitted Fox, pushing his half-eaten dish away and folding his hands on the tabletop. "But this is too important for me to doubt myself. I know things ... about them, about where they are and what's coming to them. I can save my valley from an immeasurable hurt."

Kaldora folded her hands in a mimicry of Fox's, and leaned forward. Every intimidating inch of the woman, without her saying a word, whispered, *Prove it.*

Slowly, confidently, Fox said, "At exactly the moment that I've taken my last bite, the very sky will open up on us. A storm of such ferocity, you'll hear the very mountains cry out in pain."

"It is Deep Winter," parried Kaldora. "Not exactly a stretch of a prediction, is it?"

"The blizzard will last exactly seven turns," continued Fox, using the Doffian measurement of time, referring to the period of one shift or "turn" in the mines. "And the majority of the damage will be focused on the western end of town." With that, he drew his plate near again and continued to eat. For a moment, every eye at the table was on him. As Fox took careful, measured bites, his companions began to shift uncomfortably in their seats. All except Kaldora, who continued to watch Fox with a calculating severity that made it difficult to swallow his food.

Nevertheless, he found he enjoyed the strange discomfort he'd affected upon the candlemakers. They watched him as though he were about to catch fire at any moment, and they weren't quite sure whether to throw water on him or laugh at his neat little trick.

And then, Fox took one last, dramatic bite, scraping his dish clean. The group collectively held their breath. And in the silence that wrapped around their table, they could hear it: the distinct, unmistakable sound of hailstones and thunder. All at once, the candlemakers scrambled to their feet, even Kaldora. Many of them wound quickly through the public house, warning their fellows of the incoming weather and hastily paying their tabs for dinner. Kaldora took both Topper and Fox by the elbows and hauled them across the room. They ducked outside, keeping themselves pressed to the stone to avoid getting pelted by ice.

"Seven turns, you say?" shouted Kaldora over the howling of the wind.

"Afraid so!" Fox replied at the top of his lungs. And then he felt a tug on his arm and Kaldora was leading them away, as quickly as she could without stumbling on the already icy stones. It was only once they were safely barricaded in the Flintstock home that Fox found himself worrying about Farran.

But, as it turned out, there was no need. As Kaldora lit a handful of lanterns hanging from the ceiling, a form detached itself from the shadows, making the woman drop into a fighting crouch and pull out a stone knife so quickly that Fox couldn't see where she'd been hiding it.

"It's alright," Fox said quickly. "He's with me."

Farran bowed low, sweeping his ludicrously bright blue cloak out in a dramatic whirl. "Donovan Parcelview at your service, my lady! Purveyor of fine —"

"Quiet, you," interrupted Kaldora, relaxing her stance somewhat but not lowering her knife. She did not take her eyes off Farran as she addressed Fox. "This is the one you travel with?"

"Yes ma'am," said Fox.

"And how did he know where to find you?"

"He has his ways," explained Fox, shrugging apologetically. Inwardly, he was trying very hard not to laugh at the situation. Had Kaldora known she was speaking to a god, Fox was fairly certain she wouldn't have behaved any differently.

For a moment, Kaldora continued to scrutinize the flamboyantly-dressed man standing in her home. Then, as she made her knife disappear beneath her robes once more, she said scathingly, "Men should not wear yellow."

Farran looked past her to grin at Fox. "I think I'm beginning to like her," he said.

"Maybe I should have let her kill you," teased Fox.

A BED WAS SET UP FOR Fox in Topper's room, as it had been on his last journey. Farran was put up on a bedroll in the workshop, and as Fox burrowed himself into his blankets, he found himself wondering if the god would have to simply pretend to sleep tonight. Or if he really *could* sleep, just didn't *need* to. But he could hear low voices from the workshop late into the night. Voices he was sure were Farran's and Kaldora's. Words like "Blessed" and "Windkissed" floated to him and fought their way through his fuzzy, exhausted mind. But when he awoke next morning, he couldn't be sure if he'd simply imagined it all.

He and Topper spent a good part of the day playing cards as the storm continued to rattle the mountain. Kaldora worked, wrapping packages of candles to be delivered, or else carving elegant details into the fancy, statuesque candles that were shaped like cats or people or buildings. And Farran appeared to doze off in the corner, stretched out on his bedroll with his feet propped up on several of his traveling bags.

None of them mentioned Fox's prediction about the length of the storm. In fact, none of them spoke of the storm at all, instead passing pleasant conversation on the eborill mating that season, or gossiping about who might secretly be courting whom. But every so often, Kaldora's eyes would stray to the tall, wide candle perched in its solitary bracket in a corner of the room. It was the candle that measured the time, with marks dyed into it to track the passing of hours. One "turn," Fox remembered from his previous visit to Doff, was a third of a day. There were three mining shifts, divided evenly, and it was by these that the town kept time. And so seven turns equaled just over two days. And Fox was sure that Kaldora was counting.

That night, the winds blew harder. Fox feigned a headache and excused himself to turn in early, crawling into bed and pulling the blankets tight about his ears. He buried his face in his pillow and breathed slowly and carefully, trying to keep the shivers at bay. But still they came, and he could feel the whole of Doff pressing in on his senses.

Eborills fought for spaces high up in the stone nests, pecking viciously at one another as they crowded in for warmth. Fights broke out between many of the hot-blooded fledglings, and more than a few wings were broken as they tried to grapple in the confined spaces. A southern woman who had married into a mining family was crying, miserable in the cold mountain weather and inexplicably terrified of the earsplitting roars of the blizzard. The western-most mine entrance was caving in, its stones shrieking angrily, and no fewer than five houses on the western slopes were buried beneath the towering snowdrifts. By the time Topper made his own way to bed later that night, Fox's nose was bleeding from the ferocity of the assault on his body and mind.

But by morning, Fox had managed to scrape together several hours of sleep. And so, he supposed, perhaps he was finally learning to control even these storm-driven shivers. It might have been the sort of control he wasn't entirely aware of; in fact, he wasn't even sure he was initiating it. But it was helpful nonetheless, and he was grateful.

The second day of the blizzard passed in much the same manner as the day before. The only notable exception, in fact, was that Farran actively joined in the conversation. He spun extravagant tales for them about his life on the road. And while the character of "The Incomparable Donovan" might have been false, his stories sounded so genuine that even Fox found himself wondering if they might be true.

But no matter how colorful the stories were, no matter how some of his tales had even Kaldora heaving with laughter, they weren't the stories Fox wanted to hear. The story of how Donovan had made a small fortune by successfully bartering away scraps of the cheapest peasant fabric to an exceptionally spoiled and gullible prince was truly hilarious, but Fox longed to revisit the Gossamer Sea. He couldn't wait until the next time he would be allowed to see part of Farran's story, for he didn't dare ask here. Not in such close quarters, with Kaldora and Topper watching. Fox would simply have to wait until they were back on the road.

IT HAPPENED EXACTLY as Fox had predicted. Exactly seven turns after the storm had begun, the winds quieted. A weak winter sunlight fought its way through the clouds, and the Doffians began to emerge from their homes once more. Farran disappeared, making excuses about "running errands." Topper dragged Fox away the moment they could go outside again, and the boys went to help clear some of the damage on the western end of town. It wasn't until that night, as the candlemakers took their normal places at the pub table, that Kaldora finally addressed Fox.

"Alright then, little trapper," she said. "Tell me about this Blessing of yours."

A collective tension rippled around the table, like a breeze bending the reeds along a riverbank. Their companions seemed to be trying to act casual, as though they weren't hanging onto every word. But glances were thrown up and down the table, and chewing slowed almost to a stop. Only Wick succeeded in his feigned nonchalance, continuing to steadily eat his way to the bottom of his dish of stew without so much as a skipped breath.

"The wind speaks to me," said Fox simply. He didn't bother to ask how she'd known, sure now that the snatches of conversation he thought he'd heard between Kaldora and Farran were real. "It's a Shavid gift, and I am called one of the Windkissed. Born into the Shavid way of life, without a sha in my bloodline. It's how I knew your blizzard was coming. And it's how I know my father and his caravan will be buried alive by an avalanche if they travel home the way they mean to."

Kaldora rested her chin on her folded hands, surveying Fox with something he almost thought was approval. Fox returned to his own supper, knowing well enough by now that Kaldora would speak when she chose to, and not a heartbeat before. "Fine," she said at last. "If someone escorts you down into the mines, can you make your way south from there?"

"A natural instinct for direction comes with the Blessing," Fox assured her.

"Very good. We will help you resupply as best we can, and will be waiting to receive you again on your way back. Is tomorrow morning early enough for your departure?"

"Yes ma'am," answered Fox.

"Excellent," said Kaldora.

"Your gift helps you speak to the wind, you said?" Wick still didn't look up from his food as he spoke, instead appearing to casually address the entire table.

"It does," said Fox.

"And this wind helps you track and hunt," said Wick. "And your self-proclaimed sense of direction."

Fox shrugged and scraped the dregs of his stew with a thick chunk of bread. "It doesn't hurt," he said. "I've been trained as a trapper all of my life, so I wouldn't say it's the *only* tool at my disposal."

Now, Wick finally looked up. "But under the mountains, you'll have none of those tools." He and Fox locked eyes. And in the briefest moment where Fox opened his mouth to refute him, he realized that Wick was right. He closed his mouth again, and Wick returned to his food. "I'll join you," Wick said.

"Wick —" said Kaldora sharply, but her younger brother interrupted.

"Kal, he can't make it on his own and we shouldn't expect him to."

"He won't *be* on his own," argued Kaldora. "His traveling companion Donovan will be going as well. And I can't spare you."

"Neither of them know the mines like we do. You may forget, I've *been* south before. I know the roads, under and over the mountains, and if you send them out there without a guide then the boy might as well be traveling alone."

Not one of the candlemakers was even pretending not to listen anymore. All eyes were locked on the Flintstock siblings. Kaldora looked ready to split stone with her bare hands, while her brother's face was placidly indifferent to her anger. Finally, Kaldora gave the smallest of nods, and the whole table relaxed.

"Could I —" began Topper eagerly.

"No," said Kaldora, and there was a finality in her voice that no one would dare argue with. And then, to Wick, "You will take them there and see them back, safely and quickly. But when you return, I am working you harder than you've ever been worked. You will make up for the lost time, agreed?"

With a smile and an mock-imperial nod, Wick swiped one last hunk of bread from the center of the table and stood. It was only after he'd left the public house altogether that Fox realized he might have saved both siblings the trouble of arguing. He was traveling with a god, after all. What better guide did he need?

But even as he thought it, Fox remembered something he'd read in his book, *Asynthum*. Something about how many gods were only truly strong in their own area of expertise. Gods had specialties, just like any merchant or waresman. And how much help would a pirate god truly be so far from the ships and open waters?

KALDORA MADE SURE THEY had everything they'd need for a journey under the mountain. She supplied them with fresh candles and lanterns; tinder; raw, glowing chunks of blue lymnstone ore. She gave them wrapped packets of salted meat, then sent everyone straight to bed. Farran had reappeared with packages of his own, but joined Kaldora in ushering Fox off to bed when he tried to ask what they were.

That night, Topper didn't speak much. He went to bed sullenly but obediently, and Fox was sure he was pouting over not being allowed to join them. The next morning, after a hearty breakfast of boiled eborill eggs and winter mushrooms, Topper briefly shook hands with both Fox and Farran, and then excused himself, saying, "Off to my chores then." And he darted out of the house, disappearing around a corner before the rest of them had even set foot outside the door.

Wick was waiting for them three levels up, perched on a boulder just outside one of the entrances to the mine. As Farran introduced himself and the two men started to get acquainted, Kaldora pulled Fox aside and handed him a leather pouch. Curious, Fox opened it. Tucked neatly inside was a set of new arrows. Their heads and shafts were black, and there was something strange about their fletching. Where other arrows were fletched with feathers, these were stone. A thin, iridescent and semi-transparent stone that Fox had never seen. He pulled one of the arrows from its home and balanced it delicately on one finger. It was weighted perfectly, and Fox was amazed at the intricacy of the design. These were more than arrows, they were flawless sculptures. Carefully, lovingly, Fox slipped the arrow back into its leather pouch and looked to Kaldora for explanation.

When Topper's adopted mother spoke, it was with a low and quiet urgency Fox had never heard in her voice. "There are things that live in the Beneath that will not take kindly to your being there," she murmured. "Travel well, and travel fast. Make no more noise than you must, and do not give them a reason to think ill of your presence." And then, she squeezed his shoulder in an almost affectionate manner, nodded farewell to her brother, and made her way back down the mountain path.

Fox turned to the men waiting for him. "Lead on," he said to Wick.

He followed the candlemaker through the stone crevice, with Farran at his heels. They passed briefly through an active division of the mine, teeming with workers and the ringing melody of metal on stone. But all too soon, they left it behind, exchanging the noise of hard labor for the empty, echoing beat of their own footsteps. Lantern lights faded, and only the shimmering veins of ore lit their way.

It was like descending into the very skeleton of the mountain. Abandoned mining structures and equipment seemed to grow right out of the stone like stalagmites. Great gaping shadows marked the entrances to other paths, other roads to the gods only knew where. And Fox realized as they walked that Wick had been right. He could not feel the wind. Fox tucked his arms tight around himself as he walked, resisting the urge to reach out and grab a grown-up's hand like a frightened child.

And they walked, all three in a row, down into the heart of a world where Fox felt crippled, deaf, and blind. And inexplicably afraid.

THERE WAS AN UNSETTLING quiet about the mining roads. It was as though darkness and starlight had been frozen in time, with the black twisting shadows of rock stretching in all directions, sprinkled with countless strains of glittering ore. Sound was all at once echoed and swallowed, with each footstep resounding ten times louder than normal before immediately being lost in the stone.

Fox kept close behind Wick. So close, in fact, that he had to be careful not to tread on the candlemaker's heels. But he couldn't help himself; he could feel the mountain closing in all around him. He could sense something ancient and alive, something trying to speak to him. And he felt that if he could only listen hard enough, he might be able to understand. But here, without the wind to whisper the world's secrets to him, Fox was no more than a frightened child trying not to get lost in the magnificent, terrifying beauty of the Beneath.

And he knew that the adults could feel it, too. He could sense it in the way neither of them spoke unless they had to. The way Wick always had one hand on the sword at his waist, and the way Farran gripped his carved staff. The group moved quickly, with an air of silent urgency about their pace. For more than half a day, they traveled in almost complete silence. Down winding, wooden stairs built by miners long ago. Through deserted caverns littered with the remnants of past mining communities. Scraps of old living quarters and public halls that made Fox wonder what had driven the miners of Doff out of the caves and onto the mountainside.

And then, he heard it. Something behind them on the underground roads. Something following them. Fox saw Wick's hand tighten on his sword hilt. Something was scurrying through the tunnels, not far behind them. Fox could feel both men tensing up, the same way they might if they were preparing for a morning sparring practice. It was a familiar sensation, and Fox felt his own muscles humming with taut awareness, ready to spring into action if necessary. But none of them turned back just yet. They kept their pace as their path twisted, taking them from a tight stone tunnel to an open hall. Let whatever was following them think they were an unwary prey; but Fox was a hunter. His eyes darted through the grand cavern, marking everything from the distance to the nearest ledge, to the location of the five tunnel openings he could make out in the faint glow of the lymnstone. They seemed to be crossing over an abandoned mining shaft, with carved pits and jagged pathways twisting deep below them before disappearing into the total darkness.

It happened all in an instant. Something shifted behind them, causing a shower of stone rubble to cascade across the stone floor and bounce down into the yawning mouth of cavern far beneath them. As one, the travelers whipped around, and without even realizing it, Fox had put one of his new black arrows to the string of his bow and drawn, holding steady with the point of his arrow straight at the source of the disturbance. On one side Wick had drawn his sword, of the same black stone as Fox's arrows. And on the other, Farran gripped his staff in one hand while he produced a handful of glowing lymnstone powder in the other. And with one quick, powerful breath, Farran scattered the blue powder into the darkness, where it clung to the air and the stone, illuminating their follower. A small someone with a mop of blond hair, and freckles visible even in the dim blue glow.

Topper had his hands raised over his head in a gesture of surrender. "Don't shoot?"

WICK WAS BEYOND LIVID. Fox could never have imagined how much Wick could resemble his older sister, but in his fury he radiated just as much of a coldly murderous air as Kaldora ever did. As Fox and Farran set up a rudimentary camp, Wick berated Topper in heated whispers, just out of earshot. Every so often, Fox could see Topper try to argue, only to have his adopted uncle box him about the ears.

They'd descended a bit into the cavern before setting up camp, with Wick dragging Topper by his cloak the whole way. Now, tucked into an empty pocket of stone behind a towering scaffold, Farran and Fox settled in to watch the argument from a distance.

"He's lucky I didn't shoot him," said Fox quietly as he sat atop his bedroll, munching on a slab of slightly stale bread.

"After the beating he's going to get when Kaldora gets hold of him again?" said Farran. "He might wish you had."

Finally, a seething Wick and a very disgruntled Topper returned to their little campsite. Topper plopped down as far away from the group as he could while still being included in the conversation, and Wick said, "We can't turn back at this point, we'll lose too much time. The troublemaker will have to come with us." He glared at his nephew, who glared right back.

"I only wanted to help," Topper grumbled, arms crossed defiantly.

"Oh, and what help might you be, Great Master Explorer?" asked Wick, each word dripping with unconstrained sarcasm.

Topper shrugged uncomfortably and said, in an almost embarrassed voice, "Fox saved my life."

Wick didn't respond, but his face softened. After a few moments he said, "We'll stay here for a half turn or so, then carry on. Everyone should get some rest, but sleep light." His eyes flickered down into the darkness of the mines below, but he said nothing else. Instead, he shifted his bedroll to the other side of the camp, where Topper sat.

As usual, Farran volunteered to keep watch. They lit no fire that night, everyone instead taking their meal from the supplies of bread and smoked meat. It was darker here, with all but the smallest chunks of ore having been harvested eons ago. Fox could almost see the history of the mines etched in the stone, and he itched to ask questions about the Beneath. But Kaldora's parting words echoed in his head like a distant song, and there was a part of him that was sure he didn't want to know after all.

He tossed and turned long after Topper and Wick were asleep. He could see Farran's watchful silhouette perched on the edge of their campsite, feet dangling over the ledge. When Fox was certain that sleep had completely eluded him, he slipped silently from his bedding and went to join the pirate god, perching himself carefully on the edge of the stone and wrapping one arm around a scaffold support beam.

It was Farran who spoke first, in a low and quiet voice that barely stretched past their own ears. "There are things that live in the deep seas. Things that even the gods live in fear of."

"And in the deep mountains?" asked Fox, his own voice just as low.

"There is a rumor among sailors," Farran continued, as though he hadn't heard, "that simply speaking of these terrors summons them from the very depths of the ocean. From the darkest places." And then he turned, and even in the semi-dark Fox could feel the god's eyes locking with his. "We never mention their names within the cradle of the sea. It is only in port that we can speak of the monsters beneath the waves. And even there, in the warmth of tavern firelights and doxy's beds, we can never truly be free of the fear."

Farran didn't need to say more. His message was painfully clear: don't ask, don't speak of it. Whether he had sensed the curiosity in Fox's thoughts, or simply felt his keenness for knowledge, Fox did not know. But he swallowed back the hundreds of questions making his throat hum. He would save them for aboveground, and sunlight. Instead, he said pointedly, "About the sea, then?"

There was something of a smile in Farran's voice as he said, "I suppose there's time for a bit of a story." He placed a cold and slightly trembling finger gently between Fox's eyes once more. "Now then. Where were we?"

Chapter Twenty-One
Captain Worthright

The deck of the Laila was dark and silent. Bobbing along behind it was the rowboat decoy, brilliantly lit and looking remarkably like a distant ship. To anyone watching from the naval convoy, it would simply look as though the ship that had been drifting peacefully in its wake for the past few days was falling behind. Docking perhaps, or changing course. Nothing at all sinister. Nothing to warrant alarm. They had no way of knowing that a hundred armed and ready pirates were anchored in the lines and decking of the shadow of a ship steadily gaining on them.

Farran and Edwin were at the bow, crouched in the deepest of shadows. They could feel a handful of sailors standing a way off, waiting for their cue. And Edwin sat, eyes clenched tight, struggling to do his part. An earnest sweat soaked his brow and hair, and he breathed deep and even, as if trying to fill and empty the sails with his lungs. After several minutes, however, he growled in frustration and pounded his fists into his own thighs. "I can't do it, Tal!" he whispered urgently. "I can't just make them *slow down*, that's a kind of sorcery I never —"

"*Yes* you can," said Farran, fiercely but quietly. "I have seen your work with carpentry, and it is more than pure skill. There is magic in your craft, a great deal of it! You may not know how to use it yet, but *this* you can do!" He put a brotherly hand out and grasped Edwin's shoulder. "Reach out to the ships. Command them to slow. The wood will listen to you. *Trust* your own instincts. Trust *me*!"

As Edwin closed his eyes once more, Farran squeezed his shoulder ever so slightly. A comforting, reaffirming gesture, but with a little something more. He knew that Edwin could be a great carpenter mage one day; his raw, uncut skills were unparalleled. But now, in this moment, the captain's son needed a bit of a push. And so, with the barest hint of godly magic he could muster, Farran lent out just a spark of his power.

"I can feel them," said Edwin. "The ships. Great Spirit, I can *hear* them!"

"Tell them what you want," said Farran.

And then, Farran could hear what no mortal aboard the Laila, save for Edwin, would ever hear: the acquiescent, obedient moan of the ships ahead slowing their pace. They were nothing more than wooden dogs, bowing to a new and intriguing master.

Farran passed a whispered command to the nearest sailor, and heard it passed carefully down into the bowels of the ship. The Laila shuddered slightly as sliding hatches opened in her hull, making way for rows of great, long oars. The ship began to gather speed, silently and smoothly, as the rowers deep in the ship's belly pulled in unison. And as they worked, an exhausted Edwin collapsed to the deck, pressing his sweating face to the cool of the polished wood.

"Tal?" he said, and Farran was immediately at his side again. "I could hear their voices. I could hear the planks and masts and figureheads. They were so loud ... why were they so loud, Tal? Why couldn't anyone else hear them?" He was babbling like a confused child, and Farran put a cautious hand to the young man's mouth to stop his speech before he began to speak too loudly. He could feel it when he touched Edwin's skin: the spark of divine magic was gone, and had severely drained him in the process.

"You have some time," whispered Farran. "Just be still, and gather yourself together again. The next part is easy."

Farran stood once more, and gestured in the semi-dark. The pirates assigned to Edwin's team that night gathered at once. "Don't let him get up too soon," advised Farran quietly. "But be sure he's ready at my signal."

"Aye, sir," whispered one of the men.

And with that, Farran was gone. In one quick, fluid motion, he scrambled onto the ship railing and dove into the open sea. The water welcomed him like an old friend, and for a moment Farran reveled in the bite of cold salt water on his skin. He floated several feet beneath the surface, taking in the water as only gods and fishes might. He breathed deep, and smiled. *This* was beauty. This was his first love, always: the sea. Even in the midst of the most daring and adventurous acts of piracy, he couldn't help but let himself drown in the beauty of the underwater world. The sea wrapped him in comforting arms like octopus tentacles, purring alluringly that he should stay. Bidding him to linger in the shimmering currents that, while they may have seemed black and foreboding to anyone else, were teeming with life and wonder.

But Farran had to shake himself free. There was a prize to take, and glory to be had. He began to swim, letting the ocean propel him along faster than any mortal man. Schools of fish darted about him as he went, nibbling curiously and affectionately at his hair and clothes. They escorted him all the way to the flagship, his target. He could hear many of them clamoring to help, and he assured them that there was nothing they might do, but that he was grateful in any case. And he cautioned them to stay back, or some of them might get hurt.

And warn the others, he thought to them. *There will be bloodshed here tonight, and danger. All of the nearby Undersea should know to stay away.* And with that message, the fish scattered, leaving Farran alone at the hull of a king's warship.

Farran put his hand to the wood, feeling the ship's inner soul. He did not have the carpenter's magic like Edwin, but he was after all the pirate god. And all ships, whether piratical or law-abiding merchant or military, sailed through his realm. He could feel the ship's heart stirring, confused by Edwin's orders to slow and its own need to sail on. Farran could see the men on board, and hear every step they took. He could count every one of them, and tell how many were drunk or sleeping, how many were on deck or below. And he could trace their footsteps.

He waited for a moment. Waited for one of them to come near enough to the edge. And, as a tall and balding soldier made his normal watch rounds across the deck, Farran released his hold on the ship and let himself float limply to the water's surface, looking for all the world like a body thrown overboard. It didn't take long for the man to spot him and sound the alarm. Farran let himself be fished from the sea, and he felt the sea herself cling to him for a moment longer than she should have, before reluctantly surrendering his body to the king's navy.

FARRAN LET HIMSELF lay in their medical hold for awhile, simply listening. He heard the men wondering at his appearance in the water, and swapping stories about where he might have come from. Several began to whisper that they should throw him back; clearly he was an unwanted fish in someone's net, what business did they have taking him on board? These men were the same that began to circulate the rumor that he was cursed. He was a criminal. He was a plague-bearer. Renegade. Mutineer.

Still others claimed that even if it was bad luck to pull a drowned man *out* of the sea, surely their luck would be just as bad if they threw him back *in*. For just as an albatross was only a bad omen when a sailor slaughtered it, so would it be a curse to send a dying man back to his grave without so much as a helping hand.

And then, there was quiet. The sailors were called off to their duties, and even the medical officer had other things to attend to. Farran was left alone in the hold, his spine grating against the flat examination table every time the ship pitched and rolled with the waves. He could hear footsteps along the deck far above him, and the clanking of dishware as somebody cleaned up after the evening meal. But there was no one within reach. No one to see as Farran hoisted himself from the table and set his feet solidly on the floor.

He briefly took stock of the room around him. It was of middling size, as far as shipboard med quarters went. He could see no less than a half dozen hammocks hung around the room, as well as a handful of proper beds solidly bolted into place. Supplies hung from the ceiling, swaying gently with the movement of the ship. Rags and buckets. String bags full of uncut splints and bandages. Dried medicinal herbs. The hanging things cast strange, amorphous shadows as they danced in the lanternlight.

But the medicine was not here. Farran had assumed as much, although he could never be quite sure. After pocketing several of the more wicked-looking surgical knives for his own amusement, Farran stole carefully from the med quarters and began to scurry down into the depths of the cargo hold. He might have been nothing more than an overgrown rat, lurking in the shadows and winding his way down into the ship's underbelly, searching for something the sailor's didn't want him to find.

However, as with all the cleverest of rats, Farran found his prize with no trouble at all. It was there, as he ducked around an artificial corner made of stacks upon stacks of canvas bags labeled as chicken feed. In the heart of the cargo hold, surrounded by barrels of rum and sacks of potatoes, was a haphazard castle of medicine crates. Towers of boxes, ramparts of trunks, all spilling over one another as if eager to be picked and noticed and delighted in. And Farran obliged, going quickly to them in the darkness and running his hands lovingly along the wooden slats and rope bindings. As he pried open one small chest to look inside, he knew the captain's mission had been worthwhile. The medicines lying in their bottles before him were of the highest quality. And there were so many, one small town could hardly use them all in a generation.

Farran took another quick glance around the cargo hold, taking in fine sugars and ales. Foreign spices. Imported silks. All the riches and finery a king could ask for. And it was theirs for the taking. A wicked smile stretched so broadly across his face that it almost hurt, and he had to stifle himself from letting loose a wild howl of triumph! But the job was not yet finished, and he raced silently back to the medical hold one level up. There, he stood in the corner shadows, listening once more to the footsteps over his head.

He could hear them running drills, and inwardly rolled his eyes at the naval discipline. All the ocean in the world at their rudders, and they chose to work over marching patterns in the middle of the night. Sometimes, mortal priorities astounded him. But Farran shook his head, put on his best half-drowned swagger, and stumbled up the stairs onto the main deck.

It took several moments for anyone to notice his appearance. They were so intent on their business, that it was finally one of the cabin boys who pointed and shouted that the drowned man was walking! All at once, swords were drawn and men stood ready to fight, the whole ship at attention in case Farran proved to be dangerous.

"Might I ask whose hospitality I am enjoying?" shouted Farran to the hesitant masses. As he'd lain below, listening to the talk around him, he'd caught a great bit of Marsenna dialect in the men's voices. Now, he allowed himself to slip easily into their accent as though it were his own.

A ripple began at the heart of the gathered men, like a great wild cat passing through tall grass. The sailors were bowing out of the way, tipping their hats and saluting for the man making his way forward. A man who could only be the captain.

He was a highly decorated man, and he stood with the air of one believing he was much taller than he really was. He could not have been a stitch taller than Farran's elbow, although he carried himself as though he were towering a solid foot above the god's head.

"You are aboard the Merry Doll," said the captain. "Location, King's orders only. Mission, King's orders *only*."

He eyed Farran shrewdly and as he did, Farran was fascinated by the way the captain had mastered the art of staring someone much taller in the eye, without having to tilt his head back. It was unnerving, even to Farran. But instead of dwelling on it, he bowed respectfully and said, "All hail the King's Navy, then! Didn't mean to be sticking my nose in. Promise I won't be in anyone's way."

"How did you come to be half-drowned in our remote little piece of the sea?" asked the captain cooly.

"Remote?" asked Farran, feigning confusion. "No no, we're just off the coast, isn't that right?"

As the captain calmly raised one smooth, disbelieving eyebrow, Farran put on an air of confused panic, and scrambled to the nearest shipman. In an instant, he had the confused sailor's spyglass in hand, and he'd trained it over the railing and out into the empty sea. For a moment, he let himself appear flustered and lost as he turned back to the captain and anxiously fiddled with the spyglass, although he did not return it to its owner. "But we were by land!" said Farran. "The last I remember ... it's all gone a bit hazy ..."

The captain sighed. "So you were drunk, then."

"No sir," said Farran. And then, a bit more jovially, "Think I'd have a bit more of a headache, were that the case."

A handful of the men laughed, and began to let their guard down, but the captain continued to scrutinize his ship's newest man. Finally, after a moment of unbalanced quiet, the captain said, "Alright, then. Tell me your name, and how you came to be here. If your story agrees with me, I'll drop you safely at the nearest port."

"And if not?" asked Farran.

"Then I'll drop you quite a bit sooner," said the captain coldly. He folded his hands behind his back and settled into an expectant stance. And Farran, continuing to play the confused but endearing rescued man, began to spin a tale about his life aboard a merchant ship. And he smiled to himself, taking pride in the intricate beauty of Captain Worthright's plan, like the polished wheels of a clock.

It was Farran's job to draw attention. To keep the men listening, to keep them watching him. To keep the *captain* watching him. But across the waters he knew, other pirates were sneaking on board the enemy ships. Silently tampering with the steering or sails. Pilfering swords away from those sailors less attentive than they should have been. Making each and every ship in the small armada completely unfit for battle. And, hidden at the heart of it all, the Laila sailed, silent as an owl's shadow across the snow. While Farran, planted aboard the flagship laden with riches and medicine, was their ringleader. They would be waiting for his cue.

"You know," said Farran as he fiddled absently with the stolen spyglass, "the more recent times – the fuzzy parts of my story – they're starting to come back to me now."

Even the captain seemed grudgingly intrigued by the false tales Farran was expertly weaving. Every man and boy on board had gathered to listen to the drowned man's stories, laughing when he told them of outrageous misadventures with the mayor's daughter and cheering when he spoke of his ship's loyalty to the king! But it wasn't long before his fiddling wasn't absent anymore. In fact, every twitch of the wrist was measured and deliberate. As he spoke, he angled the lens just so, catching the lanternlight and flashing it out across the water, to where the other ships sailed peacefully on.

"Yes," continued Farran, almost dreamily. "I believe there was a ship. It followed us for awhile, then set upon us in the dead of night. A moonless night, in fact." He glanced up at the shrouded sky, with the moon still tucked behind the clouds he'd drawn to dim its light. "A night not terribly far-off from this one."

"What ship?" asked one of the sailors, in a hushed but excited tone, like a small child hearing his first ghost story.

"An evil ship," answered Farran. And now, he was every bit the storyteller. Captain Worthright wanted a grand entrance for his lady, and Farran was giving her the perfect introduction. "Full of lawless men, who take what they wish and bathe in the riches and ruin of their conquests. Men with black hearts and a lust for adventure on the high seas."

And then a whisper like the finest sea breeze shuddered across the decks, full of the word "*Pirates*."

"She came and took us like a hurricane," said Farran. "Like the wrath of the very gods rode at her helm!"

The captain of the Merry Doll was gazing cooly at him, but Farran sensed a glimmer of understanding beginning to flicker in the man's eyes. "And how," asked the captain, his words clipped short, "did *you* manage to survive?"

And, with a shrug that was all at once playful and dramatic, Farran twitched the spyglass once more, signaling the final cue to the waiting pirates. And in an instant, four simultaneous explosions rent the air, one from each of the other ships.

"Swords!" screamed the captain, drawing his own. To his crew's credit, they recovered quickly from the shock and sprang readily into fighting stances. But Farran was already out of reach. He sprang easily up onto the railing at his back, held his arms out wide and whistled a sharp note. Two swords sprang up into his waiting hands, and by the time Farran had swung them into position, no less than thirty pirates were surging onto the decks from all angles.

"For our lady!" cried Farran. "For the Laila!" The pirates shouted back their war cries in thunderous appreciation and, with a wave of one blade, Farran released the moon once more, flooding the scene in cold light.

His men climbed over the railings and dropped from hiding places in the rigging, where they'd stowed away while all attention was on Farran. They swung in on grappling ropes and fought with a vigor that could only be wrung from a fierce loyalty and love for a woman. And in this case, that woman was a ship sailing at the heart of the battle, lit by moonlight and the harsh flare of the four blazing ships.

Edwin came scrambling over the railing last, and Farran reached out and grabbed the young man by the elbow just in time to keep him from falling back into the water. "Ready?" he asked once Edwin had steadied himself.

There was a devilish grin on Edwin's face that Farran had never seen before. He looked, Farran was astounded to realize, very much like a pirate. "Let's dance!" he replied.

They sprang from the railing, swords at the ready, and began to run for the helm. All around them, a savage battle was being fought. Despite the surprise attack, the men of the Merry Doll were well-equipped for battle and defending themselves beautifully. Every few lengths, Farran and Edwin were forced to fight their way through. But they always broke through quickly, though it was a tribute to Farran's fine sword work rather than Edwin's. By the time they reached the helm, their fellow pirates had cleared it of all enemy sailors, leaving a bloodstained but empty deck for them.

Edwin sheathed his sword and flexed his fingers excitedly before taking the helm firmly in both hands. He closed his eyes, and Farran could see the transformation glowing on his face. The ship was responding to him, and the carpenter mage within. "She's such a fine ship," whispered Edwin, though Farran could hear him even over the din of the battle going on below. And then, in a victorious purr, "And she's *mine* now."

Three of the Merry Doll's men tried to breach the quarterdeck, but Farran fought them off effortlessly. And then, Edwin opened his eyes once more, and with a sly grin he said again, "Let's dance."

Something was happening on the deck. Ropes began to wriggle to life, like so many jungle snakes. They attacked enemy men seemingly of their own accord, often wrapping themselves into nooses and hanging their prey from the rigging. The sailors of the Merry Doll were screaming in horror as the ship itself began to turn on them. Planks of wood behaved as catapults, flinging men viciously out into the sea. Whaling harpoons buried themselves in chests and legs, and the pirates began to cheer as most of the surviving enemy sailors threw up their hands in surrender.

Farran sheathed his swords and grabbed Edwin by the shoulders and shook him excitedly, like an older brother might. "You've done it!" he said. "What a prize this ship is! What a *beautiful* prize!" He gazed out on the

Merry Doll and caught a glimpse of Captain Worthright, laughing in triumph as his men began to bind the wrists and ankles of their captives. Grinning, Farran threw up a salute, and Worthright responded in kind. "Oh my fine young lad," said Farran, the thrill of the hunt still coursing through him. "We'll see you're honored right when we make port. Drinks on me, and the finest women money can buy!"

"I'll hold you to it," said Edwin, laughing and releasing the helm. Farran could see the color beginning to drain from the young man's face, and he kept one hand on Edwin's shoulder just in case he needed steadying. "I suppose this whole magic thing will get easier, won't it?" said Edwin as he let himself lean against the wheel, rather than holding onto it.

"Soon enough it'll be second nature," Farran assured him.

"Excellent," said Edwin.

It happened in that moment, just as Farran glanced out at the decks once more. There was movement behind Worthright, and all at once Farran saw it. The captain of the Merry Doll, sprinting with all his might in a last show of defiance. Edwin saw it as well, and shouted, "*Father!*" But it was already done. Before Farran could so much as brush his hilt with his fingertips, before any of the cheering pirates noticed, a sword was driven straight through Captain Worthright.

The next moment stretched for an eternity, though it was only mere seconds. Silence fell. Edwin threw out one hand, commanding his ship, and in a heartbeat the diminutive captain was dead, torn unceremoniously in half by his own flag and a length of anchor rope. And then Edwin was running, leaping from the quarterdeck and pushing men aside, finally coming to rest on his knees, cradling his dying father's head in his lap.

Farran watched helplessly from his post at the quarterdeck, gripping the banister so hard splinters drove themselves into his palms and fingertips. There were times when he had the power to save a life, and times when he didn't. There were moments when being a god did him no good. And the life or death of a mortal, any mortal, did not fall to him to decide. Instead, he watched as Edwin tried in vain to stem the river of blood. He saw the moment when defeat washed over him, and the realization that he couldn't help his father and captain.

The pirates began to hum a seaman's lament, while across the water they could hear wild cheers from the other ships. There, other crews of pirates had begun to put out the fires, and were celebrating their victory. But aboard the Merry Doll, triumph had turned to tragedy. And so muted hurrahs were accompanied by the thrum of despair.

THE CAPTIVES WERE THROWN in the hold of the Laila, guarded heavily at all times. The four burning ships were scoured for everything of worth, and their damages were measured and recorded. Two of them were deemed worth repairing, while the other two were sentenced to the very depths, to be scuttled and consumed by the sea.

It was aboard one of these that they sent Captain Worthright's body to its resting place. Dressed in his finest, adorned with his swords crossed over his chest, he was laid at the heart of a ship called "The Lavenlock." And then, with the crew watching from the deck of the Laila, a shower of flaming arrows set both sentenced ships ablaze once more.

Farran stood with Edwin on the quarterdeck, and they were silent for some time. While the rest of the men began to sing a proper farewell, Edwin said quietly, "We'll divide the crew. I want you to take the Laila under your command. I'll be sure to leave you enough men to keep an eye on the captives, in case something should happen. I'll take the Merry Doll, and meet you in Aseos. We'll have that drink, and sell off some of the cargo before heading out to Sovesta to deliver the medicine. Give the men time to decide if they'd like to stay on board. Maybe pick up some more crew."

"Are you sure you wouldn't like the Laila for yourself?" asked Farran, but Edwin shook his head.

"She's always been more your ship than mine. The Doll responds to me, and I think she always will."

They stood in silence for another few moments, watching the showers of sparks erupting from the sinking ships, like so many stars brought too close to the sea. And then Farran spoke once more. "Well, it will be done as you command me, Captain Farthington."

"No," said Edwin firmly. "Worthright. It'll be Captain Worthright." Another silence, and Edwin turned to gaze on the Laila's figurehead, glowing proudly in the firelight. "I suppose we gave her a grand entrance after all," he said. And then, as the dying ships began to sink beneath the waves, he spoke once more, a grim echo of Farran's earlier promise. "The shadows of our sails on the horizon will be a warning. But we fall to *no* man."

Chapter Twenty-Two
The Merchant's Highway

It took quite some time for Fox to recover from the latest piece of Farran's story. He kept waking up in the middle of the night, tearing himself out of nightmares filled with dead sailors and the memory of Captain Worthright's death, as fresh as though he'd been there. Not to mention the horrific vision of the enemy captain being torn in two by his own ship.

And apart from that, even when he was awake, Fox found his head was filled with things that shouldn't be there. Names of ship parts and nautical maps of places he'd never seen. His mind was crowded with all things piratical, and he even caught himself humming sea shanties that he was sure he'd never heard before.

But in the three days more it took them to travel through the Beneath, Fox decided it was better to focus on the memories of Farran's world than the very real fear that gripped him with every step. The group traveled quickly and quietly, and Farran always kept watch while they slept, but Fox couldn't wait to escape back into the open air. Couldn't wait to leave these indescribable terrors behind him. Whatever it was that lurked in the shadows, Fox felt sure it was always watching them.

And so it was, that at the start of the fourth day, when Fox began to sense a tingle of something familiar, he began to run. Not out of fear, but out of joy and relief. Somewhere ahead, the wind was waiting for him with open arms. He ran without caring how loud his feet were on the stone, and without a scrap of thought as to where he was going. All he knew was the wind was there, and she would never lead him astray.

He burst out into foreign foothills like a waterfall finally breaking through the winter ice, and collapsed flat on his back. He stared up at the impossibly clear sky and breathed deep, taking in the smells of fresh spring grass and unfamiliar wildflowers. *Spring.* Here, on the other side of the mountains, it was already *spring*!

Fox simply let himself lay there, sun on his face and skin being tickled by the grass as he waited for everyone to catch up with him. When they did, Farran kicked him in the ribs a little harder than Fox thought was necessary.

"Don't do that again," said Farran, and left it at that.

They decided to rest here for awhile, feasting on an early but hearty lunch and enjoying the simple pleasure of talking at a normal volume again. Topper and Fox pelted the adults with questions as they ate.

"How often have you been out here?" Fox asked Wick.

"And where are we?" added Topper.

The men chuckled, and Wick took his time in answering. "Sovesta is just the rooftop of a large community of countries, called the Central Continent. So named because, in the days of early exploration, no one knew what shape the world was. And this group of nations always seemed to be at the heart of every map and chart. Even now, though mankind has circled the very world for generations of trade, our name has stuck. And so here we are, in the eaves of the great house that is the Central Continent."

"It's a country called Mirius," said Farran, by way of a simpler answer. "For those of us who don't care to know the whole history of the thing," he said, rolling his eyes at Wick.

"Oh yes, that's right," teased Wick. "Frivolous merchants have an aversion to scholarly pursuits. Tell me, sir, can you even read?"

Everyone laughed, and Fox found he was glad that Farran and Wick had developed such a friendly rapport during their journey from Doff.

"How big a place is this?" asked Topper through an oversized bite of bread.

"Smaller than Sovesta, but still a sizable nation," said Wick. As he began to lecture them on the divisions of land, words like "fiefdom" and "barony" were thrown about. Things that no one in Sovesta ever needed to worry about. There was no fighting over land, no ruling class. Fox wasn't even sure if there was a king. Old stories and rumors claimed that there was a deserted city at the very northern peak of the land; the Lost Capital, they called it. And if ever a king or queen lived there, they certainly didn't trouble themselves to rule over their people now. No, every city and village and hamlet and town in Sovesta was on its own, and had been since the start of the great curse.

But here, on the other side of the Highborns, things were entirely different. And Fox could feel that familiar tickle, the wind whispering to him that there were new things to see and learn here. It was the part of him that was Shavid, and longed to wander.

Finally, they set off again, this time with Fox in the lead once more. He could feel the wind leading him as though there was a fifth member of their party, walking arm-in-arm with him. There were sounds and smells just off to the east, beckoning him onward, telling him just where to go. And so, with the wind leading Fox, and Fox leading the group, they made their way to the place he'd heard stories of since infancy, the place he'd always been told was his future: the Merchant's Highway.

THE LAND BEGAN TO FLATTEN and smooth out beneath their feet. What started as empty green foothills now became little farmlands and scattered windmills. They passed fields full of great, smudge-coated animals Farran called "cows." They wove around great fields of newly planted crops, and waved good day to planters and farm workers. Slowly, the farmlands turned into outlying towns. Fox craned his neck at every turn, as fascinated by this new country as he had been by Doff and Whitethorn. Perhaps even more so. For, while those had been places within the familiar borders of his own land, this was something entirely different. *Mirius*. A place with new customs and cultures, and even new weather. A place with *cows!*

And cows weren't the only new discovery. The windmills were contraptions Fox only knew by Wick's explanation. In the raging winters of Sovesta, such things would never have survived. And the great, towering buildings they could see sometimes in the distance, overlooking the towns from far-off hilltops. These were small castles, homes to the lords and barons who ruled these little towns.

As Fox asked question after question, Wick laughed heartily at his eagerness. "You'd think he was a political apprentice, the way he goes on asking about the ruling class," the candlemaker said to Farran, speaking over Fox's head as they walked. And then, to Fox himself, "Is there nothing you *aren't* curious about?"

Fox gave this some serious thought for a moment before answering, quite honestly, "No, sir."

Another good-natured chuckle, and Wick promised to buy Fox a detailed book on the workings and divisions of class in the Central Kingdoms. The towns began to grow larger and closer together. Afternoon began to sink into a light, cool evening. Buildings stretched higher into the sky, and the sounds and smells of a thriving city began to wrap around Fox, like a cat winding around one's legs, demanding attention.

And then they passed beneath a wooden archway with a hanging sign, informing them that they were now entering ... Fox couldn't read the language it was written in.

"Hawthorn Proper," said Wick. "Home of the first notable marketplace on this side of the Highborns. A modest but prospering city, and the farthest south I've ever traveled."

But Fox was only half listening. The road had widened beneath their feet and, without any other sign but his own instincts, he knew they had arrived. Here, finally, the son of Timic Foxglove had made it to the Merchant's Highway.

It might have been any other road. Pitted with generations of wagon tracks, the earth had settled and hardened almost to stone. Persistent and determined weeds sprang up here and there, and riders on horseback jockeyed for space with those city folk who walked or drove carriages. Some pushed small, two-wheeled carts laden with wares. Men sold cheese, shouting out prices and offering bargains. Women sold fabric and sewing needles. And, everywhere, there was a pervading sense of flowers in the air.

Fox had noticed it before, but put it out of mind. In a world with so much new to discover, flowers seemed rather insignificant. But now that the towns had turned into a city, he could *feel* flowers everywhere. In the tiny patterned details of women's dresses and the fresh scents wafting on the breeze. They sprang up on vines that crept up shop walls and grew in planters on the windowsills. Even the names of stores and eateries, once Fox had Farran or Wick translate for him, seemed to be heavy with flowers.

The very name of the city, "Hawthorn Proper." Fox was sure that he'd heard "hawthorn" as the name of a plant before.

It bothered him in a way he couldn't quite put his finger on until that night at supper. They'd found a cozy little inn called The Willow's Wife, built mostly above a bakery that fed directly into the marketplace. The dining room was on the second floor, and Fox sat himself at a window seat, overlooking the market below. He ate his biscuits and fish quickly and then sat staring out the window, absently fingering the flower petal embroidery worked into the curtain.

"Bubble in your wax?" asked Topper from across the table, pulling Fox's attention from the window.

"Excuse me?" said Fox, puzzled by the phrase.

"It's a candlemaker expression," explained Topper with a grin. "It's sort of what happens when an air bubble gets into your candle when you're making it. Makes weird lumps and pits in the finished product, and you can't sell it that way."

"Well, look at you!" said Wick appreciatively, pulling his nephew into a rough hug and ruffling his hair. "Talking like a proper Doffer now, aren't you?"

"Aw, go on then," said Topper, shoving away from Wick and blushing. "I was bound to pick up *some* things eventually, wasn't I?" But he looked pleased with himself all the same, and Fox chuckled before looking back out at the market.

"I was just thinking," he said. "These people would have been our neighbors if it wasn't for the mountains. And with everything they do, all around us, there's flowers."

Topper shrugged and scooped a handful of biscuits onto his plate. "It's springtime. Everywhere's got flowers, right?"

"It's just," said Fox, "I've been wondering ... Back home in Thicca Valley, most of our names have to do with plants. Even flowers, you know. Foxglove, Bracken, Lillywhite ..." He looked over at the men, and Farran in particular. "It's been said that it's because of our past. Those were our family names then, when Sovesta was prospering and green. Do you think," he continued, now meeting Farran's eyes directly, "that we would have looked like this? If it weren't for the curse and the mountains and the ice, that Sovesta would have looked more like Mirius?"

"I think," said Farran slowly, "I would *imagine*, that one day long ago, Sovesta did look very much like this." And then, he shook his head ever so slightly as he said, "But I daresay even the gods couldn't tell you what it would look like now."

"It's odd, isn't it?" said Topper, entirely unaware of the silent questions both asked, and answered. "If it wasn't for the curse of Sovesta, what cities would be where the mountains are?"

"Oh, Dream have mercy," said Wick. "I'd probably be a *farmer*. How excruciatingly dull."

A steady stream of conversation carried them all the way through the rest of their supper, and then Fox excused himself to go wander through the market. He could feel Farran watching him as he went, but he didn't turn back. No matter *this* god's intentions, or the silent apologies Fox could clearly read in his eyes, the gods were the reason Sovesta was a country of grey and snow and devastating winters, instead of a land of flowers.

THEY LEFT BEFORE DAWN the next morning, following the Merchant's Highway southward, away from the mountains. Fox took the lead again, carrying on with an eager spring in his step and often raising his voice in song, joined quickly by the others. They walked through the early mist, occasionally running across another early-morning traveler as they journeyed farther away from the city and back into sprawling farmlands.

Fox had been surprised the previous evening to realize how many things in the marketplace were familiar. He'd half expected foreign tools and inexplicable contraptions that wouldn't have made sense in Thicca Valley. But apart from everyone speaking a language he didn't understand, the goods and wares were remarkably ordinary. And far from disappointing him, Fox found it to be oddly exciting. There were so many things waiting for him out in the world that he did *not* understand, and not nearly enough days in a lifetime for him to learn them all. At least some things might remain the same, no matter where he went.

Fox knew from Father's many stories that the Merchant's Highway passed all the way through the Central Kingdoms. It even had wayposts throughout Sovesta, though they'd been abandoned generations ago. Now, the highway stretched and serpentined across the rest of the land, gracing every country, passing through countless large cities and leading its travelers from market to market.

And somewhere down the road, Father was waiting. Fox could feel himself drawing closer every day, and he pushed the pace of his little group to the very brink. The Thicca Valley caravan had moved since Fox's shiver, warning him of the coming avalanche. But Fox could still see them, if he breathed very carefully and was able to sort out all the cascading sounds and smells and feelings that were a constant accompaniment to his Blessing. And there were times, usually late at night, that Fox could feel *exactly* where Father was, down to the very color of the stone beneath his feet.

Spring rains often slowed them down, making Fox frustrated and irritable. If they'd found a place at an inn or tavern, or had even rented lodging in someone's barn, the men would insist they stay inside until the weather cleared. And Fox would pace, and glare out at the rain, and continuously un-pack and re-pack his things.

If they were sleeping outside, however, Farran and Wick allowed them to travel only so far, stopping once they'd found someplace dry.

"You'll be no good to anyone with a spring fever," said Farran, when Fox got particularly upset at their constant delays on the fifth day. "You and your father are both traversing the same road. We'll find him, I promise."

"What if something happens?" said Fox. The group was settled beneath a wide bridge, keeping mostly dry from the rapidly thickening rainfall. Not far away, Topper and Wick were playing cards on a flat rock. They had long since given up on trying to invite Fox to join in the game when he was in such a mood. "What if they change course and we can't adjust to catch up in time? What if *this* mess keeps us stuck here, and they keep moving through it?"

Farran didn't answer, instead pretending to pick dust from his fabric merchant's cloak.

"What if he doesn't believe me?" said Fox, almost timidly.

"Ah, there it is," said Farran. "I knew we'd get around to the real reason for your attitude *one* of these days."

Fox didn't bother to argue. He stared moodily out at the rain, half convinced that it was torturing him on purpose. "I've gone over and over it in my head," said Fox. "And I'm *sure* I can convince him. But then I remember the way he looked at me before he left, and I wonder ... Will he still just see a silly little boy who wouldn't listen to his father?"

"I wouldn't put so little faith in him," said Farran. "And besides, don't forget who you're traveling with. You're not the only one with tricks up your sleeves." He grabbed Fox by the shoulder and steered him over to join Wick and Topper. "Now, enough moping around. You travel like a man, you play like a man. Deal him in, boys!"

The rain didn't clear until early evening, leaving them just enough time to make it to a tiny little orchard village and rent a room for the night. But from that day on, Fox stopped brooding about the rain. He stopped worrying about how long it would take to reach Father, and instead began worrying very much about what he would say when he got there.

THERE WAS A COMFORTABLE sort of routine about traveling. Each morning, the group rose before dawn to practice combat and knife-throwing. It had started out as Farran and Fox simply carrying on their normal patterns, but Wick had soon joined them, and Topper hadn't wanted to be left out. And if either of the Doffers wondered how a dandy fabric merchant knew so much about fighting, they kept it to themselves.

They traveled with the morning mist, taking to the road just as the sun began to warm the spring grass. A fine dew would cling to their clothes and skin, and a light haze thickened the air. And, more often than not, they were not alone on this early morning road. The farther they traveled along the Merchant's Highway, the more crowded the path became. Caravans from all over the Central Kingdoms were traversing the highway, filling the air with unfamiliar scents and languages. Tents and wagon camps sprang up along the side of the road each night, and a tentative sort of camaraderie developed between those groups that found themselves traveling together by accident.

In between towns and cities, the highway was home. And it might have been a dangerous and lonely road. But instead, the spaces between became one long, winding campground. Two or three caravans would share campfires, and music could often be heard from some of them. Everyone more or less spoke "The Marked Speech," or "Trader's Tongue," the common language among waresmen and merchants that allowed them to communicate wherever they went. Fox himself had been trained to speak it from the cradle, though it was unnecessary in a valley where everyone spoke the same language. But here, he found the words rolled off his tongue as easily as though he'd never spoken anything else.

"It's not a trader's gift," said Farran one night, as they shared a spice trader's fire. Not far off, one of the waresmen was trying to teach Wick and Topper some of their words, and the Doffians were laughing even as they struggled. Their mountain home was routinely visited by other Sovestans, but their community as a whole rarely ventured outside the Highborns. They never had a need to learn something as complex as Marked Speech. But the companies on the road were more than willing to try and communicate with them either way, and Topper especially was catching on rather quickly.

"Sorry?" said Fox, torn away from his dinner by Farran's comment.

"Your gift with speech," said Farran. "It's not a natural trader's talent, if that's what you were thinking."

"I may have been," said Fox, shrugging. He knew the god far too well by now to wonder at these occasional insights to his thoughts. "It just made sense, didn't it? Father was always good at it, he's the one who taught me. Thought it might run in the family."

"Your father was good at it because he *practiced*," said Farran. "Because he had to be. But you pick up new words and speech much quicker than that. Even on the road, haven't you noticed how more of the signs make sense to you? You understand more in every passing market than in the one before."

Fox had noticed, in a way, although he hadn't given much thought to it. He assumed it was something in every trader's blood: an instinct, just as natural as tracking or reading a stranger's body language. "If it's not a trapper or a trader's mark," said Fox after a moment, "then —"

"The Shavid travel all across the Known World," said Farran, "and even beyond at times. They've got to be quick, picking up customs and languages and words. There are places where one wrong step could get you hanged, and the Shavid set foot in all of them."

They sat in silence, watching as Topper fumbled over a complicated set of numbers in Marked Speech, while this newfound facet of Fox's Blessing sank in. Finally, Fox asked, "How fast?"

"Hmm?"

"How fast can I learn?"

Farran chuckled and winked knowingly. "That, my dear boy, is entirely up to you."

As they settled in that night, Fox looked around at the lights dancing up and down the streets, and this wandering community he'd found himself a part of. How were they any different from the Shavid? Perhaps the two cultures were not as dissimilar as he'd once believed. But then, at the end of the road, these traders had a place to call home. And Fox wondered if the Shavid ever settled down one place long enough to think of it as home.

Restless, he tossed and turned long into the night, into the hours where light snores and the soft hiss of dying fires were all that could be heard, and even the animals seemed to be asleep or hiding. Finally, he sat up and scooted closer to the remains of their campfire, where Farran was sitting up as he always did.

"It's a beautiful night," said Farran softly. "We've been lucky with the weather of late."

Fox grunted in agreement, following Farran's gaze up to the cloudless sky and the stunningly bright blanket of stars flung across it. He sat there for a moment by the god's side, watching the stars winking in their secret language from above. Then he said casually, "Couldn't sleep, despite the beautiful night and lucky weather."

"Oh?"

"And I thought, maybe a story might help me sleep?"

Farran's answering laugh was so soft, the man sleeping three feet away couldn't have heard it, even had he been awake. "Such a child sometimes," he joked. "A bedtime story to scare the nightmares away?"

"Pity you can't see my face," answered Fox dryly. "Then you'd realize that no one else thinks you're funny, and what a shame that would be."

"Ah," said Farran fondly, placing two fingers on their familiar perch between Fox's eyes, "but *she* thought I was funny. And hers was the only laughter in the world I ever needed."

Chapter Twenty-Three
The Chancellor's Daughter

Two weeks at sea had brought them to landfall in the city of Aseos. And within only two days in port, the pirates had made their presence known in every brothel and drinking house in the city. Farran and Edwin had even joined them that first evening, drinking away the memories of Captain Worthright's death in a little pub just off the docks.

But come sunrise, it was all business. The two left their gallivanting crew to enjoy their shore leave, and turned their own attentions to matters of profit rather than pleasure. There were goods to sell, and repairs to be made. And, before a scrap of work could be done on either ship, they had to agree on the fates of the naval prisoners kept under constant watch in the hold of the Laila.

"Fish bait, every one of them," said Edwin bitterly as the two ambled up the gangplank. The handful of pirates left aboard the Laila tipped their hats or bobbed their heads by way of a casual salute. "Chop them up and throw them to the bilge rats. Or the sharks, if you'd prefer it."

For two weeks, Farran had heard his men saying much the same thing, along with suggesting other, more colorful means of torture. But Farran had always insisted that the prisoners be treated with an aloof sort of respect. And now, he told Edwin what he'd been telling the men for a fortnight. "These are the King's own officers, and they are gentlemen. Treat them as such, and they will respond much better."

Edwin snorted. "No king I'm beholden to. To me, they're nothing but men. Lower than men, in fact."

Farran turned a knavish grin on Edwin as they descended into the hold. "Aye, sir," he said. "Lower than men. But the humblest earthen stone can be a tool." And with that, he strode purposefully down in to the heart of the ship with Edwin in his wake, to where a single man stood guard over more than forty barred and shackled prisoners.

"Right then!" shouted Farran, rousing the naval officers from their vague stupors. Some of them glared mutinously at him, others that were no more than boys seemed terrified to the very core. But all eyes were on Farran as he continued. "You lot have two choices! First, you forfeit your freedoms as men and allow yourselves to be indentured sailors aboard one of our fine ships. You'll work like dogs for the barest wages until such time, if any, that we see fit to release you. Elsewise, I let this gentleman here," and he gestured to Edwin, who stood with his arms crossed in an almost eerie shadow of Captain Worthright's favorite stance, "tear you limb from limb with his bare hands. And I might add that your captain was responsible for the murder of his father, so I wouldn't test his anger, lads."

Farran let these choices sink in for a moment, but a moment was all it took. There was a desperate clamoring within the cell as men scrambled to offer themselves up as slaves, and Farran winked at Edwin. The two left the man on guard with parchment and charcoal pen, charged with taking down the names of each sailor who volunteered. And with that, Farran and Edwin climbed back out on deck, both laughing heartily at the panic they had caused below.

THEY AUCTIONED OFF the two smaller commandeered naval ships, even managing to drive up the price by promising to include a handful of able-bodied, indentured men with each. Edwin and Farran would each take their pick from among the sailors in the brig, and leave the rest to new captains and strange horizons. And, as Farran constantly reminded Edwin, none of them had handled the sword that killed his father. They were not the enemy.

There was only one man who refused to join with the pirates. A sailor who stood staunchly at the back of the hold, adamantly declaring that he would rather die a loyal servant than live a traitor to his crown. The man was taken aboard the Merry Doll, and Farran left Edwin to do as he would.

The man's dying screams could be heard across the dock, and when Edwin emerged, no questions were asked.

The plundered goods were sold off bit by bit, scattered between the black market and those sorts of nobles who didn't give a second thought to where their goods came from. By week's end, each pirate had a hefty bonus weighing down his pockets, along with the promise that they would not set sail again for at least a week. The indentured prisoners were divided between the Laila and the Merry Doll, or else sent with the auctioned vessels. And then, with business done, Edwin and Farran were happy to join the men in their revels. They drank and sang the nights away. And it was in these hours, tucked between the starlit darkness and the sun's waking breaths, that Edwin seemed himself again. A laughing, somewhat shy young man, much beloved by the men. Almost a younger brother to many of them, and happy to let himself be picked on and laughed at.

But it was only in these moments. Only when the song and companionship could begin to drive away the memories of his recent tragedy. And then, the sun brought its harsh glare to rest upon the city, and Edwin was the captain once more. Untried and unsure. Inexperienced and isolated. Edwin Farthington lived and laughed in the night. But he was Captain Worthright when the sun rose. And Farran, watching his young friend struggle to find his footing, couldn't quite be sure which man the pirates needed most.

SHORE LEAVE ALWAYS made Farran restless. While it was a beautiful privilege to be able to wander strange roads and discover new places, even for a god, it wasn't where he belonged. Even a place such as Aseos. It was a beautiful puzzle of a city, tucked on the edge of a mysterious land of bamboo forests and paper lanterns: Vathidel. The gem of the Gossamer Sea. Farran had wandered its roads and rivers countless times, and was always eager to be back. Still, the ocean called to him like a chorus of sirens, in voices only he could hear. Its discordant song crept into his dreams whenever he bothered to sleep, and whispered in his ear like a lady of the night. Beckoning him back, lovingly and desperately purring in his very heart.

Farran began to forsake his men in their evening pleasures, choosing instead to wander the moonlit beaches or pace up and down the water-worn docks. And, in the moments when the songs tore at him in a way he simply could not resist, he would take a swim. He would throw himself from the figurehead of the Laila, enjoying one brief moment of sharp wind on his face as he plunged downward, before he disappeared beneath the water's surface.

Tonight, he emerged from his swim covered in seaweed , starfish and barnacles clinging to his hair and clothes as the ocean tried to entice him to stay. But Farran stepped out onto the shore, and the bits of sea that had followed him fell with soft thumps into the sand, letting themselves be washed away by the drifting tide. Farran himself collapsed onto the powdery grains, caring not a stitch for the ocean waves lapping at his boots like an old dog seeking attention. He ran his fingers through his hair, drying it instantly as only a god might.

And he sat, listening to the waves and watching the skies grow steadily lighter as dawn approached. His restlessness had subsided somewhat, dampened by his swim. He watched the black, skeletal silhouettes of the ships in the harbor, and could hear the gentle creak of wooden beams even from a distance.

It would have been so simple to head out to sea again by himself, leaving Aseos and his men behind. He'd done it before, in different lands and with different crews. He was a god, after all, and not bound to the same rules as men. He had the power to disappear, to sail off alone and seek grander adventures that men could only imagine. But as he listened to the distant sounds of a city beginning to wake, Farran knew he wouldn't be going anywhere. This crew was the finest he'd ever sailed with, and Edwin was one of the most decent mortal men Farran had ever met. A friend, even. If the pirate god was content to sail the world as a man for a time, these were the sea dogs to do it with.

Besides, he thought as he stretched himself out lazily, every god drew some of their power from their worshipers. And what better way to be steeped in power than to surround himself by the very men who paid tribute to him? He closed his eyes, letting the rising sun bathe him in warm light and paint the sand a brilliant orange. They would be out to sea again soon enough, and until then he could wait.

And then, Farran heard it. A dull, pounding beat making the sand beneath his head quiver and throb. He sat up, scanning the horizon, his every muscle taut and expectant. One hand was already on his sword, his other whipping a hidden blade from his vest. Somewhere down the beach, a shadow drew nearer. A black shape thundering down the shore, throwing up sand and ocean spray in its wake.

A horse. Black as night, and bearing a rider wrapped in such dark robes that they might have been the steed's own mane. As horse and rider galloped closer, Farran could see that the horse did not wear a saddle. And there was a laugh. A wild, unburdened hollering from its rider. A woman's laugh. Farran sat up even straighter, watching as the woman came ever closer.

Behind her, struggling to catch up on his own yellow steed, was a round and anxious-looking man. "My lady!" he called. "Please, your decorum! Wait!"

But instead of heeding him, the woman bent even nearer to her horse's neck and put on a burst of speed. Again she laughed, and for the briefest moment, the sound rang in Farran's ears even louder than the ocean's call. Horse and rider roared down the coastline, their path an arrow-straight line to where Farran lay.

An ordinary man might have moved out of the way. But Farran simply leaned himself back on his elbows and waited. And, at the last moment, the horse leaped, clearing Farran as easily as though he were a sandbanked scrap of driftwood.

The woman reined her animal to a slow trot and turned it around, clicking gently in its ear as she pulled it to a stop at Farran's side. And then she sat up straight. Her hood fell away, and Farran could see her face.

He had walked the worlds and the places between for a hundred lifetimes of men. He had danced with beautifully dangerous women and dined with the goddess of love. He had swum alongside sirens so lovely then men leapt into storm-tossed waters just to be with them, and he himself had let his heart wander with more than a few mortal women. But Farran had never seen someone, be it goddess, monster, or mortal, as beautiful as this woman.

Her hair was black as the hood that now hung roughly from her shoulders. Her skin might have been the exquisitely polished mango wood of a figurehead, and carved by a craftsman so skilled that he ought to have built ships for Spirit's own armies. And her eyes ... The whole world of shipwrecked treasures in the ocean's heart did not hold a gem so pure, nor a color so deep. It was as though the richest of greens and the most dazzling golden-blues had joined in secret, to create a brand new color just for this woman's eyes.

And then she spoke, and it was a music that Farran had never known existed. "This early in the morning, my horse and I don't normally have to fight for a place on the shore."

"It's a shame," said Farran playfully. "How could anyone be asleep in their beds when they could watch the dawning light paint the shoreline?"

"Perhaps they are all fools," suggested the woman, with a smile on her lips and in her voice.

"That must be it," said Farran. "Everyone in the world, except you and me."

The woman smiled coyly, and looked as though she were about to respond. But the thud of trotting horse hooves and a heavy panting announced the arrival of her plump escort, and she kept silent.

The man was wiping sweat from his brow and neck, dabbing anxiously with a green handkerchief. "You *promised* your father!" the man said fussily, pulling his horse to a less-than-graceful stop beside hers.

"No, *you* promised my father," said the woman airily. "I can only *imagine* his disappointment if he found out how you let me run amok all across the shoreline," she teased. "I mean, after all of your promises that you'd keep an eye on me, to let me go *again*? Whatever will he say, Antos?"

The man, Antos, didn't seem to be aware of Farran sprawled out just inches from their mounts' hooves. He straightened his collar petulantly and muttered, "I should have had that wretched animal of yours hobbled years ago. Then, perhaps, you'd start acting like a lady." But even as he said it, Farran could tell there wasn't a malicious bone in this man's body. And even the woman smiled.

"Alright Antos, you'll have your way. Let's get back before your poor nerves give out." She pulled her hood back over her hair, and glanced down at Farran one last time. They exchanged the quietest of smiles before she wheeled her horse around and set off at an even trot.

As he straightened his own reins with a sigh, Antos finally noticed Farran. He took note of the ill-concealed laughter written on Farran's face, and snorted. "You think you could do better with her? Be my guest. It would take the very gods to tame that woman, and I daresay even *they* would have their work cut out." And with that, he turned his own mount and followed her, grunting with every jostling step.

Farran watched her until she was nothing but a dark smudge against the sand, and even then he could swear he still heard her laugh ringing through the air. It was only when she had disappeared completely that Farran became aware that he was soaked to the skin. The tide was up to his chest, churning angrily and humming with jealousy.

"Hush," said Farran, brushing the water and driftwood away with a gesture of his hand. As the tide retreated moodily back to its proper place, Farran stood, dusting sand and stray scraps of seaweed from his clothes. It wasn't until he began to make his way back to the early-morning bustle of the city that he realized: he hadn't heard the ocean while the beautiful woman was there. Or, rather, he had heard it from afar. Like listening to the sound of waves crashing in a seashell, instead of from the deck of a sailing ship. It was the first time in all his years that someone's voice had drowned out the sea.

THE PLUNDERED GOODS were all sold. The indentured men were given new positions and tattooed with the mark of their new ship home, and many of the pirates had emptied their pockets of almost every scrap of prize money. Repairs were finished, and fresh supplies tucked neatly aboard both the Merry Doll and the Laila. Departure was set for three days hence, and a whisper about a new threat on the Gossamer Sea began to trickle through town.

A new pirate ship. It sailed in the shadows and bore a siren as its figurehead. Farran heard rumors on the air like an incomplete song, with everyone telling a slightly different tale. Some made them seem deadly and ruthless, others made them out to be heroes, fighting in the darkness against an evil king and his navy. Still others said it was a powerful magic that sailed with them. The magic that nightmares were made of.

Eyes began to turn to the new men in town. Those claiming to be merchants, who had sailed in just weeks ago. Farran could see the suspicions following his men in and out of taverns and harlot houses. Stories came out of the black market. Accounts of the goods Edwin and Farran had sold, and the sudden inquiries as to where they had come from.

Of course, the traders had known when they'd bought them. Only a fool wouldn't realize it. But now that piracy was the talk of the town, everyone was eager to add their bit to the tales. And as for the pirates themselves, they walked with a certain added spring in their steps. Their legend was just beginning, and they could all feel it. Just as their captains had promised, they would be loved and feared and admired and sung about.

But first, according to the notices that appeared overnight just before their departure, they would be hanged.

FARRAN READ THE SCROLL once before ripping it from the door where it was tacked. Then he whistled for his nearest men, and two of them came hurrying to his side.

"Get everyone out," Farran said, low and urgent. "We meet at the ships, *now*. Leave tabs unpaid, don't kiss your women goodbye, don't even lace your boots." He brandished the scroll at them, letting the men read it for themselves. And then, without wasting another moment, the two were off. Farran watched them go, silently urging them to go carefully, before he swept off toward the docks. He could feel the townsfolk watching him go, and he knew they'd all read the notices. He knew they were waiting for the arrests.

All who were accused of piracy were to be tried at the mercy of the chancellor. Those found guilty were to be hanged at dawn the following morning. A hanging meant nothing to Farran — he'd been hanged in the name of piracy enough to retire even the busiest of hangmen. But there wasn't enough power in the entire ocean to save his men's lives once they walked the gallows. Their souls would belong to the High Executioner. A god who wouldn't be bargained with. A god to whom Farran had lost more than enough men already.

Farran slipped through the dawning shadows to the wharf, a pounding urgency playing an unbalanced duet in his heart with the ocean's call. To save himself, or save his men. To flee as a god, or escape as a mortal. Even as he quickened his pace, anxious to reach his ship, he knew his mind was already made up. It had been made up long ago, the moment he'd begun to consider Edwin as a friend. In fact, from the very moment he'd set foot on board the Laila. He would sail her to world's end, and her crew was his family. The ocean would never stop calling him, but a lone pirate was nothing. And a god without his disciples was even less.

But Farran stopped, listening to the ocean's song more closely now. Something wasn't right. Something outside of the ordinary, the usual luring temptations and soothing coral croonings. The sea was warning him.

In an instant, Farran dropped to his knees, concealing himself behind a pallet of crates stacked on a long and winding pier. He could just see the Laila, nestled at the far end of the harbor. Not far away was the Merry Doll. Many of the fishing boats seemed to have left for the day already, leaving the waterfront relatively clear. Still, most men wouldn't have noticed anything strange. But Farran did. He saw the colors on the decks of the pirate ships, and knew they weren't his. He could see clearer than any mortal man that both vessels were under guard, captured by men wearing military silks and bearing the chancellor's crest.

He could hear a handful of his own men approaching, and waved them quickly over, gesturing to stay low. There were eight of them altogether, and the rat-like kitchen boy Jethhat was the first to speak up.

"They took 'em, sir!" he said with ill-concealed panic. "Everyone except us, what managed to escape!"

"Where are they?" asked Farran at once. "What have they done with my men?"

"Taken right to trial," said Jethhat. "I heard everyone talking about it. Seems this chancellor of theirs is cursed set on seeing them all hang as soon as possible."

"East," said one of the other men, a rather beefy medic called Vat. "They've taken them to the chancellor's own estate."

"We've got bigger problems," said Farran. "I'll handle the men, and the chancellor. But I've got important chores for you."

IT WAS A SIMPLE ENOUGH matter to gain access to the chancellor's land. Farran had been impersonating a merchant for quite some time, and it was easier to disguise one pirate as a well-bred tradesman than it was to explain away a whole fleet of them at a local tavern. In fact, it was even simpler than it should have been. It seemed the chancellor was eager to showcase this particular trial. He'd invited the whole city to come and watch, and people were flocking in from every gate. Farran let himself be herded to the long, open courtyard at the heart of the estate. In any other circumstance, Farran might have let himself admire the beautiful stonework and the blossoming cherry trees. As it was, he found himself mentally calculating how much such a grandiose estate would cost, measuring each flawless pillar and pagoda in chests of gold and sacks of precious gems.

But then his eyes fell on the line of prisoners facing the crowd, and all thoughts of the chancellor's estate were driven from his mind.

His men were shackled in a long line on a raised veranda, along with a handful of other men who Farran didn't recognize. Some looked disheveled and tousled, as though they'd been dragged straight out of their beds without being allowed to finish dressing. Others had clearly put up a fight, and bore signs of struggling against their captors. Here and there Farran spotted a bloody lip or a black eye, although no one looked worse than Edwin. He was bleeding freely from a long cut across his forehead, and one of his arms was roughly bandaged. One eye was swollen almost completely shut, and his jaw was starting to swell in a way that suggested he might have lost a couple of teeth.

But everyone seemed to be accounted for, which was a relief to Farran. In fact, the only men he was unsure of were the indentured sailors aboard the Laila and the Merry Doll, and those few of his own men who had been left to watch over them. Were they now among the Chancellor's men, those guarding the decks? Or had they been killed or taken prisoner?

There was no time to worry about them now, or to think back on the ships floating in the harbor. Farran stood, concealed by the crowd but able to see his men perfectly. He waited as the buzzing tension in the crowd grew, and finally broke like a wave crashing into the side of a stone cliff. And then, as the people around him squawked at each other like chickens fighting over feed, the sound of a struck gong echoed through the courtyard and silence fell.

To the left and several stories up, a man stepped out onto a balcony and addressed the crowd. "Presenting the Voice of the Emperor for the seaside city of Aseos, Chancellor DeMorrow! And with him, his daughter and heir, the Lady Adella DeMorrow!"

All heads bowed low, and when they looked up again, a man and woman had joined the crier on the balcony. They were both draped in regal silks, and the man sported a long braid like a tail draped over his shoulder. He was otherwise clean-shaven and bore an expression of unrelenting stoicism. His whole demeanor said that this wasn't a trial: this was a sentencing. His mind was already made up.

But it was the woman who caught and held Farran's eye. Her black hair was piled on her head in a series of complex knots, instead of falling wildly about her face and shoulders. And she'd traded in her rough black riding robes for silks of the purest green and finest gold. But it was her. And Farran felt his very soul sink. The most beautiful woman in the world was going to stand by while his men were sentenced to death.

The chancellor began to speak, but Farran hardly listened. He stared up at Adella DeMorrow, trying to make sense of the confusing emotion that swept over him like a rising tide. For though he'd only met her for the briefest of moments, Farran felt betrayed. And he couldn't understand why. And when the chancellor's daughter looked down from her post on the balcony and met his gaze, a flicker of recognition shone on her face, accompanied by the slightest of smiles.

Farran turned away, all attention on her father now. "To keep our waters safe!" the chancellor was saying. "And to keep our people protected! This scourge should be burned from our oceans!"

A cheer rose from the gathered crowd, but with a simple gesture of his hand, the chancellor silenced them again. And then, he pointed a single accusatory finger at the shackled pirates. "These men shall hang at dawn. And let their deaths be a lesson to any pirate that crosses our borders: Aseos is the gateway to the Emperor's own kingdom! And we will *not* let it be tainted with the evils of piracy, and the dark magic they bring with them! Though the pirate god himself may sail through our waters, we will not be overcome!"

More cheers, and Farran raised an eyebrow incredulously. Ordinary men did not threaten the gods so lightly. And while *other* gods might have better things to do than seek revenge on inconsequential mortals, Farran couldn't think of a *better* way to spend his time. He extricated himself from the crowd as the final moments of the so-called "trial" commenced. And as he did, he felt Adella DeMorrow watching him. He turned, just before he disappeared from her sight, and bowed grandly. Then, on a sudden whim, he blew her a rakish kiss. Such a beauty belonged on the figurehead of a ship, or immortalized in statues and paintings in the grand halls of the most magnificent palaces. But she was the enemy now, standing peacefully by the side of the man who would have Farran's crew executed.

A heavy fog began to roll in from the sea, and a sudden breeze brought with it the promise of rain. What had been a bright and clear morning was rapidly greying as thick clouds began to roll across the sun. As the pirates were officially sentenced to hang at dawn, a low rumble of thunder in the distance shook the trees, shedding soft pink petals like snow. The crowd began to disperse, many glancing up nervously at the sky and wondering aloud at the unexpected shift in the weather. All except Farran, who stood in the farthest corner of the courtyard, watching as his men were marched off to spend their final hours in the estate's prison keep.

And like a shadow in the fog, Farran followed.

EVEN WITH THE GLOOM that had fallen over Aseos, Farran waited until it was properly evening to break into the prison. A change of the guard granted him ample opportunity to slip through a side gate and tuck himself away in a neglected storeroom. There, he sat crouched behind a wall of powder kegs, listening to every footfall and taking in every man's scent. He could tell which of them had been drinking by the rice wine on their breath or the slight hitch in their steps. And he knew exactly where his prisoners were being held. All he had to do was wait for the perfect moment. For the right guard to take too long on his rounds, or for a game of dice to break out and distract the guards from their duties. Every prison was the same in the end, and Farran had been in enough of them to feel almost at home here.

But he hadn't been waiting long when something else happened. The door to his storeroom creaked open ever so softly, and someone else came in, accompanied by the soft glow of a lantern. Farran stayed quiet, drawing one of his hidden knives silently and expertly. The door clicked shut once more, and Farran could hear soft and hurried breathing. Ever so carefully, Farran eased himself into a hunting crouch, waiting concealed behind his wall of kegs. The newcomer was slowly creeping deeper into the room. In an instant, Farran pounced, his arm wrapped around the intruder's neck and mouth, his knife tip pressed against their back. "You picked the wrong night for a casual stroll in the dungeons," he hissed in the shadow's ear.

Then he whipped the trespasser around to face him, and dropped his knife. Even in the flickering, shadowed light of the lantern she held, he knew her face. Adella DeMorrow glared up at him, and it was in that moment that Farran realized that she, too, was armed with a knife. A long, wickedly curved blade that was pointing directly at his throat.

The two stood for a moment, Farran still holding tightly to her, and the chancellor's daughter apparently fighting to reconcile her determination and her shock. And then, they both relaxed. Farran released her, and Adella sheathed her knife with shaking hands.

"I suppose it would be presumptuous of me to ask what in *Dream's* reach you're *doing* here?" asked Farran in a heated whisper.

"It's my father's land!" she hissed back, hooking her lantern onto a low-hanging chain. "I have the right to be wherever I wish!"

Farran smirked. "Then why are you whispering?"

Footsteps outside made them both fall silent. A passing guard. It was only when the footsteps faded away that Adella spoke once more. "You're with the pirates, then?"

Farran bowed low, scooping his knife off the floor in the process. "Guilty as charged," he said. It wasn't quite a whisper, but low enough that his voice wouldn't carry past their door. "Why, planning on stringing me up with my men?"

"Not for piracy," said Adella cheekily. "For ruining my morning ride, absolutely."

Farran chuckled, and swept his arm out in an over-exaggerated mockery of offering one a seat. But Adella took one anyway, swinging herself up onto a rough wooden crate. Farran in turn leaned up against the wall, arms crossed as he scrutinized her.

This woman was much more like the creature he'd met on the beach. Wild and untamed, with a hint of unquenchable fire in her eyes. She was not the painted, pampered young heiress in silk who he'd seen mere hours before. She was once again in simple robes, though they still seemed the most royal attire in the world, simply because they were wrapped around her. In fact, Farran found his imagination wandering to what she'd look like with even *less* wrapped around her.

Something of his thoughts must have shown on his face, because Adella raised one perfect, dark eyebrow and crossed her arms. Farran cleared his throat and smiled somewhat apologetically, running his fingers nervously through his hair. Why was he acting like a teenaged mortal farmboy? He cleared his throat again and focused instead on the situation at hand.

"So," he said, glad that his voice at least sounded sure and unaffected. "I'm here to rescue my men, and I feel it's right that I mention up front that you won't be able to stop me. Your turn."

"I'm here to rescue a ... friend. And it's only right that I also mention, *you* won't be able to stop *me*." Adella shifted on her makeshift seat, and Farran frowned slightly.

"A friend?"

"She's more like family," admitted Adella.

"Family that your own father thought to throw in the dungeons?"

For a moment, Adella did not seem so determined and sure. Her face fell, and she began to twist her hands in the fabric of her robes, looking for all the world like a lost and frightened child. Finally she said, as though every word hurt her, "My nursemaid. And Antos's wife. You remember my —"

"I remember," said Farran, recalling the portly man who had been accompanying Adella on her ride down the beach. "Go on."

"She's been with me since my mother died, which is before I can remember. And she is family, closer than blood. But yesterday, when the news of pirates reached my father, he ... didn't react well."

"Why, though?" asked Farran. It had, in fact, been bothering him ever since he first saw the notices. "Piracy is nothing new. Parts of this continent were built *by* pirates! It's a part of your history, and your future. Why is he fighting it?"

"Just piracy he can turn a blind eye to," she said softly. "But dark magic he cannot. And the new ship they speak of ... it's said to hide in the shadows and be captained by powers not of this world. And my father ... reacted badly." She stopped twisting her robes and instead met Farran's eyes. "He accused my nursemaid of practicing dark magics. Evil witchcraft. Not the healing spells and potions, the ones she's been Blessed with. But the kind that killed my mother."

That, Farran could see on her face, was a different story. And Farran found he wanted nothing more than to hear it. He wanted to hear everything this woman ever had to say, dull or exciting and everywhere in between. But instead, he asked, "So, your father had her sentenced."

"Her and several others," said Adella. "Men and women who've never done him any wrong, but who he's now convinced have something to do with the same magic that's brought pirates to our waters." Now, she began to grow irritated again. "I wish I could say it's the *first* time he's done this," she growled. "And if I had my way, it would be the last."

"As charming as it is to hear the inklings of patricide in your voice," said Farran, "we've got to be ready to move when the moment is right. So, this nurse of yours. Do you know where they've got her?"

"Right next to your men, in a cell with the rest of the accused commoners," she supplied helpfully.

"And how exactly did you plan on getting her out of the city?"

"I have my ways," said Adella. A coy smile was playing at the curve of her lips, and the untamed spark had returned to her eyes.

"This isn't your first jailbreak, is it?"

"Certain of my father's condemned have been known to disappear from their cells from time to time," said Adella casually. But it was with an entirely new level of fascination that Farran looked the young woman up and down.

"Why, Lady DeMorrow, you are something of a vigilante, aren't you?"

Adella sighed dramatically. "If you *must* call me by such a common name, then yes."

"And what would you prefer I call you?" teased Farran.

She paused, then answered cattily, "I haven't given myself a proper title yet, thank you."

Farran laughed quietly, but fell silent again almost at once as another set of footsteps made its way toward them. Not a sound filled the storeroom, not even breathing. And then, as the slightly staggering footsteps disappeared, Farran gestured for her to follow and strode quickly to the door. "We should have a few minutes until he comes back. If he comes back at all – I swear he gets drunker with every round."

The hallways were empty, but both Adella and Farran drew their knives just in case. They could hear the quiet, defeated muttering of prisoners down the hallway, as well as the distant laughter of lazy guards who had foregone their posts. Farran let the woman lead, keeping close on her heels and marveling at the nimble silence of her feet. They turned a corner, and Farran held up his hand at once to stop his men reacting.

They were split between two cells, and they began to perk up when they saw him. Adella went at once to the next cell over, where she gripped her nursemaid's hands through the bars. "We're here to get you out!" said Adella with barely a whisper.

"My lady, you shouldn't have come!" the old woman answered, but relief and gratitude were painted clearly across her face.

Without wasting another moment, Adella set to picking the prison lock with a practiced hand. Farran left her to it, instead gesturing to his own men to stay back as he addressed the lock on the first cell. For a moment he hesitated, then motioned for Edwin to step forward. "Stand right at the lock," he muttered, so only his friend could hear him.

Edwin obliged, his body blocking the lock from view of the other men. Farran placed the palm of one hand flush against the keyhole.

"What are you doing?" hissed Edwin, but Farran ignored him. Within seconds, the whole mechanism heated up and began to melt, and with a quick twist Farran yanked the now-shapeless blob from the bars and swung the cell door open. For a moment, Edwin met his gaze, and an unspoken question hung in the air. Edwin's eyes spoke of confusion, and the merest hint of accusation. And then, the pirates surged past them, and the moment broke like a severed string. But as Farran moved to the second door, he could feel Edwin watching him. And he knew that, not now, but someday very soon, he would have to explain himself.

Farran didn't have a human shield to hide his magic with the second door, but it wasn't necessary. No one was watching him anymore, the men were too busy with whispered clamoring and looking around corners on the chance that their guard would return. And by the time Adella was finished picking her lock, both cells of pirates had been opened and emptied. The hall was filled with a fierce whispering like an overexcited breeze, and Farran gestured for silence.

"They will know we're gone," said Farran, in a low but commanding rumble, echoed by the thunder outside. "There is no way for nearly fifty prisoners to simply walk through town unnoticed. And so, we fight. I will take you as far as the side gate, where I've hidden weapons, and then I have business to attend to with the chancellor." There was a supportive growl at this, as well as a sharp intake of breath from Adella, but Farran continued quickly. "We meet at the ships. You'll have a better chance of escape in small groups, but *don't get left behind*!" he said urgently. "Once we begin, the ships can't wait in the harbor for long, they'll be soft targets, waiting dead in the water."

"What about the others?" asked Edwin, nodding at the cell of commoners Adella had freed.

"They will come with me," said Farran. Then he pointed at a handful of his men, all strong fighters and trusted officers. "You five, you will make sure they all make it safely aboard the Laila." There were general nods of assent, then Farran took a moment to look over all of his fine crew. Then, he saluted them like a proper navy gentleman, and they returned the gesture. With that, he took Adella by the arm and led the way through the halls.

They came across three guards on their way outside, and each was quickly silenced before they could raise the alarm. No need to draw attention until they had to. As they went, Adella let herself be dragged alongside Farran, but as he quietly ushered the men outside, she held him back.

"What 'business' do you have with the chancellor?" she demanded. When Farran didn't answer right away, she said imploringly, "He is still my father, and this is *my* town. And my life, once I make sure my people have made it safely out of the harbor. I have to live with whatever choices you make here tonight."

There was a pleading in her eyes, but it was a mark of strength rather than desperation. Farran nodded once, and squeezed her shoulder briefly before ushering her outside to her waiting escorts. Wind-driven rain spattered against the stone walls of the keep, and thunder made the whole city vibrate like a loosed bowstring. But beneath it all, they could hear the shouts of the exterior guards. They'd been spotted.

The men began to take up arms from where Farran had hidden them by the gate, tucked beneath rocks and in thick patches of shrubbery. The pirates began to scatter, making it impossible for the guards to chase them all at once. As Edwin prepared to run, Farran took him by the arm, and pulled him into a rough, brotherly hug.

When they pulled away, Farran kept hold of his friend's arm for a moment more, and met his eyes with a fierce determination. "We will meet at the Magistrate's Harbor, my captain!" he said over the sounds of the rapidly growing storm. "This I promise you, by the pirate god's own sails!"

They let go, and Edwin smiled wolfishly. Then he raised his own sword high into the air, and shrieked a warcry the likes of which Farran had never heard from the young man. His pirates took up the call as they ran, fighting their way down to the docks. Farran could hear them as he turned to venture back into the chancellor's land. Their yawls made sweet harmony to the thunder and the rain, with the clash of blade meeting blade and the occasional pops of black powder explosions.

But Farran kept them all at his back. Let his sea dogs take all the prizes they liked. The lord of all pirates had but one prey tonight.

WITH EVERY STEP OF his thick leather boots, Farran left behind a footprint. But it was not the footprint of a mortal man, an easily discarded impression in the dirt or a muddy scuff on a stone walkway. Each was the deep, powerful footprint of a god on a mission. An angry god. Wherever he stepped, he left behind a small crater. A charred, glowing cast that would forever be burned into the earth where Farran walked. A smouldering trail that led through Chancellor DeMorrow's estate, and to the most opulent rooms in the western tower, overlooking the harbor. There, the chancellor lay sleeping, blissfully unaware that his most valued prisoners were fighting for freedom in the city streets, and that his own daughter was proudly in their midst.

Farran watched the sleeping chancellor for a few moments, listening to the storm rage outside, and fighting his own furious urge to incinerate the chancellor right where he lay. But the pleading in Adella's eyes kept him in check, and instead, he issued a sharp kick to the frame of the bed, startling the chancellor into wakefulness.

The man looked up and saw Farran standing over him, and scrambled away from him across the silk-strewn bed. He shouted for his guards, but Farran smiled nastily at him.

"Your lackeys are otherwise occupied," he said, a false calm in his voice. "It'll be just the two of us, I'm afraid."

"Who are you?" demanded Chancellor DeMorrow. "What do you want from me?"

"I?" asked Farran. "I want nothing from you. *You* summoned *me*, don't you recall?" Farran drew closer, taking deliberate, measured steps around the far corner of the bed, where the man sat cowering with his back to the wall. "You dared the pirate god himself to challenge your rule over this town and these waters. Our names are not to be thrown about as lightly as your death sentences and executioner's rope. How can you seem surprised when he answers your call?"

The chancellor's face grew sickly pale, and he tried again to call for help, but all that emerged was a mewling squeak. Farran was mere feet away now, and Chancellor DeMorrow was gazing up at him in petrified disbelief.

"You're not ..." he whispered. "You can't *possibly* be!"

In one motion, Farran seized the huddled man by the front of his sleeping gown and hauled him upright, slamming him against one of his gilded bedposts. "I am the shadow that sailors fear," growled Farran. "I am the storm in the heart of the sea, and the greed of every privateer." As he spoke, the floorboards beneath his feet began to spark and smoke. "I am the soul of every black flag, the weight of every stolen coin, and the heart of every shipwreck!" And then, Farran's very countenance began to change. Faint hints of scale patterns began to show just beneath his skin, and seaweed began to weave its way through his unruly black hair. Farran could feel saltwater coursing angrily through his veins, every inch of him raw and volatile power ready to burst forth like a dammed river. And Farran roared, "I am the First Sailor, God of All Pirates! I am Farran Arthelliad, and you will *kneel*!"

He released Chancellor DeMorrow, who fell to the floor with the resounding crack of at least one broken ankle. The chancellor hunched himself over in supplication, hands clasped before him, horrified tears flowing freely.

"Forgive me," he whispered. "I was foolish, and I beg you to spare me."

Farran breathed deep, forcing the brimming pool of his powers back, taking control of his shape once more. When he was certain he appeared human, he went to the window and gazed out at the storm. He addressed the man on the floor.

"My men may be far from innocent, but they are still my men. I do not fault you for trying to have them hanged. You're not the first, and you certainly won't be the last." Farran could see his ships in the distance, and see his men beginning to raise the sails. With a quick mental whisper, Farran eased the storm over the Laila. No need to make it harder on them. "But there were many in that keep tonight that shouldn't have been," he continued. "You'll find I've taken them as well."

"Anything, you may have anything, my lord," gushed Chancellor DeMorrow.

Farran smiled and turned away from the window, pocketing a set of silver candlesticks from a nearby table as he did so. "I will take you at your word on that," he said. And then, he crouched to the chancellor's level, looking him straight in the red-rimmed eyes. "I planned to drown you in your sleep," he said conversationally. Almost gently, even. "Just there, lying on your bed as you were. I could fill your lungs with ocean brine and watch you flail like a fish on a wire." And then, he leaned in closely and said, so quietly and deadly sweet that it made the chancellor cringe, "But I made her a promise. You're her father, after all, and that isn't her fault."

At this, the chancellor found a spark of his nerve again. "Adella? Where is she? What have you done with her?"

At this, Farran ran an almost tender hand down the long, black braid hanging over the chancellor's shoulder. He stood, letting the hair run slowly through his hand like a twisted snake. And then, he straightened his vest with a sharp tug, saluted the chancellor, and said with a wicked grin, "You *did* say I could take anything."

THE DOCKS WERE A MESS of bodies and flooding and the final, lingering moments of battle. As Farran rode in on Adella's fine black horse, with her manservant Antos perched precariously behind him and clutching tightly around his waist, a triumphant cheer rose from the pirates, and sails began to fly. Adella herself rushed forward to embrace Antos, and then she ushered him aboard the Laila to join his wife. Then she turned back, uncertainty and unasked questions painted across her face.

"He is alive and unharmed," said Farran as he dismounted, and Adella relaxed noticeably. He handed her the reins, and Adella followed as Farran made his way down the docks to where his ship waited for him.

"I know he doesn't deserve it," admitted Adella. "The things he's done to some of the people in this town, in his own household ..." She reached up and absently stroked her steed's cheek. "But he's my father. And ... his life will be mine, someday."

"It doesn't have to be," said Farran, turning to face her. And then he purred, "That's not a life for you, back there. *Come with me.*"

A feverish excitement filled Adella's eyes, but she shook her head jerkily and held tighter to her horse's reins.

Farran smiled and leaned in close. "The whole world is waiting for you, Adella DeMorrow. Where would you choose to see it from? The deck of a wave-tossed adventure, with the wind in your hair and every shoreline ripe for a sunrise gallop? Or reading about it from behind the chancellor's desk?" He held out his hand, and whispered once more, "*Come with me.*"

For a moment, Adella looked back at the rain-washed streets of her city. She turned her gaze on the stone towers of her father's land, and the storm-tossed wreckage of the ships in the harbor. When she turned back to Farran, there was an eager smile tucked in her perfect lips, and the spirit of adventure glowing on her rain-soaked face. She took his hand, and Farran brushed his own lips against the back of hers like a proper gentleman. As he led her and her black horse on board, the Laila set off. The storm lifted, and the clouds parted to reveal a brilliant sunrise. A playful breeze danced through the rigging and across the decks, starting to dry the pirates' clothes and making Adella's hair furl back like a black pirate flag. And as they left the coast behind and sailed off into the Gossamer Sea, Adella laughed. And the music of her laughter was the only song Farran ever wanted to hear again.

Chapter Twenty-Four
The Nightmarket

In town, at the markets and shops and fairs, each merchant was on his own. The friendships that were born in the spaces between disappeared like morning dew in the midday sun, only to be rediscovered again as soon as the cities were left behind. But at market, it was all bartering and knocking elbows and shouting louder than your neighbor. And for a man simply playing at being a merchant, Farran was a surprisingly adept tradesman. He was charming with the ladies and joked easily with the men. He traded for fresh supplies and new socks and some sort of heavy, moist bread simply bursting with nuts that seemed to be popular in the area. Fox found himself watching "The Incomparable Donovan" in awe.

But apart from the occasional pangs of envy at Farran's easy manner, trading was growing farther and farther from Fox's mind. He could feel the caravan, practically hear their voices on the wind, and it thrilled him. They were so close he could smell it, and even the very spring breezes seemed to be excited for him, bounding about like an eager dog as Fox picked up the pace on the road a little more each day. The waking hours were full of song and laughter and races between himself and Topper. Soon, Fox would be bringing Father home.

By his reckoning, they were just two days from crossing paths with the Thicca Valley caravan when they stopped for the evening in Florint. It was a crowded little city tucked at the base of a small fortress, with a thriving nightmarket at its heart. Fox could hear the seasoned merchants on the highway swapping tales of the city. From the sounds of it, Florint was one of the more diverse markets, pulling in waresmen and entertainment from all across the Known World.

Fox and his company trailed into town with a spice merchant, Harris, and his wife Tara. Harris was a moody but friendly enough old man, who'd welcomed Fox's group into the warmth of his fireside. And from the way he spoke, he'd been everywhere on the Merchant's Highway. Twice.

"Florit's a right little hub of madness, it is," said Harris as they passed through the city gates. "Trade from all over the continent, not to mention foreigners of every sort. But the Lord Camerontine loves his shopping."

"Sorry, but who's this Lord Camerontine?" asked Wick.

"Lives up in the fort," said Harris. "Runs it, actually. Spoiled little military brat he is, but he keeps us employed. Always buying new things and hiring new chefs right out of the Nightmarket. They haven't got a decent weapon up there to defend the city, but Spirit knows he's got enough fine jewelry to keep an entire royal court in fashion."

Every inn and tavern in the city was quickly filled as the merchants bought their keep for the night. Fox and his group were among several small companies who found room at the Pocket Frog, a cozy inn right at the edge of the square where the Nightmarket was to be held. The rooms were larger than Fox had expected, and the dining room was in reality an open courtyard out back with long tables set up beneath a lantern-hung tree. Fox didn't mind, though. It provided him a perfect spot to sit and watch the Nightmarket begin to come to life. As late afternoon wore into evening, a tangible expectation began to grow. Fox and his group took their supper early to watch it all come together.

Lanterns were lit on every corner and hung from every tree. A discordant, ghostly sort of music drifted through the air as instruments were tuned somewhere out of sight. As twilight fell, brightly colored awnings began to spring up, and wooden booths filled the street. Some were complex, wheeled in from back alleys and unfolded to reveal built-in shelves and carved niches for displaying goods. For others, it was a simple matter of bringing out a long table draped with a blanket or decorative cloth. Some, including several companies who'd been traveling on the highway, were planning on trading right out of their trunks. They lugged crates and great chests of merchandise down into the Nightmarket square, tucking themselves and their wares into any empty corner or gap between booths. And above it all, stretching between the upper rooms of shops and the rooftops of houses, was colored fabric of every sort.

Browns, golds, sky-bright blues ... every pattern and every color was stretched across the rooftops in scraps of fabric, like one haphazard tent. As Fox watched, more colors were run out on clothes lines like flags. He leaned over to Harris, sitting at the next table nursing a small vat of rather awful-smelling soup. "What's that all about?" he asked, pointing at the patchwork of color above the square.

Harris glanced up. "Just the Symbol," he said, returning to his meal almost at once. "It says to those in the fort that the Nightmarket is alive and ready for business. On nights when there aren't enough merchants in town to make it worth his while, the colors don't fly."

Fox grinned and leaned across his own table to tug on Topper's sleeve. "Do you see those colors?" he asked, and the younger boy nodded. "*That's* what the Shavid are like. All bright and varied patterns and sometimes you can't even keep them all straight!"

"But they're beautiful!" said Topper, a smile pinching his freckles.

"They are," agreed Fox. "Imagine it, Topper! A world with no more greys and blacks and whites, not like back home. It's all ..." Fox waved his hand vaguely at the Symbol, running out of words to describe it.

It took a moment for Fox to realize that the men were laughing at him, and he blushed and settled back into his seat.

"Don't be ashamed," said Wick placatingly. "We just enjoy your healthy curiosity, that's all."

"Old men like us sometimes forget what that feels like," added Farran, and Wick chuckled in agreement. Then, Farran gently nudged Fox's shoulder with the booted foot that was propped easily up on the table. "Go," he said with a smile. "Enjoy the Nightmarket. Your father will have to pass through Florint soon, this is as good a place to wait as any." And then, from a hand Fox was sure had been empty a moment before, Farran tossed each of the boys a thick silver coin. "Have fun," he said, winking.

Before another word could be said, Fox and Topper sprang up and rushed to the edge of the dining yard, where only a narrow strip of alley stood between them and the heart of the Nightmarket. And as they stepped beneath the brilliantly colored canopy, it was as though the entire world came to life around them. Music that had been muted and distant was now all around them. Colors and smells and the shouts in every foreign language bled together like wet paint. Topper and Fox clasped hands as easily as though they were brothers, and Fox let Topper lead the way.

If Fox had thought any other market grand or impressive, he had been wrong. This was no mere bazaar of goods and trading: it was like its own little country, tucked beneath a patchwork sky. A dozen different languages hit his ears with every step, and fresh smells welcomed him with every breath. There were not only merchants selling their wares, but *making* them. Workshops and smithies opened right up into the market, throwing their doors and windows wide and turning the streets into one long, twisting hallway.

Fox and Topper wandered seamlessly from shop to open-air booth, each restraining themselves from spending their entire fortune in one place. They purchased sweets and meat pies from bakery windows and tossed some of their change to a street performer twisting his body in impossible ways. They even stood at the heart of a crowd watching a spirited play put on in the middle of the Nightmarket. And as Fox watched the performers, a strange twinge began to pull at his heart. It was an odd, disconcerting feeling. Like someone had plucked at a harp string, and the string had simply forgotten to play.

"They're Shavid," said Fox finally, his eyes glued to the man on stage. They were not *his* Shavid, Radda and the company that would be back in Thicca Valley any day now. No, this was a different group. But they *were* Shavid, Fox could feel it. Their colors were somehow separate from the wild patterns above, and they smelled foreign in a way that nobody else quite did. Like they were from everywhere and nowhere, all at once. And the feeling, the sureness that these were indeed Shavid, was echoed in the odd rhythm in his chest.

"You alright?" asked Topper, elbowing Fox gently in the ribs, but sharply enough to draw his attention.

"What?" asked Fox, tearing his eyes away from the performers. "Yes, fine, why?"

"You were mouthing the words of their play," said Topper with a small laugh. "Have you seen them before? You must be a fan of their show to have it memorized like that. You were spot on."

"I was?" asked Fox shakily. He turned back to look at the brilliantly costumed performers once more. "I've never seen this play before," he added, almost to himself more than Topper. And, as his friend didn't seem to hear him, Fox let it go. But as he watched the play come to a close, he was extra careful to keep his lips pressed tightly together. And when they had finished, Fox quickly separated himself from the crowd and headed away from the Shavid, dragging Topper with him.

"Something *is* wrong!" said Topper, finally managing to free himself from Fox's tight grasp around his wrist. "Come on, tell me! What's got you shaken?"

"Nothing, it's nothing," Fox insisted, digging a handful of sweets from his pocket and munching anxiously on them. But the truth was, something wasn't wrong. Something was very, very *right*. And every one of Fox's muscles was humming, urging him to join the Shavid. To run, right now, and ride away with them to wherever they might be going. It was an urge so strong that it terrified Fox, and he simply *had* to tear himself away.

But instead of attempting to explain all of this to Topper, who was watching him with wide-eyed concern, Fox changed the subject.

"You think if you bought your Mother that necklace over there, she'd forgive you for running off with us?"

That did the trick. Within minutes, Topper was telling stories all about Doff, and Fox's problems were forgotten as they wandered through the Nightmarket. Topper went on and on about his adopted family and the candlemaking business. He bragged about the first flawless candle he'd made, and how Kaldora had kept it on her shelf ever since, saying it was too precious to burn.

"Sounds like you've really found your place," said Fox.

"My place," said Topper fondly. "You know, I've never been able to say that about anywhere." And there was something of an extra swagger in his step as he added, "Feels right nice, it does."

As time wore on, the Nightmarket began to grow ever more crowded. Topper and Fox were easily buffeted by the crowds, and they began to keep more to the outskirts of the marketplace. After awhile, they simply perched themselves on a mid-level scrap of roof. A sort of low set of eaves halfway up a shop building, so they were above the crowds but still more-or-less tucked beneath the Symbol. Here and there, the levels of colored fabric dropped lower, and patches of star-dusted sky shone through

"Reminds me of when I used to live up on the rooftops," said Topper, grinning up at the great swaths of patterns and colors. "Never had views like this, though."

Fox laughed and pointed up at a cluster of embroidered birds on one of the cloth pieces. "See, that's not too different from back home! You've got birds, you've got stars, it's practically identical!"

Both boys laughed again, and settled in to watch the Nightmarket dancing below them. They snacked on their leftover sweets and pointed out curious booths to each other. They made guesses on what country people were from, which was something of a joke since neither of them knew the name of many countries at all. But where they couldn't guess, they simply made something up. "Flat Hat Land" became a favorite, named after those traders who wore circular hats that looked more like baskets. Also, "The Nation of Pies" for the overly round gentlemen they saw wandering from bakery to sweet shop all night. They even saw Farran and Wick wandering about the place, deep in conversation about something. Topper tried to wave and get their attention, but the noise in the streets easily drowned them out, and he quickly gave up.

"So where'd you pick up that trader friend of yours anyway?" asked Topper as the men disappeared into the heart of the crowd. "He's a mite too colorful for our parts, isn't he?"

"He sort of ... found me," said Fox uncomfortably. And then, surprised he hadn't thought of it before, he added, "He's my best friend's ... uncle." It was close enough to the truth, in any case. Farran might have been Lai's true father, but she would never see him that way. Borric was her father, and always would be.

"Well, every family's got the odd one, doesn't it?" said Topper sagely. "I like to think mine is Wick. Because if it's not, it's surely bound to be me!" He laughed, and Fox shook his head.

"I *know* the odd one in my family is me," he said. "First one in generations to be thinking of another life besides trapping."

"Yeah, but it's *you!*" said Topper genially. "You've got talents that aren't meant for a life in Sovesta. You've got *magic!*" He said it with a childish awe in his voice, like he couldn't believe such a thing truly existed.

"Maybe," said Fox, shrugging. "But I couldn't make a decent candle if my life depended on it."

But Topper's no-doubt ribbing response was drowned out by a sudden shiver. Fox could feel something approaching, something that wasn't meant to be here. It smelled of blood and anger, and something that might have been desperation. Fox scrambled to the edge of their perch and looked around, scanning the crowds for anything unusual. The Nightmarket was so packed, it was hard to pick any one smell out. But if he listened very closely, he could hear a jarring note that set his teeth on edge. Something that sounded, and felt, wrong.

Fox swung down easily from the ledge, dropping onto the street like a feral cat. Topper followed, asking anxiously what was going on. But Fox held up his hand against the questions: he had to focus. He was on the hunt.

The Nightmarket seemed even louder and more hectic than before. The colors nearly blinded Fox in his heightened state of awareness, but he continued on, weaving expertly through the crowds the same way he might have dodged through trees and thick underbrush. Topper kept close on his heels, no longer questioning him. In fact, Fox thought his friend seemed downright excited.

They wound through shops and back alleys, all the while following a scent only Fox could smell. There was something sour in the Nightmarket, and Fox could feel himself getting closer. But their urgent progress was slowed when they hit a solid wall of people. A clamoring crowd of shoppers who didn't seem to be buying anything, but were all facing the same way, straining to get a look at something neither of the boys could see.

Fox tried to push his way through, but there was hardly a gap large enough for him to fit one arm through. And each time he tried, he was rebuffed with a glare or a harsh word. Finally, Topper grabbed Fox by the elbow and tugged at him, saying, "This way!"

With a practiced ease, Topper led Fox through one of the open side alleys and up onto the rooftops, where they scurried along to the head of the crowd like rats. Oftentimes, their heads brushed up against the patchwork fabric of the Symbol, or else they had to part it like curtains to move forward. Finally, they came to the edge of the crowd and looked down, at once understanding what everyone was staring at.

"It's Lord Camerontine," said Fox. "It's got to be!" They were looking down on finely-curled, golden locks of a young man who simply dripped with wealthy foppishness. He was gazing on every trinket as though it were simply a toy, and not someone's hard-earned living. Here and there, he stopped to buy a piece of jewelry or a sugar-spun candy, laughing joyously at the simple little things. Fox could hear him saying things like, "Oh yes, this is delightful! I *must* serve these at my next party!" or "Fifty crowns? Oh, why not then! I'll just use it as a paperweight somewhere." But everywhere he went, merchants and vendors were thrilled. Those who were lucky enough to sell him their wares would likely be able to feed their families for an entire season.

"They're all watching to see what he buys," pointed out Topper. "Look!"

Fox followed his gaze back to the crowd. Topper was quite right; it seemed as though whatever Lord Camerontine bought was considered highly fashionable, and there was often a mad rush behind him as shoppers hurried to try and buy exactly what he had. To this, Lord Camerontine seemed completely oblivious. He was surrounded by his guards and personal shopping aides, all carrying his packages and telling him how grand he looked in every hat and scarf he tried on.

"Is he what you've been looking for?" asked Topper.

"No," said Fox, glancing around for a hint of anything unusual below. "But it's close, whatever it is." He breathed in deep once more, and with a sudden rushing certainty, he knew exactly *where* it was, although he still had no idea *what* it was. He eased carefully away from the edge of the roof, and lay on his back against the shingles for a moment, letting the feeling sink in. There was something here that wanted to *hurt* someone. And, in Fox's mind, it felt an awful lot like the Desolata. Sick, and powerful, and hungry for death.

If he could find it, whatever it was, he could send Topper to find the men. Farran, at least, would have no problem with it. And even Wick seemed a capable fighter. But if it was anything like the Desolata, there was no part of Fox that wanted to fight it on his own.

He motioned to Topper to stay silent, and then began to belly-crawl across the roof, away from Lord Camerontine and his adoring masses. Closer and closer they grew, until Fox could hear something, hidden behind the now-distant cacophony of the Nightmarket. A growling, spitting language, in many voices. Whatever Fox was hunting, there was more than one.

Fox let himself be led to a dilapidated rooftop, partially obscuring a narrow alley. It was tucked in a less-crowded corner of the Nightmarket. Here, the colors of the Symbol were faded and water-stained. The alluring smells of foreign soaps and spices and fresh-baked bread were gone, replaced with the sharp, sickening scent of stagnant grease and sweat.

Below, in the light of a crude lantern that popped and sputtered, a group of men were conversing in that strange tongue. Only, they weren't quite men. As Fox leaned carefully over the edge of the rooftop, peering down at the little group, he thought their faces looked a bit too pointed. Their chins and cheekbones were overly pronounced, and the skin that stretched across them was pockmarked and a strange shade of brown that was almost red. They wore their blue-black, matted hair in braids down their backs, or else piled in knots and horse tails on top of their heads. But even more than that, Fox's eyes were drawn to their weapons. Ugly, roughly wrought things that were not designed for smooth slices; they were designed to decimate a body on the way in, and out.

Fox scurried back from the edge, far enough that they would not be able to hear him as he whispered, "Go find Farr – Donovan. And your uncle. Get them back here."

"Do you think they mean us harm?" asked Topper, but his face said he knew the answer already.

"I think they mean harm to anyone they get their hands on," said Fox honestly.

"We could just leave," said Topper urgently, visibly shaken by the men below. And though Fox knew that Topper could not feel them in quite the same way, he was sure that his friend knew *something* wasn't right about them. "We can get back on the road, right now! We can hide out somewhere ..." And then, in a small and terrified voice, "They make me feel naked. I don't like them, Fox."

"That's why we have to stop them," said Fox, squeezing his friend's shoulder. "Do you remember when I told you about the Desolata? The bandits I had to face back home?" The hint of a nod in the dark. "I have never been more frightened in my life. But I saved my village. This might not be *our* village, but as merchants every market is our home."

He could feel Topper quivering beneath his hand, but finally, the younger boy whispered, "I will bring them." And he backed slowly away from the roof's edge and began to scramble, in a hurried crawl, across the roofing tiles and out of sight.

Fox was left alone, with the sound and smell of the darkest corners of the Nightmarket pressing in around him. He lay on his back, flush against the crumbling shingles, and listened to the alley. The men-things below seemed to be arguing. Fox did not have to understand their language to recognize the universal sounds of fighting. He listened to the shuffling half-steps of someone restraining themselves from attacking somebody else, and the low hisses punctuated by the occasional raised voice. Until finally, one speaker seemed to win. The others fell silent, and a single voice spoke up. It seemed to be ordering the rest of them, demanding something.

There was the dull shriek of a blade being sharpened, and the hum of a bow being strung. And then, footsteps out of the alley. Fox scurried to the edge of the roof and gazed down at the dimly-lit back street, and his heart sank. Three of the men were leaving, creeping out of the alley like feral dogs on the prowl. That left four men behind, speaking amongst themselves once more in low, hurried voices. Fox could feel his heart thudding wildly against the shingles, beating a tattoo Fox was sure the men below could hear as he struggled to make a quick decision: to stay and wait for Topper to return with help, or to follow those three and catch them in whatever mischief they were planning.

The rotting span of roofing beneath Fox's belly creaked, and shifted under his weight. There was sudden silence from below as all the men looked up, and Fox scrambled back from the edge, his decision made for him. With graceless panic, Fox slid down the slope of the roof, away from the alley. Given his odds, he would much rather take his chances with the three who *hadn't* seen him than with the four who had.

He more-or-less fell to the cobblestone street, then picked himself up just in time to see the three hunters rounding a corner not far away. He ran, as eager to catch up to his quarry as he was to put distance between himself and the four men-things behind him. Fox could hear them in the alley, scrambling to sharpen their own weapons now and throwing stones at the piece of roof he'd been stationed on. It wouldn't be long until they discovered he wasn't there.

He kept the three man-things within his sight, following closely behind them as they ventured out of the abandoned corners and into the heart of the Nightmarket. A ripple of fear began to pass through the shoppers as they caught sight of these men, and people began to back away or hurry to the cover of workshops and dining houses. But the hunters paid them no mind, and Fox realized that they must not be the target. They had to be hunting *someone* though, he thought, slipping behind a meat stall to watch. And then, a roar echoed through the Nightmarket, and Fox turned to find the remaining four men from the alley standing at the end of the street. And the biggest, nastiest brute of the lot was pointing his wicked blade right at Fox.

Screams echoed through the streets as a true panic began, and everyone scrambled to clear the area. In the dancing lights of the Nightmarket, it was clearer than ever that these were not men. They were monsters.

The three hunters picked up their pace, running now through the market, seeming to have realized they were being followed. But Fox could not trail them anymore; he was pressed with his back against a rough wooden stall, with no way of escape from the four creatures advancing on him.

Their leader — he was sure that the big one had to be in charge — growled something in that strange language. "I – I don't understand!" said Fox desperately. "Please, this was a mistake. I didn't mean to get in your way."

The big one laughed. A horrible, grating sound that made Fox's stomach churn. "He does not understand?" he said in harsh, broken Trader's Tongue. "Little rat spy, couldn't keep your nose to yourself! I will remove it, along with your head!" And with a roar, he and his men charged, and Fox darted to the side without thinking, running wildly through the Nightmarket. A knife whizzed past his ear, narrowly missing him as he dodged into a bakery. He wound through it, apologizing over and over as he knocked breads aside and spilled flour across the floor. He escaped through the back of the shop, into a now-deserted street that had earlier been filled with eager shoppers. He ran, making for the Pocket Frog, all the way at the other end of the marketplace.

The inn was quiet and dark when he arrived, panting, at the back door. He could hear the whispers of frightened patrons, hiding in the common room. Their silhouettes were just visible, tucked up against the walls or beneath tables outside. They spoke in hushed, terrified voices, saying there were bandits in the market. They could hear them drawing nearer, roaring angrily through the streets and trashing stalls and booths as they went.

Fox knew he didn't have much time. They would be looking for him. Quickly, he darted through the common room, looking for the innkeeper. Or a member of the staff. Anyone who might know where Farran and Wick had gone. He asked no fewer than seven different people before, finally, he had the slightest bit of success. A terrified young kitchen maid, crouched in the shadows of the empty fireplace, said she'd heard them talking about going to see the Shavid players. "They said they fancied some entertainment," she squeaked. Fox thanked her, but as he started to go, the girl grabbed his sleeve urgently. "Do you know," she whispered, then cleared her throat. "They say the bandits have started killing people. Have you seen — "

"I'm sorry," said Fox, "I don't know how many. I didn't witness any of them."

She let him go with shaking hands, and said quietly, "My brothers are out there, tending to the shop." She twisted her apron between her fingers, worrying at the lace edging. "They run the smithy." After that, she seemed to be done talking. And Fox, not knowing quite what to say, stood awkwardly and left.

He took to the rooftops again, peering cautiously down at the streets below. All was clear, though he could hear distant screams that indicated the bandits were still about. Fox kept still for a moment, perched on the roof's edge like a gargoyle. He breathed deep, taking in the smell of panic, the sticky and sour scent of fear. He could almost taste the bite of the oils the bandits used to sharpen their blades. And still, beneath it all he could just sense the smell of fine Doffian wax that was the Flintstock men, and the ever-present hint of saltwater that was Farran.

Fox began to race, across the rooftops and down onto lower balconies. He made his way closer to the street level without ever touching it, ready to spring back to the safety of the shingles at a moment's notice. But when he reached the abandoned wreckage of the square where he'd seen the Shavid perform, he finally let himself drop to the cobblestones, and ran panting to Farran's side.

"Thank the gods," said Wick, grabbing Fox in a rough hug. "Topper found us and told us what was happening. We were on our way, but that's when the rioting began."

"What are they?" asked Fox, rubbing at his arm. It was bleeding — he hadn't realized he'd cut it during his mad dash. Or perhaps one of the man-creature's weapons had grazed him after all. He couldn't remember.

"Ryegout assassins," answered Farran gravely. "The term you might use is 'goblin.' Trying to masquerade as men."

"We killed one!" said Topper cheerfully. But even through the bravado in his voice, Fox could hear an underlying tremor. He clapped his friend on the shoulder with an approving nod before turning back to Farran.

"But what did they want?" asked Fox.

"Lord Camerontine," said Farran. "Ryegout politics are complex and dirty. Should I have had to guess, I would say they were looking for a ruling house to call their own."

"And did they — "

Farran shook his head. "He was here when they attacked, and we were able to help buy the guards time to spirit him away. He might be a spoiled little dandy, but better him than a Ryegout, I promise you." Now, he looked Fox up and down with fatherly concern. "Can you keep moving? Much of the Nightmarket is still under attack, we shouldn't linger."

Fox nodded and wiped sweat from his brow with his arm.

"We'll get you two safely to the outskirts of town," said Wick. "And then, Donovan and I are going to help clean up. These people aren't equipped to fight, and there have been far too many deaths already tonight."

"The outskirts?" argued Fox even as he let himself be led out of the square. "I can help! Besides, you'll waste too much time! All the way out of the Nightmarket and back, half of Florint could be dead!"

For a moment, Farran looked as though he wanted to argue. But one look at Fox's face, and he heaved a sigh riddled with frustration. "Keep up, and don't get yourself hurt. You're under no obligation to these people."

"And neither are you," said Fox stubbornly. And then, because he knew the dangers of battle were nothing to a god, he turned to Wick and added, "Not either of you."

But the men were not given the opportunity to respond. There was a crash of wood behind them, and the whole group wheeled about. A nasty, scowling Ryegout burst straight through a shop door and ran at them, his weapon out before him like a twisted pike.

"RUN!" shouted Wick, and the boys didn't waste a moment. They took off, putting the fight at their backs and darting through back alleys. They could hear the clash of blade-on-blade, and the angry screeching of an injured beast. It was only when they heard a triumphant crowing from Farran, echoing through the empty streets, that they began to slow down.

It was in a twisting side street that they finally stopped, collapsing against the wall of the sweet shop where not so long ago they'd been purchasing candies like eager children. They sat, chests heaving as they gasped for air. And then, inexplicably, Topper began to laugh. It began as a chuckle at first, and then began to swell. At first, Fox stared wildly at him. And then he, too, began to laugh, until they were both no more than giggling puddles on the alley floor.

"Some fighters we are!" said Topper through tears of mirth.

"Spirit's Fire, could we *run* though!" said Fox, coughing as he laughed a bit too much.

They laughed until their breath ran short, and then finally began to calm again. As they did, they could hear footsteps running their way.

"Here!" shouted Fox. "We're over here!" And then, beginning to laugh again, he said, "Don't you worry, when you say run we *run!*"

Topper had another fit of the giggles as he added, "Take your time, men! We've only gotten about a week ahead of you!" He snorted at the cleverness of his own joke, and then made to start pulling himself to his feet. But as he stood, the color drained from his face. Even his freckles seemed to disappear, until he was pale as the moon.

"What's wrong?" jibed Fox, struggling to his own feet and dusting off his rear. "Stand up too quickly, you know, and you'll make yourself faint like a pretty little woman!" And then, when Topper did not answer, he turned to find what his friend was looking at.

He only caught a glimpse of red skin and blue-black hair before Topper shoved him out of the way. Fox went crashing into the wall of the shop. There was a cry of pain, and a blur of straw-colored hair as Topper fell, a crude blade buried hilt-deep in his chest.

At the other end of the alley, the Ryegout who had thrown it suddenly dropped like a stone, a black-hilted knife straight through his throat. Fox didn't bother going to see if he was still alive, instead scrambling to Topper's side. The younger boy stared fixedly up at the fabric-strewn skies above him, eyes wide. His breath came in shaky, painful gasps, and Fox reached out to clasp his friend's hand.

"Just hold on," Fox said reassuringly. "Your uncle will be here soon. And Donovan – he'll know what to do."

Topper smiled and squeezed Fox's hand. "Oh, how we ran, though," he whispered, each word sounding labored and tiresome. "We ran too far — they won't find us. We ran across the whole world."

"Hush," said Fox, wiping teardrops from Topper's forehead. It took a moment for him to realize they were his own. "Any moment, they'll be here. Just you wait —" And then, though he knew he was no longer speaking to anyone, "Your mother will be waiting for you. You've got a whole, wonderful life ahead in Doff."

He kept speaking, nonsense words and impossible stories, until Farran and Wick came hurrying into view. And then, he said nothing. He watched as Wick ran to his dead nephew, and cradled his head on his lap. He met eyes with Farran, and mouthed silently for him to do something, but the god shook his head, true pain and regret in his eyes.

After a few minutes, Wick stood, sword in hand, and turned away. With no explanation, he disappeared into the night. Still, Fox knelt at Topper's side, clutching his hand. Farran stood on the other side of his body, looking down on them like a watchful shadow.

"Bring him back," demanded Fox.

"I can't," answered Farran simply.

"You're a *god!*" said Fox desperately.

"I've told you before," said Farran quietly. "The ways of the gods are beyond your understanding. And had he lived, you most certainly would be dead."

"Is that supposed to comfort me?" asked Fox, anger creeping into his voice now. "Knowing that he died, for *me?*"

"Topper's time to die was long ago," replied Farran. "The day he crossed Meat Man Mallard, he should have been murdered. You changed that. You saved *him.*"

"So I bought him a couple of months," said Fox bitterly.

"You did so much more than that," said Farran. "You took what might have been a brutal, meaningless death, and made it so much more. Topper was always going to die, but now his death means someone else's life. That is a deep and powerful thing, and it should not be taken lightly."

Fox couldn't decide on his next words. His tongue was so full of angry accusations and frustrated curses, he couldn't settle on just one. He began dabbing at the blood pooling around Topper's wound, anything to stop himself shaking and throwing things.

Except, it wasn't blood. "Is that ... ink?" asked Fox.

"Yes," said Farran quietly.

"How?" said Fox, a note of disbelief creeping into his voice. "Why is he bleeding ink?"

For a moment, Farran didn't look as though he was going to answer. Then, slowly, he said, "You are a man of maps. And he owed you his soul."

He said it like it was a matter-of-fact. He said it as though it were the simplest thing in the world to understand. And a creeping realization began to come over Fox. He dropped Topper's hand. "You knew," he whispered. "You knew that he owed me his ... soul?"

Fox nodded, one slow downward tilt of the head.

And then, Fox snapped. "Fix it!" he shouted. "Bring him back! Go back and save him! Something! *Anything*!"

"I tell you, I *can't!*" said Farran, beginning to sound as angry as Fox. "I wish that I could, trust me! But I —"

"All those stories of the gods I read in my book," spat Fox. "They tell of great and miraculous things, of powers no mortal can have! *They* can bring back the dead, or save them before they die! What kind of god are you?"

"I am one of the *great* gods, little one," growled Farran, "and I would advise you *not* to try my patience!"

"If you're so great," said Fox, standing and glaring at the god, "then why are you so useless when it matters? Why couldn't you save him?"

"Because that was the price of loving her!" shouted Farran, and Fox fell silent. Farran was visibly shaking as he continued. "Those powers were taken away from me. It's why ... why I need you." He ran his fingers through his hair in frustration. "I cannot restore them myself. Who I was — and who Adella was — are hidden from me. And *you* can find things!" He looked at Fox with pleading eyes, and his desperation was so overwhelming Fox took a step back.

"Enough," he snapped, his voice low and harsh. "Enough of your stories and your riddles and your useless powers!" He took another step back until he could feel the wall just inches behind him. "You can find another pawn, we have no more deal." And then, when Farran did not move, he shouted, "Go on! Get out of here! Leave me alone!"

"But, you are my captain," said Farran beseechingly. "I follow you."

"Then jump overboard," said Fox. "I am done with you." He knelt by Topper's side once more, and when he looked up, Farran was gone.

DAWN WAS JUST BEGINNING to warm the Nightmarket when Wick returned. The man offered no explanation as to where he'd been, but Fox could see in the colored light that filtered through the Symbol that Wick was covered in blood. And when Fox asked if there was any more word of the Ryegout, Wick answered simply that they'd been taken care of.

They sat in the rising dawn, listening to the marketplace as it started to come back to life. But it wasn't the joyful, thriving sound of shop doors opening and customers beginning to trickle through the streets. Instead, it was the sound of hard labor as merchants and traders began to pick up the pieces of their ruined stalls. Funeral arrangements were made for those who had fallen, and a great bonfire was set to burn the bodies of the Ryegout. The stench of rotting flesh washed through the streets, but still people carried on. The Nightmarket would live again. Perhaps not tonight, but soon. And there was work to be done.

Topper's body was taken out of the city, far from the graveyards of Florint. Fox and Wick carried him between them, laid out on a ruined wooden door they had taken from the wreckage. Just before they left the alley, Fox went to retrieve the black-hilted knife that had brought down Topper's murderer; it was one of his own, although he didn't remember throwing it. They did not speak, and they did not stop until they reached a stretch of isolated moor, dotted with little hills and odd tumbles of stone. There, they laid him down at the foot of a grey heap that looked like a crumbled and ancient tower.

"He should have been buried in the mountains," said Wick, turning his face up to the sky. "He should have been taken deep into the mines, where so many of our ancestors have slept."

"It's my fault he came," said Fox quietly.

"Nobody will blame you."

"Kaldora will blame me," said Fox.

Wick took a deep breath before he answered, turning back to look down at his adopted nephew. "Yes, well," he said, with something in his eyes that, under any other circumstances, might have been a smile. "We've a long road before you have to face her wrath. Let's do what we've come for and be on our way."

"Tell me about the Doffian funeral ceremony," said Fox. "Tell me what I need to do."

They built a barrow for him out of fallen scraps of stone, laying on one top of the other around Topper's frame. But they left the center open, so they could still see his body tucked peacefully within its stone border. Once the walls were set a foot high on every side, Fox took a great hunk of strange, blue wax from the satchel Wick had brought, and laid it, as instructed, on Topper's chest, just over his wound. The offending knife had long since been removed and wrapped up.

And then, Wick began to sing. A strange song, in a language that sounded older than the stone itself. Words Fox could not understand, but that nevertheless spoke of great pain and sorrow. And as Wick sang, the wax lump began to melt. It pooled and spread and stretched like a fresh layer of skin, following every line and curve of Topper's body. It even kept the contour of his face, until Topper was nothing more than a statue laid out in a bed of stone.

It took until evening, and Wick sang all the while. His voice hummed and murmured like a river, bubbling over rocks and boulders on its way. The stone structures scattered across the moor began to pick up the song, echoing it back until it sounded as though a hundred men were singing. And even when Wick and Fox had finished, and they left Topper's wax figure in its lonely grave, the stones continued to hum their sorrow.

They sat at an isolated table at the Pocket Frog that night, each indulging in a large pint of something Fox knew he wasn't allowed to drink, but he did not care. The city of Florint was quiet, with many people choosing to stay within their homes tonight.

"What was that wax?" asked Fox eventually. His tongue started to feel fuzzy halfway through his drink, and not long after he found he felt like talking again.

"Lymnwax," muttered Wick. "S'got lymnstone powder in it, that's what makes it so blue. And what gives it such special powers." He was more than a quarter done with his second drink now, and already raising his hand to order a third. As he spoke, he absently spun the empty tankard from his first, twirling it on its side on the tabletop. "I never meant to bring it, you know, but your friend said I should. And so ..." He let his sentence trail off into nothing as he took another great swig.

As Fox turned his attention to his own drink, he suddenly stopped. He had thought, for a moment, that he saw Farran standing by the lantern tree, watching them. But he blinked, and the vision was gone. It must have been the drink, or the fact that Wick had mentioned him. But Wick started speaking again, and Fox tore his gaze from the tree.

"Should have known, then," said Wick. "*He* always knew Topper was going to die, whoever he was. *What*ever he was."

"Why do you say that?"

"We only use that wax for funerals," said Wick. "There's one piece per Doffian. Only responds to their body, and theirs alone. We had Topper's made about a month after Kaldora claimed him."

"And Donovan asked you to bring it?" asked Fox, ignoring yet another flicker of a shape standing by the tree. Farran was gone — it was just his imagination.

Wick nodded as he took another drink, managing to spill a great deal of it down his front. And then, he pointed his tankard at Fox and said, "Someday, when I can remember what you say *very* clearly, you'll have to tell me who he really is. And how he could have known." And then, he stood and stretched and said, "But not now, I'm afraid. More pressing matters call." And then, beginning to unlace the front of his breeches as he went, he stumbled off to the privy, leaving Fox alone at the table.

He chose to ignore the shadowy figure of Farran who was now clearly sitting beside him. The god was not quite solid, but definitely there. He didn't say anything, and Fox responded in kind. He went to his room early, shoving Topper's bags under the bed so he didn't have to look at them. And as he tucked himself between his blankets, he knew the ghost of Farran was standing watch at the door.

Wick never came to bed that night, instead falling asleep at the table in the courtyard. Fox found him the next morning and helped him stagger upstairs, where he fell into bed fully clothed. Then Fox took his journal and his pens downstairs, settled himself down at their table once more, and began to write. He spent all day drawing maps of the places they'd been, and taking notes about everything he could remember. He continued to ignore Farran as he worked. He ordered both lunch and dinner from the kitchen maid, the one whose brothers worked the smithy. He was told they were all alive and well, and congratulated her. And, as the afternoon stretched into evening and the lanterns were lit, Fox continued to work with the silent ghost of a god never far from his sight.

And it was here that nightfall found him, just as the Thicca Valley caravan rode into town.

Chapter Twenty-Five
The Parting of the Ways

It was with a detached sort of fascination that Father listened as Fox told his story. Fox could read the emotions clearly painted on his face; as though it was a truly captivating tale that *must* have happened to somebody else, because the mere thought that it had happened to his own son was impossible to grasp. But nevertheless, he made a wonderful audience, listening patiently, and interrupting only a handful of times with valid and interested questions.

They sat where, not so long ago, Fox had sat with Topper; on a low rooftop, overlooking the Nightmarket. Below, the lights flickered and burned, and above, a faint patter of rain met the great tent that was the Symbol. The Nightmarket itself seemed but a dim shadow of its former radiance. Fox had a feeling it would, one day, return to normal for the people of Florint. But for him, it would always be haunted by the echoes of Topper and the Ryegout. Even as he spoke, Fox could almost hear his friend's laughing voice. He heard things that Topper might have said, had he been listening to the story. Comments he likely would have made, or additions he would have eagerly supplied.

Fox ploughed on, ignoring the imagined commentary and focusing instead on every detail of the months Father had missed. He talked and talked, more than he had since Topper had died. He started with the day the caravan had left him behind, and talked Father through everything from his trips to Doff, to his discoveries about how maps spoke to him. And, eventually, to the journey south, down the Merchant's Highway, to find Father and bring him home.

The only part he had omitted was the part involving Farran. He mentioned briefly that there had been another companion traveling with them, a merchant called Donovan, but that he'd recently left them to pursue his own path. And while Fox could manage to tune out the false voice of Topper in his imagination, much harder was ignoring the flickering pirate ghost on the rooftop just across from theirs. It sputtered in and out of focus like a guttering candle, but it was there, and it grew briefly stronger when Fox mentioned the name "Donovan."

Finally, with his voice raw and mouth dry from storytelling, Fox fell silent. He watched as Father struggled to come to terms with everything he'd been told. After several long moments, where they could hear nothing but the drumming of the rain above their heads, Father said quietly, "It is never an easy thing, to lose a friend on the road. May you never have to experience it again." And then he pulled his son into a tight embrace, and Fox wept on his shoulder. Father hummed quietly, as he had whenever Fox had been frightened as a child, and let him cry. After a few minutes he said, "It wasn't your fault."

Fox pulled away and wiped his streaming nose and eyes on his sleeve. "But it is," he said miserably. "I can't really explain ... it has to do with my magic, and I don't quite understand it myself. But I think ... I think it truly *was* my fault."

To this, Father had no response. Fox watched as Timic Foxglove struggled to find something comforting to say, and then gave up and changed the subject. "How long do we have until this avalanche of yours?" he asked.

Fox sniffed, coughed, and tried to focus. "It's unclear," he said finally. "All I know is, it could happen at any time. And all of my instincts are telling me, you *can't* go back through the pass."

Father ran his thumb across the curve of his left ear, as he always did when he was thinking. Finally, he said, "You've traded on your own, fought on your own, traveled under the very Highborns and across the Merchant's Highway to find me. You've become more of a man in one winter than I ever was at your age, or for many years after." And then, a warm and gloriously proud smile stretched Father's beard and made his eyes twinkle like the lantern light. "I think that earns you a man's rank with the caravan." He held out his hand, and shook Fox's in a firm grip. "Welcome aboard, Trapper Foxglove."

THE NIGHTMARKET WAS closed. The faintest hints of a drizzling dawn were just beginning to brush the city streets, and the Thicca Valley caravan had all turned in for the night. As they descended from the rooftops, Father promised Fox that they would meet later in the morning, with the rest of the caravan. "When they've had a chance to sleep, and eat a decent meal," said Father. "They're much more agreeable with food and rest, and there will be those who need convincing."

As they reached the door of the Pocket Frog and Father turned to leave him for the morning, Fox said quickly, "I don't want them to know about me." When Father turned an inquisitive look on him, Fox continued, "About my Blessing. Not many know about it and I just feel ... I know if we tell them, soon the whole valley would know."

"Would that be so terrible?" asked Father sincerely.

Fox did not respond, but Father must have sensed the answer in his silence. He sighed and began to rub his ear once more. "That will make things a bit tricky," said Father. "Explaining why we want to change course so drastically, with no solid reasoning?"

"We can think of something," said Fox. "Can't we?"

"I suppose we'll find out," said Father.

They bid each other good night, and Fox made his way upstairs to where Wick still slept, sprawled out across the bed. Fox didn't want to bother with moving him. Instead, he went to dig his bedroll from their bags, and stopped. Farran had been the one carrying the camping gear, including Fox's bedding. And all of Farran's packs had vanished.

Shivering somewhat from walking in the rain, Fox looked around for something else to curl up under. His eyes fell on a wadge of blanket peeking out from beneath the bed, and he started to pull it out. And as he did, Topper's things came tumbling out with it, freed from the darkness where he'd stuffed them. Clothes, shoes, things he'd bought along the road for Kaldora ... all came spilling out as Fox pulled Topper's bedroll out into the middle of the floor.

For a moment, Fox tried to ignore them. He'd put them away later. Or he'd simply leave them here — the group would be leaving Florint soon enough, let the innkeeper deal with a dead man's relics. But then, without thinking, without caring, Fox began to throw things. He hurled scraps of food from Topper's pack into the fireplace. He shredded shirts and breeches with his knife, and even his bare hands. He tore the straps from every offending piece of baggage that had dared to escape from beneath the bed.

It was as Fox began throwing candlesticks across the room that Wick finally awoke. He coughed and sat up, looking blearily around the room for the source of the noise. His eyes fell on Fox, sitting among the wreckage of his nephew's things. Wick's face remained a perfect blank as he grunted, pulled a bunched-up blanket from beneath his head, and tossed it at Fox. "This was his, too," he said. Then he rolled over, turning his back to Fox and, by all appearances, fell back asleep.

Fox looked down at the blanket that had landed just beside his left knee. It was ragged, and thin, and Fox was sure he'd seen it on the rooftop that had once been Topper's home, back in Whitethorn. This, Fox did not ruin. He folded it carefully and tucked it beneath his own head as a pillow. And then, because there was nothing more to be done, he slept.

FOX WAS HAPPY TO DISCOVER that Wick had returned somewhat to his normal self by the time they awoke. The sun was high, and a timid clock somewhere was placidity chiming midday, when they both began to rise. Wick was more chatty than he'd been for days, and even made a handful of casual jokes as they dressed and headed downstairs. Behind it all, however, there was a deep, broken sorrow in his eyes. But Fox tried to keep the conversation light and easy, not wanting to think even for a moment about the sorrow he might see in his own eyes should he happen by a mirror.

Father was already in the dining yard, shoving mis-matched tables together at the foot of the lantern tree to make one great, sprawling table for the caravan to sit around. Fox sprang in to help, introducing Wick as he did so. Father and Wick got along at once, and were soon swapping songs and laughing like old friends. It might have been a bit forced on Wick's end, but Fox was pleased to see it happen either way. By the time the rest of the caravan began to trickle into the yard, kitchen girls were bringing out huge platters of food. Spiced sausages; rolls bursting with fruit; trays of ham, both hot and cold; a cinnamon pie that Fox was sure he'd seen as dessert at one of the Nightmarket stalls, but he was sure it could pass very well for a breakfast dish.

There was no ceremony about the meal, people simply dove in. Their cobbled-together table became a mess of shouting and tossing food about. It was a scene that could only be played by men who had traveled too far and too long together to have any more shame. Even Wick slipped right in as though he'd been a part of their company from the start. Insults filled the air as easily as jokes, and raucous whoops and hollers filled the air whenever one of the married waresmen got a bit too friendly with a kitchen maid. In fact, when poor Fire Merchant Terric so much as said "Thank you," to the woman who brought him his drink, the table erupted in dirty rhymes and suggestions that made the young man blush.

"Oh go on," shouted one of the flint merchants, an older man called Ellegar. "Leave him alone, we all know he's pathetically shackled to that wife of his." And then he grabbed the woman as she made her way around the table and pulled her down onto his lap with a hearty laugh. "Me, all I've got to go home to is that witch who grew into her *mother!* Spirit save me!" More laughter around the table. Ellegar planted a huge, wet kiss on the kitchen maid, and was promptly pelted with scraps of food and whole biscuits from his companions.

Father lowered his voice so that only Fox could hear him beneath the hubbub. "Everyone's in a good mood," he murmured. "Now's your best shot. Let's play out this tune."

Fox had only a moment to prepare himself before Father stood with his back to the tree and addressed the table, and a comfortable hush fell over the group. Ellegar and his kitchen maid emerged, breathless, from their passionate embrace, and the man sent her off with a wink. All eyes of the caravan were on Father now, and he spoke. "You know how much I hate to break up a celebration," he said, and his companions laughed agreeably. "We've done well this year, and we should all be proud!"

A brief round of cheers and self-congratulations and boasting circled the table before Father raised a hand to signal for quiet once more. "But now, I bare grave news. It concerns our passage home." He glanced sideways at Fox for a moment, and Fox internally pleaded that he wouldn't be asked to speak to these men. But then Father went on, and Fox breathed easier. "I have reason to believe that the Tessoc Pass will be too dangerous to traverse this year. There have been whispers of a coming avalanche."

At this, nobody spoke. Even other groups at nearby tables seemed to be listening in; for everyone knew what an avalanche meant. It was more than a death sentence: it was the destructive tool of the gods. A means of wiping out everything in its path, burying offending travelers, beasts, and whole cities with its wrath. People grew cold just thinking about them.

"You're sure of your sources?" asked one of the men.

"Without a scrap of doubt," replied Father.

And then, all talk broke out at once, with every man trying to speak over his neighbor.

"... nowhere to go but into the Desolate ..."

"We'll be butchered if we go there, you fool!"

"But if there's no other way ..."

"I say we wait here until we're sure! If it comes, so be it! We're safe on the other side!"

"And what, have our families starve without us?"

" ... risk it anyway! Our caravan has been traveling that pass for generations, without once being caught in an avalanche."

And then, there was no telling who was speaking or what they were saying. Something someone had said seemed to have sparked an outrage, and men were standing and shouting at each other, everyone trying to argue his point. Through it all, the Foxglove men remained silent and watchful.

"There's another way," said Wick. He spoke quietly but, somehow, this hushed the rabbling madness. He was calmly eating his way though the remains of his meal, seated right at the heart of the debate. All eyes turned to Wick, and Fox smiled to himself. "Through the mines, beneath my city."

"And where exactly are you from, boy?" asked one of the older traders, fixing Wick with a mistrusting eye.

"Doff," said Wick proudly. "And I promise you, we can make it easily through the Beneath and get everyone home safely."

Fox watched as a strange array of reactions played over the group's faces. Some of them nodded to each other, clearly convinced that this would be a perfect solution. Others still looked skeptical. But many of them, almost half, went pale. They began to look nervous, or even slightly ill.

"We'll take our chances with the pass," said Ellegar softly. "There is darkness in the Beneath that makes even an avalanche seem like a chance worth taking."

"Why?" asked Terric. "What's the Beneath?"

A flurry of anxious whispers and hisses *shhhhhh*ed through the group. "The deepest mankind has ever traveled," said Wick evenly, and the company hung on his every word as he continued. "It is the very soul of the mountains.

"And we do not speak of it if we can help it," said Ellegar, with an anxious energy that made him hunch his shoulders. It was as though he expected something to spring upon him out of nowhere, and Fox recalled Farran's talk about sea monsters: *There is a rumor among sailors, that simply speaking of these terrors summons them from the very depths of the ocean. From the darkest places.* And he remembered Kaldora's warning as he'd entered the mines, urging him to travel quickly and quietly. Fox himself began to shudder as Ellegar continued, "It is full of a dark and dangerous magic that mankind can never hope to understand."

"But it *is* traversable," argued Wick. "If you walk lightly and don't disturb the darkness, you have nothing to fear. Can you say the same for this avalanche of yours? Or the Desolata?"

A flurry of arguments began to break out again, this time much quieter than before. The afternoon began to wear on, as pros and cons and worries were bandied about. One faction of the group was demanding that they leave now and take their chances with the Beneath. Others argued that there was far too much risk. This second group was the same that began to question where Timic Foxglove had gotten his information in the first place.

Even other trade caravans and merchants began to join in the conversation, overhearing from their own tables and chiming in. Some were scheduled to head up into Sovesta themselves, and worried about the possibility of an avalanche, or else wondered if they could brave the Desolate as a larger group and rely on strength in numbers.

Finally, after more than a half hour of back and forth between the men, a fire merchant called Druacc stood and slammed his hands down on the table. He was a rail-thin man with a close-cut beard, black as coal. Fox knew him well enough from Father's stories: unspoken leadership of the caravan was generally split between the two. Now, he spoke more to Father than anyone else, but all were listening.

"What you're suggesting is that we abandon the cities we have left to visit, and leave *now*, to journey into the heart of danger, is that correct?"

Father stared him down calmly, but it was Wick who answered. "Timing is essential. Once the passes and high snows begin to melt, whole chambers of the mining trails flood. If we don't move quickly, we'll be just as cut off as we would be trying to navigate the Tessoc Pass in Deep Winter."

Druacc glanced sidelong at Wick with sneering contempt on his face, and then continued to speak only to Father. "That's weeks of fine business we're losing. Markets we usually turn beautiful profits in. And all on what, some brat kid's hunch?"

Fox wished more than anything that he could melt into the bench he sat on as every eye turned on him. At his side, Father tensed, but didn't respond. He barely would have had the chance. Almost at once, Druacc continued, "Come on, Timic. We all heard the stories. You told us yourself, at the start of the season. All about how your boy said he was having visions, and tried to stop you coming. Even you admitted he was going buggy."

Father glanced quickly at Fox, with an apology in his eyes that said they'd talk about it later. But even so, Fox found himself inching away from Father on their bench. He took a shaky breath, then stood and turned to look at the men, keeping Father out of his eyesight. Just behind Wick, he could see the familiar, ghostly figure of Farran, always silently watching.

"It's true," Fox said, with more assurance than he felt. "The information is mine, and I am even more sure now than I was before the caravan left, that it *cannot* return the way it came."

"And how are you *sure*?" spoke up one of the other traders, a younger man who had only married into the valley last year. "How do you *know*?"

"The same way I knew when the caravan would be coming home last season, or exactly when it will begin to snow," said Fox. "It's the same part of me that makes my tracking flawless. No doubt my father has told you stories of some of my *better* attributes, not just my tantrums."

At this, many of the traders began to nod in agreement or glance knowingly at Father. They had, indeed, heard about the Foxglove son and his enormous talent. Many who had been looking skeptical before now started to watch Fox as though they might actually believe him. With a surge of confidence, Fox went on.

"Those who have traveled with me know, there's not a storm or a change in the weather I can't feel coming. Call it instinct if you like, but I'm standing here as living proof. *I* found you on the Merchant's Highway. And I'm here to bring you home!"

Once he was finished, Fox wasn't quite sure how to excuse himself from the conversation again. He wanted to sit, but it felt like a weak ending to his speech. So instead, he continued to stand and stare at them all, making many of them squirm in a visible discomfort that echoed his own.

Finally, Druacc spoke once more. "Men," he said evenly, "you have heard both arguments. You may choose to travel home with the Foxgloves, through dangers we have never faced, and lose valuable time earning our families' keep. Or, you may stay behind with me. And I will lead you home by the roads that have never failed us." He took a swig from his drink and then set it down on the table once more — not quite slamming it, but hard enough to make a statement. Then he bowed himself sardonically away from the table, saying, "Do as you will, men. I'll see you at market."

As he left, Father addressed the men once more. "My company leaves at dawn. We meet here as the Nightmarket closes. I hope — I pray that you join me, my friends."

The group began to disperse, many looking wary, all looking thoughtful. Ellegar stayed behind, nursing his own drink and scrutinizing Fox with a closed, unreadable expression on his lined face. Even as the Foxgloves and Wick left, going to pack their things and prepare for departure, Ellegar remained in his seat. Fox could see him every time he passed the window in his room, and there the man sat all through the afternoon.

DAWN CAME PAINFULLY slowly. Fox lay awake all night, restless and completely incapable of sleeping. He tried for a handful of hours, tossing and turning while trying not to wake Wick at the other end of the bed. Outside, he could hear the discordant melody of the Nightmarket. Hawking cries of the vendors mingled with music from a dozen different performers and the drunken songs of just as many taverns.

Eventually, Fox gave up on sleep and pulled out his journal once more. He flipped it open to the glowing, familiar map of Doff, and traced its many lines with his fingertips. He let himself sink into the dream-like state that let his mind wander through the faraway paths as easily as if he were really there.

The little village was aglow with rivers of ore and the clear, almost painfully bright ocean of stars above. A hint of spring was in the air, and a handful of particularly stubborn mountain flowers had begun to creep up here and there. Fox had no destination in mind, he simply meandered through the village like a breeze. He sat like a shadow in the public house and watched drinking contests and card games; he visited the eborils in their stone nests and watched them soar in the moonlight; he sat in the open window of Kaldora's workshop, and listened to her haggle on prices and take orders for specialty candles; he lay outside the entrance to the mines and listened to the rhythmic chiming that accompanied the art of harvesting ore.

It was the hint of dawn bleeding into the mountain light that made Fox flee back into his own body. When he awoke in Florint, it was still fully dark, but he knew morning was just around the corner. He shook Wick awake and the two gathered their things, already packed from the night before, and headed downstairs.

The Nightmarket was beginning to clear. Traders and waresmen and traveling merchants were packing up their wares and heading off for some much-needed rest. Lanterns were doused, and the chimneys in every inn and tavern began to smoke, filled with the scent of early breakfast preparations. And in the dining yard at the Pocket Frog, beneath the still-lit lantern tree, a small company of men had begun to assemble. Many of them hailed from Thicca Valley, but here and there Fox spotted a face that was unfamiliar. They came with their bags and carts and pack animals, and milled about in the pre-dawn.

Fox counted almost twenty men in total, with even more heading their way, and caught Father's eye with a grin. Father returned the smile briefly before returning his attention to the gathered crowd and starting to arrange everyone in ranks to make the travel easier. Then, as last-minute preparations were being made, a group of merchants fresh from the Nightmarket passed them by, and Fox looked up to see Druacc at the head of a sizable party.

They said nothing to each other, but Druacc's sneer said it all — that he was sure they were all fools, and he would be perfectly content not to travel with such people anymore. But Fox's eyes slid past Druacc's and fell on the man some paces behind him. Terric, looking exhausted from trading in the market all night. Fox recalled how eagerly the fire merchant and his young wife had reunited last season, when the caravan finally came home. Steeling himself, Fox stepped forward to address Terric.

"And what should I tell your wife when you don't make it home?" he asked casually.

Terric stared at him, a tired uncertainty in his eyes.

"Ignore the little whelp, Terric," said Druacc, but Fox ignored him and continued to hold Terric's gaze.

"Five suitors fighting for her that year," Fox said, "and she only wanted you. I watched her cry all winter, that first season you were gone. She's a woman lost without you. So, what shall I tell her? That you didn't care enough to come home safely?"

"Stop it!" growled Terric suddenly. "Don't you think I want to go home to her, more than anything?" He rubbed his face vigorously, out of exhaustion or frustration, Fox could not tell. "I want nothing more than to go to her and hold her, and never have to leave her side again! But —" Here, he glanced about nervously and lowered his voice. "The way people speak about the Beneath ... Everyone who knows of it is terrified! How can I — "

"Terric, *I've* been there! A boy! And I survived it!"

"And then there's all the money we'd be losing! We can barely scrape by as it is, without sacrificing weeks worth of markets and ..."

"And think on how hard it'll be for her to survive on her own," said Fox evenly. "The choice is yours, but before you go with Druacc, instruct me what to tell her." He knew he was being cruel, and unfairly playing on Terric's emotions. But Fox had already made enough widows for one lifetime — he was *not* going to let this man's fear add to his ledger.

Behind him, Father's caravan was preparing to leave. Terric seemed torn, glancing uncertainly between Fox and Druacc. Then, finally, he said to Druacc, "I'm sorry, but if there's *any* chance he's right about this ..." And then he grabbed Fox by the shoulders and said, "Make sure they wait for me! Please! I'll run and get my things now and ... just, wait for me!" And then he was gone, running out through the streets to whatever inn he'd found space at.

Druacc raised one dark eyebrow at Fox, something slightly more respectful than a sneer on his face now. "Big words for such a little man," he said smoothly. "And when you've been devoured by the soul of the mountain, what shall I tell your mother then?"

And with that, he was gone. Not long after, Terric came racing back, haversack thrown haphazardly over his shoulders and still lacing his vest as he went. He fell into line with the rest of the caravan, and grinned broadly at Fox. Fox laughed and gave him a companionable wave. Then, he took his own place at the head of the group, with Father and Wick by his sides.

They headed out of Florint, back the way that Fox's group had come mere days before. Dawn was fully upon them as they broke free of the city gates, and the open path lay before them. Here, the group halted for the briefest moment as Fox waited for Father to take the lead. But Father shook his head, and gestured with open arms at the Merchant's Highway. "This journey is yours," he said softly. "Lead on, and we will follow."

And so, with two dozen men trailing behind him, Fox followed the wind: the caravan was going home.

Chapter Twenty-Six
Darkness

"Bartrum stayed with us for quite awhile," said Father. He and Fox were grooming Cobb that evening as the group stopped to make camp. While they worked, Fox had asked about his colorful friend, worried that he hadn't been among the caravan. "But when we arrived at Athilior, it turned out there was an opening at the university. A professor of ... something useless I've already forgotten." He chuckled to himself and began to work a comb through a stubborn set of tangles in Cobb's mane. "So, he said his goodbyes, and I can only assume he's doing well."

Fox sighed and scratched Cobb fondly behind the ears. "I had hoped to see him," he admitted. "Maybe someday, I'll call upon him in Athilior."

"Perhaps next year," suggested Father. "The caravan always pays a visit, it's a thriving trade city."

"I remember the stories," said Fox, and then he fell silent, pretending to be focused on his attentions to the pony. But in actuality, he simply wanted to avoid carrying on that trail of conversation.

In the distance, he thought he could hear the echo of Shavid songs on the wind. But whether they were from Radda's company or the players back in Florint, he could not say. The music spoke of promises, adventure, and a new life. A life that was so close, Fox could almost taste it. A life that he was ashamed to want.

Trapping was a steady business. It was a luxury trade, bringing finer things to the valley than mere firestones and ore. Father had never left his wife and son wanting for the comforts and necessities of life. Without Fox to carry on the family business, what would happen to the valley? Or his family? It was a thought Fox couldn't quite bring himself to dwell on, and so he tried to put it to the back of his mind, as he had been doing for months now. He kept up a steady stream of meaningless conversation with Father, and turned in early. He lay on top of his bedroll, staring up at the cloudless night sky and enjoying the spring breeze. Around him, the air was filled with the light snores of men who had already fallen asleep, the low hum of talk from those who hadn't, and the comfortable shuffling of animals settling in for the night.

It was a good life, being a waresman. A difficult life, perhaps, but rewarding. Fox had grown up wanting nothing more than to join his father on the caravan. And now, surrounded by that very dream, Fox was not so certain. A life on the Merchant's Highway was all very well and good. But a life on *every* highway ... a life with every sea and city and marketplace ...

Fox hummed along quietly to a familiar Shavid tune that he could hear fluttering on the wind, and rolled over onto his stomach, smooshing his makeshift cloak pillow into a more comfortable position beneath him. He didn't have to think about it now. He had a long journey ahead, and for the time being he would simply celebrate the fact that he was bringing his father, and many others, home safely. And he would revel in the joy of his first — and possibly last — caravan.

BETWEEN BOTH OF THE Foxglove men and Wick, the company had little time to rest. Fox led the way with Wick often several lengths behind him in the ranks, and Father brought up the rear. Between the three, they drove the company hard. They ate on the move, and often slept under the stars instead of taking the time to set up a proper camp. The spring rains seemed to have finally cleared away, and the weather was fair and peaceful, making tents thankfully unnecessary. But even with the pace, the company was a lively group. They filled the air with raucous songs and bawdy jokes. Every market they passed should have been a reminder of the trade they were losing, but instead the men seemed to see each missed bazaar as one less barrier between themselves and home.

Fox was often alone at the head of the group, with the nearest rank of men several dozen paces behind him. But the wind was his constant companion, fetching him smells and snatches of conversation like a pup with a stick. He could hear the men talking about everything from reuniting with their wives and wagering on the genders of children that had been born while they were away, to arguments about which marketplaces deserved to be skipped next year.

And, far more often than he would have liked, Fox overheard talk about himself. Whispers about just how the Foxglove boy knew what he did, and how he'd always seemed a bit strange. The men began to watch him more closely at every turn; Fox could feel their eyes on him, and it reminded him all too much of how everyone in Thicca Valley had watched him after the attack of the Desolata.

Most of these whispers, he quickly realized, were started by Ellegar. The usually jovial old trader was rather pensive and quiet these days, murmuring questions to the other men about Fox's strange instincts. The words "not natural" and "cursed" were often carried to Fox on the wind. He could see Ellegar and his small band of followers each evening, watching him from within their glowing pool of firelight. And even though he began settling himself at the farthest end of the camp from them, he could still hear the rumblings, lulling him to sleep like an unsettling cradlesong.

And every night, he dreamed. They were memories that were not his own, brief scenes of life on the high seas. They were not as lengthy or as detailed as they had been when Farran had been at the helm of his mind, but they were unquestionably the pirate god's. Fox found himself wandering the decks and rigging of the Laila every night, watching like a forgotten ghost as the ship took prizes and the pirates went about their daily lives. He woke from these dreams just before dawn each morning, regular as milking the goats, and continued to actively ignore the shadow of Farran.

His regular morning combat practice with Wick helped to clear his head somewhat, where they were often joined by whichever members of the caravan happened to be awake and interested. It helped Fox to focus his mind, and push the dreams away. It was also easier, he realized, to control his shivers when he was disciplining his body. He pushed himself harder each day, wishing for new techniques and challenging the men to wrestling matches. And as he improved, he thought of Neil, and how many things his friend could still teach him.

And the caravan continued to ramble along the Merchant's Highway, back up into the foothills, until the Highborns stretched into the sky above them like stone teeth, casting a shadow over their feet and their hearts. On the other side was home. But between them and Thicca Valley, an unknown peril lurked. And for Fox, another peril altogether lay just beyond that. No force in all of the Beneath could possibly be as terrifying as Kaldora Flintstock.

THEY WERE CAMPED JUST outside the mouth of a large cavern. It was still only late afternoon, but Wick decided the company needed rest before descending into the mountain. Cooking fires were lit, and tents pitched in a quiet echo of the caravan's usual joviality. The shadow of the mountain seemed to make the men nervous, and they spoke in hushed rumbles and whispers, rather than their usual songs and bellows.

As night sank in around them, supper was eaten quietly, and tools and weapons were drawn. The men sat in small groups around their fires, sharpening blades and counting the arrows in their quivers. Every sound seemed to be swallowed by the yawning cave mouth at their back, so that the scraping of whetstones and twang of bowstrings seemed more like the ghosts of sounds, indistinct and unfinished.

Fox and Wick sat alone at the fire closest to the cavern maw. Wick was slowly turning two fat brush rabbits on a spit, a focused expression of thoughtfulness written in the shadows on his face. Fox sat nearby, meticulously polishing the black shafts and carved stone feathers of his arrows. His knives were laid out on a flat stone by his side, awaiting the same treatment.

"We're going to be alright," said Fox quietly to Wick. He said it as a statement, rather than a question, because he had to believe it was true. "We made it through last time just fine. We'll walk quietly, and get through just as well as before."

Wick didn't answer immediately. He tossed another log on their fire, watching as fresh sparks licked the roasting meat. Then he said, carefully, "Our road was easy, before. We traveled only by foot, not wagon or pack animal." He looked out at the assembled caravan, and Fox followed his gaze.

"There is another path. A deeper one, where the light of the ore and lymnstone disappears. It is the only road that will accommodate so many."

There was something in Wick's voice that made him look away from the gathered men. Slowly, tremulously, Fox said, "You don't think we're going to make it."

"It is a quicker path," said Wick, rather than answering directly. "It carves about a day and a half out of our journey."

"But there's a reason we didn't take it, last time," Fox concluded.

A nod from Wick, and Fox knew there would be no more talk about it. After all, sailors didn't speak of their worst monsters.

Fox did not sleep that night. He lay awake, listening to the mountain. He heard tiny rivulets of water, trickling down and into the thick layers of moss and lichen that grew up where the foothills finally met the stone. He heard the dry scrape of wind-tossed leaves against the unrelenting mountainside as the breeze plucked them from nearby trees and scattered them against the rock face. And then, in a much deeper place in his own mind, Fox could hear a sound that could only be described as a heartbeat. It was in the same ancient, wise voice in which Fox had heard the neighboring mountains scream out in pain at the coming avalanche. It was a heartbeat that echoed every step of every traveler to cross its paths, and the vibrato of every axe that had ever struck its ore.

Fox drank in every sound like it was water in the desert. For, come the dawn, they would step within the mountain, and he would be deaf to the wind. And, because he was listening so closely, he knew he was not the only one lying awake.

Dawn found the entire company already alert, packed, and lined up in rank. No one spoke. Even the animals seemed to know to keep quiet. All eyes were on Fox, who stood at the head of the group with Wick by his side. With the simplest gesture of his hand, the company surged forward as one. The creaks of wooden wheels and leather boots on stone were the only sound, and there was nothing menacing in that. Still, Fox was not the only man who had one hand on his weapon.

Wick took the lead, and Fox followed close at his heels, once again plagued by the sickening feeling of missing his senses. Behind him, many of the traders were awed by the shimmering beauty of the lymnstone veins that ran through the stone all about them. Fox could see the wonder in their faces, even from those who had been down into the Thicca Valley mines before. After some hours, the men began to relax, and even seemed to be quietly enjoying themselves. But then their path turned, down a different road than Fox and his small group had traveled before. They wound down and down, past the skeletal remains of abandoned mines and beneath the hanging chandeliers of ancient pulleys and machinery. With every footstep, the glowing, shimmering orelights seemed to grow dimmer until, finally, there was nothing but darkness.

"We camp here," said Wick in barely a whisper, but everyone heard him all the same. "No lanterns, no lights. Not even lymnstones. We will rest for half a turn only, so make the time count. But do it in silence, and without light."

There were hints of disgruntled mumblings as the men began to settle in as quietly as possible, feeling around to get their bearings. An occasional curse escaped the silence as someone stepped on someone else's foot, or else ran into a stone pillar. Fox settled down where he stood, as did Wick. Neither of them bothered to try and find food, or bedding, they simply sat.

"The darkness should last for three more turns, after this," said Wick, again just loudly enough to be heard, although this time only by Fox.

"*Should* last?" asked Fox, just as softly. "Don't you know?"

Something that might have almost been a muffled laugh came from the spot Fox imagined Wick must be sitting. "It should," repeated Wick. "And if the light comes any sooner? We run."

ONE TURN PASSED PAINFULLY slowly. The company stumbled along their way in the dark, traveling with hands pressed against the cold stone wall. They traveled as best they could while trying not to make a sound, but every so often there was a shuffling or a whispered "Ouch!" as the men collided with each other or the stone. They moved slowly upward, the path an easy but constant incline beneath their feet.

It was a darkness that was more than a simple lack of light. It was darker than Fox had ever experienced, even in the tightest grips of the deepest winter nights. It was a darkness that did not lend itself to the possibility of light, ever again. It swallowed up sound in a way that mere stone simply should not. And, to a young man who had grown up his entire life in the mountains, it felt *wrong*.

All that existed, it seemed, was the ground beneath their feet. At times, Fox was sure he was walking alone, and that the rest of the company had disappeared into the black. But then someone would cough, or he would brush up against Wick's arm, and he would relax, if only for a moment.

The first turn ended. He heard Wick whisper the time, counting down until they were free of the darkness. Halfway through the second turn, Fox found it was growing harder to breathe. He began to sweat and shake, gripped with a discomfort he could not explain. He felt as though something was crawling over his skin, but when he went to slap it away, he found nothing there.

And he was not the only one. He could hear the men and animals beginning to grow restless, and a quiet hum of grumbled conversation began to grow. Goats and ponies snorted anxiously, and men cursed at the darkness, muttering about evil spirits and whispering their longing to stop and rest. Wick kept hissing at them to be quiet, and the silence would descend again for a brief moment. But then, they would inevitably begin to chatter quietly again, sounding for all the world like a small hoard of irritated snowflakes.

The second turn was dwindling down into mere minutes when Wick called them to a halt, hissing a warning. Silence fell once more, complete and unmoving. Fox could feel Wick at his side, tension radiating from every muscle. He tried to ask what was wrong, but before the words could find their way to his mouth, he knew.

There was light, dimpling the darkness far below. Just a small glimmer, like a lonely star lost in an empty sky. But the glow was enough, and they could see the grey shadows of their surroundings now. They stood on the edge of a great chasm that stretched at least half a league across. The space between the wall they had been traveling along and the jagged edge of their path was a mere five feet wide. Several of the men pressed themselves closer to the wall, suddenly much more afraid of the drop than they had been when they couldn't see it. But Wick and Fox, along with a handful of others, edged closer to the drop, leaning over to look down into the black depths of the mountain's heart.

"What is it?" whispered Fox.

For a moment, the single light twinkled almost cheerfully. It might have been miles below them, or maybe it was only a handful of inches. They watched it, some men with their hands on their weapons, others merely curious. And then, another light winked into existence. Then three more. A dozen. A whole fleet of infinitesimal, jewel-bright shimmers was swimming below them, and it was as if the whole night sky had been flipped on its head and trapped deep within the mountain.

"Move," said Wick, low and insistently

"But what —" started Fox.

"Move!" shouted Wick. The pinpoints seemed to be growing larger, or perhaps just drawing nearer. Wick drew his sword as he led the group forward, up their winding path in a steady and urgent march that was not quite a run. As they went, Fox had just enough time to realize that the little sparks were not the silvery-white of stars; they were *blue!*

Their path twisted upward and began to widen. The glow grew brighter, and they could hear a sound, like the rustling of dry leaves being tumbled in the wind. Something was moving upward, through the bowels of the mountain toward their group.

"Keep moving!" shouted Wick, no longer seeming to worry about silence. And then, something burst from the chasm, straight into the air. Many of the men, Fox included, stopped and held their weapons ready, prepared to fight. But they were not attacked. It wasn't one something, it was a thousand little somethings. Were they birds? Or bats? Fox couldn't tell, they were moving so quickly and there were so many of them. But they *glowed!* It was as though blue lymnstone ran through their veins and in their feathery wings and tails.

They surged upward, shrieking at each other or at the caravan in tiny, high-pitched voices. They filled the caverns with a luminescent blue light, illuminating every shadow, every stone. Here, there were no scars in the rock from generations of miners. No abandoned machinery or rickety scaffolding. There was nothing but unnervingly smooth stone, and the black chasm erupting with tiny creatures of light.

They could barely hear Wick shouting at them to keep moving, so loud was the sound of wings and inhuman shrieks. But the men surged forward once more, fighting to keep their pack animals moving forward. Fox could see Father at the end of the ranks, trying to wrestle a panicked and rearing Cobb back onto all fours. Fox pushed his way back down the path, hurrying to the pony's side and holding tight to his harness. Not only was Cobb a danger to himself, but the small wagon he pulled was rocking perilously close to the edge. If it got much closer, there was a decent chance that Cobb would drag himself, as well as both of the Foxglove men, down into the depths with it.

"Get back up there!" yelled Father. Far above, the rest of the company seemed to have stopped on a plateau, weapons drawn. Wick was shouting something, but the Foxglove men couldn't hear it.

Panting with the effort of grappling with Cobb, Fox called back, "You first!"

Even in the midst of all the mayhem, Father smiled and laughed heartily, every inch of him dripping with a pride that Fox knew was aimed at him. Together, the two managed to get Cobb's front hooves back on solid stone, and they began to hurry him up the path to where the others waited.

The light was beginning to fade. Fox glanced over at the wall of bird-things, and noticed their numbers were thinning out. High above, they seemed to be disappearing. He could only assume they had found a tunnel to vanish into, or another cavern, or even a path into the open air. The darkness began to fall once more, and Father and Fox slowed, hesitant to run when they couldn't see where they were going. Silence wrapped around them again, swallowing up even the echoes of the flying creatures as the last few disappeared from sight. Fox could feel himself panting, feel his heart beating a warning so strongly it made his ribs vibrate, but he could not hear it.

For the longest moment of Fox's life, they stood rooted to the spot, still as the stone itself. And then, a rumbling began, deep within the black pit. Mere seconds later, the cavern was filled with light once more as something, one glowing, *enormous* something, came tearing up the far wall across the chasm.

Fox had an arrow on his bow before he even had a chance to think. At his side, Father was scrambling to pull a heavy hunting knife from his belt, one hand still wrapped around Cobb's harness. Fox could see them out of the side of his vision, but his eyes were trained on the thing that had just appeared. He watched it as a hunter, down the shaft of one perfect black arrow.

It was a beast like nothing Fox had ever seen, read about, or dreamed of. It was nightmare itself, come to life and clinging to the opposite wall with claws the size of pickaxes. Whether it was darkness held together by glowing veins of lymnstone, or lymnstone light held captive by darkness, Fox couldn't tell. Something about it was reminiscent of an immense mountain cat, or at least the skeleton of one. But it was carved of black stone, or else the very blackness of the Beneath itself, and there were parts that didn't belong. Massive wings of a glowing blue membrane that ran the length of its front legs, so batlike that Fox wasn't surprised that the creature's ears appeared to be borrowed from the flying rodents as well. There was a tail that was long and thin like a whip. And a face, inspecting its prey across the chasm, that was sickeningly human.

It was stretched and hollow-cheeked, and the nose was wider and longer than any man's nose Fox had ever seen. But its eyes, echoing the empty darkness of the Beneath, remained unaltered. Perfect, human eyes in a monster's body. Fox swallowed back something that might have been fear, or illness. To see the Desolata, disfigured and mutated as they were, was horrible enough. But to see human parts and expressions on a creature never meant to walk on two legs, that was an entirely different sort of *wrongness*.

High above, Fox could hear Wick shouting something to the men, but he couldn't quite make out what it was. Between the pounding of his own blood in his ears and the angry shrieks of the glowing beast, all other sounds were merely distant echoes. And then, the creature's gaze shifted down to where Father and Fox stood, and time seemed to hold its breath like the woods after a blizzard.

Whether the creature decided that he and Father were the weak members of the heard, or if something intrinsically magical drew it to Fox, he didn't know. But before he had a moment to think about it, the creature *pounced.*

It was instinct that drove Fox to dive toward Father. Not instinct as a son, running to a

parent for safety, but the instinct to *protect*. He had come so far to find the caravan, he was not returning home to Mother without her husband by his side. Before Father could react, or argue, Fox heaved with all his might and toppled Father backwards into the cart. Then he slapped Cobb on the rump with the shaft of his arrow, driving the pony forward in a frenzied race up the path.

And then he turned, just in time to duck as one of the creature's massive claws swiped at him. The creature crashed into the wall behind Fox, giving Fox a moment to scramble away and pull himself up again, arming himself once more with an arrow poised to shoot. The beast propelled itself back and flew several feet away, hovering as best it could over the chasm. Fox didn't waste a moment, he simply fired. One perfect arrow soared straight through the beast's left wing, punching a hole in the glowing membrane and making the creature cry out. It was a cry that sounded unnervingly like a woman's sob.

And then, the wound sealed itself. It clouded over with blue lymnstone dust and the creature was whole once more. It hissed and dove again, and Fox ran. He ran up the path, sure to stay close to the wall. The creature was so huge, Fox guessed it would have trouble grabbing him from the air without crashing into the stone again. Sure enough, twice the beast charged at him, clawing at the stone fruitlessly before finally it grasped tightly to the stone wall and looked down on Fox, every inch the frustrated predator. The bear desperately trying to pluck a rabbit from too small of a hole. And, feeling emboldened by the beast's distress, Fox began to run faster.

He had forgotten about the tail. It whipped around from behind and caught him about the ankles, bringing Fox crashing to his knees and sending his bow skittering away on the stone, toward the edge of the chasm. Fox tried to scramble for it, only to feel the tail pulling him back down the path, while Fox clawed helplessly at the smooth stone beneath him and at the wall rushing by.

And then, just as abruptly, the creature let go. Fox didn't hesitate a moment, didn't stop to wonder what had happened or look around for where it had gone. He half-crawled, half-ran to his bow, rescuing it from where it lay, mere inches from the irretrievable depths. He scooped it up and turned to face the beast once more, fumbling for an arrow. As he watched, it suddenly became clear what had drawn the beast's attention.

A hailstorm of arrows, spears, and even a handful of pots and pans came raining down on the beast from above, where the rest of the company stood. The beast roared in anger, a jumbled combination of men's screams issuing from its grotesque human face. It began to claw its way up the stone face toward them, more catlike than ever in its advances. Fox sent his arrow soaring to bury itself deep in the creature's spine, desperate to draw its attention once more. He knew it was foolhardy, but somehow he thought that even alone he stood a better chance than the caravan above. They were on an open plateau, and all the beast had to do was reach them and they would be easy prey. But Fox, one small target tucked on a winding ledge, might prove harder to deal with.

The arrow hit home flawlessly, making the beast hiss and fumble in its journey. Steeling himself, Fox ran forward and grabbed hold of the whiplike tail. As the creature surged upward once more, Fox ripped one of his knives from its home in his vest and drove it straight through the black, lymnstone-laced tail, pinning the creature to the very stone. And then he scurried out of the way once more as the creature came crashing back onto the path, anchored unexpectedly.

As the creature struggled to regain its balance, Fox noticed something; not all of the beast's injuries healed themselves. The places that were not lymnlight, but the strange black that might have been the Beneath itself, seemed to *crack* somehow when they were hit. And, somehow, they seemed less empty. Almost vulnerable.

The rest of the caravan was beginning to surge down the path once more. They were still a ways away, but Fox could hear them approaching. If only he could hold the beast off until help arrived ...

The beast had other plans. It tore itself free of Fox's knife and leapt from the path into the chasm, flapping its enormous wings and shedding blue lymnstone dust as it went. And then it doubled back, diving at him like a hawk about to seize a particularly fat and juicy mouse. In less than a heartbeat Fox had another arrow to the string, but it wasn't quick enough. The creature bore down upon him, claws outstretched, and Fox braced himself.

There was a sound like thunder rattling a forest of icicles as the creature slammed into something right in front of Fox. Something pearlescent and almost invisible. Something that looked like a man, with his arms crossed high over his head. Farran turned his head to meet Fox's eyes, strain and agony carved even in the ghostly hints of his face.

The unspoken message was clear. Fox didn't waste another moment, but raised his bow once more and fired a single, perfect shot. His arrow buried itself right where he imagined the creature's heart would be. There was the briefest moment of calm as the creature's shrieks were abruptly cut off. And then, from the place where the arrow sprouted, a thousand razor-thin cracks started to spiderweb away from the wound. It was like watching ice begin to shatter, and Fox instinctively took several steps back, hitting the cold stone wall with enough force to knock his own wind out.

But the creature didn't burst. It hung in midair, face stretched in a grotesque exaggeration of a human scream. From the jagged cracks, and especially around Fox's arrow, clouds of thin, lymnstone-blue light began to escape from the creature's skeleton, like tiny geysers of steam breaking through a frozen tundra. They floated out and drifted away, ghostly petals on an intangible wind, before fading into darkness. With each one, Fox could hear something that sounded like a long-past sigh of relief, or exhaustion, or sorrow. And he knew, without any explanation but *certain* that he was right, that whatever the diaphanous smoke things were, they were *free*.

In the glow of the creature's final moments, Fox could see Farran's spectral shadow collapse onto its knees, and then fade away into nothingness. Fox tried to cry out to it, but he couldn't find the words. Instead, he watched in silence as the beast of the Beneath finally vanished, leaving the heart of the mountain dark once more.

WICK ALLOWED THEM TO light torches for the remainder of their trek through the Beneath. In the flickering firelight from half a dozen pillars of flame, the stone walls looked unexpectedly plain and harmless.

They made camp for what Wick assured them would be the last time within the mountain. Everyone crowded around one brilliant bonfire, rather than a scattering of smaller ones. And everyone, it seemed, wanted to talk to Fox. Wanted to know what he'd done, how he'd fought it off, and what magic he'd been using to shield himself. And Fox telling them all that he hadn't done anything was nothing more than a waste of breath. None of them had seen Farran. Not even Wick. And so, in their eyes, Fox was a hero.

In the remaining journey to Doff, half a day's march, not one ill word was spoken of him. And while Fox was grateful for the pleasant turn of the men's attitudes, his mind was elsewhere. It was ahead, on the reunion with Kaldora Flintstock that was drawing ever nearer. And it was behind, where the shadow of Farran had disappeared.

Chapter Twenty-Seven
Reunion

The open air felt like the first breath of spring, refreshing and far too long in coming. All of the men were eager to break free of the mountain's heart, but none were so happy as Fox. He stood just outside the mine's entrance and simply breathed, soaking in every smell and sound, no matter how common. The wind welcomed him back like an old friend, rustling his hair and tugging at his clothes and bags.

But his moment of relief was short-lived. As the caravan wound its way down the mountain path, everyone intent on a proper meal at the public house, Fox was seized by an overwhelming urge to dart back into the Beneath and simply live there. He could smell *her*, tucked in her workshop several levels below. And as the men found their way into the low stone dining room and began to fight over bread and shout orders to the barkeep, Wick and Fox hung back.

"It wasn't your fault," said Wick quietly.

"I'm not so sure she'll see it that way," Fox replied.

"I can speak to her alone," offered Wick. "She's my sister, after all." Here, he attempted a shaky grin. "She can't stay mad at me forever, and she would miss me far too much if she killed me."

But Fox couldn't be moved to smile. "It's my responsibility," he said. "Topper was — " He swallowed a painful lump in his throat and tried again. "It's my fault he came. I may not have slain him, but I'm the reason he was in the Nightmarket."

Side-by-side, they trudged down the path, a growing dread in every step. Fox's brain went into a frenzy, frothing like an overboiled pot of soup, bubbling with excuses and apologies and pleas for forgiveness. But as they approached Kaldora's workshop and the woman herself came rushing out to meet them, every word of it was wiped from his mind.

"Where is he?" she asked at once. Kaldora was pale with fury. Suddenly, Fox's instinct to run and hide didn't seem quite so childish. But then, as he looked closer at Topper's mother, he saw something else tucked behind her rage. A warm, loving worry. It frightened Fox even more than the anger.

"What nerve, to run off without even a note!" continued Kaldora. "I had to hear about it from one of the miners who saw him sneak after you!" She was wringing her hands anxiously, as though she couldn't decide if she wanted to strangle or embrace her son. "So, where is the little scamp? Tell me you haven't let him go see the birds, he's to report right back here at once so I can flay him alive!"

Something in their faces seemed to make Kaldora pause. Her expression softened, and she looked at Wick with a hint of pleading in her eyes. "Where is my boy?" she asked, much quieter than before.

Something unspoken passed between brother and sister. And then, Kaldora began to shrink like a melting icicle. She seemed to crumble in on herself, and it appeared to be only a lifetime of stubbornness and the strength of leadership that kept her from simply dissolving into a puddle of tears. Wick reached out to hold her, but she slapped his hand away, eyes wide but somehow unseeing. Her brother opened his mouth, perhaps to say something comforting. But before he could speak, Fox cracked.

"It's my fault!" he squeaked, his voice breaking. "He stepped in front of a knife meant for me!" He did not cry, but he hovered right on the edge. He forced himself to look Kaldora in the eyes as he continued. "He saved my life, and I owe him a debt that I can never repay."

Kaldora did not respond at once. She stared at Fox as though she didn't quite see him. Or, rather, as though she didn't *want* to see him. And then, in an empty and strangely childlike voice, she said, "I trust you can find your way out of Doff on your own, yes? Very good. I trust you and your men will be gone in the morning. They are welcome here at any time." And then, a single tear broke past the wall she had dammed it behind. It trickled down her cheek and settled in the corner of her mouth as she said, "But the honored village of Doff is closed to you, Forric Foxglove." And without another word, Kaldora let herself collapse into her brother's arms.

As Wick led Kaldora inside, Fox turned abruptly on his heel and strode purposefully back up the mountain, all the way to the top, where he sat pressed into a stone crevice among the eboril nests. But even all the way up here, watching the dark birds soar overhead, Fox could still hear the piteous moaning of a funeral song, sung by Topper's family.

For the first time since Topper's death, Fox desperately wished that Farran were by his side. For comfort, or friendship. Or even for answers. Fox glanced around the mountaintop mews, hoping for the familiar flicker that meant Farran was watching over him. But there was nothing. And Fox closed his eyes, head throbbing with exhaustion and the pain of being attacked by an enormous monster. He wanted to fall asleep for about a month, and wake up when life made sense again.

THEY LEFT DOFF BEHIND as the late afternoon sun painted the sky a brilliant orange. The men were well-fed, and eager to see their wives and families. Fox took the lead once more, assuring the men that they were less than two days from home. Hearts were light all around, and the men continued to treat Fox like the conquering hero of legends past. They began to write a charming little song about his defeat of the "Underbeast," as they had dubbed the creature Fox had fought in the Beneath. And Fox, while he disliked the fact that he was the champion of the piece, found it very catchy. He even caught himself humming it as he walked, much to the amusement of the men. That night as they made camp, Fox even contributed a verse, singing about how he'd been dragged by the beast's tail, like a floundering fish on a hook.

The caravan sang and talked and played dice late into the night, excitement and expectations running high. Apart from the primal eagerness to be reunited with their mates, the men were also anxious to find out if anyone knew the fate of the other caravan yet. Thicca Valley might have gotten a message from them by now, or else heard if something had happened on the mountain trail. But, as far as Fox could tell anyway, the company that had chosen to travel with Fire Merchant Druacc had not yet reached the Tessoc Pass. They might still be safe, for the moment. Even so, he tried not to dwell on them. He avoided reaching out on the wind for their group, dreading the possibility that one day he might hear them perish.

And then, dawn broke over their camp. It was as clear a signal as if someone had hammered on a gong. It told the men that it was time to go home. Those who had slept at all were awake and packing within moments, and those who hadn't bothered with sleep cobbled together a hasty breakfast for everyone else. The group was on its feet and marching into the first light before many of them even had a chance to finish their food. But they ate as they walked, and threw the scraps to those birds and rodents who hunted in the early hours of the morning.

Fox was no longer alone at the head of the caravan. He was constantly escorted by two or more men, all eager to talk to him and ask him about the strange powers he had and the amazing talents that had helped him defeat the Underbeast. And while this was a marked improvement from the days when Ellegar and his companions would whisper rumors about him, there was a part of Fox that simply wished for solitude. His insides were churning with the anticipation of his return to the valley. And, he stumbled upon the realization as they walked, about seeing Lai again.

He had not thought about her since he set out from Whitethorn; it had simply been too painful. Had she forgiven him? Was she even still his friend? Had she told Borric that she knew the truth? So many questions weighed on his mind and heart, even heavier than the worries about the other caravan.

Morning stretched into afternoon, and the sounds and smells of home lay thick in the air. Woodsmoke and goats and rosemary bread. Fox could hear the familiar sounds of the pre-Homecoming preparations. The whip and snap of the colorful banners on the breeze. The pounding of wood on packed earth as the wrestling pen was erected in anticipation of the Courter's Contests. He could hear rugs, beaten with broomsticks, and rooftops being repaired. Every mundane sound and scent flitted to Fox on the spring zephyrs, and he suddenly realized how very much he missed home.

Explosions of song accompanied them for the last league of their journey. No one seemed to be able to decide on one song at a time, and as a result there were often small vocal battles raging on within the caravan, each man or group trying to sing his tune the loudest. And then, they rounded a curve, and there was Thicca Valley, nestled below them like a single egg in a nest of mountain and forest and field.

Someone far below saw them coming and began to sound a cry. By the time they descended onto even ground, the whole valley was out in the streets and screaming their welcomes. Wives rushed to their husbands before they'd even stopped moving. Children clambered into their fathers' arms, and Ellegar's many grandchildren began to climb all over him like he was an old but loving tree.

Fox hung back. He knew Mother always waited at the house, preferring to welcome Father home in private. And so, Fox enjoyed watching the passionate embraces and friendly reunions from afar. *He* had brought them home. *He,* Forric Foxglove, had created this joy.

And then, something registered in Fox's brain. He looked closer at the faces of those hugging their loved ones. There was more than simple rejoicing in their expressions and attitudes; there was an almost painful relief. His eyes swept the crowds who still remained in the streets, those who hadn't rushed forward at the sight of their men. Here, there were mournful and tear-streaked faces. Faces that still turned upward to the mountain path, as though waiting for something. Something, or someone, that would never return.

It was in a disconnected daze that Fox began to shuffle his way through the crowd. He would find Borric. Or Picck, or even Moss. Someone who could tell him what had happened. Someone who could confirm Fox's fears. But before he got very far, Fox felt someone grab his arm and pull him into a tight embrace.

"Thank you," whispered a tearful female voice. A mess of curly blonde hair obscured his vision, but when the woman pulled back, Fox recognized her at once as Fire Merchant Terric's wife. "When we heard," she said, "I was *sure* Terric would be dead. But he says you saved him. *You* made him go another way, and oh Fox I can't tell you how —" She dissolved into tears once more and threw her arms tight about Fox's neck, nearly cutting off his air. Behind her, Terric grinned and wiped away a stray tear of his own. And then, he began to tell another man's wife the story of how young Forric Foxglove had saved them all. And more of the men began to spread the tale to their wives and children and friends. Fox could hear the conversation buzzing all around him, but it was nothing more than a dull cascade of words to him. He let Terric's wife hold him in a tight embrace, all the while searching the crowd for Father.

He found him, saying hello to a few miner friends of his several yards away. They seemed deep in conversation, and after a moment Father looked up to meet his son's eyes. An unspoken question passed between them. And, with a drawn and agonized look, Father shook his head. There had been no survivors.

Fox couldn't breathe. He finally managed to peel himself free of Terric's wife, only to be hugged and kissed by one of Ellegar's older granddaughters. She, too, had heard his story it seemed. Fox disentangled himself from this young woman as well, and had barely made it three more steps when he was set upon by no fewer than a dozen valley folk, men and women alike. People were thanking him and begging for him to tell his story. He was caught in a hailstorm of well-wishes and hugs and kisses on both cheeks. His head was spinning with the closeness of his admirers and the visions of Druacc and his caravan being buried in the avalanche.

There was a familiar and comforting scent, and a set of fingers wrapped themselves through his. Lai began to pull him free of the knot of people, saying they would see him at the Homecoming, and to let the poor boy get some rest! Then she led him out of the crowd, dragging him several lengths out of earshot before she finally dropped his hand and wheeled around to face him.

"Go and see your mother," she said fiercely.

Fox was taken aback. He had expected a fight, or even a relieved welcome. A slap in the face wouldn't have even been unexpected, but ... "Mother? Wha — "

"Everybody thought you were dead, Fox!" Lai said urgently. "We got the news two days ago about the avalanche, and she's not here to see you've arrived! She's been holed up in that house ever since! She probably still thinks —"

But Fox wasn't listening. He tore across the valley, running faster than he'd ever run in his life. Faster than he had when he and Topper had run from the Ryegout, and faster even than his mad dash away from the Underbeast. He burst through the cabin door completely out of breath, his chest on fire, and summoned just enough energy to shout, "Mum!"

There was no answer. Stumbling over his own feet, Fox rushed upstairs and charged through the closed bedroom door with enough force to knock it completely free of its hinges. She was lying in a huddled heap on the floor, just beside the fireplace. She didn't move.

Fox ran to her side and collapsed onto his knees, grasping her shoulder in terror. "Mother!" he cried. Her eyes were closed and her face was paler than the purest snow. Gently, tenderly, Fox smoothed a wisp of hair from her face and said, tremulously, "Mother?"

Her eyelids flickered open, slowly, as though they were too heavy for her to manage. She looked up into his face, but it was as though she hadn't truly seen it. She blinked. Twice. And then, it was as though life had surged back into her. In one swift motion she pulled herself from the floor and wrapped her arms around her son's neck, squeezing him even tighter than Terric's wife.

And then, true to form, Mother pulled away and slapped him hard across the face. "How could you?" she shouted. "Letting me think you were dead! Running off like that with no warning, no — " But Fox hugged her again, grinning with relief. She might have made herself sick with worry and misery, but it was nothing so terrible that she couldn't scold him. And that meant she would be just fine.

When Father came rushing into the room moments later, Fox traded places with him, letting Mother wrap her arms around her husband's neck. She took turns hitting him about the face and shoulders and weeping openly into the collar of his shirt. But when she kissed him, it was with a tenderness that told Fox, more than any words ever could, how happy she was to see him. Quietly, Fox backed his way out of the room and left them to say their hellos in private.

He began to head back to the heart of the valley, where the Homecoming would soon be underway. His parents would be occupied for longer than usual this year, he imagined. And besides, Fox had his own reunions to take care of.

LAI WAS WAITING FOR him by the river. She sat on a tangle of exposed roots from an old and weathered oak, her bare feet dangling just over the water's surface. The tree was perched on a scrap of mossy ground that dropped sharply into the riverbank, and its roots twisted and rambled down into the water itself and across the face of the river-worn earth. As young children, Fox and Lai had treated this tree and its labyrinthine fortress of roots as their personal play kingdom. It was their castle, or their pirate ship. Their jungle war zone, their dragon's nest, and even a haunted barrow.

But now, as they sat side-by-side on the cusp of adulthood, it was just a tree. Mementos from their childhood could sometimes be found hung in high tree branches or stuck between the gnarled roots, the tree itself having grown around them. For quite some time, they sat in silence, watching the river below their toes as it teemed with life. Schools of fish darted here and there, tiny scales catching the sunlight as it filtered through the thin spring foliage. Turtles emerged from the mud every so often to lazily float about, or sun themselves on the bank.

Fox had made so many apologies in the past few weeks that it was starting to become second nature to him by now. But as he opened his mouth to try and apologize to Lai, he found he couldn't. Different words than he'd meant to say came out instead. "The Shavid return at dawn."

Lai didn't respond immediately. She absently twisted a piece of bark free of the roots and dropped it into the river, where it floated away like a tiny brown ship. "Will you go with them?" she said finally. "If they ask?"

"I have to," Fox answered simply.

"You don't," argued Lai, and she finally turned to face him. "Things will be different for you here. It's not like before, when people were watching you after the Desolata attack. Now, you're a hero! Women in town are already talking about offering you matches with their daughters. Everyone from the caravan owes you his life."

"Exactly," said Fox firmly. And then he smiled. "You always were the better storyteller, but I think it's my turn now."

He started from the moment she had left him in Whitethorn, and he told her everything. His return to Doff and the first journey through the Beneath. How Farran had disguised himself as The Incomparable Donovan. He told her of the Merchant's Highway, and tried to explain what cows were. On and on he talked as the Homecoming began far off in the distance, and music filtered through the air.

When he reached the part of his story including the Nightmarket, and the murder of Topper, Lai silently took his hand in hers. And when he told her of the dreams he had of Farran's life, and his meeting of Adella, Lai's whole face glowed with an eager hunger that even she seemed ashamed of. When he finally stopped, his throat raw and scratchy, it was dusk. He could hear the wolves waiting, just out of sight.

Lai had asked no questions as he spoke. She had simply listened to his story like a fascinated child might listen to a bedtime tale. Now, however, she asked far too casually, "What is he like? My f ... your friend, Farran?"

"Lot like you," said Fox honestly. "Clever and charming. Stubborn to a fault." And then, because he thought he saw a familiar flicker out of the corner of his eye, he said, "Would you like to meet him?"

More emotions seemed to dart across Lai's face that instant than there were fish in the river. But finally, she said softly, "Maybe someday."

When Fox looked for the flicker once more, it was gone. Perhaps he had simply imagined it. He put it out of his mind and began to speak again. "He said Topper owed me his soul."

"What does that mean?" asked Lai.

"I've been wondering myself," admitted Fox. And Farran hasn't — I haven't had the chance to ask yet." And then, he tried to put into words something that had been working to put itself together in his mind. "I think there's something in the magic that ... sort of *tied* Topper to me after I saved him."

"And now you've saved half the valley," finished Lai. "And you're afraid."

"Wouldn't you be?" asked Fox, with a humorless laugh escaping into his words. "What if everybody who I've ever saved owes me their soul?" The image of Topper bleeding thick, black ink onto the alley floor was still fresh in his mind. It was an experience he never wanted to repeat.

Lai met his gaze unflinchingly, searching his face, though for what Fox didn't know. Then, she said quietly, "You have to leave."

"I *have* to leave," repeated Fox.

And then, she stood and balanced herself carefully on the tree roots, then pulled Fox to his feet. She grinned impishly, though there was something deeply sad hiding behind her smile. But she began to scamper back up the path of roots and onto the moss, just as they had when they were little, shouting behind her, "Come on, then! Your adoring public awaits!"

Fox followed after her, and they ran hand-in-hand to Fox's last Homecoming. Fox was welcomed with a raucous and appreciative applause, and his night was a colorful snowstorm of celebration. Fox danced with almost every young woman in town, and Lai twice. He played dice and cards at the Five Sides over an incredible meal, which was mostly made up of desserts and cheese. His song was sung time and time again, and he was dragged into physical re-enactments of his defeat of the Underbeast no less than a dozen times.

He met Picck and Rose's daughter, who had been born while Fox was away. She was a tiny, pink thing bundled up in a patchwork pinafore. She was the spitting image of her mother, except for her dark hair, which was already showing signs of being an eternally tangled mess, just like Picck's. They called her Rivena.

Fox took in everything. From the sound of dice hitting the wooden tavern tables, to the soft, indescribable scent of baby Rivena's head. He held tight to the thanks of every wife whose husband he had brought back, and mourned for those children whose fathers he had not been able to save.

Many of the revelers began to trickle back to their homes and beds as dawn approached. Those few waresmen who had joined their caravan from other towns and valleys took rooms at the Five Sides, and the common room was all but empty by the time sunlight began to filter through the streets and distorted glass windows. But Fox did not go home. He climbed to the tavern rooftop, his back to the mountains, and watched the horizon.

And as the sun began to lift mist from the grasses, blanketing the valley in a spring morning haze, the Shavid rode back into town.

AS THE REST OF THE Shavid set up camp in the same place they'd been the previous spring, Fox joined a select few of them in the tavern common room. Radda, Neil, Aubrey, James, and Otter sat with Fox at a long table in the center of the room, snacking on leftovers that Fox scavenged from the kitchen, and listening as Fox recounted his tale for them. It was a story that rolled easily off his tongue now, though he was careful to leave out the parts involving Farran. For while it had seemed only right to tell Lai about her father's role in his tale, something made Fox want to keep his relationship with the god to himself. At least for now.

When he had finished, Radda was watching him with a calculating expression. It was James who finally asked, "So, have you discovered your Blessing, then?"

"Yes," said Fox. "It's maps. They speak to me, and I can see things."

A stunned and disbelieving aura fell over the group. Fox, confused, said, "Is there a name for someone like me? Something other Shavid could call me?"

They didn't seem to be entirely listening to him. Aubrey was whispering urgently to Otter, and Radda continued to simply stare at him. And Fox, heart suddenly sinking, was sure he had said something entirely wrong.

"But it's impossible!" said James. "They all died out! Their gift was taken away from us."

"And now, it has been returned to us," said Radda. "In the form of this wonderful young man."

"What's going on?" asked Fox, completely baffled. "What does this mean? What am I?"

Radda smiled warmly at him. "Son, you don't know how strong a Blessing you have been given. It means, you are more than just a Windkissed. More, even, than merely a Shavid. You, my boy, are a legend."

Chapter Twenty-Eight
Cartomancer

"They were called the Cartomancers, or Mapweavers," said Radda. "And their gift was, in many ways, valued above all others. They were said to be the most honored among Rhin's chosen children."

"Why were they so special?" asked Fox numbly. Him, a *legend*? The hero of a small valley was unbelievable enough ... but a Shavid legend?

"They knew things that even the finest Seers couldn't know. And stories say they could command the very wind, while the Shavid merely harness it."

Aubrey cut in. "We haven't heard of one for over three hundred years. It's something we even began to believe had never existed in the first place."

"But ..." Fox was confused. He was overwhelmed. He tried again. "Where did they go? Why — "

"We don't know," said Radda. "We have a hundred different theories and half-remembered stories. Some say they grew too powerful, and the gods became jealous. Others claim that they learned something they shouldn't have, and were punished for it." And then, Radda seemed to falter a bit. "We're not even sure about everything they could do," he admitted. "It was so long ago, and there are hardly any records of them."

"Still," said Otter firmly, "the boy should come with us. He should be with people more like him, not stuck in this stone hole in the mountains."

"But we're *not* like him," argued Aubrey. "None of us could begin to teach him what he needs. It would all be guesswork and — "

"And it will be better than what education he could get here!" said James. "Shavid is in his blood, and you know we're not meant to settle in, put down roots. He'll go mad by the time he's seventeen, if not sooner."

Throughout all of this, Neil had remained markedly silent. Now, however, he shifted down the bench to sit closer to Fox. "You've had quite the year," Neil said quietly.

"Has it only been a year?" asked Fox. "Seems like so much longer."

Neil glanced around at the adults, shaking his head, and then turned back to Fox. "You've had more adventure in a year than most people have their whole lives. Most normal people, anyways. But that's life with the Shavid. And no matter how unique your blessing is, it is still a Shavid blessing."

"But what if they're right?" said Fox, worry creeping into his voice. "What if they can't teach me anything?"

Here, Neil smiled. "You've forgotten who you're talking to. The Un-Blessed of the group. The *honorary* Shavid." He said the word "honorary" like it was something akin to a horrible swear word. "There's not a drop of magic in my blood, and yet they still find new things to teach me every day. Besides," he said, clapping Fox on the shoulder in a brotherly manner, "you seem to have done quite a decent job of teaching yourself. So, what it comes down to is, do you *want* to come with us, or would you rather live out your life here?"

"Yes," said Fox quietly. And then, louder so the whole group could hear, he said, "Yes. Yes, I want to go with you."

The group fell silent, all eyes on Fox as he addressed them.

"No matter my Blessing, I'm still a Shavid at heart," he continued. "And if there is a place for me in your company, I would be honored to travel with you."

Radda stood, and took one of Fox's hands in both of his massive ones. "And I speak for all of the Shavid, the whole world over, when I say it would truly *be* an honor to have you." And then he bowed his forehead and touched it to the back of Fox's hand. When he straightened again, there was a boyish excitement in his eyes. "Spirit help me," he said with a laugh. "Just when I thought I'd seen it all, a Windkissed *Cartomancer* drops into our laps!"

And then, Fox was swept up in a small sea of hugs and shaken hands, and he could see Neil smiling a congratulations. He was dragged out into the Shavid camp, where Radda delivered the good news to the rest of the company. Mindi, Radda's middle daughter, welcomed Fox by planting a gigantic kiss on his cheek — rather closer to his mouth than Fox was entirely comfortable with.

The streets were beginning to fill with valley folk once more as the Homecoming continued, and excited cheers were raised when they saw the garish Shavid tents and wagons. By the time the players began to put on their first show on the makeshift stage, the story had already begun to spread like wildfire: young Forric Foxglove, the hero of the caravan, was going with them. He would be leaving when they did, at the close of the Homecoming. He was one of them.

But Fox himself was already heading back up the hill, exhausted from all the excitement and from staying up all night. He was going home, to take a very long nap and to begin packing his things. As he walked, the wind brought him pieces of conversation from the valley square below, and he smiled to himself. Hearing the Thiccans talk so excitedly about it made it more real, somehow: he was *one of them*!

AN INCREDIBLE SMELL woke Fox from his deep and surprisingly dreamless slumber. Groggily, he fumbled his way downstairs. He could hear both of his parents in the kitchen, talking in hurried and almost anxious tones.

"Should we have made the fish as well?" asked Mother.

Something thumped onto the counter top, and Father said, "You spent too much time with the mushrooms. *And* there's the soup, plus the goose ... I think we'll be fine."

When Fox slipped through the doorway, he found Mother and Father both busying themselves around the fire pit. They didn't notice him right away, instead continuing to stir pots and chop vegetables.

The kitchen was a glorious sight. It seemed that every one of Fox's favorite foods was there. Roasted mushrooms and goat cheese; a plump goose turning on a spit; two different kinds of soup; heaping piles of smashed potatoes mixed with beans and onions. He smelled spiced turtle jerky and rabbit pie, as well as a half a dozen of Borric's best pies.

Mother spotted him first, and ushered him into the kitchen with a grin. Streaks of flour freckled her cheeks and forehead, and multi-colored berry stains danced across her apron and the rolled-up sleeves of her dress.

"What is all this?" asked Fox, his mouth watering slightly.

"It's your farewell meal," said Mother fondly, joyful and proud tears threatening to break the dam behind her eyes.

"All of your favorites," said Father, who was ladling up a steaming hot bowl of what smelled like mussel stew. "Sit! Eat!"

As Fox obeyed, the first knock came at the door. Terric entered, a heaping basket of roasted potatoes in his arms. Behind him were his wife and his brother, a miner Fox only knew by sight. They offered their thanks, added their potatoes to the feast, and Father offered them a place around the fire. Ellegar came next, his excitable pack of grandchildren swarming around him like ducklings. He brought flat, delicious corn cakes that his wife had made, as well as a finely-spun garment that was something between a shawl and a cloak. This, he offered to Fox with genuine and heartfelt thanks before he, too, joined in for dinner.

And all evening they came and went. Valley folk bearing platters of food and gifts of well-wishing and thanks for Fox. The cabin became home to one massive party, all in Fox's honor. Borric himself stopped by before too long, bringing even more of his best pies. He managed to pull Fox aside from his many admirers for a moment to speak to him quietly.

"She told me that she found out about her true parents," Borric said, so that only Fox could hear him.

"And where does that leave you two?" asked Fox.

Borric smiled wanly. "She was mad at me something awful at first. But in the end, she says I'm still her father."

"I didn't want her to find out," said Fox apologetically.

"Oh I know you didn't, lad. But these are the ways of gods, after all. And what we say, or do, often has little merit in their eyes." And then he shook Fox's hand firmly. "I know you tried."

Borric didn't stay long. He said he had to get back to the tavern. But he made Fox promise to say a proper goodbye to Lai before he left, and Fox said he would. And then, he was surrounded once more by food and gifts and grateful families. It was as though the Homecoming had split in two: the part happening down in the valley square, and the part that was constantly ebbing and flowing through the Foxglove house. By the end of the night, Fox's family had enough food to keep them fed in leftovers for two weeks, and Fox himself had a small mountain of gifts piled beneath the front kitchen window.

His parents wouldn't let him help clean up. They told him to turn in early. Tomorrow was his last day in Thicca Valley, after all. There was much to do. Fox started to head off to bed as suggested, but then remembered something. While Mother and Father were busy sorting out what food would keep and what food should be eaten at once, Fox pocketed several slices of turtle jerky and hid an entire roasted hare behind his back. Then he slipped outside quietly and headed to the nearest patch of woods, right at the outskirts of his family's land.

The wolves were waiting for him. They lay like patient old dogs, lounging just within the safety of the trees. When Fox approached, a few of them perked up, their ears twitching and noses beginning to snuffle the air. Completely unshaken by their powerful jaws and deadly teeth, Fox crouched down to their level, holding the hare out as an offering.

The wolf he was sure was the alpha male came forward first and began to lick and gnaw at the carcass. Fox wasn't sure if wolves enjoyed cooked food, but he figured it was better than nothing. As the wolf ate, Fox cautiously reached out and scratched him behind the ears. "I just wanted to say thank you," he said quietly. "And, if it's possible ... watch out for my family while I'm gone? And Lai."

The wolf looked up from its meal and licked Fox's nose, almost affectionately. Almost at once, Fox was surrounded by the rest of the pack. They licked his ears and picked at the roasted hare and begged strips of turtle from him. He hugged them around the necks and scratched them all behind their ears, digging his fingers into the remnants of their thick winter coats. And then, once they were finished being fed and groomed, the wolves turned to head deeper into the woods, and Fox knew they were going to hunt. For a moment, the alpha male hung back, as if waiting for Fox to join them. But Fox said quietly, "Perhaps next time I'm in town, friend." And the wolves disappeared into the night.

FOX'S LAST DAY IN THICCA Valley dawned clear and chill. It was cold even for early spring, but it didn't keep people inside. They flocked to the Courter's Contests, bundled in their finest scarves and shawls. The usual flurry of bets and wagers filled the air, and Fox was accompanied by Neil and Lai. His two friends got along remarkably well, and they passed a pleasant afternoon watching the contests.

When Neil tapped him on the shoulder and pointed out that he'd better finish packing, Fox started. It was already evening. Everything had happened so quickly, and he hadn't even noticed. He let Lai escort him home, and they sat on the front porch rail for some time, watching the sunset and talking about nothing in particular. Finally, as the sounds of crickets mingled with the Shavid music that had flared up in the square below, Fox said, "Don't come to see me off tomorrow."

Lai looked hurt as she asked, "Why not?"

Fox struggled to put it into words. Finally he said, "I don't know when I'll be back. You'll look different, I'll look different ..." He rubbed his head, almost hoping that it would somehow bring the right words to mind. "I just don't want to think about you changing. And if you're there when I leave ..." He trailed off once more. And he knew as he turned and looked at his oldest and closest friend, that he didn't need to finish it. She understood.

The moment hung between them like an ethereal strand of a spider web. Lai reached over and tucked her arm in his, then leaned in, slowly, and kissed him on the eyebrow. When she pulled back, a flush had risen in her cheeks, visible even by the moonlight. She slid from the railing and straightened her skirts, then said, without looking at him, "You'd better come back one day. 'Cause I'm not marrying anyone but you."

It was the only goodbye Fox was going to get. She was gone, running down the hill, leaving a very confused Fox alone on his front railing.

HIS THINGS WERE PACKED, and loaded into one of the Shavid wagons. His parents said goodbye at the kitchen door. He promised to write, and often, before heading down the hill with his haversack strapped to his shoulders. True dawn was still a ways away, but a thin greying light began to wash out the sky as Fox set foot in the valley square.

He stopped, his feet frozen on the packed earth. He could hear the Shavid company making their final preparations, and an eagerness twisted his stomach. But there was something else, something he didn't have a name for.

"Are you afraid?" asked Neil, and Fox jumped. He hadn't realized his friend was there.

"Yes," admitted Fox.

Neil detached himself from the shadows. "Of life on the road?"

"Of ... not being who everyone thinks I could be." Fox stood rooted to the spot. He stared straight ahead at the place where, across the shops and streets at the heart of the valley, the Shavid were waiting for him. "Wouldn't it just be easier to stay where I have a place?"

"You could do that," said Neil casually. "Or you could make your own place."

Fox tore his eyes from the distant, colorful blur his eyes had been fixed upon, and looked instead up at the lightening sky. "Were you afraid?" asked Fox.

There was a pause and then, "Every day."

Fox closed his eyes and breathed deep. A barrage of sounds and smells greeted him, each one connected with a memory or fear or hope or possibility. And when he opened his eyes again, he took a step forward. Neil walked with him, one uncertain step at a time, down the center street of Thicca Valley. With every footfall, a new question came tumbling into Fox's mind. When would he see the valley again? Where was Farran? What if Fox couldn't live up to his own burgeoning legend?

But with every footfall, Fox found his resolve growing stronger. And by the time they reached the company, there wasn't a doubt in Fox's mind: he was a Shavid. And Shavid were meant to roam.

They began to walk, warming the morning with song. Here and there throughout the valley, Thiccans stuck their heads out of doors and windows to shout farewell, and farmers already in the fields waved their goodbyes. A single goatherd high on a wildflower-strewn hill stood watching them go, but did not wave. And even without looking too closely, Fox knew it was Lai.

And, as the ground beneath their feet began to rise, taking them up and away from Thicca Valley, a shimmer caught the sun in the corner of Fox's eye. He turned quickly, afraid it might disappear again, but it didn't. It was fainter than before, but it was unmistakable. Fox smiled, and Farran saluted him before flickering into nothingness once more.

But Fox didn't mind. He took it as a good omen, and besides, he knew the god would be back. In the meantime, he had new roads to wander, and new paths to tread. He thrust his chest out and sang with the rest of Radda's company, as they marched away into a fresh and brilliant dawn.

ACKNOWLEDGMENTS

In the decade it took to pull this story from my brain and force it onto paper, I've been supported by countless people. A HUGE thanks to the Cards, for their constant love and care. You are my second parents, and I would not be here without you both. To my uncle specifically, thank you for being my mentor. On stage or page, I'd be lost without your direction. Thank you for giving me such a high standard to aspire to as an artist, and for believing in me before I even knew I had the potential for talent.

To my parents, and my siblings: Thank you for being dreamers. None of you ever tried to tell me, even as a child, that I *couldn't* do something. I became this creative person because of all of you. I am forever grateful to have been surrounded by literature and the arts my entire life, and it's thanks to all of you. The painters, the writers, the readers, the actors, the singers, the musicians ... You are all my personal Shavid tribe.

Begrudgingly, I must thank You-Know-Who-You-Are, for saying "cartographer" when I asked for a stupid profession. But that's all you get.

To Fiona Jayde, my cover designer ... what can I even say? You were willing to work with an INSANE deadline to help bring my vision to life. You were willing to hold my hand through the entire process, and put up with my complete lack of publishing experience. I can't wait to see what you come up with for the rest of the series.

To all of my friends who suffered through my MANY panic attacks, the warmest, most loving thanks. To my beta readers, peer readers, and creative writing classmates, thank you for suffering through every typo and early draft. You helped me build the very world my story is built on, and you always asked me for more. For that, I can't thank you enough. This book would not be what it is now without your faith in my storytelling.

For Cody, I have no proper words. You have been there for me through the hardest, darkest moments of my life. You always find the perfect balance between tough love and comfort, and you make my life richer every day. You got me back on my feet (literally and metaphorically) and this book would STILL not be finished if it wasn't for you. "Thank you" is not enough, but it's all that I have. Thank you.

For Dad, who truly inspired my love of words. No book will ever be as good as The Chronicles of Prydain, as you read them to us. My favorite memories of you from my childhood were those storytelling nights, and I will always trace my love of literature back to our old living room couch, and Caer Dallben.

And, finally, for Mom, who never got to see this published. There will never be the proper words in any language, real or imagined, to express how grateful I am to you. For everything that I am, and everything I one day hope to be, thank you.

If you enjoyed what you read, please consider reviewing on Amazon or Goodreads! Every review of an indi author helps more than you can imagine, and we are grateful for each one!

About the Author

Kaitlin Bellamy has always been a storyteller. She grew up in Greensboro, North Carolina, where she discovered a passion for the stage, and spent her youth performing in a church community theatre ensemble. From there, she moved to Buena Vista, Virginia, to study Shakespeare and Musical Theatre at Southern Virginia University. Through a series of life-changing events, Kaitlin then found herself in Orlando, Florida, where she now enjoys an eclectic and vibrant life as an actor. She has continued her education at a snail-like pace that would make molasses jealous, choosing to add Anthropology and English majors to her scholastic wishlist. She doubts whether she will ever actually finish any one of her degrees, but making this book deadline gives her a small glimmer of hope. In the meantime, you can find her performing in local theme parks, narrating audiobooks from her home studio, and playing Dungeons and Dragons with her closest friends.

To keep up with all her adventures, feel free to join Kaitlin on any one of her social media platforms, or her website.

Facebook.com/KaitlinBellamyOfficial
Twitter.com/KaitlinBellamy
Instagram.com/Executive.Geek
www.KaitlinBellamy.com

Made in the USA
Las Vegas, NV
02 June 2024

90635986R00229